CLOSER...

Griffin's face had gone as empty of expression as she'd ever seen it, but his eyes were dangerous. She stood and strode toward the door, shaken by her anger—and his. "If you will excuse me, it has been a long day. I am tired and—"

He was in front of her, pulling her into his arms. She did not dare push at him for fear of hurting his injury. Or that's what she told herself as she slipped closer.

"I was so bloody worried," he growled into her hair.

Before she could explore the interesting effect of those words, his mouth came down hard on hers and demanded deep kisses. Oh, Lord, his touch was instantly intoxicating. Passion flared in her, hot, sudden and intense as an electrical charge. She arched up to meet him. This was what she'd longed for, what her body demanded.

He pulled her closer and groaned. "Now, Araminta. Please."

<u>BOOK YOUR PLACE ON OUR WEBSITE</u> <u>AND MAKE THE</u> <u>READING CONNECTION!</u>

We've created a customized website just for our very special readers, where you can get the inside scoop on everything that's going on with Zebra, Pinnacle and Kensington books.

When you come online, you'll have the exciting opportunity to:

- View covers of upcoming books

- Read sample chapters

- Learn about our future publishing schedule (listed by publication month *and author*)

- Find out when your favorite authors will be visiting a city near you

- Search for and order backlist books from our online catalog

- Check out author bios and background information

- Send e-mail to your favorite authors

- Meet the Kensington staff online

- Join us in weekly chats with authors, readers and other guests

- Get writing guidelines

- AND MUCH MORE!

Visit our website at
http://www.kensingtonbooks.com

SOMEBODY TO LOVE

KATE ROTHWELL

ZEBRA BOOKS
KENSINGTON PUBLISHING CORP.
www.kensingtonbooks.com

For Michael—and just not just because of January.
For all those months, too.

I am grateful to the wisest of forced bats,
Bronwyn Clarke,
Julie Korzenko,
Anne Lind.
You, too, Pam Gitta.

Of course, as usual.
I owe Linda and Nan big time.

CHAPTER 1

New York City, 1883

Araminta Woodhall left the kitchen, slipped to a back room and donned her most stylish gown, a rose-colored satin and velvet creation. She should have felt elegant in the damask bodice, with the swaths of plain satin and damask that draped the skirt. Instead she felt even more like a circus act.

She reminded herself that no matter how much she despised being on display for her employer's wealthy, leering clients, at least she could be proud that her *ris de veau aux pois avec haricots verts sautés au beurre* and *saumon aux concombres, sauce homard* had been exceptionally good tonight.

She hung her cotton work dress on a hook in the small storage room, and then pushed through the door separating the servants' quarters from the main part of the mansion. After a satisfying yet hectic day's work producing sixteen courses, she craved quiet, but first she must greet Linder Kane's foolish guests. Wearing a smile as artificial as the silk roses at her waist, she would curtsey at their applause, and then head back to her territory, the kitchen.

But as Araminta walked past the thick, polished door

barring Kane's private sanctum, she heard a woman's shout. She froze.

In the office, the woman gave another cry, and Araminta recognized Olivia's voice. Oh, Lord no, not Olivia. Not again. Her protective instincts surged, but she'd interfered before and it had not helped.

Olivia must have ventured down onto the first floor of the Park Avenue mansion, and Linder Kane didn't allow his mistress anywhere near the parlors where the well-heeled gamblers gathered at the card table or the roulette wheel.

A more muffled cry, followed by a sharp crack, forced Araminta into motion. She shoved open the unlocked door.

The normally immaculate Mr. Kane stood red-faced and disheveled in the middle of the room. Hands on knees, he bent over the sprawled figure of Olivia, a frail figure crumpled in a heap on the wine-colored Aubusson carpet.

Her heart beating double-time, Araminta cried, "Are you trying to kill her?"

Kane straightened and looked over at her, his usual affable smile fixed in place. "Ah. Araminta. No need to worry. Miss Smith is fine. She tripped. Knocked her head on the table."

Araminta bit back a retort. She elbowed him aside and knelt on the carpet. Olivia's blue eyes frowned up at her. Touching her friend's cheek, Araminta saw bruises already beginning to form on the porcelain skin.

"See? I told you she's fine." Kane tugged at his waistcoat and adjusted his perfect, starched white cuffs. "You'd better pay attention to where you are stepping, Olivia," he said. "And Araminta, we've got a most select group of customers tonight and so in five minutes—"

She clenched her teeth to keep from screaming in his

face, and her voice was tight with the effort. "No, Mr. Kane."

His smile didn't disappear, but it seemed less wide, and the amiable eyes held an unpleasant glint. "But our clients enjoy the chance to congratulate you on your superb creations. You know that I expect you to do us this favor."

Araminta knew he enjoyed the chance to show off the fact that he had snared this year's novelty, the French-trained girl with the café-au-lait complexion and an upper-crust British accent. Once upon a time, the ridiculously high salary he paid her would have stopped her from telling him what he could do with his expectations. Now concern for Olivia kept her mouth shut.

She drew in a breath to steady her temper, and risked an insolent stare into his face. "You might inform them that I'm ill."

He ran a hand over his glossy dark hair, and his lips compressed. "I most certainly will not tell them that the chef is sick."

She raised her voice. "Mr. Kane—"

He held up a hand, palm out, in mock surrender, once again wearing the air of the jolly, good-natured fellow who wouldn't hurt a fly. "Yes, yes. I know you chefs are temperamental. I'll make your excuses. You will be a little late, yes?"

Araminta opened her mouth to protest, but saw the challenge in the wide crocodile grin.

"Yes, sir. I'll be down before they rise from the table." Araminta helped Olivia to her feet—an easy job, for the slight girl felt as if she weighed no more than a bushel of apples. "Excuse me, Mr. Kane. I need to take her upstairs."

Olivia moaned, and her thin fingers grabbed onto Araminta's arm.

Kane's smile didn't waver. "Good plan. Let me make sure the hall's empty."

"Naturally we don't want the patrons to see this," Araminta muttered.

His sleek demeanor nauseated her. She should have known that anyone that greedy for power would be corrupt. She rued the day she'd allowed herself to be lured into accepting his offer of employment. Kane wasn't the only despicable man she'd encountered in his gambling hall. The wealthy customers who frequented the Park Avenue establishment might not have his streak of violence, but as far as she could discern from the conversations she'd overheard, they cared more for their money and pleasure than for any honorable pursuits.

She half carried the girl up the back staircase to Olivia's bedroom, a few doors down from where Kane slept when he stayed in the house.

After she helped Olivia change out of the blue satin gown, she settled the girl into the bed with the dark wood headboard, which towered over Olivia and made her look even more like a child. Araminta sat on the edge of the bed and brushed a few pale hairs from her friend's forehead. The heart-shaped face might have been an echo from Araminta's past. Darling Charlotte, Araminta's mother, had almost the same face, the same fragile form as Olivia.

And really, Olivia was not so different from Charlotte. Frail yet loving women, trapped by heartless "gentlemen."

At least Araminta's grandfather hadn't beaten Charlotte.

"I know you dislike it when I tell you to leave this place, but more and more I'm convinced he's dangerous." Araminta spoke softly, though she still wanted to shout.

"This is the third time this week that he's hit you. That I know of."

"No. Really, I'll be all right."

"You could stay in my house."

"I can't leave." Olivia's face, which had been screwed up in pain, relaxed but grew even paler. Her blue eyes opened wide, and Araminta thought she saw fear in them. Olivia shook her head and then grimaced again. "You mustn't ask me to."

"Why not?"

But Olivia had closed her eyes. "I can't," was her only answer, and Araminta knew she'd get no other.

Her friend fell asleep almost at once. As Araminta drew the ugly puce cover over the girl, a knot of frustration and anger formed in her chest. She needed to rescue foolish Olivia, but she could not do it alone—and no one she knew would dare challenge Linder Kane. The men wasting money downstairs likely kept mistresses of their own and would have more empathy for Linder Kane than for a poor lost girl.

She extinguished the flickering gaslight. Closing the door firmly behind her, she wished she could lock it to make sure Linder Kane stayed out.

She walked slowly toward the stairs. Whenever she had broached the idea of leaving, Olivia had grown panic-stricken, so she must fear something outside the walls of Kane's mansion. Araminta would need to find some source of protection for the girl here and once she managed to get the girl out from under Kane's thumb. Charlotte's daughter could not walk away from a lost soul like Olivia.

Griffin Calverson strolled from the dining room through the middle parlor, careful to keep his face a mask of indifference. Behind him, the soft slap of cards punctuated men's conversation and raucous laughter. He shoved open a massive oak door he suspected was meant to discourage any member of the public from wandering out of the first-floor gaming rooms. Cigar smoke thickened the air and trailed him into the empty corridor.

Griffin rubbed his chin and pondered his next move. A friend had brought him to this gambling parlor, and so far, he'd managed to avoid being introduced to Kane, who would recognize his last name. Kane's greedy hands were trying to dip into the Calverson Company coffers.

The man had to be stopped.

A few minutes earlier, Kane had reappeared in the dining room after a long absence, the fixed smile more pronouncedly false. Something back here had ruffled the man, and Griffin decided to indulge his piqued curiosity. Just a quick snoop round. And he'd heard a rumor he wanted to confirm.

The air in this deserted back corridor was only slightly less rancid than that in the parlors, but Griffin breathed deeply, putting his thoughts in order. He became aware of a slight prickling, like a soft touch on his skin. Someone watched him.

He glanced up, his gaze following the sweep of an ornate stair that led to the upper chambers, to the shadows at the top where a woman's form stood, unmoving, looking down.

Good God, so the rumor was true. This was where the woman had ended up. There was no mistaking the lovely curve from waist to hip. The elegant set of the slightly tilted head, seen in silhouette, matched the memory that occasionally distracted him.

Araminta.

What the hell was she doing working here?

If he knew her, perhaps she recognized him. He'd have

to speak to her. He started toward the stairs, tamping down his sudden, unexpected eagerness.

The oak door behind him opened. Araminta vanished into the shadows of the upstairs hall.

Kane's starched and impressive butler stood and frowned at Griffin, who set his shoulders and stared down the man with frigid hauteur.

The butler immediately showed an apologetic smile as wide and false as Kane's. "Sir? I'm sorry, but we prefer our customers remain in the front parlors. Coffee is being served in the dining room."

"Of course." Griffin strolled past him. "I beg your pardon."

In the dining room, Melrose, the odious but useful acquaintance who'd brought Griffin here, lounged in a chair, three sheets to the wind, bragging about his recent mining deals in Colorado. Griffin knew the dark-haired, oily man listening and beaming was Kane, and so he took a chair well away from the two of them.

He fell into conversation with a thin stick of a lawyer who looked dyspeptic.

"I enjoy a few hands of vingt-et-un, but mostly I come for the dinner," the lawyer confided. "She'll be out soon."

"She?"

"The gal who does it. Wish I could steal her, I tell you. All the rage just because she cooked for a duchess and that eccentric whatshername. Timona Caleston."

"Calverson," Griffin muttered. He didn't bother to add his sister's name was now actually Timona McCann.

"Yeah. For all the fuss, she's as skilled in the kitchen as any Pierre or Jacques—better even." The stick smiled. "And tastier to look at."

Kane's raised voice rumbled over the conversations. "Ah, Miss Araminta."

Griffin leaned back. He draped his arm over the top of the chair and examined Kane's cook.

She had the voluptuous hourglass figure of a Bowery actress, but the demeanor of royalty. Her eyes were dark, delicious, exotic, her skin the radiant color of dark clover honey in sunlight. Her hair, a mass of curls, had been drawn into a tight knot at the back of her head, but enough raven locks had escaped to frame her face. He fancied that the last time they'd met, her hair had been shorter.

She looked straight into his face. Her full lips parted slightly and she blushed. He narrowed his eyes, hoping she'd see his warning. Perhaps she did, for she looked away at once.

The men, filled with her excellent cooking and Kane's good wine, applauded, stamped their feet and whistled at her. She murmured some nonsense about "enjoying their visit," though Griffin was amused to hear that she sounded as if she cursed them all.

And then for another long moment, her glowing dark eyes stared into his face. Several of Kane's other patrons turned to see where her attention had focused. Amused, and a bit rattled, Griffin frowned, then shifted his gaze from her eyes to the wineglass he held. He felt almost as if he'd broken physical contact.

Damn the woman for showing the room she recognized him. He already knew Araminta Woodhall displayed every emotion on that lovely face. And as far as he could tell, every emotion for her was a strong one. Luckily Kane had been distracted by Melrose and didn't notice.

When Griffin looked up from the ornate crystal glass, Araminta had disappeared.

He'd endure a few hands of cards and then go seek her out. He needed to make sure she wouldn't babble to Kane. And, he reasoned, he owed it to his sister to find out why her former employee worked for that unscrupulous twit. He took a gulp of wine and wondered why the blazes she'd stared at him in such a marked manner. The possibilities were intriguing.

As soon as she escaped the smoke-filled dining room, Araminta let the door close behind her and leaned heavily against the wall. Her instincts had proven correct. The frisson of recognition that had shot through her had not been a lie. She'd only had a glimpse of him in the dark hallway, and had doubted her eyes—the Griffin Calverson she remembered would not be dim-witted enough to throw money away at Kane's crooked gaming hall.

Araminta had met Calverson only twice, but had a clear picture of him in her mind as a cynical man who should have seen through Kane's air of bonhomie at once.

Those remarkable eyes, green and cold as chips of emerald ice, had captured her gaze across the dining room. Even though she'd felt the heat rise to her cheeks, she hadn't been able to tear her gaze away from the stern, handsome face. He'd looked out of place among the other men, and not just because he was clearly sober and alert. She could not put her finger on what set him apart. Something perilous.

She knew from that stare he recognized her, but his eyes had narrowed as if in accusation. What message had he wanted to convey?

As she pondered that, a second thought rose to her mind: despite his own mysterious and perhaps murky dealings, Calverson might be the answer to her problem. His influence and power far exceeded Kane's. She needed a wealthy, ruthless man to help Olivia. He did not seem to be friendly with Kane—in fact, she could swear Calverson had directed a look of contempt at the man.

She walked toward the kitchen, wondering how she could approach him to ask for help. Lost in her thoughts, she started and gasped when, from behind, strong hands grasped her upper arms.

At first she suspected the regular customer who'd twice come searching for her after he'd downed several brandies. "I've already told you," she said in the voice that could subdue the cheekiest kitchen assistants, "I'm not interested, and my employer has assured me that I might . . . oh." Her indignation died away, replaced by something more complex.

The hands that held her arms were stronger than that customer's pudgy fingers. And the scent of this man much more subtle.

"Good evening, Miss Woodhall." The soft voice in her ear set her back rigid and tingling with awareness. "I expect you recognized me in the back hall?"

She managed to catch her breath again, but her whisper was ragged. "Yes, Mr. Calverson. Please let go, sir."

She turned and found he stood too close. She backed away at once. Looking up into the austere face nearly hidden in the shadows, she grew light-headed. That had to explain her next words.

"I'd have thought that you had better sense than to come to a place like Kane's," she whispered. "Sir."

"If it comes to that, I thought you were too intelligent to work for a man like him." He took a step closer, and the dim light shone upon the man's clear eyes, his high cheekbones, the harsh set of his brow. The lines next to his mouth hinted at dimples, except the blighter never smiled.

Oh, bother. As she looked at him, her insides melted into jelly. She hadn't left behind either one of her peculiar reactions to the man: lust and incivility. Why would he create such nonsensical responses in her?

Calverson frowned down at her. "Do you come out and greet the customers every night?"

She heard his odious disapproval. "No, sir. Perhaps once a week. Only when the most elite clientele visit." She reined in her servant's reaction to his commanding tone. Why should she explain herself to him? "Or as some of the men who work here say, when high-flying mugs come to be parted from their cash."

He raised his eyebrows. "And you associate with the men who work here?"

Annoyance overpowered the uncomfortable curling awareness of him. How dare he, of all people, condemn her? "Did you have anything else you wished to discuss, sir? Might I ask why you grabbed me?"

An odd expression flickered across his face. Guilt, perhaps? Not likely. "I wanted to assure myself that you wouldn't tell Mr. Kane that you saw me in the hall tonight."

"Certainly, no, I won't." She remembered her mission and chewed on her lower lip. She drew in a deep breath. "What are you doing, sir?"

"In a few moments, I shall go back and lose some more money in Mr. Kane's front parlor at the roulette wheel."

"I meant why are you here, sir? Are you friends with Mr. Kane?"

"Not at all." His voice was filled with disgust.

The vision of Olivia's bruised cheek and temple came to her, and her own weakness in his presence seemed a petty concern. She realized she'd been holding her breath and allowed it to escape in a deep exhale. "Then I own that I'm glad to meet you—"

Footsteps and voices echoed in the corridor from the back of the house.

Araminta twisted around to see who was coming. Probably some of Kane's assistants, on their way to the gaming rooms. When she turned back, Griffin Calverson had disappeared.

She had a flash of disappointment, but she dismissed it. There was work to do, and she didn't want to be caught fraternizing with a customer. She'd pushed Kane far enough tonight. If he raised a hand to Olivia because of her, Araminta could not bear it.

She continued on to the kitchen, feeling absurdly glad she was not wearing her usual work garment. She smoothed the velvet on her sleeve, mussed from Calverson's grip. Her arms remembered the strength of his hands.

He was up to something here. Though she didn't know the man well, she guessed his presence meant trouble for Kane. And perhaps salvation for Olivia.

Tomorrow she'd track Calverson down in his lair and find out.

CHAPTER 2

The next afternoon, Araminta slipped into the spare room off the kitchen. As she changed into her plain navy walking skirt and matching overdress, her nervous fingers fumbled on the pearl buttons of the bodice. She poked her finger with the hatpin while she pinned the matching blue felt hat to the bun at the back of her head. Silly of her to be rattled by a man like Calverson. He was a businessman. She would speak to him in a businesslike manner and ignore the fluttering sensation in the pit of her stomach.

She told her kitchen staff she would return in an hour, and set off on her errands. She'd stop in and set up deliveries from the new butcher and then go in search of help for Olivia.

As the streetcar rolled downtown, Araminta considered why Griffin Calverson had caused an internal uproar in her from the first time she'd set eyes on him two years earlier. Not even the man. His image. She'd surreptitiously studied a portrait of him that his sister, a talented photographer, had taken.

The picture by Timona, her friend and former employer, revealed a glimpse of Calverson's personality. Anyone glancing at the image would see a typical prosperous entrepreneur: his full mustache trimmed, his clothes fitting as if he'd been born to wear the wealthy businessman's suit, complete with gold watch chain across the midriff. Yet even that small portrait showed more: the cleverness and the arrogant authority. In the eyes, perhaps, or the angle of the clean-shaven chin. The strength was there, too.

Strength she'd need for Olivia.

The Calverson Company offices were housed in a towering granite building in the financial district. How appropriate, she thought, amused, that her potential knight in shining armor worked in this castle-like structure. Or perhaps he was more of a feudal lord—a capricious tyrant who'd lop off her head.

The brisk wind tugged at her dress and her hat, yet the air held more than a hint of spring, a hint of hope that braced her for the challenge of facing him again.

The company occupied two floors of the building. Araminta walked up the large staircase to the door that had a gold-plated plaque with "Calverson Company" etched on it.

A supercilious clerk immediately approached. "Pardon me. What do you need?"

When she said she wished to speak to Mr. Calverson, the clerk sniffed and studied her for a few seconds before he disappeared. A few minutes later, he emerged from somewhere in the back and, looking almost chastened, led her into Mr. Calverson's private office. He left, shutting the door behind him.

Alone in the cavernous office, Araminta distracted herself by studying her surroundings. Disappointing, really, that she found nothing quirky about the room. She'd hoped for something odd, such as a stuffed crocodile, a mummy's sarcophagus or perhaps a butterfly collection. She'd settle for something personal, perhaps evidence of Calverson's wide travels.

Like the man, the room was cool and polished. A large, uncluttered desk, nearly devoid of any decoration, stood near the window. A few tasteful landscapes hung on the wall. A thick Turkish rug covered the polished wood floor. No hint of the occupant's character—other than the obvious facts that he had a great deal of money and simple taste—showed in the furnishings or decorations.

For fifteen minutes she sat in the overstuffed armless chair designed for lady visitors, twisting the gloves in her hand into shapeless wrecks, staring out the window at the splendid view and regretting her blasted tendency to act first and think later. Rushing over here had to be a mistake.

She could easily imagine his cold amusement as he turned her down. How many other women had come to Griffin Calverson for aid, for money—or for needs her body understood, but her mind refused to contemplate.

Surely he was no different from the other men who prowled Kane's gaming parlor. Griffin Calverson was not a knight in shining armor.

Just as she convinced herself she was on a fool's errand and rose to leave, the door to the office opened, and he strolled into the room.

His splendid green gaze rested on her, and he stood as motionless as a gravestone. Of course he would show no emotion.

The man hadn't changed and—Araminta halted her ungracious thoughts. After all, she wanted a favor from him.

She reminded herself it was not truly his fault she had trouble breathing or behaving sensibly in his presence.

For a very long minute he inspected her. "Good afternoon, Miss Woodhall. Please, sit down." His strong, clear voice startled her. She half expected the soft murmur she'd heard in the hallway the night before.

She sat and smoothed her skirts over her knees. "Good

afternoon, Mr. Calverson." Fine—she sounded normal. "Er. I hope you are well?"

He took a seat behind the desk, his commanding air nicely adding to her image of him as lord of all he surveyed. He leaned back, the better to scrutinize her down that patrician nose of his. "I hope I didn't startle you too badly last night? You seemed rather breathless."

She shook her head, uncertain. Did he know the reason she'd been so rattled? If he guessed at her idiotic attraction to him, she would have to leave at once.

He tilted his head as he scrutinized her, as if viewing a questionable work of art. "To what do I owe the honor of this visit?"

She straightened her already poker-straight back when she heard the hint of sarcasm. Honor of this visit—by his sister's ex-cook. All thoughts of asking directly for aid for Olivia dissolved like smoke. She would take an indirect route, feel him out. "I thought perhaps you could give me some advice. I've come seeking a favor."

How on earth could she explain to Griffin Calverson that she wanted a man who could act as threatening and remorseless as . . . well, as Griffin Calverson?

"A favor that your employer, Mr. Kane, cannot grant?"

She grimaced. "No."

"Tell me, what will happen if I don't help you?"

His slow voice insinuated some sinister meaning. She pulled on her gloves and tried to smooth the wrinkles from them, stalling for time. Calverson waited, as tranquil as someone with all the time in the world.

"I don't know. Nothing, I suppose," she admitted. "But a dreadful wrong won't be corrected."

"A wrong against whom?"

"I can't tell you." Olivia was Kane's mistress. What if Griffin's anger toward Kane encompassed those in Kane's immediate circle?

"Yet you come to bargain on this person's behalf?"

When he put it like that, it seemed absurd, but she would still say nothing more. Araminta nodded.

"And if I don't do as you ask, you will tell Mr. Kane that you saw me in the corridor when—"

"Oh! You thought I was threatening you?" She felt absurd and wished she had not come. She despised feeling foolish in front of him.

Olivia's safety was paramount, she reminded herself, worth suffering some uneasiness. "Of course I won't tell him, even if you choose not to help me. I came today because I am worried about a friend of mine. And I thought . . ."

She clamped her lips tight rather than blurt out the request she'd considered. *I thought you might convince the horrible Mr. Kane to go to the devil.*

He wore his usual rigidly bland expression, but he could not hide the striking details. His skin was tanned almost to the same soft golden-brown color as his hair— not so much lighter than her own skin, really. Perhaps the reason he appeared too vivid was the sheer energy of the man, an icy glow to him.

His eyebrows raised slightly. "It appears you are agitated, Miss Woodhall. Perhaps you might take a moment to catch your breath before telling me what you thought. And this, ah, friend. What sort of trouble is she in?"

She heard mocking amusement, or perhaps mere scorn. The tone of a man who knows his effect on a woman. Good heavens—perhaps the scorn was for her friend because he assumed a woman in trouble could mean only one thing.

Reckless Araminta, her mother had fondly called her. And in Griffin's vivid presence she could see now that this was yet another ridiculous impulse. She did not want to be in debt to this man for anything, particularly if he sensed her reaction to him.

There had to be another answer for Olivia's plight. She could ask Timona for another name. Her sociable friend had many acquaintances in this city.

"Please excuse me, sir. I don't think you can help me after all. I was wrong to bother you. I bid you a good day." She picked up her beaded bag and made ready to stand.

He held up a hand in an imperious gesture. "Not yet."

Araminta, normally not a dithering weakling, found herself sitting down again.

"I interrupted a meeting to see you," he said. "I expect you might at least tell me what it is you require."

She scowled, but did not answer.

"When we met in Minnesota, Miss Woodhall, you had no trouble telling me my family's business. You expressed your opinions on any number of issues. And yet you will not tell me now what you want? Why is that?"

He was as imperious as Kane, as certain he knew best as her blasted grandfather. Good God, Araminta despised tyrants. But she still managed to hold back her temper. She clenched her fingers around the padded edge of her chair's seat. "Thank you for your concern. I merely changed my mind."

His mouth tightened. "You were inclined to reject my help when you decided to come to New York, I recall."

She would leave before she said anything she'd regret. "Thank you, yes, I also recall that time, and I didn't need your help. I found employment on my own."

"You could have done better. I know a great deal about Mr. Kane. None of it good."

"Then why did you visit him last night?"

"He has requested money from this office for his help

in keeping various business contracts and associates, ah, secure."

Araminta stared, momentarily diverted. "Do you mean he's threatening you?"

"Yes. And I will not tolerate this behavior." His voice was sedate, quiet and entirely bloodcurdling.

It struck her that asking the ruthless man for help with Kane might be the equivalent of unleashing a hurricane to deal with a load of hot air.

Another reason to leave as soon as possible. Not enough that the man's self-contained presence gave a sharper blow to her sense than she'd expected—there was the matter of protecting her beastly job.

The work she did for Kane paid better than any position she'd held before. And she needed only a few more months of salary in her savings to realize her dream. She'd have enough time to convince Olivia to leave. Four months more should cover a half-year's rent for an establishment, though not in one of the best locations.

His voice, even icier now, broke into her calculations. "Miss Woodhall. You are quite silent, yet I see that you appear to be in distress. Let me assure you that I would feel a need to assist anyone who's been in service to my family."

Araminta had had enough. The man couldn't bother to be polite but believed that because he had once paid her salary, she should allow him to decide what was best for her. And, of course, he expected her to feel gratitude for his effrontery.

She jerked to her feet, her heart beating fast as the anger built. "Ah, then you need not bother with me. I worked for your sister."

He rose from his chair, too, far more smoothly, of course. "No doubt Timona would require me to help her friend."

The bored tone, his horrible spirit of noblesse oblige, choked her breathing. And the dam holding back her temper broke.

"*You* owe me nothing. I thought I made myself clear, I was not in your employment."

The corner of his mouth twitched. "That's an understatement. I recall that in Minnesota you would not relay a message from my sister without first subjecting me to your opinions. You clearly consider yourself above taking orders from me."

"If you mean I would never be one of the unctuous toad-eating sycophants with whom you surround yourself, you are right." The appalling words seemed to tumble out on their own.

His face showed no emotion, although she noticed that his hands, which had rested palms flat on the desk, closed into tight fists at his side.

"No, you wouldn't. I prefer to surround myself with people who treat me with basic respect."

She had taken two steps toward the door, but now she turned back and leaned across the desk toward him. "Respect breeds respect, Mr. Calverson. You obviously recall our meeting a year ago."

His hands relaxed, as did the set of his jaw. "Vividly."

The way he examined her now made her skin feel warm, but she could not stop to consider it. "Do you recall that when you came into that house in Minnesota, you did not bother to return my salutations? Not so much as a 'good morning' passed your lips. And when I offered you refreshment you never bothered with a please or thank you. And rather than bidding me a simple hello last night you lurked in the hallway—"

His calm voice interrupted. "I regret startling you, and apologize for that."

"Yes, all right. But your actions are generally of a

piece: you have no need for manners because the people around you think you walk on water. You must start to believe it yourself."

The eyes went hard again. "Of all the imper—"

She drew in a deep breath and plowed on, determined to finish having her say. "The worst of it was that even Timona, God bless her, thought your every word a pearl of wisdom. My heavens, the nonsense you'd poured into your sister's ear before I met her. 'There is no such thing as love,' you told her. Oh, I heard some of the things you told my darling friend, the things she grew up believing. Oh, how I wanted to . . ." Her voice died away.

"Wanted to do what, Miss Woodhall?" The hard eyes challenged her.

She was tired of intimidation by detestable men and ignored the danger in his soft and smooth-as-cream voice. Years of swallowing her words and mumbling "yes, sir" "no, sir" had built up inside her. Women like her were not permitted to say anything more. About time one of those men who thought he was the right hand of God listened to her. "To tell you what you are, Griffin Calverson. I know your sort of arrogant gentleman. You discount servants, poor relations, fools and yes-men. And since that describes every single person with whom you have contact, Griffin, you respect no one. I've wanted to tell you for years that you are a nincompoop. No, worse, a brute, who'd attempted to turn Timona, a happy young girl, into as scornful a monster as—"

Araminta's mouth snapped shut. She closed her eyes. And wondered when she'd lost her mind. Last night, perhaps, when she decided to come see him.

He spoke at last. "Now that you have had your say, are you satisfied?"

She put her hand over her mouth, wishing she could stuff the words back inside. She'd heard stories about

Griffin Calverson. Plenty of them. Oh Lord, this was perfect. She had yet another powerful, ruthless man angry
with her. At least this time she deserved his fury.

The clatter and voices of a busy workplace outside the
office barely registered; the silence inside the room
weighed on her like a boulder. And all she could hear
were her own reckless, asinine words echoing in her
head.

"No. I'm only mortified. I—I do not know what—"
She drew in a breath and tried again. "I can only say I am
sorry. I do not know what came over me. I have no excuse. I think it—"

Amazing that his dry, impersonal voice again managed
to cut short and roll right over hers. "Is there any reason
I should accept your apology? You march in here, saying
you have a matter of some urgency, and then when I attempt to find out the problem, you begin to abuse me."

She gave a shaky laugh. "Yes. Well. It's a good thing
that I don't need your help after all, isn't it, sir?"

Araminta clutched her bag tight, disliking the way her
hands and voice trembled, but not caring that he witnessed it. She swallowed hard and stepped back from his
desk, toward the door.

"Tell me," he said, and she was amazed he did not
sound angry. Indeed, there might have been a note of
amusement as he spoke. "Do you always give near-
strangers a list of their shortcomings?"

His hands were relaxed now, and she noticed his blunt
nails and the scars on his skin. No rings, no manicure.
The only part of his surface that did not quite fit his businessman's image.

She considered asking him if he always sneaked up on
near-strangers in corridors and grabbed them from behind, but decided she had been rag-mannered enough.

Instead she smiled. It did not feel entirely forced this

time. "Oh. Naturally. You should see how I exert myself for my friends."

His eyes widened. And then he gave a brief, startled chuckle. She had never heard his laughter before, and the sound's warmth shocked her.

It gave her the courage to speak—less like a harridan this time, thank heavens. "But you think I don't know you? Let me explain that to know Timona is to know her brother, Griffin. The girl loves you and talked of you often. And to find someone so chill—"

She drew in a deep breath and made another attempt. "Griffin—" Good heavens, she had called him by his first name twice. That confirmed what she suspected: her mind was slipping into madness. "I—I mean, Mr. Calverson. I again apologize for behaving badly, and for interrupting your work."

He'd regained his normal bored manner. "Despite your impertinence, Miss Woodhall, I am willing to be of service to you."

She inclined her head. "No, but I thank you for your time and . . ." Despite her best effort, her voice quavered. "Well. Never mind, then. Good day."

She was not brave enough to look him in the eye before she turned and bolted for the door.

He watched her stride away. And the fire that burned in his gut wasn't entirely anger.

Last night he'd been unforgivably rude, and she must still be upset by his effrontery.

In a way, he might consider his seizing her in the dark hall fair payback. A year earlier when they'd met, he'd been thoroughly taken aback by the woman. After months of letters from his sister filled with "Araminta says" and "Araminta thinks," he'd been prepared to face a managing, loud-mouthed female with no grace and too much influence over his sister.

In the past he'd had to quietly get rid of a couple of other leeches who'd latched on to the kind-hearted Timona, hoping to get their hands on a piece of the Calverson fortune.

Araminta was indeed managing. She was also energetic, intelligent and beautiful.

He dropped into the chair where she'd sat and allowed himself a smile.

A few months earlier, Griffin had bedded a woman who resembled Araminta—an intelligent and talented creature, the only kind with whom he bothered to waste time. But she had not suited him. Pleasant but indolent, the well-paid lady had held no heat outside the bed.

Last night the sight of Araminta at Kane's had made his pulse race again. Today he'd been almost excited to hear that she wished to speak to him. And thus annoyed at himself and on edge, for he did not like unrestrained eagerness.

Her accusations had blindsided him, and surprised him into retorts, instead of the more intelligent answer to such nonsense—ignoring the woman. He frowned, remembering her words. Did he discount servants?

Clearly her grudge lay in the fact that a year ago he had not greeted the cook as if she were an old family friend. Yet he sensed more in her: she felt attraction, too.

Griffin stared out the window at the street below, where the midday traffic was snarled by a broken-down hay wagon. The discomfort she showed as she talked about "the friend." Clearly she was in some sort of trouble herself. Her indignation meant it wasn't the sort of trouble that females so often got into. If not a pregnancy, what else could it be?

He knew that a chef's work was arduous and occupied

most of a day's waking hours. Griffin was willing to bet the trouble had something to do with Kane or his household.

Eh, he'd already decided to hire Galvin to infiltrate Kane's empire. One more assignment wouldn't hurt.

He rang the bell that summoned a secretary, and then propped his booted feet on the desk, as he composed a plan and waited for someone to take a letter to Galvin.

Despite her refusal of help, he'd step in.

If Kane were as bad as the rumors he'd overheard the night before, Griffin would make sure his sister's friend was safe. He'd planned to allow Williams to take over the Kane matter, but now he'd maintain a personal interest. For Timona's sake. And perhaps, eventually, to his own advantage. He thought of Araminta's plump mouth and the curving body he longed to explore. A very personal interest indeed.

CHAPTER 3

In Kane's huge and sunny kitchen, Araminta reached for her apron. Her hands didn't tremble, but they were still not entirely steady after her latest meeting with the self-important Mr. Calverson.

She pulled the apron over her head, shoved back the thin curtains covering the windows and opened the back door that led out to the garden. A chilled draft swept through the kitchen, but the room would soon be filled with heat from the two ovens and the ranges.

Araminta stopped for a moment to catch the scent of early spring, a welcome change from the usual New York stink of waste from horse and humanity. The garden would soon be lovely, and for a moment, she regretted having to leave, but she consoled herself with the thought that when she finally found the perfect place, she'd plant her own garden, and include herbs for her future restaurant's kitchen.

She made her way to the dark back pantry to fetch the pastry shells she'd made earlier and began to mix the ingredients for the filling. And to come up with another plan to deal with Kane.

Her staff had taken advantage of her unusual absence and had disappeared. Araminta enjoyed the peace.

Olivia drifted into the kitchen. She wore a flowing morning dress. She usually dressed formally, but today her girlish figure was unbound by stays—likely the bruises inflicted by Kane pained her too much. She drew back from the sunlight, and Araminta guessed her head still hurt.

She gave Araminta a tentative smile. "I looked for you earlier. Where did you go?"

"To see an acquaintance who's visiting New York." Araminta flipped open the lid on the smaller icebox to check the ice supply. The block was nearly gone. She'd have to put in an early order.

She straightened and surveyed her friend. Olivia's soft blond hair still rippled down her back like a china doll's. "I forgot Kane dismissed your maid. Do you need help with your hair?"

Olivia shook her head. "He wants me to wear it down."

"Oh? There is nothing elaborate planned for tonight's meal. Is he expected back here?"

Olivia's ivory brow furrowed. "He—he doesn't tell me when he'll come back. I don't dare ask."

Araminta made an impatient noise and dropped a head of garlic onto the counter. God knew she wanted to help Olivia, but sometimes she wondered if the poor thing could be rescued. "Olivia, I lose patience with you. Grow a backbone, my girl."

She seized a heavy knife and pressed down on the cloves to loosen the skin.

A quiet sniff made her look up. Olivia's china-blue eyes had filled with tears.

"Araminta, please, don't. You sound like you would leave. I am trying, truly. I would—" Olivia's voice broke off. A tear rolled down her cheek.

Araminta's anger dissolved. She wiped her hands on the apron and pulled the girl into a hug. All bones. Olivia needed to eat, and she needed to be distracted from her troubles.

"Come on, now, never mind. I'll teach you to make a proper béchamel sauce, shall I? Or better still you can help me get some work done. Maggie's off doing errands, and I don't know where Jack is."

Olivia, lovely despite the tears, wiped her eyes and nodded.

Araminta set her up in the corner with a chopping board and a knife and a bunch of parsley.

Olivia clumsily hacked at the parsley. "When I came into the kitchen you looked positively grim, Araminta. Was the visit with your friend unpleasant?"

Araminta heaved a huge pot of water onto the top of the range, then shoved more coal into the firebox next to the oven.

"He isn't actually a friend."

Olivia stopped chopping. "Ah, a man then."

Araminta shuddered. "Oh, indeed he is."

"You are interested in him."

Araminta opened her mouth to protest but knew there was no point in denying it. She'd had several dreams about Griffin over the last year. Disturbing and lingering dreams. And just thinking of his touch last night could make her feel as if her skin had been brushed by a warm feather.

"Well! Is he interested in you?"

She laughed. "Perhaps as target practice."

Olivia's uneven thumping stopped again. Her eyes widened. "What can you mean?"

Araminta opened the clay butter holder and scooped several spoonfuls into the pan. "At our previous meetings, he was terribly rude. He did not answer my 'pleased to meet you.' Ha, he didn't even bother to smile or nod. I greeted him and he stared at me as if I were a—a talking dog or something. No, it was worse. He stared right through me."

Araminta considered telling Olivia about the strange meeting the night before. Better not, for she knew the girl had no defenses against Kane, and she didn't want any reports getting back to him. She opened the glass jar of flour and continued, "And today. I went to speak to him and, uh, rather lost my temper."

As she stirred the sauce, she told Olivia all that she'd blurted out at Griffin.

Olivia gasped. She put her hands over her mouth and began to laugh. "Truly, you couldn't have."

"I did."

Olivia, still laughing, shook her head. "Araminta. What were you thinking?"

"I wasn't, obviously."

"Oh, I could never speak to anyone, certainly not a man, in such a manner. I have to admire your strength."

Araminta wrinkled her nose as she recalled the tirade she'd directed at Calverson. "Strength? You mean bad manners."

Olivia giggled, but then the smile faded from her face and she gave a few hard whacks with the knife. "Perhaps, but if I have learned anything in the last year, it is that in some situations, it is best not to behave like a lady."

"Not so difficult for me, for I was never one to begin with."

"Oh, pray stop, Araminta. You are as much a lady as any woman I know. You have . . . presence."

Araminta gave her a smile. "Thank you. I shall have to remember that word. Presence. So much more impressive than shrewishness."

They both laughed.

Araminta stirred the thickening flour and butter as she added cream. "So your troubles began a year ago?"

Olivia's smile disappeared. "Forgive me," she said softly. And Araminta knew that she meant she wouldn't say anything else. The girl refused to discuss anything about her past.

"Fine, fine. I shan't bother you about it." Araminta shook her spoon at Olivia, who ducked her head with a slight smile.

After she finished with the parsley, Olivia left to "go for a nap," she said, but Araminta saw the pinched, haunted look in her face. She looked unhappy or even ill, not tired. For a few minutes Araminta considered what this could mean, until the pace of work picked up and her thoughts turned to preparing the day's meal.

As usual, when she threw herself into cooking, she could forget anything else. Only occasionally was she tweaked by the memory of Calverson. The image of his face, his body reclining in the chair as he examined her, or his strong, limber hands would flash into her mind.

Every few weeks, the Park Avenue mansion lay silent and closed up for twenty-four hours. On those quiet days she did not have off, Araminta caught up with the bills and orders or experimented with new recipes or created dishes that would not spoil to be used the next day.

One of those mornings, Araminta went to Kane's, glad for the quiet. Still chafing at the memory of their peculiar encounter, she'd awoken that morning thinking of Griffin, knowing he must have haunted her sleep again.

She mixed and kneaded dough for some loaves of bread, and then she checked the supplies to make a list for the next week's menus. Alice, the younger scullery maid, stood at the basin, scrubbing out the last of the servants' breakfast dishes. Every now and again, Alice twisted sideways to stare out the kitchen door into the garden. Plainly the girl longed to be outside.

Araminta put down her pencil and stood up. "Leave it,

Alice, and trot round to the Miltie's pushcart and see if he has any cucumbers." She pulled her purse from her pocket and put some coins in Alice's hand. "And I think that the corner store where he parks his cart has made some ice cream. Stop and get yourself a dish."

Alice bobbed a curtsy and, grinning, ran out the door.

A few minutes later, Araminta went to build up the fire for the ovens, but the scuttle was empty. "Alice? Would you fetch some coal? Or get Bill to do it?"

No answer.

She gave a click of disgust—the girl was on the errand, of course. Araminta grabbed the scuttle's handle and started down the steps to the dark basement room where the coal was kept. The lamp Jack was supposed to keep trimmed and ready at the bottom of the stairs was out of fuel. She was just starting back up the stairs for the kerosene and scissors when a soft shuffling sound stopped her.

Rats. Oh, how she despised rats.

But then a man with a peculiar wheezing voice spoke at the other end of the passageway. "Christ almighty. I told you to do him by the river. We wouldn't have to go through all this fuss if you'd follow directions."

Araminta clenched her teeth to keep from crying out.

Another man spoke. "Yeah, and Kane'll have our guts for garters if he finds out we're here. Dammit, Bacon, this ain't private enough. We'll have to find somewhere else for storage."

Heart pounding, Araminta pressed tight into the dark corner by the stairs. She didn't move, not even to brush away the cobweb tickling her cheek, until she heard the two men, thumping and cursing quietly, shoving their way out the basement hatch door.

What could they be about? Something so wicked they

didn't want Kane to know of it? A quiver of fear ran through her.

She counted to one hundred. Then, determined to appear as normal as possible, she walked with shaky steps to the room that held the bin. Her eyes had adjusted to the darkness and she had no desire for light as she filled the scuttle, scrabbling at the chunks of coal in her rush.

When she returned to the kitchen, she couldn't concentrate on her work, and almost sliced off her thumb.

Someone had to be told. She had to make a search. At last she forced herself to creep back down to the basement holding an oil lamp. Squatting, she scanned the hard-packed dirt floor where the men had stood. She found nothing—no drops of blood, only a rock lying in a corner, a polished bit of pink rose quartz that she slipped into her pocket.

For the rest of the day she worked automatically, her mind lost in disturbed thought. Whom could she tell? The police? Oh, certainly. A man named Bacon and his friend had dragged something into the house and then hauled it back out again. And her evidence that there was foul play?

Nothing more than a peculiar conversation, and perhaps this pretty pebble, officer.

She could imagine what might follow. The police would mark her down as a hysterical woman. Or worse, if she'd interpreted the whole thing correctly, she might be the next one dragged to a basement.

Even if the police believed her, they might not act. Timona had blithely told her about how the police were paid off by businesses like Kane's. Griffin had told his sister about the corruption.

Of course. Calverson.

Griffin Calverson would know what to do. He said he

knew a great deal about Kane, after all. The thought drifted through her head, but she tried to ignore it.

Even work could not keep Araminta from thinking of what she'd heard in the basement. Restless, and then at last discouraged, she knew she would ask Griffin Calverson whom to contact. He'd tell her if her story was even worth telling.

She'd send round a note. Anything rather than face the man again.

That evening, she crumpled sheet after sheet of paper, trying to think of how to apologize and ask for advice without groveling or further insulting the man.

She at last settled for "May I call upon you at your hotel?"

The answer came the next day in the form of an unsigned note on Fifth Avenue Hotel notepaper, delivered by messenger.

"Tomorrow morning."

CHAPTER 4

Calverson rose and walked to the front of the desk. "Have you come to apologize?"

Araminta stood in the sunny library of his hotel suite and wished she could think of someone else, anyone else, in New York who might be able to help her.

He waved to a velvet chair near the fireplace. She walked over to it and ordered her legs to bend so that she might sit.

"Yes. I am sorry," she said, her voice as rigid as her body felt. "Mr. Calverson, once again I must say that I am dreadfully sorry to have bothered you. The only reason I have is that I do not know to whom else I might turn. Thank you for agreeing to listen."

Rather than look up at the man standing near her chair, she focused on the huge circle of sunlight that lit the gleaming elaborate parquet floor in front of her, and seemed to set the wood on fire.

He sank into the chair that matched hers. "I suppose I should be grateful that you don't mind returning to visit an upper-class mannerless nincompoop."

She tried hard not to squirm or blush, without success. "I wish you didn't recall what I said that day."

"I assure you, I remember it well." He pitched his voice slightly higher, not a crude mockery, at least. " 'In the Calverson organization when Mr. Griffin Calverson even implies a thing, it's truth straight from the mouth of God. No wonder he's come to believe he's better than the rest of mankind.'"

She winced. Why had she said that to a man she barely knew? And a man like him!

He went on, his voice as cool and slick as silk. "In truth, Araminta, I am not sure why you would seek advice from, ah, 'a heartless brute.'"

Oh bah. She had hoped he would not remember that particular phrase. She absently pulled off her gloves and squeezed them tight, trying to dismiss her discomfiture.

"Why are you frowning? Don't you recall those words?" he asked.

"I am fighting the desire to apologize yet again."

"Please, feel free to beg my pardon."

She glanced over at his face at last. His gaze did not seem particularly pleasant, but then again, it was not angry. Unreadable, naturally. She'd allow herself one bit of recklessness. "I know I was unspeakably ill-mannered, but I don't think I'll apologize again." At least she managed to keep from uttering the rest of her thought: *for I was also correct.*

And before he could continue with this dreadful conversation, she rushed ahead. "I need to ask you, or rather tell you—or someone—I suspect that Mr. Kane has some evil men working for him. I do not know what I should do."

Not a particularly smooth way to pose her dilemma, but she got his attention diverted from the subject of her last visit.

He leaned back, rested his elbows on the arms of his chair and steepled his fingers. "Go on," he said gently. "Explain."

And she managed to get out the story of the two men with what she thought might be an inconvenient corpse.

Griffin did not exclaim in horror or laugh at her or even widen his eyes. He waited until she'd finished her tale to ask, "You didn't see them?"

"No." She felt in her pocket and pulled out the small stone. "I went back later and found this."

He bent forward. "May I?" He took it from her palm, and she started as his warm fingers grazed her bare hand.

Her gloves lay forgotten in her lap. She quickly thrust her hands back into them.

Griffin apparently didn't notice, for he only studied the stone. "I'll keep this, if you don't mind."

Something like relief filled her. At least she wasn't wasting their time. "Then you do think the men were up to no good?"

He still stared at the stone. "I don't know."

"What should I do? I mean, ought I tell the police?"

He raised his head. She steadily met the considering gaze of the green eyes. When he spoke, he sounded almost tender. "I think it is best if you forget what you overheard, Araminta."

The relief gave way to a shudder, and cold dread trickled through her again.

Her distress must have been obvious, for he remarked, "You look as if you need some tea."

She straightened her back and groped for her bag. "Thank you, but I must return to work."

He rose from his chair. "You say you want my advice? Leave Kane's household, at once."

She'd considered that idea, of course, but wasn't about to admit it to Calverson. "Even if I did overhear something . . . horrible, Kane wasn't in the basement. And they said he'd have their guts for garters."

"Perhaps only because they planned to keep whatever or whoever it was in his house. Had that occurred to you?"

It had. She'd carefully watched every nuance of the swaggering, noisy Kane's manner. "He is behaving exactly as he always does. I know he is a bully. And I can easily imagine him beating Oliv—someone to death. But cold-blooded murder? No." She reflected a moment. "Nor do I think he is a good enough actor to hide such a thing."

He dropped the pebble into his jacket pocket and said in his usual brisk manner, "I hope you are right. I will make sure, if you don't mind." He waved off her protest and said, "I have my own reasons. Call it curiosity."

She nodded and got to her feet, glad to have told someone. "Thank you for your offer of tea, Mr. Calverson. But I think . . . there is nothing I can do but wait and watch."

When he walked to stand near her, she was almost astonished that she did not have to lean back to see up into his eyes. She had forgotten he was only a few inches taller than she. The clean, strong lines of his features and body held so much power he might have towered over her.

"You called me Griffin last time we met," he said. "What has changed?"

She had to smile. "Perhaps I've learned some manners?"

"I hope not."

Araminta gazed into his unreadable face. She had thought a man like Griffin did not indulge in banter, but there was the unmistakable gleam of humor in his eyes.

"Come," he said. "We'll take some tea in the sitting room."

This new facet of Griffin made her too curious to walk away. "Yes. Please. I think I would like a cup of tea after all."

Clutching her handbag tight, she tried to stroll rather than scurry past him as he waited by the door. She would not feel like a mouse around the man. Or rather, she would, but she would not let him see her timidity.

As they walked across the spacious apartment, Araminta admired the huge arched windows, the thick, soft carpets, the armloads of fresh flowers. She had worked in stately homes before and could tell the difference between real and false elegance. Kane's mansion was all show, with wood painted to look like marble in the fireplaces and pressed veneer rather than carved mahogany furniture.

The appointments of this hotel's apartment were less lavish—far less ornamental molding or gold and silver leaf—but she was certain that the details were real. The urn by the huge mantel, for instance, was surely ancient Chinese. Her mother would have known, for she adored antiquities.

She turned her attention to her host and studied him covertly, or so she thought until he spoke.

"Why do you stare? Have I a smudge on my brow?"

"I—I am searching for any resemblance to dear Timona."

"And do I look like my sister?"

She hesitated. "No, though you both have brown hair and green eyes."

"No other difference?"

Was the man trying to goad her? "Very well, then. Timona smiles easily, but you never do. In fact, your face never offers anything like encouragement."

"I have no need to encourage anyone," he said and shot a sidelong glance at her, as if waiting for her response.

No doubt about it. He wanted to irk her. She pasted a smile onto her face, determined not to allow herself to fly off the handle again.

He put his hand on her arm, a light touch but one that

shimmered through her whole body. She held her breath. Remaining here for tea was not a good idea.

He'd been of help to her—furthermore, she felt certain that he would take some sort of action. Because of him, she could return to work and pretend she'd never heard that strange conversation in the basement. She owed him her gratitude.

But she'd be safer nosing around Kane's business than staying too long in this man's presence. "Mr. Calverson, I beg your pardon. Thank you for your offer of tea, but I think I should take my leave."

Griffin grasped Araminta's elbow, determined not to let her escape. "You act as if you're afraid of me. Do you believe I'll offer you a tirade with the tea? Only bread and butter, I assure you."

She hesitated a moment, then gave him a small, almost shy smile. "You're right, I am being silly."

Over the last few days, since her last, unexpected visit, Griffin had wondered how he could approach her. Instead the fly had walked straight into the spider's parlor. But no, not an apt analogy, for he did not plan to destroy Araminta. For one, his sister would never forgive him if he hurt her friend. For another. . . Well, Griffin had the pedigree but didn't call himself a gentleman—he had spent too much time in too many ungentlemanly situations. Yet he had enough breeding not to hurt a woman, especially not a servant. His plans for Araminta involved far more pleasurable pursuits.

He led Araminta to the sofa. She gave a regal incline of the head in acknowledgment. Queen Araminta. When she wasn't Termagant Araminta.

He waited for her to take a seat before taking the chair across from her.

The door opened and Annie, the maid, entered, pushing

a cart laden with the teacups, two steaming silver pots and plates of small sandwiches and biscuits.

"Oh," breathed Araminta. Her expressive face lit like a child's upon spotting a longed-for plaything.

Griffin swallowed a smile. "Homesick?"

She shifted her dark gaze to him. "How do you manage to read minds, Mr. Calverson?"

"I have seen the same longing cross a number of English faces. And remember, I'm Griffin. Araminta."

He enjoyed the way her face flushed with interest and suspicion at his words. Araminta Woodhall was remarkably easy to read, but an interesting subject nonetheless. Far more interesting than her dull maternal grandfather, the only other member of her family Griffin had met. A starchy British banker, Woodhall had been puffed up with his own self-worth.

Too bad he couldn't ask Araminta what she thought of her grandfather. He wasn't certain if she even knew the man's identity. He was reasonably sure she'd be offended if Griffin revealed that he did.

She murmured her thanks to Annie, who retorted with her usual cheeky, "Oh, sure. You're entirely welcome."

Araminta sank back into the cushions, clutching a delicate Meissen china plate of food and her tea. She watched the maid, her curiosity obvious.

Griffin nodded, and Annie left.

"Are you enjoying New York?" he asked.

"Somewhat." She picked up the teacup, took a sip and closed her eyes and gave an audible groan. Dead easy to imagine that passionate look and sound elsewhere. He watched, fascinated, as she nibbled a crustless sandwich. Such a luscious mouth.

She gave another tentative smile. "The tea is perfect, though I should not be surprised. Calverson food and drink always appears and tastes perfect."

"That was why my sister hired you once, after all."

She looked over at him again, and her grin widened. He'd never noticed the way her eyes shone when she beamed, possibly because she hadn't favored him with such an expression before.

Araminta sipped her tea. "That was only one reason she hired me. Perhaps I would work for her still if she had not insisted on living so far from civilization."

She looked around the apartment as if searching for a topic of conversation. He waited, curious to see what she managed to scrape up. "Your maid . . ." Her voice trailed off.

"Annie."

"Yes. She is, er, pretty."

Griffin hid a smile at her diplomatic way of putting "wears far too much face paint and looks like a tart."

"She is well aware of it."

Araminta bent her head over her teacup rather than meet his eye. "She's unusual."

"Indeed. And Becky is even worse. I hope you notice that Annie is not particularly deferential? Not what you'd call a toadying servant."

She blushed, and he enjoyed the sight of her confusion for a moment before continuing. "But I'd rather not discuss my domestic staff."

"Oh." She seemed less bold than the Araminta he remembered.

Perhaps Kane and the city diminished her vibrancy, or perhaps she was dampened because she held a leash on her fiery temperament. He did not want to bother with polite small talk—not with her—and since she would not come to the point, he would drag her there. He already knew she wasn't Kane's mistress. What kind of trouble had she landed herself in?

"I'd rather talk about you. Why would a woman as, ah,

scrupulous as yourself about your employers associate with a dangerous fool like Kane? Why do you stay with him?"

She pressed her delicious full lips together. "I don't think my reasons are particularly interesting."

What the devil could that mean? He tried another tack. "Do you enjoy working for him?"

"Why do you ask?"

He decided he'd keep her slightly rattled. "The question was purely of a social nature. Chitchat."

Her eyes narrowed. "Yes, you excel at polite conversation, don't you?"

Ah, this was the woman he knew. "No more than you do, Araminta."

He expected she would apologize again, or perhaps grow offended. Instead she burst into laughter. She laughed so hard she had to pull out her handkerchief to wipe her eyes. After she tucked her handkerchief back in her bag, the amusing and irksome woman looked him up and down with one of her bold examinations, her eyes still bright with laughter. "I really must apologize. I'm sorry. I don't understand why I'm driven to be rude to you, sir."

"I am glad it entertains you."

The smile still wavered on her lips. "Are you?"

Griffin decided it was time for the next move. He was usually a patient man, but he had already grown tired of waiting.

He placed his delicate porcelain cup and saucer in the middle of the polished table next to his chair. He got up and settled close to her so his thigh lightly touched hers. She watched him and appeared wary of him, but not afraid, thank goodness. Not the fierce Araminta.

He had imagined the moment she would give in to him, but he would not rush her. No, he intended this to be more than a single seduction. Though he did not have specific plans for her yet, he wanted her in his bed. Eventually. He reminded himself not to push too far too fast. Self-control and tenacity usually won him anything he desired. And for whatever reason he very much desired this woman, and he had for far too long..

Araminta did not move away from Calverson. She followed the rise and fall of his chest, and the light lemon scent of him teased her. This is what she'd feared when she'd agreed to stay to tea. No—from the moment he'd touched her in Kane's dark passage.

The hair on the back of her neck rose as she suddenly realized she sat alone in a room with a ruthless, strong man who could easily overpower her and hide any ill deed he chose to perform. But even as that thought occurred to her, she realized she wasn't afraid of him. She trusted the white devil.

It was her own self that she did not trust.

The way her pulse quickened and her belly filled with strange, heavy pleasure told her she hadn't lost a jot of longing for him. At that moment, she wished she had never heard of him or heard the voices in the basement. She placed her cup and saucer on the table next to her and lightly clasped her hands in her lap.

He spoke at last, his voice light but filled with meaning. "I believe I have missed you."

Ah, not a good sign: her insides gave another small but insistent shiver of agreement. Pure *lust*, she reminded herself. And the word lust echoing in her made the queer sensation that much stronger. Bad to even acknowledge how much she wanted the man.

He reached over and picked up one of her hands. As he touched her, a strange heat of longing blazed through her—so intense it threatened to cook her good sense.

"Your skin is so lovely," he said in a husky voice. She pursed her lips, ready to scold him for mocking her.

But he shifted closer. She breathed in more of his scent, felt the heat of his body envelop her. The looming presence of the man swamped every thought.

She desperately tried to push her thoughts back into order, but only grew dizzy. "I came today because I'd supposed you'd give me advice about whom I might turn to. I have no desire to . . ." Her voice trailed off as he peeled away her glove, leaving her hand feeling obscenely naked. "Oh, my," she said. "I am not sure . . . That is . . . Mr. Calverson, do stop. I wish to talk about what I might do."

"We will talk," he assured her as if she were a small child. "Of course."

"But I am not at all sure this is what I want. Oh—"

He lifted her hand and put his lips to her wrist. His breath warmed her, and his soft mustache grazed her tender skin. She had wondered what that hair above his lip would feel like. Not harsh or bristling as she had suspected. Silken. She cleared her throat. "I'm not certain this is a good idea."

Her body grew heavy with thick longing even as she reminded herself that Calverson was not comfortable or warm. During the dark years following her mother's death, she had promised herself that she would not associate with anyone who was not kindhearted or did not easily laugh.

His gaze remained fixed on her face as he pressed a firm kiss into her palm. He overset her senses, made her a less-than-sensible woman. She could not ask him for anything that might give him more power over her.

"Mr. Calverson. Griffin," she croaked. "I must go."

He studied her for a moment, gave a single nod and released her hand. "Of course." He rose to his feet with unconcerned grace. "But you'll come back."

He sounded so certain, and appeared so detached compared to her—her legs turned wobbly when she was near him—she wanted to snap, "Never." Yet she also didn't want to eventually look like a fool.

She felt him stand close behind her as he helped her with her jacket, but then he stepped back politely as she readjusted her hat. "You were right to come to me about what you witnessed at Kane's," he said.

Araminta could breathe again, now that he no longer loomed behind her. "Thank you. I agree. I'll try to ignore what I overheard, since you believe I ought not contact the police."

"Has Kane ever threatened you, Araminta?"

"No. In fact when I began work for him I thought him a pleasant gentleman."

Griffin made a rude noise at the back of his throat.

Araminta had to smile. "Yes, it did not take long for me to understand that under that amiable smile, he's horrible. Though he's not the worst employer I've had, I do not like the way he—he treats other women."

He regarded her face thoughtfully. "Ah. And do you inform him of your opinion?"

"Of course not."

"No 'of course' about it, Araminta. Remember to whom you are speaking."

"Oh." She hoped he didn't see her blush. "But those things I said to you . . . You were different."

"Explain."

She rubbed her gloved finger hard on a jet bead on her bag and didn't look at him as she admitted, "I have become rather afraid of Mr. Kane. And I suppose I knew that you would not hurt me."

"How did you know that?"

"As I told you, your sister had talked about you so often I felt as if I knew you. And I know that you are actually harmless."

"And you are a fool."

She considered acting offended. Instead, she waited to hear his meaning, but he said nothing else. When she at last glanced over at him, his face showed no emotion.

For a moment, they lingered near the front door. He watched her, plainly expecting something, so she hesitantly reached out a hand. "Thank you for your time, Mr. Calverson."

He was in front of her, opening the door. "Allow me."

She hesitated, and then walked toward the back staircase.

He'd followed her and now lightly grasped her forearm. She swallowed hard, ready to fight him off, but he merely said, "We'll take the elevator."

"Mr. Calverson, I don't mind—"

"I will escort you to the lobby, Araminta."

"Oh." She wasn't sure she liked this plan. She still felt the heat he'd wedged into her with that mouth on her skin. . . .

He must have seen her dismay, for in his usual dry voice he said, "I shan't make any grabs at you. I am a host escorting his guest to the door. Not a ravening wolf."

She wasn't sure she believed that last statement. The elevator arrived, the man pulled open the gates, and Griffin waited for her to step in. As they made their clanking way down, he stood close to her and spoke quietly. "If you require my help, please don't hesitate to call upon me again. In the meantime, I advise you not to tell anyone what you, ah, might have witnessed, especially no one in Kane's household."

At the wide marble columns flanking the entrance of the hotel, he bowed over her hand and bade her a pleasant farewell. She settled into the cab, an unusual luxury, although this one smelled as if it had been shut up tight too long.

For the first time she noticed he had treated her with common civility.

Unlike most men.

As the cab made its slow, halting way uptown, she sat back and argued with herself about Griffin. He wanted her. But why? He could have nearly any woman in New York. Perhaps he wanted to teach her a lesson. Or perhaps he enjoyed the abuse she had heaped on him. She closed her eyes and saw him as he'd looked at her in the shadowy hallway. His face had had the intent, sharp quality of a hunter that night. The expression she thought could be desire. He'd wanted her then, too—and the thought made her stomach flip and settle in a new spot.

She'd do better to avoid the selfish man, of course. But the frightening exhilaration that hunter's look sent through her . . . Oh, Lord. On the other hand, she did not have to actually fear he would overpower her.

The man might be selfishly indifferent to any needs but his own, but he had listened to her this morning. She had told him no, and he had stopped at once.

He had not treated her like a menial today.

Araminta did not fool herself. No matter how much education or money she acquired, to most of the world she would always be a servant or worse. But for a few minutes she had forgotten her often demeaning place in society.

In the fuggish interior of the cab, she laughed aloud. Griffin Calverson either irked her or seduced her into acting outside of her role. He was not a dull gentleman, at any rate.

CHAPTER 5

Griffin stood on the sidewalk, hands clasped behind his back as he watched Araminta's cab disappear into the stream of traffic. The annoying and seductive woman still had not gotten around to asking for the favor she'd wanted when she'd first approached him.

If Griffin didn't hear from her again, he'd find some way of seeking her out. To his own advantage, as well.

He'd seen the desire flare in Araminta's eyes. Her transparent face showed her reluctant interest—which she displayed when she wasn't giving him holy hell.

In the meantime, Griffin had another job for his friend Galvin, whose men had infiltrated Kane's: increase their protection of Araminta.

Griffin had heard about the disappearance of a man called Pushy Pete. Perhaps Araminta's story confirmed who was responsible.

If Kane had had Pete murdered, Griffin would have to apply more pressure, work faster. And it also meant that Araminta could be in trouble if Kane should discover the connection between the Calversons and her.

He wished he could grab the woman and talk some sense into her, drag her out of Kane's house to safety. But Miss Woodhall would never tolerate that sort of treatment.

Griffin handed several coins to the doorman. "Send

someone up to my rooms to tell my associates I've gone to the office and I'll meet them there."

He strode up the avenue in the opposite direction Araminta had gone, and attempted to dismiss her from his mind. He was faintly annoyed that he had trouble concentrating on other matters: the memory of her powerful eyes and delicious figure interfered.

Though he did not despise his appetite, he rarely indulged it. Perhaps that was why he had such difficulty concentrating on other matters. He had suppressed himself too long.

As he entered the building that housed the Calverson Company's offices, a man greeted him with a gruff, "Hey! Mr. Calverson."

Griffin turned and surveyed the broad-shouldered gray-haired man with the battered nose and even more battered homburg: Gregory Galvin, one of Griffin's favorite businessmen.

"Galvin. Walk up with me."

"I'm just here to drop off yer report."

"Yes. But I hope you can spare a few minutes?"

Galvin eyed him briefly, then turned and waved at the two bull-like young men lurking behind him.

They made their slow way up to the fifth floor using the curving stairway rather than the elevator. Griffin knew the older man didn't trust those boxes.

After he settled at his desk, Griffin held out a hand. Galvin fished through his pockets and pulled out a crumpled and grubby sheet.

Griffin read the paper, then folded it up and tapped it absently against his palm.

Galvin stood in front of the desk and shifted his weight from foot to foot. "That what you want?"

Griffin nodded. "Yes, it'll do. Three gambling halls and

two brothels more than I'd known about. Well-covered connections, too. It seems I underestimated Mr. Kane."

"Not like you, boss," Galvin said. "You're not usually stupid, are ya?"

The two men with him shot horrified glances at him and then at Griffin, who stared back, entertained. Perhaps the two expected he'd pull out a dirk and stab Galvin for mocking him.

"Ah. Neither are you. Usually," he said softly to see what the young men would do. They took a step away from Galvin as if disassociating themselves.

Griffin had had enough playing around. "You two, excuse us. I need to speak to Mr. Galvin alone."

After his employees had scrambled out the door, Galvin rolled his eyes and remarked, "Puppies. But Buckler's loyal enough. And Hobnail, well, he's a special case, ain't he? They both follow my orders well enough."

Griffin pointed to an armchair, and Galvin grunted as he eased himself into it.

"Tell me anything else about Kane's households and domestic arrangements that wouldn't show up in here." Griffin flapped the paper he still held.

The older man fingered his tobacco-stained mustache. "He got the usual bunch of assistants, all bigger than dray horses, and at least one at all his establishments. Mostly to protect him, pick up cash, guard the door. He got an honest-to-God butler, maids, the works. Kane's come a long way from running a couple of gin mills and a rat pit. And that mistress he installed at Park Avenue. Very classy female."

"Miss Olivia Smith."

"Yah. Whatever her name is, it probably ain't Smith."

"What is she like?"

Galvin's blunt features were wreathed with wrinkles as his face curved into a smile. "Gorgeous. Perfect, bit thin but with a figure like . . ." Lost for words, he drew the in-evitable curves.

Griffin grew impatient. He'd glimpsed the girl the night he visited Kane's mansion, and he had the impression of a trembling blancmange. Not a jot of fire in her. "I want to know about her personality."

Galvin rolled his eyes again. "Hold yer horses. I'm getting to it."

No unctuous underling here, Griffin thought with amusement.

"She's polite. Classy, like I said."

"You make her sound horrifyingly respectable. Why do you suppose she's Kane's mistress?"

Galvin shrugged. "I dunno. She isn't like most of the whores. Too innocent like, you know? Kane doesn't let her around the other girls, but she's friendly with the cook there. The one that used to work for Miss Timona."

Interesting—Araminta had found herself a lost puppy. A weakling who needed rescuing. He almost smiled. No wonder she and his sister got on so well. Ah, and perhaps it explained her mission to find help for a "friend."

He pulled a roll of bills from his pocket, peeled off a few and handed them to Galvin. "Good. Stay awake. And remember, don't let that cook get in trouble. She's a friend of my sister's."

Galvin leaned forward as he tucked the bills into a back pocket. "That Timona. She makes the oddest friends. A woman who's just a cook, of all people."

Griffin restrained himself from arguing that Araminta, though she could be infuriating, was a great deal more than just a cook.

"She might also be a source of information." He tossed the smooth quartz onto the ink blotter, and told Galvin everything she'd told him about the men in the basement.

Galvin picked up the rock and turned it over in his

thick fingers. "Hell. This is Pete's. One of his lucky rubbing stones." Galvin gave a low hum. "Hell. I heard Kane say he thought Pushy Pete worked for you."

"Ah. That's interesting."

Galvin rolled the stone back onto the desk. "That cook will make a good on-the-spot witness."

An unwelcome realization flashed through Griffin. Even more than he wanted to bring down Kane, he wanted to keep Araminta out of danger. "No. Not her. Her usefulness to us is over."

He'd spoken with too much heat, and Galvin, who paid close attention to everything, blast the man, sniffed, amused. "Well, well. Is it now?"

He watched Griffin a moment or two before adding, "I think I'll put Hobnail onto watching the cook, since he's at Park Avenue, and I'm on Kane much of the time. That a problem?"

Griffin shook his head.

Galvin grunted and leaned back in his armchair. He fingered his mustache and his gray eyes focused on Griffin again. "Funny that a little matter like Kane would grab your attention. Wonder why you suddenly decide to bother with me and so many of my boys? And ask a favor of Inspector Byrnes, no less. Before poor old Pete, who isn't even one of ours, it wasn't like Kane was a big threat to anything of any importance. Yup, fellow's got to wonder what you discovered that night you went gambling at that Park Avenue house of his."

"You are presumptuous, Galvin," Griffin said mildly.

Galvin winked. "Want I should crawl out of here so Buckler and Hobnail think you've beaten me?"

"If it would amuse you." He watched his friend amble from the room. It was rather amusing, the foolishness people associated with him. Galvin's men clearly thought

Griffin a bully. And Araminta was not the first to call him a brute.

Even his own sister had sometimes implied she was disappointed in his nature. Not the first female in his family to dislike his blunt manner.

A picture of his mother arose, unwelcome, but he didn't bother to fight the very old memory of her severe face. No point—after all, he saw her every time he looked in the mirror. And truly, he must be grateful for her legacy, for Griffin had little respect for untrammeled passion. Success in any endeavor called for cool minds.

He pushed away from his desk. He ripped up Galvin's folded report of facts and figures and dropped the shreds into the trash. He'd already committed the report to memory.

Some men collected stamps. He collected information about people who interested him, like Araminta. Or people who threatened him, like Kane.

But leisure time was over. Now he'd take action. Perhaps he'd even take an active role with Kane. Cultivate the man. Keep an eye on his cook.

He pushed the button that summoned Williams, his second in command of the New York office.

Williams knocked and entered at once.

Griffin didn't trust the ambitious young man, but then he trusted very few people. "I'm not leaving for London as soon as I expected. I'm going to personally address some of the local issues."

Williams, slender and fashionably dressed, raised a respectful eyebrow. He gazed over the top of his gold-rimmed pince-nez. "Might I ask, sir, which projects you mean?"

The man appeared understandably rattled. Griffin did not normally take over any work he'd already asked others to handle.

"No, no need to look so worried, Williams. I'm not about to march in and bungle any of the negotiations with the mining company. I mean some, ah, less formal business."

Williams smoothed a hand over his slicked, carefully parted dark hair and cleared his throat. "Before you arrived in New York, I had already spoken to several of our friends at Tammany informally about Mr. Kane and—"

"Good. The next time you meet with any of them, I will attend."

Williams had been with him long enough to know when to stop pushing. "Yes, sir." He bowed and left.

Griffin knew Williams wore a puzzled look for a good reason. The New York branch of the Calverson Company and its associates had been threatened before, usually by larger and more menacing problems than one nasty little criminal who wanted to muck about in its concerns. Griffin had let his employees handle these problems.

He was scheduled to board ship to London in a fortnight, but he wouldn't use those tickets. And why was that?

Araminta. Galvin, damn his shrewd eyes, had spotted the truth.

Griffin wrote a note to be wired to various offices—he'd hear some grumbling that he'd canceled his plans for the next month. But really, his actions weren't unreasonable.

Timona's friend was very important to her. It only followed that he would go to some lengths to protect the woman.

He looked forward to future meetings with Araminta. He hoped to channel her fiery spirit into another, more satisfying sort of encounter. Just the thought could stir him.

Yet really, he would have taken these same steps for anyone Timona valued. His silent argument was so effective he almost convinced himself.

CHAPTER 6

Olivia perched on a stool, watching, as Araminta finished placing the decorative sugared violets on a cake. Araminta, lost in thought, stared at the elaborate creation without really seeing it.

She knew from his sister that Griffin rarely expressed amusement. Why was the man so bleak? Despite her indignation at his unreasonable approach to life, she felt inordinately proud that she could provoke his laughter. She realized she wished she could attempt to make him laugh again and see his striking face express something other than stony indifference.

"Did you hear my question?" Olivia's voice pulled her from the reverie.

Araminta bit her lip.

Olivia leaned forward. "It wasn't important. Why are you lost in thought?"

"I was thinking about my friend. The one I visited."

"Oh, so he's a friend now, not just an acquaintance." The girl grinned. "Have you been to see him?"

"Yes."

"And he's forgiven you?"

Araminta shrugged.

She was pleased to hear Olivia sound like any happy, chattering young miss as she went on, "Surely he has. I knew he would never hold a grudge against you! You are too wonderful. Oh, what fun! You have a beau! But you haven't told me. Who is your gentleman?"

"Calverson. Griffin Calverson."

Olivia's exquisite forehead furrowed. "No."

"I assure you, that is his name."

Olivia's frown deepened. "Oh, Araminta. I've heard of him. I think he's—he's, ah, in the same sort of business as . . . as him." She didn't seem able to say Kane's name.

A wave of nauseating dismay washed over Araminta, but she showed no sign of it. "Nonsense. Why do you say that?"

"I overheard one of—of *his* assistants say something. Something about Calverson wanting territory."

Araminta had learned that Kane was a gambler, a pimp, a thief, a man who preyed upon destitute, desperate women and drunkards. When she was particularly fretful, she added possible murderer to the list. She had known Griffin was ruthless but had never thought him as terrible as Kane.

Could that be why he wanted her to keep quiet about what she might have overheard that day in the basement?

No. She closed her eyes, saw his hard, handsome face as cold as winter. But she knew better, didn't she? Her instinct told her the truth. She could trust him. She could only hope what she thought of as instinct was based on something more than severe lust for the man's body.

Dudley, the butler, came into the kitchen to discuss the evening's arrangements. She said good-bye to Olivia and followed Dudley into his pantry, glad for the distraction.

That night, after she and the two undercooks and the scullery maids cleaned the kitchen, she rested on a kitchen stool before walking to her snug home, eight blocks away. Kane had wanted her to live in, but she refused. And she was so much in demand as a cook that she could make some unusual conditions.

"Miss Araminta."

Oh, bother. Kane's bulky form blocked her kitchen door.

"Good evening, Mr. Kane. I hope tonight's fare was satisfactory?"

"Better than satisfactory. As always."

He lurched across the room. The way he picked his steps made her suspect he'd had more to drink than usual. Sure enough, when he stood near her, she was enveloped in a thick fog of alcohol. He beamed at her, his large eyes and smile giving him the appearance of a handsome, dissipated cherub.

"Miss Araminta," he breathed into her face as he began what she suspected was a practiced speech. "I have enjoyed having you in my employment. I would like to personally offer my appreciation and affection."

She resisted the urge to reach for her meat chopper to show him what she thought of his personal offer.

She slipped down from the stool. She knew she ought to be frightened, yet she rarely felt fear in these situations. Only useless belligerence. "Mr. Kane, not only am I not interested, but if you come into my kitchen again with this sort of suggestion, I will walk out the door."

His face flushed an ugly red. "This is my kitchen."

She took a deep breath to cool her flaring temper. "Yes, indeed it is. But you won't have me cooking in it. And I know you like having me work for you because of those times I have to come out and prance around like a show horse in front of your guests."

The hard red face relaxed, but she was not fooled into thinking he was amused when he showed his usual toothy smile. "Nice picture you paint there, Araminta. But I think most of the women in my employment would gladly give more than a simple curtsy."

She opened her mouth to reply, but remembered the lesson her mother had attempted to drum into her. She did not always have to speak her mind. Araminta pressed her hands together. Only a few more months, she reminded herself. Then she would leave forever, dragging along Olivia if she must. And Maggie, too.

He watched her. "Yes?"

She didn't speak and stared down at her hands.

"Smart girl." Kane unsteadily perched himself on the edge of the stool she'd abandoned. "I wonder if you could tell me about your last employer."

Ah, now she understood why he hadn't allowed himself to explode into a rage when she'd told him to leave her kitchen, perhaps even why he'd set out to seduce her. He wanted something from her. "You want to know about Mrs. McCann?" she asked.

He grunted impatiently. "I mean Mr. Calverson."

Had he somehow found out about her visits to Griffin? Had he beaten the information out of Olivia? How foolish she'd been, to speak Griffin's name so freely to the girl. She swallowed and managed a cool "I have met him, yes."

Kane chuckled. "You don't think much of me, do you? Did you like him? Let him get to know you?"

"Mr. Kane. I really don't think that is—"

Kane leaned close to her. "Because Calverson is bad news, Araminta. Not a gentleman despite that classy accent of his. He's colder'n a whore's heart. Do you know he's killed at least three men? Eh? And he don't think much of women, either. They're nothing but playthings to him."

She was proud of herself for not asking if Kane thought he was any better.

He bent even closer. "So, tell me. Do you know what the bastard is like? Got any weaknesses, eh?"

She took a few steps back to get away from the unsavory mix of cologne and alcohol wafting into her face. "I did not socialize with him, Mr. Kane. I am afraid that I am busy just now and I can't—"

"I can't see why you're so riled up by my interest. You don't exactly got a line of men waiting at the kitchen door."

As if on cue, a voice at the outside door interrupted. "Miss Araminta?"

On edge and startled, Araminta spun around. "Mr. Hobbes, you have startled ten years from my life."

The large, broken-nosed and somewhat dim flunky ambled into the kitchen. Hobbes was an even more recent hire than herself. He probably did some kind of rough work, judging by his size. Perhaps he worked as one of the burly doormen set to watch the front of the house, to keep out undesirables and warn of police raids.

He tilted his hat at Araminta and then to Kane.

"Evenin', sir."

Kane glared. "What the hell do you want?"

"I was wondering if I might walk Miss Araminta home."

The glare turned to a smirk. "I see I was wrong. You do have someone after all."

Araminta opened her mouth. Hobbes's meatloaf of a hand descended on her shoulder and gave a light squeeze. She closed her mouth.

Hobbes still clutched his hat. " 'Night, sir. I'll be back in a tick."

But Kane had already pushed back through the kitchen door.

She turned and examined the large man with brown,

close-cropped hair and sideburns, and an amiable though slightly vacant expression in his pale blue eyes.

She was not sure she wanted to go anywhere alone with him. "What on earth are you doing here, Mr. Hobbes?"

"Like I said. Walking you home."

"I have no trouble making my own way home."

He shrugged, but didn't move.

Araminta watched his placid face. They'd be on public streets—surely he would not attempt anything. And really, he had a calm, stolid air about him. Hard to imagine him turning into a raging maniac. Rather than argue with him, she pulled on her gloves, hat and cloak and went out the door, locking it behind her.

Though it was almost midnight, the streets bustled with people. Mr. Kane's establishment closed early on Sunday nights out of respect to the upper-class neighborhood, though Araminta thought the neighbors would barely notice the gambling den's activities. Many of the residents held huge fetes of their own on a regular basis.

The night air was chilled, and she risked harming the feather on her brown hat by drawing her cloak's hood over her head.

The gas lamps on the avenue made the first part of the walk easy. Araminta tended to speed up once they turned the corner into the less well-lit street. But she had to admit that with Hobbes at her side, she wasn't as worried about what might lurk in the darker corners she passed.

"Your appearance in the kitchen at precisely that moment was suspiciously fortuitous, Mr. Hobbes."

"Call me Hobnail. Everybody does."

"Why did you show up, Mr., er, Hobnail?"

"M'boss told me to keep an eye on you."

She slowed down and glanced up at him. "Mr. Kane is your boss. And he didn't seem pleased to see you."

"I got another boss. But that's neither here nor there."

"It isn't? What do you mean by that?"

He shrugged, and she understood that he wasn't going to give out any more information.

Another boss. She thought of Griffin Calverson. Who else would bother to interfere in her affairs? Annoyance at his meddling blended with a strange excitement. He cared enough to intervene for her.

Perhaps she should attempt another visit to Calverson and ask him if he'd set Mr. Hobbes on her like some lumbering watchdog. She rejected the idea as an excuse to see him again. Of late Araminta often found herself manufacturing excuses to contact Calverson. Something that put him in her debt rather than the other way around suited her best.

"I should have asked if you would prefer to take a hansom cab, Mr. Hobbes—Hobnail. But I do like to walk home."

"Makes no difference to me. I'm used to a fair amount of walking," he assured her.

"Do you enjoy it?"

He shrugged.

She looked around at the dark buildings, with only a few windows glowing here and there. "I love seeing the city mostly asleep. And the air this time of year. It can have such a wonderful scent. Under the usual reek of the city, I mean."

He grunted.

"And in the mornings, it is even better. Just as the sun is coming up, even the worst places seem full of potential beauty. Rather the flip side of 'Roses have thorns, and silver fountains mud/clouds and eclipses stain both moon and sun,'" she recited. "Though really, come to think of it, despite the theme of sin, the rest doesn't fit at all."

"What's that, anyway?"

"The sonnet? Shakespeare."

"Oh, him."

She continued to talk, while he only occasionally mumbled a reply. Perhaps she annoyed him with her sudden need to fill the silence.

"Am I disturbing you by chattering?" she asked.

"No. I like it. But we're just about there, ain't we?"

"How do you know where I live?"

"Er. Just heard the address somewhere, I reckon."

Griffin again, most likely. She had been pulled into his sphere of influence, and had become another subject in the feudal lord's kingdom. Yet even that thought did not rouse resentment; instead she felt protected by his shadow.

So much for keeping that subject from haunting her, she thought as she offered her hand to Hobnail for a shake goodnight.

CHAPTER 7

The next day was what Maggie called one of their "fancy days." Araminta thought of the nights the most important clients attended Kane's as nuisances, though she did occasionally enjoy creating the more elaborate meals.

Araminta checked a mirror to make sure her dark curls had not turned too unruly in the steam and heat of the kitchen. She pulled her mother's pearl drop earrings from the little shelf under the mirror, screwed them on, fixed a smile on her face and pushed open the swinging door separating the servants' quarters from the rest of the house.

On the nights she changed into a fine gown, she left the cleaning up to her staff. Since many chefs never lent a hand in the tidying of their kitchens, she knew that her help most evenings was more remarkable than her occasional neglect.

She dropped a swift curtsy in response to the applause, and when she gazed through the blue haze of cigar smoke over the crowd of black-suited men seated at the long damask- and silver-laden table, she looked straight into the bored, heavy-lidded eyes of Griffin Calverson. A curious dizziness seized her as she examined him, and then noticed his companion.

Lola, who occasionally visited in order to "entertain"

the gambling clients, lounged beside him. It would be more accurate to say that she was practically draped across his lap. Araminta had little contact with the light-skirts from Kane's other establishments. She dearly wished she could grab the young creature and march her to the front door. She'd order Lola to wipe off that dreadful—and unnecessary—rouge and go home.

Araminta's gaze traveled up from Lola's pretty young face, and, as her eyes met Calverson's again, her heart thumped hard. He clapped like the others. Yet he appeared so profoundly uninterested, she could swear his mind was elsewhere.

"Thank you all for your generous appreciation." Araminta launched into the short speech Kane demanded she give. Her employer did not appear to mind that she usually adopted as dismal a tone as possible. Tonight she aimed for the voice of an undertaker announcing a viewing. "And once you have enjoyed your port and cigars, we ask that you retire to our exquisite"—she paused, and in an even more hopeless tone finished—"gaming rooms in the front parlor."

Another round of applause. Griffin's eyebrows raised slightly, and his eyes glimmered with a tad more interest. As close to a look of hilarious amusement as he'd allow on that face, she supposed.

She turned and marched out of the dining room. If he wanted to play with the likes of Lola, it was none of her business.

The garden door stood open, and unseasonably warm weather beckoned her to the only part of Kane's establishment she enjoyed. She wandered the paths of the small pleasure garden that lay behind the kitchen garden. A full moon shone; the soft music floated through open windows. A night for enchantments, not rankling thoughts of men who had too much money and too little to occupy their hands.

A couple slipped from the French doors of the rear parlor, beyond the terrace and into the garden. A soft breeze picked at her skirts as she backed away from them and went to the vine-covered pergola, where she sat down in the shadows. In a few weeks, the little shelter would probably be redolent with the heady perfume of the wisteria.

Someday she'd have a garden as enchanting as the one her mother had cultivated. Charlotte, who'd never so much as touched dirt before her banishment, had had a gorgeous garden behind their small cottage. Araminta smiled at the memory of her mother's gift of quiet happiness. If only she, Araminta, could have been content to remain in that small village. But that was a child's memory of paradise. She could not fit life there, and though her mother had never complained, Araminta realized Charlotte had not either. Poor Charlotte must have been lonely.

"May I take a few minutes of your time?"

She jumped up from the wooden bench. He appeared to be a looming shadow, though the shape of his crisp white shirt stood out clearly.

"Good evening, Mr. Calverson," she said. "Where is your dinner companion?"

"Not with me."

Her heart should not have lifted at that. "Did you follow me out here?"

"I have been waiting for a moment when I could slip away."

Not an answer to her question, of course.

He sat down across from her. In the darkness behind her, creatures—birds, she hoped—rustled sleepily in the vines.

"Why are you out here, Araminta? Do you have an assignation?"

"Pray do not be ridiculous. I come out here to slip my bonds."

"Now you are speaking nonsense. Even Kane would not hold you against your will."

She smiled. "No, indeed. He is a monster, but still, I enjoy my work. I mean bonds of a different sort. Mostly my own making, I suspect."

He made a small rumble of disbelief, or perhaps mockery. He shifted on his seat, leaning toward her slightly. Her hand rested on the bench. She shivered as he absently stroked the side of his thumb over her fingers.

She knew she'd been hoping he'd seek her out. Even after she had seen Lola in his lap, she could not contain that distressing eagerness. She could only be grateful that the shadows hid her reddened cheeks, as well as her difficulty maintaining a steady breath. "What can I do for you, Mr. Calverson?"

"I am merely enjoying your company."

"Hmm."

"No, I am not lying, Araminta. I am not sure I should admit this to you, but I have rather admired you since that day in Minnesota when we, or rather you, discussed my sister's marriage. My interest was furthered during your two more recent visits."

Could he be serious? She assumed he meant the day she'd informed him that he was a worthless specimen of a man.

"I had no notion." She was dismayed at her breathless voice. She'd hoped to sound arch.

"I did not want you to."

Her heart beat far too fast, and she had trouble with her breathing. "Coward," she whispered, unsure if she meant herself or him.

"Yes, I am." His voice was dry as three-day-old bread.

Amazement helped her regain some of her composure. "Griffin, have you learned to laugh at yourself?"

"I have learned to tolerate your laughter," he said, his face and voice still so deadpan she could not read his mood. "Araminta."

She'd always disliked her name, but not when he spoke it. He made it a poem—about lust for her, perhaps, but still fairly beautiful. He shifted so that the outside of his leg touched hers. She grew dizzy with anticipation waiting for the touch her skin almost felt, or the kiss she could almost taste. But before he'd bent close, another voice interrupted.

"Hist, sir. He's coming now."

Griffin bounded to his feet. His dark shape blocked the dim light from the garden as he peered out from the doorway, but then he backed away and stood in the shadows next to her. He yanked off his jacket and tossed it to her. The wool garment still warm from his body landed across her lap, but before she could ask him what he was about, he'd pulled his shirt from his trousers. A moment later he unbuttoned his trousers, then rebuttoned them obviously wrong.

Araminta half rose from the bench. "What do you suppose you—"

He leaned close to Araminta and whispered, "Stay in the shadows and keep quiet."

"But I—"

"Keep quiet."

Griffin trotted down the steps and was greeted by a cheery outcry. Kane.

"Good evening, sir! Have I interrupted something?"

"A few minutes earlier you might have."

"Oho, so you have taken a fancy to one of our ladies? Which do you have in there?"

Araminta shrank against the vines, at last understanding Griffin's actions. She hoped.

"The one called Lola, I believe?" Griffin sounded as cool as ever, though perhaps faintly lazier. "I was just on my way inside. Did I hear you mention that you have a faro table upstairs tonight? I was going to try my hand at that."

The men's voices grew faint.

Araminta rubbed her hands together; her palms had grown damp. She picked up his jacket, a heavy, well-tailored piece of clothing. Almost reluctantly, she pressed the jacket against her face and inhaled his scent. Then she folded Calverson's jacket and left it lying on the bench.

She stood in the arched doorway and glanced around the now-deserted garden, and then descended the stone steps to the path.

"Miss Araminta," a voice hissed from the boxwood hedge next to the arbor.

She started and gasped. "Mr. Hobbes, you have removed yet another year from my life. How do you manage to pussyfoot about the place?"

"I'm Hobnail," he reminded her. "Haven't snuck around at all. Was stationed here."

"Oh."

She leaned against the thick wooden arch and considered this confirmation that Griffin had set the man on her. If Hobbes was supposed to look after her, maybe he'd be willing to threaten Kane about keeping his battering fists off Olivia's body. After all, Calverson had said he would help.

"Mr. Hobbes—"

"You ready to go?"

"I'd like to hire you. To protect someone. Do you know Miss Smith, Mr. Hobbes?"

"Hobnail. Nah, don't hire me. Do my best, but can't do much. Can't annoy Kane. Ready?" He stood and waited.

She clicked her tongue impatiently. "It is still early, well before midnight, and I do not think I'll require—"

"He'll have a fit if I don't."

"Mr. Calverson?"

"No, not him. Want me to fetch your bag?"

He was sedate, but as stubborn as Araminta herself on a good night. Since this wasn't one of those nights, she gave up. "I shall collect my belongings and be ready to walk home in five minutes."

"Meet you at the door, then."

He paused. "Do you mind Mr. Kane thinks I'm courting you? 'Cause I would. Court you."

She felt the stirrings of a headache. "I understand. But please, it's unnecessary to feel you must—"

"Like to," he said.

"That's extremely kind of you, er, Hobnail, but I think not."

He shifted his feet and spat. "Huh. Change your mind, tell me, eh?"

"Of course."

Really, she reflected, turning him down had not been nearly as awkward as it might have been. And when they walked toward her house, she made a couple of cheery remarks about the people up and loitering on the streets.

Hobnail answered with, "When I worked at night, met all sorts, most of them running away from me."

"Yes, I can imagine they think you're a dangerous sort of a fellow."

He seemed to think that was particularly funny.

When they lapsed into silence, it felt companionable rather than stiff.

* * *

Araminta had just fallen asleep at two in the morning when a light tapping at her front door brought her abruptly upright.

She yanked on a dressing gown over her nightgown and thumped down the stairs in the dark. Had someone fallen ill? Or died?

When she tugged open her door, Griffin Calverson stood on her doorstep, pristine again in his dark evening suit, complete with wool coat, gloves and silk top hat. He'd donned an overcoat to ward off the chill. Protected only by her thin gown and robe, Araminta shivered and stared at him through the wisps of cold fog that had settled on the city.

He peered over her shoulder into the dark house. "May I come in? I do not wish to harm your reputation by standing on your doorstep."

She wordlessly opened the door wider. He slipped past her into the hallway.

As he sauntered into the front parlor, he pulled off his coat and hat. He turned and held them out to Araminta. She took them, surprised by the coat's bulk. After a moment's thought, she flung them onto the sofa.

"That will do." He sounded amused. "Tell me what you plan to do."

"What are you talking about, Mr. Calverson?"

"Your visit to my hotel the other day. I know you said you would pretend you did not overhear those men in the basement, but I want to make sure you're not getting into some other sort of trouble. You or your friend."

Annoyance flooded her. In four hours she would have to walk back to Kane's establishment and begin her day's work.

She pretended to give a wide, audible yawn.

"Very nice," Griffin remarked.

"Can't this wait until regular calling hours?"

"I am afraid not. It is best if Mr. Kane not know that you and I are acquainted. And I would rather not be seen visiting you in your home during regular hours. Your reputation, as I mentioned."

"Oh." She wondered that he was jesting. Didn't he know what people usually thought of her? She was too aware of the world's notions about a woman like her. "It is too late—about Mr. Kane, I mean. He came into my kitchen and asked me several questions about you. I told him that I barely knew you."

Even in the dark she could see how he folded his arms and stared down his nose at her. "I am still convinced you should leave Kane's establishment."

"No. I can't."

"Come now, you do not require his money."

The quiet, canny note in his voice told her he knew about her private funds. The money she loathed.

The man and his encroaching ways almost frightened her, and she allowed her temper to take over. "There is no reason for you to care whether or not I continue working for Kane. You don't need to know my reasons for doing so."

"Perhaps. Nevertheless, I am interested."

He walked over to the gas lamp and drew out a tin of matches from his pocket. The lamp started with a soft pop and hiss.

He turned slowly on his heel, inspecting her parlor as if he were a potential buyer of the small watercolors her mother had painted, or perhaps the landlord's rich, well-maintained furnishings. "Very nice. You have fine taste."

Griffin turned and examined her with the same acquisitive air. The glow of the gaslight cast dangerous shadows on his face and turned his hair to spun dark gold.

Araminta folded her arms and wished she'd worn her

winter flannel nightgown and thick dressing gown. Not the batiste gown and matching robe. More than just the chill and anger gripped her now. Her breasts prickled with awareness of the man.

"Nothing here is up for sale," she said, meeting his gaze steadily.

His eyes sparkled. Could it be humor? "No, of course not. It might surprise you to learn I am not a covetous man. There are very few things I value enough to add to my permanent collection."

Well, that was a warning of sorts, wasn't it? She backed away from him.

Coffee. If he would insist on prolonging this strange nocturnal visit, she'd have to make some coffee. Or rather do something to keep herself from moving too close to him.

Without a word, she padded into the kitchen. The stove had enough embers, so starting a fire would be no problem. She fed it some coal, and then got down the mill from the shelf. She opened the sack of beans, put them in the mill and turned the crank. He leaned in the doorway and watched.

"Yes, good idea. Thank you, I would like some coffee."

She snorted. "Fine time for you to start in on proper etiquette. Sit down and tell me what you want from me."

He obliged; as he drew back the plain wooden chair it scraped loudly on the floor. "I don't want anything. Yet."

He leaned back in the chair, the habit of controlled sprawling, Araminta thought as she watched from the corner of her eye. Calverson relaxed was as tense as a normal man ready for battle.

"Go on, tell me what you don't want, then."

"No need to sound so defensive, Araminta. I think we are not at cross-purposes. I wish to thwart Linder Kane. Without calling in too many favors from my New York friends, that is. And you wish to protect your friend, Miss, ah, Smith and somehow remove her from the house."

The rasp and crunch of the grinder stopped as she turned and gaped at him. "How in God's name did you ever—"

"I am not unobservant."

"Hobbes. He must have told you."

"I have never discussed the matter with him. No, I recently thought about your attitude toward my sister. You seemed to treat her more as a protégée than an employer. You appointed yourself her protector."

She gave a humorless chuckle. "With a family consisting of you and that worthless father of yours, she needed some protection."

"No longer."

"No." She agreed with a sigh and recalled Timona and her husband. McCann's tender smile showed how he adored Timona. . . .

Araminta went to the kitchen sink, pumped water into the coffeepot and set it on top of the stove. Oh, my. She would give away her favorite recipes just to get a man she cared about to look at her with a smile like McCann's. Ridiculous thought, since fate seemed determined that she care about a man who rarely indulged in smiles of any sort.

Griffin's cool voice interrupted her yearning. "And so when I understood another lost lamb worked in your employer's house—"

"She does not work there," Araminta said.

"I beg your pardon. When I understood you had encountered another stray, I thought I'd discovered why you would continue working for a man you disliked. Am I wrong?"

She sat down as far from him as possible to wait, but the kitchen table, like the kitchen, was not large. Both seemed far too small at the moment. Griffin's presence filled every corner of the room.

"No. You're partially right," she admitted at last. "Although contrary to what you think you know, I do need the money. And I also care about the people who work for me." Fine. She decided it would not hurt to tell him more. As long as it would not give him any hold over her, she would share. "I agree, Smith is not her real name. I had thought perhaps . . ." Her voice trailed off, and she tried again. "I once thought of contacting a detective and hiring him to uncover the truth of Olivia's past, but the poor girl seemed so eager to hide it. It hardly seemed fair to drag it up."

"Who do you suppose she really is?"

She rubbed her eyes and stifled a real yawn. The gurgle of the coffeepot was a welcome sound. She climbed to her feet and got down the thick mugs. Thin, lovely porcelain for tea, a peasant's mug for coffee. "I have no milk or cream. I don't bother keeping any at home since I'm at Kane's most of my waking hours. Sugar?"

He nodded. She placed a few misshapen lumps of sugar onto a plate. No special treatment for visitors who show up in the middle of the night.

"Olivia Smith," he reminded her. "Tell me what you know of her and why you care about her."

She waited, staring down at the coffeepot. What kind of interest could he have in Olivia? But nothing she knew would hurt the girl. After she'd poured coffee for each of them, she sat down again. "She's the daughter of someone wealthy."

"Why do you believe that?"

"She's well educated and she has that air of a girl brought up with wealth. Furthermore, I think she's afraid someone will discover her real name and somehow contact her family."

He swigged his coffee and watched her over the rim of his mug. "Perhaps. Although your theory has some problems." He put down the mug. "If she is the daughter of a wealthy family, then why haven't we heard of her disappearance? Why aren't the police searching for her?"

"Maybe she's lied to them? They might well think she's safe in some school or on a journey."

"How old is she?"

She wanted to demand his reasons for all of these questions, but perhaps he needed the answers to protect Olivia. "I'm not good at judging age. I suppose less than twenty, more than sixteen. And she refuses to tell me. She's an innocent, though. A sheltered girl, or she was until recently. Oh, and she has recently contracted some sort of illness, I think."

She described the way Olivia occasionally turned ashen and shook. "Sometimes she perspires so freely I worry for her."

He was silent for a long moment, staring into the flames. "I wonder if it could be the sort of, ah, illness brought on by need."

"What can you mean?" The only thing Olivia really needed was to get out of that place.

He shrugged. "Is she Kane's mistress?"

She knew he would never pose such a question to a woman of his own social class. She swallowed a mouthful of coffee along with another sort of bitterness. "Yes, although he doesn't spend many nights with her. She lives above the gaming rooms."

"Does she love Kane?"

Araminta took a larger gulp of coffee and scowled. The coffee was too strong. And the idea anyone could love that man too absurd. "She is afraid of him."

"You do not answer my question."

"Can you truly love someone you fear?"

"Oh, yes, indeed you can, Araminta." A corner of his mouth quirked.

"I suppose you'd know," she retorted, fighting the quiver of awareness running the length of her spine. "I imagine some woman or another has passionately declared her love for you, and anyone sane would be at least slightly afraid of you."

His face maintained its usual deadpan, but even in the light of a single candle she could see the glimmer of beguiling merriment in his eyes.

"Now why did I suppose you would not keep your promise to remain civil to me?" he asked as if talking to himself.

She couldn't help grinning. "I'm afraid I do enjoy goading you."

"I am curious. Why?"

She wrapped her hands around her mug as she considered the question. "I feel brave when I speak my mind to you, and a coward when I remain silent. I rather like the idea of poking the tiger on the nose."

He tilted his head, and the shadow of a real smile crossed his face. "With an umbrella through the bars? Hardly seems sporting. And yet you must beware the tiger who roams free."

"Yes, and you aren't behind bars, are you?"

He did not answer, and in his silence, he reminded her of the beast she accused him of being, a waiting tiger of infinite patience and impassive jade eyes.

"You laugh at my jibes," she pointed out.

"The shock of novelty."

No, something more. Some recognition, or so Araminta guessed. Aloud she said, "Yes, I imagine the men you pay do not care to risk their jobs by crossing their master. And even your sister thinks you are close to perfect."

"My friends suffer under no such illusions."

She studied the face that might have been carved from stone. Without a trace of banter she softly asked, "Do you have friends, Griffin Calverson?"

He blinked, and a faint crease appeared between his eyes. She knew she had pushed too hard. The discussion was over. She ignored her disappointment that she'd made him angry. After all, his friends or any other aspect of his personal life could be none of her affair. And she needed her sleep. She swallowed the last of her coffee, hoping it would not keep her awake the rest of the night. Ha. The memory of Griffin in her house was probably more than enough to do that.

"Olivia," she said briskly. "What do you propose to do?"

"Kane has made enough of a nuisance of himself that I think I will have to take some sort of action eventually."

"What has that got to do with Olivia?" A sudden, horrifying thought came to her: could he be speaking of murder? She flinched at the thought.

He did not seem to notice. "I think that while I deal with Kane, I could be of some assistance to your friend."

"Couldn't we ask your friend, Mr. Hobbes?"

"Ah, Hobnail. I'm surprised he told you of our connection."

"He didn't, but it does not take a genius to see it after he stood guard for you this evening in the garden. He could simply take her out of that place."

Griffin folded his arms. "Even if Miss Smith could be removed from Kane's, where would you shelter her?"

"Here."

"And what would keep Kane from sending a few lads over to rough you up and take back his property?"

"Oh." She fell silent. "Nevertheless, I'm willing to risk it."

"I am not, however. I have already sacrificed a part of Kane's trust in Hobnail."

She frowned. "How?"

"By having him to keep an eye on you, of course."

She already knew that Griffin was responsible for Hobbes's protection, but she liked hearing him admit it.

"I thought so. Why do you have him walk me home if I'm to be protected from Kane?"

"There are other dangers in the city for a woman. And it is a small matter to see you're kept safe from more than just Kane."

Rather than feel indignant at his interference in her life, she couldn't keep from smiling. "It would have been better to protect Olivia."

"Come now, you know Kane would not tolerate any interference with her."

A chill draft over her bare legs reminded Araminta that she wore almost nothing. "Yes, but I can take care of myself."

"You already know that the men who work for him are dangerous. Pray, do not underestimate the man himself. Do you notice his slight limp?"

She nodded.

"I've heard the tale behind that limp. Apparently he accosted two women, ah, employees of his. A week later, they paid someone to break his leg."

"Good."

"I would never expect you to be so bloodthirsty, Araminta," he said, and his eyes glinted with appreciative humor. He drank the rest of his coffee.

He got up, poured himself another cup and pointed to her mug.

"No, thank you. But do, pray, help yourself."

Griffin ignored her sarcasm. He sat back down and stirred in a small lump of sugar before he spoke again.

"To continue my story, the women and the assailant they'd hired disappeared without a trace soon afterward. That was more than ten years ago. Even then the police did a lackadaisical job of investigating the disappearances. Linder Kane has gained considerable power since then. He is smart enough to pay very well for protection both within and outside the law."

Araminta shivered, and not only with the cold. "He is a beast."

"A wealthy beast."

Something like grudging admiration in his words made her at last remember what Olivia had said about Griffin. She stared into his eyes as she blurted, "Are you like him? I mean, might you consider going into the same sort of business?"

Calverson's expression didn't change and he remained silent, but a moment later, he rose from the chair again. He pulled out his pocket watch, and the gold flashed as he flipped it open and tilted it toward the light of the single candle. "I have disturbed you long enough."

"You and Kane are two of a kind—you each feel you must warn me about the other. Do you know he told me to be careful of you? He said you have murdered at least three men."

He tucked his watch away, and then placed his chair precisely at the table.

Araminta felt indignant. Bad enough that he apparently would not tell her if Kane told the truth—she disliked being ignored.

She got to her feet and carried her cup to the basin. "We have not made any kind of plans yet."

"I do not think we need to discuss the plans any further tonight. And likely I can take care of this matter without disturbing you. I merely . . ." He trailed off; she hadn't heard a sign of indecision in him before. Something had

shifted in that calm voice, though she could not read what
had changed.

He shook his head. "As you said, I wished to warn you
about Kane. And to tell you it would be best if you do not
mention any connection to me, or to appear sympathetic
to me."

"I told you, he's already asked me about you. He re-
members that I worked for your sister."

Griffin pursed his lips. "Yes, it might be a good idea to
repeat to him some of the things you have told me."

"About which subject?"

"About my faults, naturally."

Araminta blew out a breath as she tried to recall how
insulting she'd managed to be this evening. "Should I
apologize to you again?"

He gave her a slight but perfect bow. "No need, I assure
you."

She at last understood what had changed in him. His
voice and eyes held no amusement.

They walked into the front parlor. He picked up the
coat, the hat and the gloves.

Araminta watched him, and an odd disappointment
tightened her chest. When he left, the house would feel
empty. She wanted to talk to him, tell him not to go yet.
Murderer, thief though he might be—at that moment in
the silent parlor in the middle of the night, she did not
care. Once he left, she knew she'd feel lonelier than she
had for a long time.

"Griffin."

He swiveled at once to face her, and she took an in-
stinctive step backward, away from a perilous trap—the
heat she saw that leapt straight into her. The green eyes
were no longer cold.

"Um. Good night."

He moved to her then, unceremoniously dropping

everything he held. Another step forward and his leg brushed hers, but otherwise they did not touch. Then one hand moved to rest on her waist, another lightly clasped the nape of her neck beneath her plaited hair. His hands held her, and for a moment he did not move. His eyes were fixed on hers, and she understood he would let her say no, push him away. But she didn't. His gaze dropped to her lips.

He bent to her, and his mouth on hers calmed rather than frightened her.

Something in her shifted, and she knew she was entirely wrong. His hands and mouth didn't calm her—quite the opposite.

Restless, she stirred in his gentle grip, and the kiss deepened, his clasp tightened. His tongue stroked hers and a soft gasp came from her throat. As she strained forward, her melting limbs regained strength and purpose. She wanted to touch as much of him as possible, and she pressed close like a possessed woman. Her fingers touched the stubble of his cheeks, explored the silky hair at the nape of his neck.

He twisted closer and resumed exploring her mouth with his, tongue, teeth and lips all sweet and hot with the gently tickling mustache above her mouth, reminding her—as if she could forget—who kissed her.

He slid his hands to her shoulders and ended the embrace by gently pushing himself away. He bent to pick up his possessions, pulled on the gloves and coat and donned the hat.

She almost protested the end of the embrace, but she came to her senses and saw how she had already made a fool of herself. She would not give voice to the desire that had swept through her with no warning.

She cleared her throat. "Good night, Mr. Calverson."

A quick doff of the hat, a quiet, "Good night, Miss Woodhall."

At least, she thought, as she locked the door behind him, she hadn't imagined his craving for her. She'd tasted it in his kiss, heard it in his hoarse voice as he bade her good night. Her body burned, but at least he also did not remain cold to the dratted desire. She did not see how that did her any good, but it seemed to improve her mood as she made her way up to a bed where she knew she'd lie awake until sunrise.

CHAPTER 8

Griffin shoved his balled fists into his trouser pockets and strode down the sidewalk. Bored and restless, he'd wanted to see Araminta, and it had seemed a reasonable idea after two brandies. He did not usually drink more than a glass, purely as a matter of discipline, but years of self-control seemed to be slipping lately. So was his carefully built wall against anger and other strong, useless emotions. Such as the heady desire to haul her against him. He was rattled to his core. Perhaps another glass of brandy would settle the fire she stirred in him.

Araminta's insinuation that he was as bad as Kane had rankled beyond reason. It made no sense to feel even a trace of annoyance at the woman. She did not know him, for all that she claimed she did.

Many other people had assumed the worst of him—though none had been bold enough to accost him with a list of his sins, as she had.

Impertinent Araminta.

In the past he'd been amused, even encouraged the reputation. With Araminta, he had been more diverted than irked when she had launched into him that day. What had changed his amusement to annoyance?

As she'd stood close in that shadowy hall, he had impulsively decided to punish her by kissing her, and then standing back and pointing out her response to him, the one he'd sensed in her. Not truly mocking her—more a matter of showing he knew she wanted him. Taking control of the situation.

Yet his own arousal had been too strong. He'd been knocked sidelong by a simple kiss, and he did not appreciate that. He would not allow anyone or anything to breach the guard. It had taken him too long to perfect the inner strength that served him well.

He slowed his walk, despite the fact that a leisurely pace would turn him into a good target for a robber or pickpocket.

A good tussle would give him a chance to clear the anger from his system.

A dark figure appeared under the gaslight, walking in his direction. Griffin tensed, ready.

Not a cutthroat, but a cop on his beat. The cop nodded to him as he passed. "Evening, sir. Everything all right?"

Griffin nodded and felt absurd at his readiness to launch into a fight. He understood that he must call for the police—the right sort of police—in a civilized metropolis. Taking matters into one's own hands was not the best route.

It would be best to return to his original plan. He knew how to give assignments. From now on, Galvin could handle the Kane problem and keep Araminta from getting hurt. If Galvin and his men didn't work quickly, Griffin would pay more and get some larger gears moving. Whatever it took.

The damn woman wouldn't have the sense to run from a burning building if a cat was trapped in it.

He rubbed a hand over his face. Blast the stubborn Araminta and her refusal to leave her job. Devil take it, he might as well be transported back to the days when he spent sleepless nights worrying about Timona—or riding to her rescue. His sister had frequently gone to the aid of some lost soul or another, without a thought to her own safety. From boyhood on, Griffin had often been all that stood between the heedless Timona and her stumbles into danger.

He leaned against a streetlamp and waited for several horses and a carriage to pass before crossing the street. Rather than waste any more of his energy and time with Araminta, he would rid himself of the nagging desire. He knew how to ignore want.

Iron self-discipline had served him in the past. Time to employ it again, for he did not appreciate disruptions of his well-organized life.

The resolution to shrug off his craving for Araminta lasted until the next morning. As he stepped from the hotel, he caught the scent of fresh bread with a hint of cinnamon. Almost Araminta's scent. It aroused hunger in him, but not for food.

As he walked to his office, he watched the women he passed. It had been a long time since he'd allowed himself this sort of weakness. Yet though some of the women were good-looking, he detected faults in them. That one was too sallow. The other one was too thin. The one in red smiled at him, but in a sideways manner, which seemed furtive and annoyingly indirect. It took him a surprisingly long time to figure out that he was finding fault simply because none of them was Araminta.

He paused in front of a jeweler's shop and saw a string of pearls. At once he pictured them nestled against her skin, at the base of her long neck. On impulse he pushed through the door of the shop.

As he handed over the large wad of cash and shoved the small velvet pouch into his pocket, he wondered how she would respond to the gift. Not by conveniently throwing herself into his arms. More likely she'd throw them at him.

He grinned at the thought. He glanced up to see the jeweler watching him with a knowing smile. Griffin scowled, and the man paled.

Damn it, he was acting like a lovesick schoolboy. If word got around that Griffin Calverson was grinning like a mooncalf, he might risk his reputation as a heartless cad, a reputation that served him well in business, and had the added benefit of keeping much of foolish society away.

Bloody hell. He would give in to Araminta's lure, and perhaps rid himself of her control over his desires. And the power over his mind, he reflected as he nodded to the doorman of the office building. He'd thought of nothing but her since he'd left the hotel. Silly behavior for a grown man. Especially for Griffin, who did not indulge in silliness. Or, he thought as he fingered the bag of pearls, impulsiveness.

Araminta did not have to do her parade that evening, so she wore her favorite comfortable, faded chintz dress.

With her hair under a cloth and a large white apron across her, she resembled any serving girl, or so she supposed. But a girl came to the kitchen door with a note. "For you, miss," she said, bobbing a curtsy, and thrust the note at Araminta.

"How do you suppose she knew who I was?" she asked Olivia, who'd accompanied her to the kitchen for a chat over tea.

"Your bearing is too proud to be a regular servant."

"Ah, that's right. I'm not a shrew. I have presence," Araminta said, and they both dissolved into giggles.

Araminta watched Olivia as she laughed. The girl appeared less wan lately; perhaps she was recovering. But at that moment, Olivia suddenly gasped and pressed a hand to her side as if in pain.

"Are you ill?"

Olivia's lips thinned and she shook her head. Araminta had seen that haunted look before. Olivia must have received another beating. Kane had been on the warpath that week, and she knew Olivia had borne the brunt of it.

"Olivia," she began softly.

"Aren't you going to read your note?" Olivia interrupted. "I am better, I assure you."

Araminta scanned the hot-pressed paper. Another letter from a lady requesting her to come to be interviewed for a job, "offering a generous salary." Araminta had received several such offers since starting work at Kane's. She looked over at Olivia, who now stared absently into the teacup she clutched in her slender fingers. No, Araminta would not leave Kane's until Olivia was safe. The dark circles under the girl's eyes had faded, but she was not safe in this house.

At the end of the night, Hobnail waited for her by the door. The lapels of his heavy wool coat hung open in the not-so-chilled air, and he tugged the brim of his bowler hat as she walked out the kitchen door. She'd grown accustomed to his ruddy, friendly face and even begun to look forward to their homeward walks. Somehow, knowing he worked for Griffin almost made her feel as if Griffin's presence was at her shoulder.

After two blocks of silence she asked, "How long have you worked for Mr. Calverson?"

"Him? I don't work for him. I work for someone else."

After asking a few unproductive questions, she grew frustrated with his monosyllabic answers. He must be fairly low down the Calverson ladder and report to an underling of an underling. A vast organization, she thought, a peculiar spiderweb of contacts and bosses that would be hard for an outsider to trace. Rather like Kane's.

"What would you do if Mr. Kane decided to, ah, harm Mr. Calverson?"

"Grass on 'im, of course. Tell my boss."

"And if Mr. Calverson went after Mr. Kane?"

"That one?" He made a rude noise. "Hold his hat for him. Or maybe join in. Don't think he'd go for anything I wouldn't approve of. Hope not, anyway."

His loyalties were clear. That was the nice thing about a man like Mr. Hobbes, she reflected; he had no real mystery to him.

For a few moments, as she strolled at his side, she imagined the ideal wife for Hobbes—perhaps some rosy-cheeked woman who'd present him with a gaggle of sturdy children. While Griffin—could she even picture him with his child? Her heart beat faster at the thought.

But no, a gentleman of Calverson's stature would not be a father, not a real one who played with and loved his children. Perhaps he might do better than his own father, but that was saying little. Sir Kenneth had barely noticed he had offspring unless he needed them for his absurd projects.

When she worked for Timona, Araminta had spent more than enough time with Griffin Calverson's wretched father, an absent-minded nitwit. Amazing that Griffin and his sister had survived under the care of that one. Perhaps that appalling father had instilled the need for frosty self-control in Griffin. The thought saddened her, especially when she recalled the moments she'd seen his self-control slip for a moment, to reveal a glimpse of the man beneath, like an unexpected swath of tender grass beneath perpetual snow.

Mr. Hobbes interrupted her thoughts. "You have the

day off tomorrow? So happens I do, too. Want to go have a look at the bridge? Only a few weeks till it opens."

To her dismay, she knew she could give only one answer. Any other would not be fair to the man. "No, thank you, Mr. Hobbes."

"Hobnail."

She smiled. "Hobnail, then. But still, I'm afraid I must decline."

As she walked around her house preparing for bed, she felt restless, wishing for things she couldn't have. She gave herself a stern scolding. Her life was full enough without dreams of a man with green eyes. She did not need kisses that drugged her senses in order to be happy. She would eventually be her own mistress, and she did not need to marry to have enough to live on. Really, she was a lucky, lucky woman.

The next afternoon, she planned a real day off. She would make some dishes for the soup kitchen, perhaps work on sorting recipes, and then attend a concert of rarely performed music. The beauty of Bach's flute concertos would be more than enough to remind her that the world and her life held real beauty.

CHAPTER 9

The recital hall smelled of damp newspaper and old perspiration. Though the building was relatively new, gilt peeled from the elaborately frescoed walls and ceiling. If she hadn't looked forward to the concert, Araminta would have turned around and demanded her money back. But it wasn't the surroundings that made her wish she hadn't come.

Araminta had splurged on a good seat near the front, but the usher refused to lead her to it.

The young man with spots and a crimson moth-eaten coat gestured toward the balcony. "That's where you should be. I guess the ticket seller didn't notice what you are."

Araminta clenched her teeth, but didn't move. Once upon a time, she would have come close to dying of shame and crept from the scene.

After her years working for a countess, she knew how to put on the act as well as any noblewoman. With her chin tilted high, and peering down her nose as if she viewed something distasteful, she confronted the man. "I daresay the ticket seller did not see anything objectionable. He simply took my money. And now I expect to be seated or to receive a good part of that money back."

The man sputtered and shuffled his feet on the worn

crimson carpet and even turned apologetic, but Araminta's British accent had not worked as she'd hoped.

"Yes'm. I'm sure we will get some of your money refunded. If you'll come with me, please." He turned and began to lead her against the tide of incoming audience. She suppressed a sigh and followed.

A strong hand grabbed her upper arm. She twisted round, ready to do battle.

"Mr. Calverson," she gasped. "What are you doing here?"

He raised an eyebrow. "A strange question."

Griffin and music. Of course. The tension in her chest dissipated, and she almost forgot the noxious young usher hovering at her other side. She smiled at Griffin. "You play the flute. I remember now. Timona said you played beautifully."

He ignored the comment and leveled an imperious stare at her unwelcome escort. "Tell me, what does that ridiculous man want?"

The usher tapped Araminta on the shoulder. "Please, ma'am, the concert starts in less than five minutes."

Hot embarrassment flooded her cheeks. Of all people to witness this, why did it have to be Griffin Calverson? She shrugged, hoping she appeared unconcerned. "I'm supposed to sit in the balcony."

Griffin gave the usher a frigid stare that had the man shuffling his feet again. No wonder the carpet was threadbare. "The young lady will accompany me." Griffin's voice was almost too quiet to be heard over the din of the fast-filling hall. "I shall pay the difference in ticket prices."

The usher rubbed a gloved hand over his forehead. Under his maroon cap he turned a clashing shade of vermilion. "It's not a matter of the money. The girl already has paid the money."

People had turned in their seats to watch. Others squeezed past and looked back, curious.

"Then what appears to be the problem?" Griffin's voice turned dangerously calm.

"It's that she belongs up there." The usher stabbed a finger toward the balcony. "That's where she's supposed to go."

Griffin stared at the man with contempt. "No. I think not." He tucked Araminta's hand into the crook of his arm and began to lead her away. She curled her fingers around the fabric of the coat, almost giddy with the rush of gratitude as well as awareness of the strong arm beneath the superfine cloth. As a seeming afterthought, he turned to the cringing usher. "You are neglecting your work. People are waiting to be escorted to their seats."

"But . . ."

"Go. Now."

The usher went.

"You didn't have to do that," Araminta murmured. "I would have been fine in the balcony."

Griffin gave her a cool look, almost as contemptuous as the one he'd directed at the usher. "Feel free to go then."

"Never mind." She blew out a long breath. "I think I'm merely jealous at the way you handled him. I wish I could quell people the way you do."

She wondered if Griffin's eyes actually twinkled as he said, "You can, I assure you."

He led her to seats that were even better than her own. "Not a very crowded event. I wonder why that man made such a fuss," he remarked, and she knew by the way he watched her that he wanted to know what she had to say about the incident.

She waved a gloved hand in what she hoped was a casual manner. "I imagine the usher enjoys the fact that at least there are some people who are considered his inferior."

He lounged back in his plush velvet seat, regal in his perfectly tailored suit, every inch the man of wealth and taste. Not a man to be seen with a woman like her. "Thereby proving that he is the most inferior being possible. You don't seem particularly annoyed."

"I very rarely experience problems," she said, masking her discomfort by smoothing her green silk dress over her lap. One of her better gowns yet she felt sadly rumpled and unfashionable sitting next to Griffin's impeccable facade. "Many people mistake me for an Italian."

"And is that good?" The iciness had returned to his face.

Could he possibly condemn her for denying her ancestry?

"Anything that makes life less complicated is good," she snapped. "You do not know what it is like to face prejudice, do you?"

He tilted his head and eyed her for a long moment. "Touché," he murmured. "You're not one to shy from hard truths, are you?"

She was relieved when the musicians took the stage.

The music made her forget everything. The soaring lyrical flute solos brought tears to her eyes. In the quiet between movements, she glanced over at Griffin. At the same moment he turned to her.

What did she see during the brief moment when their eyes met? Radiance, peace, a quality of the man he hid from the world that was released by music, and even more intoxicating than the Bach.

Shaken, she faced the stage again. And when the music lifted her, she was curiously connected to the man next to her, because she knew that it struck the same notes in him. The almost tangible link the music formed between them seemed even as strong as the kiss they'd shared. So strong she knew she dared not mention it.

Yet after the concert, when he asked if she would join him to share a small meal, she eagerly agreed.

He pulled out his gold watch. "Blast. I forgot. I am meeting several gentlemen."

"Ah. Perhaps another time," she began.

"No, please, join us." Something of the intriguing gentle warmth lingered in his manner.

"I'd be delighted," she said, although less eagerly now, fully aware of what these gentlemen would infer when they saw her unchaperoned in Griffin's company.

As they walked down the stone steps from the concert hall, two young men bade Griffin a good afternoon and joined them.

"This is Mr. Potter and Mr. Nelson," Griffin introduced the men. "They and three other gentlemen will be joining us for dinner."

Potter and Nelson wore formal black evening wear and silk top hats, but Araminta suspected that they'd be more at home in rougher clothing. Occasionally, when either of them thought no one watched, he ran a finger between his neck and starched white collar.

"Did you enjoy the concert?" she asked Potter.

He turned slightly pink. "Nah. I didn't stick around for it."

The restaurant was smaller than Cavanaughs or Delmonico's, though nearly as fashionable. Araminta braced herself for more trouble, but apparently Griffin Calverson could bring anyone in for dinner.

The maître d' led them past the main dining room to a smaller semiprivate salon.

Thick carpeting meant their footsteps were muffled, as were the conversations. With each table surrounded on three sides by an elaborate stained-glass enclosure, this section of the restaurant was the perfect location for conducting serious business.

The chairs were large and well padded. And heavy. With some difficulty, the waiter pulled back her chair for her.

"I apologize," Griffin murmured as he paused next to her chair for a moment. "I must sit with the men who will be joining us. And I have to go over some numbers first."

He walked to the far side of the oversize table.

Araminta, who'd seen Kane's thugs, supposed these young men assumed the same function for Griffin. A sort of decoration to show the man was so important he required guards. Although in Kane's case, she supposed the guards were for more than show. Perhaps in Griffin's case as well.

As Griffin sat down, Nelson eagerly pulled a small notebook from his waistcoat.

Araminta was taken aback to see Griffin take the notebook and study it. From the little bits she could overhear, she understood the business was connected to the railroad and seemed boringly legitimate. Potter must have seen her surprise. "We don't strike you like regular gents, eh?" he muttered.

"I had rather thought you were, ah, here to make sure everything ran smoothly." That seemed like a good euphemism.

Potter understood, but didn't seem offended. "Yah, we keep an eye open for trouble, but we're more like apprentices to business. That's what I'd reckon you'd call us." He grinned at her. "Up through the ranks, like Ragged Dick."

He flapped his napkin a few times before carefully placing it on his right knee. "Nelson there was a baggage smasher at the big depot. I worked for a cotton merchant nearby. Nelson knew about Mr. Calverson and had the bal—, um, brass to stop him one day at the terminal and ask him if he had any positions open. For both of us."

Araminta enjoyed listening to his description of life in a rough-and-tumble New York until the three other prosperous-looking gentlemen joined the table.

Griffin made introductions. The stout young one called Richardson shook her hand and claimed the seat next to her. He greeted her warmly, his gaze never shifting from her bosom.

They made their order, and Richardson, who had thick, heavily pomaded blond hair and a red face, winked at Araminta.

"You been around long?" he asked her bosom.

She knew at once that he had pegged her as a loose woman. She should not have been surprised, of course, but she always felt as if she'd just been slapped in the face when men made that assumption.

Richardson's hand brushed her knee. Come to think of it, slapping didn't seem a bad notion. Would Griffin mind if she gave Richardson a good clout? She regretfully rejected the idea. Araminta had encountered many men who'd considered her fair game, but she did not think her usual direct method of dealing with them would be appropriate.

"I am a chef, Mr. Richardson," she said firmly as she shifted away from him.

"Ahh," he said, and immediately launched into an off-color joke about a cook and his cleaver.

The table was too large for general conversation. Several times Araminta attempted to speak with Potter, who sat on her other side, but Richardson was determined to have her attention.

She grew tired of Richardson's goggling at her bosom, and barely noticed the flavor of the delicious curried soup.

"Oh dear, have I spilled something down my front?" she asked him at last.

"No, I'm just enjoying one of the prettiest views in New York." Richardson leered. "Nothing wrong with that."

She knew she blushed and so pretended to drop her napkin, determined that he wouldn't see how his words affected her.

Griffin, who'd been engrossed in a conversation at the other end of the table, called out, "Is anything wrong, Miss Woodhall?"

"I'm afraid Mr. Richardson has mistaken me for a piece of the New York landscape," she replied.

Richardson chuckled. "One I wouldn't mind taking a tour of."

Everyone at the table fell silent as Griffin aimed a look of pure ice at the man. "Mr. Richardson, please do not mistake Miss Woodhall for anything other than a lady."

Even Richardson must have sensed the hostility, for he toned down his advances after that, but he still smirked enough to take away Araminta's appetite.

She had very few precious hours off, and decided she would rather spend them reading or even sewing a seam than listening to Richardson's idea of conversation.

When the main course had been removed, she stood. At once, the gentlemen all rose.

"I beg your pardon, I think I shall go home. I find I am extraordinarily tired."

Griffin glanced at Richardson and back at her. "I will escort you," he said.

The older gentleman next to him spoke up querulously. "But Mr. Calverson, we leave for Chicago tomorrow and we need to finish up this unexpected—"

"No need to bother about me," Araminta said. "The streetcar is quite convenient. I can make my own way home." In fact she could hardly wait to flee this place and return to the sanctum of her home and kitchen, the world where she was adept and confident.

Griffin narrowed his eyes. "But I hope you will not mind if Mr. Potter escorts you?"

Rather than argue, she allowed Mr. Potter to lead her from the restaurant.

She sighed and wished she'd left after the concert. The dinner did not strike her as a disaster, but it somehow detracted from the moments of magic in her day.

Griffin had waited, hoping Araminta would give Richardson one of her set-downs, but instead she had fled the scene. Now he wished he'd stepped in and stopped the idiot before he'd chased her off.

Oh, the devil with it. The meeting could wait.

He stood and tossed his napkin on the table. "I shall return in half an hour, gentlemen. Nelson, if you would go over the thoughts you shared with me about the northern corridor's requirements?"

He strode from the restaurant without another word.

Potter was just helping Araminta into a hansom.

Griffin tapped his shoulder. "Go back and help Nelson set their minds at ease."

Potter wheeled around. "But sir, this deal represents a whopping sum—"

Griffin, leaping into the cab, interrupted. "I trust you to represent Calverson's interest in this, Potter. You and Nelson can keep Richardson's inflated expectations in line. I'll be back."

He closed the door on the young man's goggling face.

In the dark interior of the carriage he leaned back and tried to make out Araminta's expression.

Her smile gleamed briefly as she smiled at him. "It wasn't necessary to come after me."

"Potter and Nelson'll do fine. Araminta, I am sorry Mr. Richardson annoyed you. I don't know if the man was drunk or just a natural boor."

"He was an annoyance, but at least he kept his hands to himself—for the most part."

"Why the blazes didn't you cut him to shreds with your sharp tongue?"

"I had supposed you did not want your dinner guests offended."

Her hesitant answer bothered him. He did not like to think of Araminta as anything but strong and defiant.

He shifted irritably. "To hell with Richardson. You were my dinner guest. And I apologize if you were offended."

She drew in an audible breath. "Thank you."

She'd been perched at the edge of the seat, holding the strap; now she slid back and settled into the corner. "It was a good concert," she said. "I am glad I saw it with you."

Her soft, measured words made the simple statement ring through him. Griffin was at a loss. If he opened his mouth, he would either say something idiotically frothy or, far worse, he'd say too much, offer more than he should. He might press too hard, too fast.

The carriage paused under a streetlamp. Some of her ringlets had fallen and framed her face. The strange light through the window cast a harsh shadow across her features. He leaned forward and tucked her hair behind her ear so he could see the fine, dark eyes. Her smile faded, though her lips remained parted. The hunger he saw in her face made him light-headed with desire. He took off his hat. And as the carriage lurched into motion again, he slipped across the seat to her and leaned in for a kiss. She gave a small, muted whimper.

For a moment he thought she would pull away and protest, but when she shifted, it was to tilt her head so their mouths fit more perfectly. He tasted her—splendid, delicate kisses that escalated into delicious moaning ones and drove him beyond pleasant anticipation to raging arousal—until the thump of the driver pulling back the hatch brought them back.

"Wait here," Griffin instructed the driver, though he hated saying the words.

At the top of her steps, Araminta held out a hand. "Good night."

He kissed her gloved fingers, and then, remembering her response the last time he'd done it, turned her hand over and kissed the inside of her wrist. Her answering gasp was gratifying.

He bowed. "Good night, Araminta."

Settling back in the cab, he considered his next move. He had never had any interest in setting up a mistress, but knew well enough how one approached this sort of business.

Surely Araminta had lived in the world long enough to understand these matters as well. Thank goodness the idea would not send her off into some weak womanly vapors. At worst, she would give him a sharp set-down. Remembering the kisses and the way she melted in his arms, he rather believed she would not.

In the restaurant, the men were deep in discussion—which stopped when Griffin entered and dropped into his seat again.

He idly wondered if they were talking about him when Richardson piped up. "Thought you wouldn't be back so soon. A fine woman, that Woodhall."

Griffin wondered how he might wipe the grin off the

man's face without spilling blood on the restaurant's carpets. "She is."

Midler, the older gentleman next to Griffin, put down his glass of wine and darted a nervous glance between Griffin and Richardson.

But Richardson apparently hadn't noticed the fury in Griffin's voice. He snickered. "I can imagine how fine she is. Tell me, is she available, or do you keep her busy to the exclusion of other gentlemen?"

To hell with the rich Richardson's interest in the steel deal. . . .

Then he recalled that the idiot was not so far off the mark. He did indeed plan to make Araminta his mistress. But surely Griffin's intentions for her were not as revolting as this imbecile implied. He appreciated Araminta's voluptuous figure, yet he would treat her as more than a receptacle for lust. She deserved a man's respect.

He swallowed the brandy the waiter had brought him and wished he had not invited her to this dinner. And he knew he couldn't entirely blame the loathsome Richardson, who must have expected Griffin to be the kind of host to provide his guests with women.

He, Griffin, had been to any number of dinners where the sponsor provided charming young girls who expected to make private arrangements with the guests. And on occasion, Griffin had even indulged himself with the more tempting females.

In a less hostile tone, he said, "You mistake who I am, Mr. Richardson. I am not attempting to bribe you with food and females. We are here to share a meal and perhaps discuss what to expect in Chicago."

Richardson, who'd been attempting unsuccessfully to light a cigar, stopped fiddling with it and frowned. "Then why'd you invite the girl?"

A good question. The answer had to be that Griffin

had experienced a moment of weakness. After the concert, he hadn't wanted to say good-bye to Araminta. But of all people, he should know how to order his life so that it would not be an untidy jumble.

"I shan't make that mistake again," Griffin replied coldly.

He was still annoyed with himself for not telling Richardson to go to hell earlier, and he wished Araminta had driven a fork into Richardson's hand when the idiot attempted to grab hers.

He wrestled his attention back to business for the rest of the long evening.

From now on, he'd remember to keep the worlds separate.

Twinges of a nameless apprehension bothered him through the rest of the evening. The memory of the delectable, though far too brief, interlude in the carriage ought to cheer him up. And certainly convince him that his plan for her was a fine idea.

The men rose to leave. They shook hands and talk reverted to trivial matters—the bridge opening, a horse race, gambling. A stray thought froze Griffin. Oh hell. What might happen if word got back to Kane that his prized chef was fraternizing with Griffin? The thought curdled his blood. If she wouldn't get out of there as soon as possible, he'd have to take some other steps.

CHAPTER 10

Two days later, when a sleepy Araminta arrived at work at her usual six in the morning, she found Olivia, white and trembling, sitting in the kitchen, clutching her arm to her chest.

Araminta sent a maid out for a doctor.

She made Olivia lie down on a sofa in the silent front parlor, which, before the gaming began, reminded Araminta of a house of mourning. Around them, two maids quietly went about their business, only occasionally looking over and whispering.

Araminta dragged over a heavy padded chair from one of the tables and sat down next to her. "He did this?"

Olivia nodded.

"Why? What happened?"

"I don't want to talk about it," Olivia whispered. Her face was white with pain, but the stubborn set to her lips showed Araminta she still had some strength in her.

"Is he still upstairs?"

Olivia shook her head. "No."

It was a good thing he was gone. Araminta knew she'd be hard-pressed to restrain her rage if she'd caught sight of the man's smirking face. She summoned a maid to fetch some tonic from the parlor and ask Jack, the other undercook, to make beef tea for Olivia.

He came out to complain, of course. Jack took every

occasion offered to him to make it clear he disliked working for a woman. He stroked his bald head and twisted the ends of his oversized walrus mustache. "We don't need no beef tea for tonight. It's a big crowd this evening. He's got a lot of big players coming—you know he warned us to make it memorable. And you don't have that pâté stuff done yet. That will take a good hour."

"We need broth, and you or Maggie will make it. And ask Dudley to fetch the Madeira wine. I shall make a panada for Miss Smith."

"But the lad has gone to fetch a last-minute market basket, and the girl who—"

Araminta waved an impatient hand. "Go. I will send for more outside help later if we require it."

Jack kicked at a chair halfheartedly and grumbled his way back into the kitchen.

The doctor arrived, a grim gray-haired man with stern, thick black eyebrows. He made a quick examination and announced that Olivia's arm was "only" cracked. After he bound the arm with a splint and cloth, he stroked his wispy goatee and frowned down at the patient. "You're far too thin and pale. I have my suspicions that you must have formed an addiction to some sort of drug, hey?"

Araminta, who stood nearby pretending to check the bowls of roses, froze and waited for the answer. Even she, who prided herself on bluntness, had never managed to form that question, which had lingered in her mind since Griffin's middle-of-the-night visit and his offhand remark about Olivia.

"Not anymore, sir," Olivia finally said.

"You there, girl," the doctor called to Araminta. Her newly formed good opinion of the man ebbed slightly.

She turned and eyed him icily. "Yes?"

"Don't allow your mistress to have any kind of pain reliever. Maybe a touch of brandy, but nothing more. Understand?"

Araminta nodded.

He rolled up the last of the cloth and shoved it into his bag. "I'll send my bill to Mr. Kane."

Olivia gasped her dismay. Kane would never approve of a doctor's visit. At once, Araminta drew some money from her pocket. "That won't be necessary, doctor. How much is your fee?"

His dark brow furrowed, but he answered. "Five dollars."

She handed him the money. "Please do not mention your visit to anyone."

He clapped his hat to his head. "No need for you to be telling me my business, girl." And with that he turned and stomped out of the house.

"What a rude man." Olivia stared down at her uninjured hand as she spasmodically rubbed the fabric of her chair.

"Yes, very, but a good doctor nonetheless." Araminta pulled the chair the doctor had used even closer to Olivia. At last she understood Griffin's words, an illness of need.

She leaned forward to study the exhausted, thin Olivia. "You were addicted to taking a drug?"

"Yes, opium and hashish. But I am doing much better. He . . ." She swallowed and at last met Araminta's steady gaze. "Mr. Kane will not allow it, and so I've—I have learned to do without." Olivia heaved a sigh. "My arm feels much better now. Thank you."

"But you've had some since you've been here?"

Olivia nodded. "I don't want to talk about it, Araminta. It's been horrible."

Araminta could ill afford the time for chitchat, yet she took Olivia's uninjured hand in hers. "Very well, we will not talk about the past. Let's discuss the future. You must leave him. I am afraid he will hurt you badly, and—and you do not belong in this place. He disgusts me more each day. I won't work for him much longer"—she ignored Olivia's attempts at interruption, including her gasp at this point, and plowed on—"and at any rate, it is clear I can't protect you. You must get away from Mr. Kane."

Olivia slowly shook her head. "I cannot," she said at last.

Araminta got to her feet. She only just managed to hold back the torrent of words building up inside her.

"If you can't leave on your own, I shall have to find a way to make you," she announced, and swept off to the kitchen to finish preparing the elaborate dinner.

Over Jack's objections, she sent a scullery maid out to help Olivia to a bedchamber and to bear her company for a short while.

The kitchen was in an uproar. The timbales and bouchées she'd created were perfect, as were the day's selections of vegetables. But the trout had not even been boned, the pigeons had yet to be plucked, the quail meat was questionable, the saddle of lamb was not large enough, the ice cream would not set, the meringue was too brittle to serve as the base of Araminta's elaborate creation—the centerpiece of the dessert—and there were not enough pistachios to finish off the Pudding à la Parisienne. And the palate-cleansing sorbet, to be served between the fish and meat courses, was too grainy.

Araminta sighed and tied on her apron, and then called out to one of the scullery maids to get started on the pigeons.

The day before she'd been befuddled by the strange incident with Griffin, and she'd not paid proper attention to her work. Today she chopped, roasted, fried and stewed with a vengeance, her anger at Kane causing her to crackle with energy. The man was too dangerous to threaten; what could she do?

Nothing other than get Olivia—and herself—out.

Hours later, as she curtsyed to the applause, she was not surprised to see Griffin at the table, elegant in his black cutaway jacket. He could have been a different man; his face showed none of the light she'd glimpsed at the concert. Or on the carriage ride home. Ice settled in the pit of her stomach.

Then she saw the attractive young woman who sat at his right. This one was not one of Kane's hired women. She bit the inside of her lower lip to counteract the peculiar sting caused by the sight of them together. She allowed her gaze to wander over the rest of the table. More women than usual attended this evening—and very few of them were professional girls visiting from one of Kane's other houses.

The candlelight reflected off the rich women's glittering diamonds and jewels and bounced around the walls. Mr. Kane had drawn a wealthier crowd than usual. Surely that was in part because of Mr. Calverson. Didn't he know that gracing the gaming parlor with his presence meant he helped its success? Kane must know, or he would not tolerate Griffin's presence. The man would dance with the devil if he could turn a profit doing it.

Araminta dragged herself wearily back to the kitchen and the small crowd gathered there. Before cleaning up, the staff had gathered at the back table to eat the scraps of the feast.

"This here's the best I've ever had," muttered a maid who'd been hired for the day. As usual, several of Kane's bagmen and flunkies had managed to escape their duties and find their way to the kitchen.

Araminta smiled, waved and headed for the garden. And the pergola.

She didn't expect him so quickly, but less than five minutes later, he stood in the arched doorway, his dark form blotting out the light.

Would he want to kiss her again? She'd thought of little else for two days. Just recalling his kisses made her feel as if warm chocolate slid through her—when the memory didn't fill her with paralyzing shame. What would she do if he tried again? She still wasn't certain she'd let him. She was too rattled by Olivia's injury, as well as discouraged at her own inability to convince the girl to leave Kane's.

That whole day—the concert, the dinner and the kisses—was an aberration. A piece of some other woman's life set down in the middle of hers. It could mean nothing. The kisses meant nothing. She had repeated those words to herself so often she was heartily sick of them. An almost as tired of reminding herself that if she gave in to him, for a time she would be happy, but he would ultimately cause her pain. What else could he offer?

"Good evening, Araminta."

She blurted. "Why did you come to Mr. Kane's this evening?"

He did not answer right away. When he spoke, he sounded unusually serious. "I think I wanted to lull him into believing I am not his foe."

Of course he hadn't come to see her, and she wondered why she felt disappointed. "You *think* that's what you wanted?"

"Yes. For once I am not sure." The habitual accent of world-weary amusement had returned to his voice. "Do you recall that you recently accused me of being like Kane?"

"Yes, but I knew it was a silly—"

"I wondered if perhaps you are not the only one who

believes I am going into the same sort of business." He sat on the bench near her. "And I was right. I think that Kane believes that I am a threat to him. This must be one of the reasons he has become such a nuisance. I hoped my visits would allay his fears that I am his enemy."

The side of her body nearest him was almost too warm. She sidled a few inches away. "Why bother with him and his fears?"

"Several reasons. You're one. The other is that it's the easier path. Otherwise I will have to take a less diplomatic approach. I *was* hoping the police would curtail his most destructive behavior."

She wanted to ask how she could be a reason. And then her insides congealed slightly at the implications of "less diplomatic approach." She asked, "What would your next step be?"

"I don't know."

She did not believe him, but thought it best not to pursue the subject. "The woman who sat next to you tonight." Araminta hesitated. "She seemed very taken with you. She is exceedingly pretty, too. And wealthy. She would make an ideal wife."

"Are you suggesting that I could be interested in the Myles girl?"

She did not like the way his incredulous words gave her a warm pleasure.

"Even if she was ideal," he said, "I am not looking for a wife." He leaned forward, and the golden glow from the house momentarily touched his face, which wore an extraordinarily grim expression.

His voice was as level and light as it had ever been. If she hadn't caught a glimpse of that bleak face, she would not have guessed he felt any pain.

Pain? Griffin Calverson? She must be tired.

"I am glad to have a chance to speak to you," she said

briskly, dismissing that fanciful impression as well as any lingering thoughts of kisses. "I have thought over what you advised. And I think it is high time I leave this place."

She hesitated. "You do know that some of Mr. Kane's aides are wondering if you are considering becoming his partner?" Certainly he might lie, but she thought she should ask one more time. Even if she managed to anger him.

"Nonsense," he said shortly. "But I might let him believe it. Keep your friends close, and your enemies closer."

She believed him, and realized that except for a single moment when Olivia first mentioned the idea, she'd never truly doubted him. A dismaying thing, her growing trust in Griffin Calverson. She feared she liked him too much. She almost wished he'd show a touch of evil. A boring sort of evil would be best, she reflected, because anything else might make him even more interesting to her.

She rubbed at the base of her neck, which ached from a long day's work. "I shan't go without my friend, however."

She wondered if she heard him groan at her words, but continued, "Might you give me a name of someone such as Mr. Hobbes, who might be able to help Miss Smith? I asked Mr. Hobbes himself, but he refused."

"I'm glad to hear it. He's got more important work."

She turned to face him. "She needs help. What can be more important than protecting an innocent woman?"

Griffin did not answer. He folded his arms and looked out toward the garden. "Who is this woman to you?"

"A friend. That is all you need know."

"Ah. The friend on whose behalf you first approached me."

"Yes."

"Very well, I shall see what can be done."

"I will pay for—"

"Do not insult me, Araminta." He answered her unspoken question almost at once. His words were soft and, for once, seemed to hold real gentleness. "I help you for my sister's sake."

And not for the sake of whatever strange thing exists between us, she silently added. It occurred to her that she had to admire the man for not trying to use his actions on her behalf to coax her into his bed. Although perhaps he didn't want her there any longer. Perhaps her embrace had not been satisfactory, and he'd lost any interest in her. Gloom struck her at this thought: she was not as a good a woman as she liked to pretend.

For example, despite all of her lectures to herself, she still wanted to feel his lips on hers again. Goodness, "wanted" was too paltry a word. She longed to press her mouth to his. Every breath ached with desire. Her body screamed for him.

Not a good woman at all.

"Why are you sighing?" he asked.

"Oh, I'm exhausted," she said. "It has been a long day."

"You produced a magnificent dinner. Even Mr. Brady commented on it."

"That salesman? He'd eat the table if he could."

Griffin chuckled. "Yes, I imagine. But he is the best source I've found of information about the rail system." His gaze followed her fingers as she rubbed her neck again. He apparently came to a conclusion, and stood. "Enough business," he said, holding out a hand to help her to her feet. "Allow me to walk you home."

She didn't take his proffered hand. "I should help my staff—"

"Nonsense. Knowing you as I do, I have every confidence you have them well trained to do their job."

"Mr. Kane. If he should see us—"

"You have no need to fear him when you are in my company." He lowered his arm. "Mr. Kane and some of his guests are about to leave the premises to go to a private entertainment."

A pang of disappointment touched Araminta. "Will you join them?"

"I pleaded tiredness. If you walk with me, we will think about what is to be done with your Miss Smith. Will you come, Araminta?" He lifted his hand again. Though the light was almost nonexistent, the invitation on his face was pure, determined lust, and she could not resist the pull.

Setting her fingers delicately on his hand, she stood and then pulled at the draperies at the back of her skirt. "That would be . . . satisfactory."

He stepped close and, for a moment, she went positively tottery, but his strong hand grabbed her arm just at her elbow, where her glove ended. His touch on her tender bare skin inside the crook of her arm made the need so great she wondered he couldn't hear the way her body clamored for him.

Perhaps he did hear her uneven breath, or feel her fast pulse under his fingers, for he did not release her right away. Heat spread through her. She uttered a small breathy sound.

"Really, I wonder," he murmured. "Is that groan one of joy or displeasure?"

"Let go of me, please."

She supposed he'd gotten his answer, for he didn't repeat the question. God save her from smirking men. Especially those who were right.

His large hands now encircled her waist. She realized they were very much alone in the quiet dark garden, and she also realized that Griffin was very solid and strong.

She gazed into his unfathomable face. Her hands,

trembling slightly, lay flat against the hard wall of his chest.

"Are you sure you want me to let go?" His whisper was a rasping growl.

At that moment she knew only that she wanted him and didn't care that wanting him was wrong, and even harmful. Her plans, their stations in life, none of it mattered. None of it seemed as real as the steady heartbeat she felt beneath her palms.

She raised her face, her lips already tingling in anticipation of his touch. She longed for him to press his mouth hard against hers, and send her into a swoon of desire so she could forget everything else. But he paused, inches from her, and only his warm, sweet breath touched her lips.

She shivered with impatient hunger. He hesitated, his mouth maddeningly close. "You are cold," he said, wry amusement in his muted tone. "Shall I get your cloak?"

She tried to say no, but he'd already drawn away.

As he stepped back, she regained too much of her sanity to remain in Kane's garden, longing for illicit kisses.

"I must leave." She swept out of the pergola and walked the winding brick path to the kitchen.

He followed—silently, of course.

"Wait here," he whispered, and was gone, leaving her to stare through the kitchen window. A good staff, she thought, distracting herself purposefully from the heat pulsing through her body. Even Jack, despite his grumbles, did more than his share. Perhaps if she opened a restaurant, they might join her. But no, if she did open her own establishment, it must be somewhere far away. Not in New York—not when it held Kane.

She watched the people in the kitchen cleaning and chattering until she was startled by a light touch on her shoulder. The man moved like a shadow.

"Let us go by way of the alley," he said, and handed her a cloak, a gaudy and shoddy purple one that had been drenched in rose water.

"This isn't mine."

"I did not want to make a show of finding yours. It belongs to one of the girls who work for Kane. She said I might borrow it."

"Who is she?"

He shrugged. "I don't recall her name. No, don't worry. I slipped her a few dollars for her compliance."

Araminta understood that for a variety of reasons, he did not want to be seen with her. Ignoring the pinch of sorrow that caused, she drew the hood over her head and they walked through the garden, out the servants' entrance in the back.

In the next block, he took her arm and led her back to the sidewalk. They walked in silence, or rather wrapped in the noise of the street. Even though it was nearly midnight, a boy's light voice called out the news headlines, trying to sell the last of the evening papers. A raucous group of well-dressed young men, partygoers, pushed along the sidewalk. Rather than attempt to plow through the group, Griffin steered her to the edge of a stoop to wait until they'd passed.

When they turned onto the quieter side street, he spoke at last.

"What will you do when you leave Kane's? You are still in demand, I imagine."

She shrugged. "I have hopes of opening my own restaurant." She thought about her dream of using her own earnings to forge her future. And never again touch the money in the trust.

"You'd give Delmonico's serious competition."

"No. I am tired of . . . glamorous dining."

"An oyster house then?"

"I want a small, *intime* restaurant. I'd like to offer more rustic French dishes."

"Ah. Crusty loaves of bread and hunks of sliced onions."

She didn't bother answering his flippant remark. "And you? Will you stay in New York much longer?"

The question seemed to bother him. He hunched his shoulders. But a few seconds later he spoke as emotionlessly as always. "No. I grow weary of being constantly surrounded by so many of my fellow men."

"Will you return to London or somewhere more exotic?"

"I await the wind and will cast off in whichever direction it carries me."

She gathered the edges of her borrowed wrap in her hands and held it closed against her chest. "That does not sound like the proper attitude for a businessman."

"Perhaps. But my family has never been one to cultivate the proper attitude."

"That's an understatement."

"And yet we manage to remain profitable in our business."

They stopped at a street corner and waited for a wagon loaded with barrels to pass. Traffic was light this time of the night.

He took her arm again. "I have been thinking about your Miss Smith, and I believe the best thing to be done is to bring her to my hotel. I'll be able to thwart Kane, should he attempt to take her again."

"In your suite?"

"I will also let the other suite on that floor. She is used to remaining indoors, isn't she? She should stay with me until she's ready to tell me who she is."

Araminta frowned. "I'm not sure that would be best for her."

"No?" The quiet word challenged her to voice her doubts.

"Olivia is . . . beautiful. And injured."

"And you don't trust me?"

Of course she didn't. Not when it came to that sort of matter. Araminta drew in a deep breath as she tried to think of how to say the words. "It is more that I am afraid she would be . . . That she would turn to . . ."

"Come now, don't hide your meaning, Miss Woodhall. You think I would take advantage of her as Kane has."

"She is very beautiful," Araminta repeated, feeling thoroughly asinine but unable to think of how to explain herself. "And timid."

They passed under a streetlamp and he studied her. "I have seen her. And I know what you think of me. You do not trust me around the beautiful and tempting Miss Smith."

She huddled inside the purple cloak and was silent. Any protests she made would only sound false, and she remembered how he had kissed her. The very memory of it made her body hum. If he did that to Olivia, the poor girl would be lost.

She reminded herself that the most important thing was to get Olivia out.

Griffin stopped in front of her house. In the soft light shed by the gas lamp, he was impossibly handsome, lean and lithe. He clasped his hands behind his back and tilted his head. "Will you invite me in?"

Please, yes, her body clamored. "No." She bit down hard on her lip, trying to hold back her desperate longing. "I shouldn't," she reminded them both.

He stepped close to her. His hands cupped her face. "No," he agreed, and brushed his lips against hers. "You know me, after all."

She would have protested the mockery in his voice, but

at once she was caught up in a delectable swooning pleasure that would not allow her to move away, that made her open her lips and press closer. Desire that had built up for two days, no, for years, poured from her body into that kiss.

A man's guffaw came from a window nearby, and she came to the surface again. "Good Lord," she groaned. "We are making a spectacle for the whole street."

"Araminta," he whispered. And she saw that the strength of their shared kiss had hit him as thoroughly as it had her, and he remained captured by its magic. The iceman had melted into heat. She had wielded that power over him. Nothing else mattered. She let him kiss her again and draw her into the shadow by the gate. Only when a clock struck one did she disentangle herself from his arms. A tawdry Cinderella, an hour after her time. No. Lovely girls like Olivia—they were Cinderella. She could only be Cinderella's cook.

She backed away, her hands out as if holding him at bay. He leaned against the wrought-iron gate and folded his arms.

"Good night," she said, hoping she sounded normal. She ran up her steps as if pursued by the devil himself and scrabbled at her heavy ring of keys.

His amused voice at her shoulder stopped her. "Allow me." He reached over and took her ring of keys, and within a few seconds had unlocked the door and held it open. She hurried into the foyer, and then stopped when she heard his footstep behind her.

"You are glorious in that gown," he said, and she couldn't look into his face as she muttered yet another farewell.

He held out his hand. Fascinated, she stared at the severe black sleeve, the edge of the white cuff, the small strip of golden wrist, the solid hand encased in the tight glove that did nothing to hide its power. If she could somehow step into that hand, let him encase her in his warmth . . .

His voice interrupted her peculiar fantasies. "The cloak."

"Oh." She ripped at the tie, yanked it off and thrust it at him. "Good night. We—we shall talk."

"Yes, we will. You come to my hotel, though," he said. "I shall leave word that you are to be admitted at any time. Day. Or night. Yes. Most especially night."

He strolled down the stairs and disappeared into the shadows.

She did not slam the door on him, but she was sorely tempted. But as she sagged against the door, she reflected that the door should be slammed on herself. He had not ravished her or made demands upon her body, though if he had, she would have quickly transformed into a willing partner.

Griffin Calverson had respected her choice. She moved slowly to the steps, sat on the third stair up and set her chin upon her fists. Oh, it was so much easier to see him, talk to him when she considered him an untrustworthy beast and not a man who could overturn her ordered existence.

When she met Kane the next day, she managed to hold her tongue. It took some effort, for he stood in her kitchen beaming around, obscenely cheerful.

"Fine weather we're having, eh, Miss Araminta?"

"Certainly," she said and attempted to get past him with her basket of steamed lobsters.

He laid a hand on her arm, and she froze.

"I wanted to thank you for taking care of Miss Smith yesterday," he said, with a hearty earnestness that made her skin crawl. "She fell down the stairs. She did tell you that, yes?"

The pressure on her arm increased. She pressed her lips tight, knowing that if she disagreed, he would take it out on Olivia. After a long silence, she nodded.

"Very good," he said, though she could see the unmistakable glint of anger in his dishwater-gray eyes.

One of Kane's assistants came to the door.

"Carriage is ready, sir."

"And you loaded my valise?"

"Yes, sir."

Kane gave Araminta's upper arm one last squeeze. She tightened her muscles under his hand, and his eyebrows rose. "My, you got strength as well as height? Won't keep me from getting what I want, though, girl." His smile was so broad she could see his back teeth. "Dear Miss Smith will eventually agree, I'm sure."

"Agree to what, Mr. Kane?"

He waved a playful finger. "Ah, ah, that would be telling. I'll leave you to it, Miss Araminta. I expect a good report from Dudley when I get back."

"You are leaving, Mr. Kane?"

But he'd already sauntered out of the kitchen, leaving her with two dozen lobsters and a sinking feeling.

She put down the basket and went looking for Olivia.

Olivia's eyes were puffy and red. "He's going to Albany," Olivia said. For some reason, this seemed to worry the girl.

"Whatever for? Why have you been crying? Has he hurt you?"

"No. And he is sorry about my arm."

Araminta wanted to shake her but instead only lightly touched her shoulder. "It was the drugs that held you here, wasn't it?"

Olivia shivered and didn't answer.

"And now that you are free of them, we will find an answer that will serve."

She could see Olivia considering her words before replying, "No, I can't. It's more than the drugs."

But Araminta had seen the girl's desire to flee, and knew that she'd soon be able to pull them both out of Kane's power.

CHAPTER 11

The desk sent up a message: "Miss Woodhall to see Mr. Calverson." Anticipation quickened Griffin's stride as he went to meet her in the vast marble lobby.

More curls than usual had slipped from the knot at the back of her head. She wore a simple blue cotton dress, but with her graceful posture and her elegant chin held high, she could pass off rags as haute couture.

Her lips curved into a nervous smile for him and she blushed. He knew at once that, unless he put a foot seriously wrong, this was the moment he would at last win his chance. But he must move slowly, so first he escorted her to the huge, nearly private chamber near the lobby, designed for guests and their visitors.

He would repress his customary manner with her. No teasing. Businesslike. Put off her guard, she would be more likely to fall to him, a piece of ripe fruit.

Her gaze traveled over the chairs and tables scattered across the room—everywhere but into his face. She pulled off one of her gloves and began to twist it. He resisted the urge to reach over and take it away from her. "How may I be of service to you, Araminta?"

"I came to speak to you on a matter of some urgency. Kane is gone. I took the afternoon off because I want to get Miss Smith away from him as soon as may be, within days. He has some plan in mind."

"He's hoping to move to state level in his sphere, or so my friends in Albany tell me." And thanks to Araminta's description of her friend as the daughter of someone wealthy, Griffin suspected he knew part of Kane's strategy. He was not entirely certain, but he was close to tracking down Miss Smith's identity.

At the moment, however, he had no interest in Kane, his goals or anything other than the woman who sat upright and nervous in front of him.

She was apparently fascinated by the button on her glove and still avoided looking at him. A very good sign. "I meant he has a plan for her. I don't know what it is, and she won't tell me. While he's gone, I think I will convince Olivia to come here. For a visit. Perhaps that is all that it will take. We could return her to where she belongs. So she needn't remain here for more than an afternoon."

He was tired of this game and risked being too straightforward. "I would agree to that. Would you care to come up to my rooms now so we can discuss plans in private? I'd serve you tea again."

Her rigid posture and shuttered eyes told him she was going to refuse. Before she could, he leaned forward and laid a hand on the edge of her chair to draw her attention, and she twisted toward him. For a long moment the large, pure brown eyes stared into his. He forgot everything—even his ambition to have her—as he gazed back, caught in the glorious fire of those eyes.

She gave him another tentative smile, and he remembered his goal. "I will offer my aid even if you say no," he said quietly. "But I would like to spend some time with you, Araminta. Alone. Will you make the time?"

She nodded, and he hoped that the way her mouth tightened meant she understood what he wanted.

Neither spoke as they made their way up in the elevator. Araminta's head spun with the hope and dread that he'd touch her, but he did not so much as lay a finger on her arm.

He led her to the sofa. She pressed her back straight and trusted her demeanor was calm, though inside she felt as if she were a small girl waiting for a grown-up to come take charge of her. Ridiculous, of course. The tension boiling through her had nothing to do with being a child.

He sat next to her, almost allowing his leg to touch hers, so close that she could feel the heat of him. He reached for her hand but did not pick it up. His fingertips swept across her knuckles. The simple contact of skin against skin undid her. She started, and began to rise from the sofa.

"No. Stay with me, please. Don't go." He whispered his plea, and Griffin begging was too much for her to resist.

She sank back down beside him and examined those extraordinary eyes. Filled with the passion of a hunter but something more: restraint, perhaps even tenderness. She thought he likely remained motionless so as not to frighten her, and she was grateful.

Enthralled by the well-dressed, broad figure waiting, watching her, the invitation in his eyes and in his unsteady breath, Araminta lifted a shaky forefinger to brush Griffin's well-cut dull-gold hair from his forehead. She traced a line from his forehead to his neck. His eyes closed, and she could see him swallow. With his head back, exposing his throat, he surrendered to her touch.

Now that was a gift. She leaned toward him and ran her lips along the line of his jaw, and stroked his face, marveling at the soft skin, the rough stubble, the fine, thick mustache.

She knew he would go only as far as she allowed, and she lost her fear. Yet as her mouth tasted his skin, his vulnerable pose vanished. He seized her and pulled her into a deep kiss. His arms and hands were stronger than she had imagined, but she didn't resist his embrace. She closed her eyes and burrowed closer, wishing he could enfold her. The rasping breath in her ear, the hands that gripped her, told her he wanted her and that he would lose himself in that desire. She smiled at the power she held over him.

As his hands skimmed her waist and hips, the now familiar heat poured through her. Lying in his arms, kissing him, was as natural as breathing, and as essential.

The kisses grew wilder; his strong hands became bolder, exploring her breasts. He pulled her against him intimately, then drew in a shuddering sigh, as if recalling his control over himself.

"Araminta," he whispered. His rough hold loosened and they half lay on the sofa, still pressed against each other from thigh to shoulder.

"Araminta," he said again. "I give in now. For now."

He surrendered? This was his idea. She opened her mouth to say so, but he at once lowered his mouth to hers for another of the sweetest kisses she'd ever tasted. It started light but rapidly grew, and by the end she came near to howling with need.

Just for now, he'd said. Yes. She had been waiting for this moment for so long. The doubt did not magically dissolve and it nagged at her, reminding her that she should know better. More than anyone, she knew what they might create: another bastard.

God, she should resist this. She'd been strong so many years—since she was very young and had seen her mother's underlying frailty.

But she'd never met a force that could match her strength, and she wanted to taste the wild freedom of letting go. His mouth demanded more, and his hands too, and she arched up to respond. Giving in. Just this once. For now.

He seemed momentarily troubled by the rage of their passion; she welcomed it. She would embrace it all.

He rubbed his face against her breast and she drew a hissing breath, dizzy with the force of her own appetite.

Yes, all of it, even a baby with green eyes, almost especially such a baby.

His fingers pushed into her hair, loosening hairpins. One clinked to the floor. His hand cupped her head, holding her steady so he could deepen their kiss, and urge it stronger and harder. Even as their mouths explored kisses, his other hand lightly circled her breast and then moved over her hips. She twisted her legs around his, trying to get as near him as possible. Her brain shut down to anything but the sensations that poured through her with every sliding friction of touch. Her skin, her mouth, even her eyelids tingled in anticipation of his touch. And between her legs. She could not refrain from pressing forward and moaning when his hand slipped under her skirt and petticoat and up her thigh.

He tore his mouth from hers. "Wild woman."

"Hush." She touched the nape of his neck to draw him back for another kiss, hoping his hand would continue its exploration. But he pulled back and stared down at her.

"The bedroom," he said firmly.

She thought the fever might pass as they untangled limbs and stood. She half hoped she'd regain her sanity and at last ignore the hunger long enough to leave, but he kept those heavy-lidded hypnotic eyes focused on hers, and she walked with him into the huge bedroom with the four-poster bed.

He came to her, wrapped his hands around her waist, and whispered, "Now, Araminta, we will take off your clothes."

"You take off yours," she retorted breathlessly as she backed away.

They stood a few feet apart. She watched with greed and fascination as he unbuttoned, unfastened, slipped out of the clothing. He was faster and she was too distracted by his body. She still wore her stockings, garters, chemise and absurd bustle when, naked and magnificent, he moved to her and began to impatiently help.

"No heavy corset," he murmured as he ran the tip of a finger across the top of her light stays, leaving a trail of heat on her skin. "I intensely dislike these things."

She pulled off her corset. "Don't wear them, then," she said, idiotically. Her shaky laugh cut off as he bent, peeled away her thin chemise and covered her nipple with his mouth. He sucked greedily.

She whimpered. He straightened, pulled her to him, heat pressed to heat. His hand stroked down her leg, then he gave a little pull on her knee to make her lose her balance. Before she could fall, he reached down and gathered her up, and hauled her into his arms.

She gasped and wrapped her arms around his neck, and reveled in the strength of his arms. "You are absurd. Put me down."

"Not yet." His face pressed into her neck as he carried her to the bed. "You smell of spice. I knew you would. I've caught hints of it. But you aren't as heavy as I had imagined."

In his arms, she had trouble thinking or feeling anything other than her craving. "You are a carnival act then? To guess my weight?"

"I have guessed many things about you, Araminta. Long past time to see if I was correct."

He threw the covers off the bed and placed her on the bare sheet and lay down next to her. Before she had even turned to him, his strong, clever hands were on her breasts and his mouth fit over hers for a kiss.

He touched her in places she'd barely imagined she had. His fingers swept over her skin and twisted into her and she gasped, sensitive and eager for more. But he did not indulge in leisurely play for long. After barely any exploration, after a few minutes of caresses and kisses, he rolled a layer of protection onto himself. She stopped him for a second to marvel at the sight of the sheath. And to admire his sleek, well-muscled body.

He sank between her thighs, kissed along her legs and her belly and, when his mouth found hers, pressed himself into her. She had a moment's panic, for he seemed much larger than her one previous lover, but the sensation of too much turned enjoyable almost at once.

Without patience, but not without skill, he moved in her, slowly at first, but soon he grew more urgent and harsh. She ran her hands over his wide shoulders, down his spine. Each time he pushed into her, her whole body grew tighter as if coiling around her center.

His rhythm changed. She arched up to meet him as he thrust harder, and her body wrapped itself even more firmly around that ache, growing thick until he stopped and, shivering, nuzzled the side of her neck. "At last. Oh God."

She writhed and clutched him, and only let go of him when he pushed up from her to balance himself on his hands. He kissed her gently and pressed his forehead to hers. "I'm sorry," he murmured.

She frowned. But why did he apologize? A moment of panic seized her. Did he regret inviting her up here? She closed her eyes against the rising mortification.

"Are you?" she said quietly. "Then I should be too, I imagine."

He pulled up and away from her. "Oh, no. Not you, Araminta. You are wonderful."

Relieved that he did not appear to be in distress, she opened her eyes again to watch him. He discarded the condom and propped himself on one elbow to look at her. The green eyes were lazier now, though the gleam of the hunter still flickered through them as his gaze roamed her. Nervous, she licked her lips, for desire still coursed through her at the sight of his long-limbed and glorious body so close to hers.

He stroked her hair. "Did you think I am sorry you are here?"

Araminta felt disconcerted that he could read her thoughts so easily, and she didn't answer. He ran his fingers feather light over her breast, and pressed his thumb into her nipple, which rose to meet his exploring finger.

"I apologized," he murmured, "because I did not mean for it to be over so quickly. I've wanted you too long, I think."

That was a reason to express regret? Araminta didn't know what to answer. She had thought of herself as an experienced woman, but her only sessions of lovemaking had been four pleasant though far faster episodes with her chef lover in France soon after he had declared he would marry her, and a single experience of groping with an Italian she'd met in England. That brief event had ended with her shoving him into the street before he'd gotten much further than a few sloppy kisses.

She had never been entirely overcome before, and the intensity of sensation still dazzled her. As she lay quiet, sprawled on the huge bed, almost too befuddled to notice the continuous throb in her belly and breasts, he caressed her nipples. Then his fingers stroked the throbbing into a sweeter and stronger ache than she'd ever recalled. She twisted, pushed against his exploring hand.

The man seemed to know what he was doing.

She felt raw and far out of her depths swept along. Her embarrassment forgotten, now she squeezed her eyes tight to concentrate on his strokes, the sound of his sighs against her skin. Then the warmth and magic of his hands were gone. She groaned in protest, but when she looked over at him, she was astonished to see that he was preparing to lie on her again. Could a man even perform the act more than once? The answer was very clearly yes, and oh, so good.

She cried out and clutched at his shoulders and back frantically when he entered her again. Even as he moved in her, he touched and kissed her.

"Araminta," he breathed. "Oh God. I lose control with you."

She didn't understand what he could mean. His hands on her were as expert as her touch with pastry. She was raw dough, sure enough. Almost immediately, the tightness inside her exploded into delicious throbs. She screamed out her surprise and joy.

"Yes, oh, yes, good." He groaned.

She could only whimper with pleasure, as he pushed harder, rubbing her sensitive flesh. The swirls again grew to the moment when she felt another exquisite blast roll through her. This time, she half heard, half felt his shout at the same moment.

She lay stunned for a time, waking from the trance when his fingers brushing the curls from her face grazed her skin. "Are you still here?" he asked, soft amusement in his murmur.

"Oh, very much." She turned onto her side and smiled. She dipped her head and explored the taste of his chest, his flat nipple, and daintily inhaled the satisfying musk of the man.

"You will kill me," he informed her as he gathered her

into his arms. "Although I'm only too delighted to die this way."

She burrowed into his chest, and soon she reveled in lovemaking that was achingly slow now, though no less intense. She felt as if she'd run for miles, and ached with the fulfilling exercise and the jolting releases her body had never known.

In the now darkened bedroom, with only the faintest sounds of the city below, she lay curled on the soft featherbed, her arm across his chest, her leg on his, her skin pressed against his. He lay on his back. She pulled away so that by the faint glow of the moon, she could admire his smooth skin, his strong but slender build, a light sprinkling of hair across his chest and on his long, solid legs. Peace flowed into her. And an unfamiliar deep ache in her throat she suspected might be the stirring of love.

Griffin broke the silence. "We shall take action on your friend's part as soon as possible, just as you suggest. She ought to come here. And then, Araminta, I will be very happy to arrange something for you."

She gave a sleepy murmur of thanks. As he talked she wiggled back over to rest her head on his chest so she could feel his deep, cultivated voice through her skin and into her bones.

"A house." Above her head his hands traced a shape in the air. "Anywhere near New York. Or London, if you prefer. And a fair amount deposited into an account each quarter. We shall discuss specifics the moment you wish to."

She jerked entirely awake. Her mouth went dry. His mistress. He was hiring her. Cold horror swept through her, and she pushed away from him so no part of him touched any part of her.

She squeezed her eyes shut hard enough to hurt, in order to ward off any angry tears that might be forming.

"No." Eyes still shut, she heard only the rustling sheets as he turned onto his side.

"It would be a generous arrangement. Very generous. I know you have an independent income, but you say you need more."

She opened her eyes, shifted to face him and forced herself to look him in the face. "I feel as if . . . oh, as if today I had created a feast. No. As if you and I had worked together to create one."

He chuckled softly and touched the end of her nose. "I am fairly sated. And look forward to feasting again at your, ah, intimate restaurant."

"And when you had finished eating," she continued as if he hadn't spoken, "you stood up and spat on the table. That's how your generosity makes me feel. You are no better than your friend from the restaurant, Mr. Richardson."

He did not so much as flinch, and his eyes remained steady and focused on hers. But in less than a heartbeat he had turned into the Griffin whose brilliant emerald eyes were sharp and cold enough to bore into her. "Nonsense. I have never offered another woman such an arrangement."

"So you mean I should be proud to be your whore?"

"That is not the word I would use. There is no reason to be offended by a mutually satisfactory agreement."

"Oh, dress it in any names you like, Griffin. The answer is no."

"Surely this would be better than staying at Kane's. You would be able to open your restaurant eventually. You will never get another offer as good as mine." The controlled voice had returned—strong and cool as carved marble. The warmth of life had fled him again.

She rolled away, slipped from the bed and bent to unwind her stocking from a ladder-back chair. How on earth had it become so entangled? Oh, God. What had she been thinking? She had to get out as quickly as she could.

She stopped yanking at her stocking to respond. "Yes, you're correct, I won't get such an offer because I am not a whore. Not at any price." She was pleased at how calm she kept her voice.

Not as tranquil as he managed to keep his, of course. "Why did you come up to my rooms with me? What do you expect from me? I hoped you would agree to meet with me again. I still hope that you will. But don't look for too much, Araminta."

Though he sounded almost gentle as he said the last words, she wished she could think of something biting to say. Something that would slash him to the quick so he'd feel as much pain as she did. No, that sort of speech would not help her. A throbbing started in her temples.

She balanced on the edge of the bed, far away from him, to pull on her other stocking and adjust the garter. "I know. I didn't think of marriage, Griffin. Your kind does not marry women like me."

He'd pulled himself up, and now his folded arms rested on raised knees. "What do you want from me?"

"Nothing, now." Her shaky fingers worked automatically as she pulled on her chemise, stays and petticoat and found her gown. From inside its folds she continued, talking to herself as much as to him. "Perhaps I had not thought of anything beyond today. I can no longer recall. I—I slipped my bonds. I shouldn't have."

"You have used me." He sounded amused.

She pushed her head through the neckhole.

He moved to the edge of the bed, where he sat, naked and magnificent. She tilted her head and examined him, up and down, hoping she looked as insolent as any man examining a woman.

The muscles of his shoulders bunched as he clutched the mattress. His fingers were white with the pressure of his grip. Not so unaffected by this confrontation after all.

Oh, God, if only he were composed of nothing but a superb body and haughty power. The strange pain she recognized in him now reminded her he was more. She'd seen too much of the man in the time they'd spent together.

A flush of sorrow shot through her and melted the anger, leaving her bereft, without even a good towering rage to hold on to. "I did not think I used you," she said at last. "But perhaps I was mistaken."

She buttoned the front of her dress, a gown designed for a woman who had no maid to help her. Knowing he watched and analyzed her every motion, she turned her back on him.

"What would you call it then, Araminta? We enjoyed each other."

Yes, indeed they had. No arguing with that, and perhaps later she'd remember only that fine time, once the hurt and anger dissipated. Already she felt empty.

She adjusted the lace at her bosom, slipped on her shoes and picked up her jacket. When she was fully dressed, she turned, ready to meet his stare. "I thought we were making love. I have been wrong about that before."

As she reached for the doorknob, he rose to his feet and reached for his trousers.

She shook her head. God, she wanted him nowhere near her once the tears started. "No need, sir. I shall show myself out. I won't embarrass you by using the lift. I know how to find the back staircase of this establishment."

"Let me summon an escort for you, then. It is best—"

"No."

The door softly clicked behind her.

* * *

Griffin stared at the blank white door, his heart thumping hard. If he went after her, she would run away from him. He knew it. And what could he say if he held on to her and forced her to listen? Agree with her? *Yes, we were making love . . . but I don't know what the hell that means. I don't want this. I want you.*

Damn it all, he couldn't go after her. He'd gibber like a fool. He pulled in a deep breath, desperate to escape from the nauseating sensation that he'd shattered something vital. Again.

As he slipped on a heavy velvet and satin figured robe, he reminded himself he had no reason to feel as if he'd just slit someone's throat. The woman had too much pride, not enough sense.

He had made it clear more than once that he had no intention of marrying, ever. What else could a woman expect from him? He had already offered more than he'd meant to, but she wanted more than he would give—he knew that about her, though she said nothing. Not money or other comfortingly familiar objects. Araminta's expectations showed in her eyes as clearly as any of her strong emotions. He tied the belt as he walked to the sitting room, where he pressed a button.

Hobbes appeared.

"Where's Wurth or one of the others?" Griffin asked.

"The other men are busy." Hobnail's voice was tight.

"Playing poker, no doubt. What are you doing here?"

"Mr. Galvin is meeting me."

"Then you have at least an hour. Go—fast—to the back entrance. Follow Miss Araminta, but don't allow her to see you. Just keep her safe."

Griffin noticed the unpleasant scowl Hobbes shot in his direction, but dismissed it as being of no concern.

He went back to his bedroom and gathered his scattered clothes. Yet he did not order a bath. He barely admitted the fact to himself, but he did not want to wash away the traces of Araminta. Not right away. As he dressed, he surveyed the disordered bed and allowed himself a minute or two of longing or regret—he didn't give it a name, for it wouldn't help to know what he felt.

Bloody hell. There could be a serious consequence to the day's events. No doubt the woman would sanctimoniously turn away any help he'd offer. He'd have to put some sort of round-the-clock guard on her to keep her safe.

He reached for his watch. Almost nine o'clock; he'd work for a couple more hours. As the watch snapped shut, the familiar click came inside him, too. Closing off anything but business. Time was up. Enough nonsense. Back to work. He did not need more.

He strode across the sitting room toward the library, where a mineral rights report waited for him. A small white object lay on the floor next to the couch: her glove. Without breaking stride, he reached for it and tucked it into a waistcoat pocket.

Araminta swept down the street, the rhythm of her heels striking the sidewalk venting some of her feeling. Her anger was directed at herself now. She should have known. All her life, she had faced the fact of her heritage, yet she had foolishly harbored some desire to hear the word *love*. She truly did know better than to imagine she'd hear the word *marriage* from a gentleman such as Griffin.

Jean-Pierre had talked of marrying her toward the end of their year together. But soon after that, he had expressed his very great sorrow that such a thing could never be. No, indeed, his family would never permit it.

And when she refused to enter his bed again, he had found himself an acceptable, middle-class white wife.

She had not regretted her lost virtue, much. After she turned sixteen and developed a rather extravagant figure, the world assumed she had experience. Once, a gentleman who had learned of her murky background informed her that God created her kind for bed sports.

Her mother had tried to teach her to think of herself as a lady. Everyone else seemed to assume she was for sale.

Her grandfather had been right. She fit nowhere and no one.

"Miss Araminta." A voice behind her interrupted her bitter thoughts.

Damn that Griffin. He must have sent along Hobbes. Reluctantly, she slowed her pace.

The big man caught up with her and pushed his battered brown bowler back to reveal a forehead creased by a scowl. For a moment she feared he would berate her, but then he asked, "You all right?"

"I am well, thank you."

"Don't seem so good."

She bit her lip to keep the tears back. After she knew she'd succeeded, she spoke. "I suppose you are right. But I have no one to blame but myself."

He briefly touched her shoulder. "I'll not have him hurt you."

"That's kind, Mr. Hobbes—"

"Hobnail," he reminded her.

"Hobnail, you offered to court me once."

He nodded. "Like the way you see things. Wouldn't ask about—about what you and him did."

"Oh, Hobnail. You are generous, far too good, but I must still say no, thank you. I just want to know, would you ever consider marrying a woman like me?"

"That's what courting often leads to."

"Despite my . . . " Her voice died away.

"Your what?"

"My color, Hobnail."

"You're Italian, ain't you?"

She pressed her hands together, hard. "No. My grand-mother was probably a mulatto," she said gently.

"Oh." He sounded uninterested. "She a good woman?"

"I never knew her." She didn't even know her paternal grandmother's name.

"Sorry to hear it," he said. "My granny's a fine old lady. I'd take you to meet her but she'd think we were courting. It's her dearest wish that I get a wife."

Araminta lost the fight against tears and pulled out a handkerchief. How much easier her life would be if she could somehow manage to fall in love with Hobnail Hobbes. But she wouldn't marry without love, and she apparently was attracted to heartless scoundrels, and not decent men.

"Oh," she managed, after she'd wiped her eyes and blown her nose. "I'm sorry, I think I shan't ever marry. But I would be honored to be your friend."

"Right," he said, unconcerned. "That's understood, Miss Araminta."

He began to whistle.

When she lay in bed, her brain would not turn away from Griffin. The hot anger had fled, and now indecision clouded her thoughts.

He was not unfair, really. He had always been clear that he would not marry. She should have known he would be businesslike about bedding her. Oh, heavens, but he wasn't anything like cold in that bed. His touch lingered on her skin, in the raw ache between her legs. She shivered, as memory of that passion rippled through her.

She even wondered if he was right to offer compensation. After all, she was the only one who would take risks, for only she would be hurt when their time together ended. His armor was too thick.

But then she abruptly recalled that she wasn't the only one at risk. There might be children. Another generation raised outside the boundaries of society. She had briefly indulged in fantasy earlier, had almost felt the sweetly perfect weight of Griffin's baby in her arms. But she could not be selfish and cause an innocent to suffer the pain she knew too well. Her early childhood had been idyllic, but once she'd understood . . .

Deep sorrow extinguished her uncertainty. The matter was settled.

She woke the next morning determined to find another solution to the problem of Olivia. Perhaps the two of them could buy tickets for a ship sailing to Europe. Ignoring the pain that had replaced a giddy passion, she made plans. A fresh start would suit her. She slowly started the familiar process of sloughing off an old life, as she had after her mother died. Now she left behind more than a small country village—what was the old-fashioned phrase her mother might have used? Araminta would put herself on the shelf, and abandon dreams of love.

As she yanked on her dressing gown, she dismissed any other possibilities. She could not settle for a man she didn't love—not after her mother had sacrificed everything for love. To settle for less would be an insult to Charlotte.

CHAPTER 12

Early in the morning, even before the sun rose, Araminta threw back the lid of her trunk and stared down at the letters. Stacks of them. All of them hers, written to her grandfather, the man who'd thrown out his daughter. He had never answered her on paper. But he'd saved the letters, and somehow, after his death, they'd made their way back to her, and for some reason she'd saved them. Evidence that she had once had a family, perhaps.

She tied the belt to her dressing gown tight, and then leaned down to open a few, pulling them at random from the thick piles and throwing them back into the trunk without reading them. She'd save a few—not a link to the past, more of a small reminder.

The rest she gathered, and, kneeling by the small fire she had started in the grate, she tossed them one by one onto the blaze. Mesmerized, she watched the paper— some of it white, some cream, depending on where she'd lived when she wrote the letters—all curl into black, then gray, ash. The solid pain remained, but rested more easily now. This end of a past marked a beginning, after all.

"Well, then, Grandfather," she said aloud, "you wouldn't allow the loss of something precious to interfere with your busy life. Maybe you can teach me something after all."

She tossed the rest of the letters into the trunk and

spoke to her grandfather again. "I must say it is too bad your lessons always seem more true than Mama's."

At work she kept herself and her hands busy with preparing a meal. The usual eight-course meal for the evening's guests—nothing extravagant. The rhythm of cooking eased some of the dreary heaviness in her heart.

Olivia came into the kitchen earlier than usual and perched on a stool to watch. Since Kane's departure, she seemed more cheerful, so Araminta decided to approach the question.

"Did you ever want to visit Europe?"

Olivia's smile vanished. "Yes, but that was an old dream."

Araminta tied up the bags of herbs and stuffed them into the trussed-up fowls. "I might return to England, I think. Would you like to accompany me? I'd buy your ticket for you."

"Araminta, you are too generous and kind."

Araminta was reminded of her own words to Hobnail.

Olivia pulled out a delicate handkerchief and wiped her eyes. "I can't. I shall never be able to travel, I think."

"It's not so difficult, you know. Simply walk up the gangplank and allow the captain and his sailors to do the work."

Olivia gave a watery smile. "Tell me, Araminta, why are you so determined to rescue me?"

Araminta began to knead some herbs into butter. "Who wouldn't want to?"

"But to go so far as to quit your job!"

For weeks it had been more a matter of going so far as to keep it, but Araminta replied, "I suppose because you remind me of my mother."

Olivia's eyes widened. "I am so much younger than you."

Araminta hid her amusement. "Yes, by a half-dozen years, I'd say. But she looked like you, even had coloring like yours—no, don't look so surprised. I believe I must take after a member of my father's family."

Olivia shook her head, bemused. "Because I look like your mother, you are willing to run all the way to Europe to protect me? You are a zany."

Araminta laughed. "It is not such a sacrifice. Nothing holds me here. In fact, I would be delighted to leave this city."

"Are you hurt, Araminta? You seem so unhappy."

She wiped her hands on her apron and reached for a tray of timbales. "I'm a trifle sad. Perhaps because I'm— I am thinking of my mother," she lied. "You are like my mother in more than just appearance, too. Lovable and"—she decided not to add "weak,"—"and under the thumb of a man who doesn't deserve to hold power over any living creature."

"Your father was a bad man? I'm sorry."

"No, my father died soon after I was born, and my mother loved him. She always said he was as fine a man as ever lived. I mean my grandfather. But it's not a particularly interesting tale."

Araminta didn't intend to share her family's story with Olivia or anyone else. She walked briskly to a cupboard and came back with her arms full. "Here, break up this bread into small pieces for me." She handed Olivia three loaves of long bread and a large bowl. "I shall make a bread pudding. With brandy and a good cream sauce, no one will know it's such a homely food."

Araminta finished preparing the timbales and went to pour a cup of coffee for herself and Olivia. The huge pot was empty, but rather than stop one of her busy helpers, she made a fresh pot herself.

She put it on the range. Across the kitchen, Jack wedged open crates of supplies with an iron bar. He gave an angry shout.

"Look at this!" He pointed at an open box full of young lettuces. "The ones on the bottom are slimy."

As she strode over, Araminta could smell them, but still she leaned down and prodded the lettuce with a finger. Disgusting. "Didn't you talk to the greengrocer about his produce before?"

Jack kicked the box. "Yeah. But he's done it again. I think you'll have to say something, Miss Araminta."

"Yes. Good idea. I'll pay the man a visit immediately."

Olivia bid her good-bye and wandered from the kitchen. Araminta untied her apron and flung it down. She was in the mood to tell the greengrocer what he could do with his rotten vegetables.

His shop was only a few blocks away, and it took less than ten minutes to settle the matter. The brisk walk and the "conversation" with the apologetic greengrocer helped improve Araminta's mood.

When she returned to the kitchen, she poured herself a cup of coffee and frowned. The pot she'd just made was almost empty.

Sure enough, five used coffee cups sat on the counter. She piled them in a corner for the scullery maids and pulled a pencil and paper toward herself to jot down a recipe detail that had occurred to her on the walk back from the greengrocer.

Olivia stood in the doorway, panting and worried. "There you are."

"Are you all right?"

Olivia peered around the kitchen as if searching for something before coming all the way in. She must have been satisfied because she came close to Araminta, bent toward her and whispered, "I'm fine. But your friend. He's not."

"My friend?"

"Mr. Calverson. I was coming down the stairs and I heard a few of the men talking in the hall in the kitchen. I hid, but I could hear the whole conversation. I think they are going to go to his office to—to kill him."

Araminta shot to her feet, alarmed. "Was Mr. Hobbes one of the men?"

Olivia looked around nervously and whispered, "You mean the big one who seems so taken with you?"

"Yes."

"No. He's not here."

Another strange thing. Araminta grabbed her bonnet and reticule. "I have to do something. I must warn him."

"Where are you off to now, miss?" red-haired Maggie shouted after her.

"I'll be back," was her only reply.

She abandoned frugality and hired a hack. By the time she had reached Griffin's hotel, he'd departed for his office. And when she managed to rush there, she was told he'd just left.

"He accompanied a large, rather uncouth gentleman," a gossipy clerk informed her. Araminta breathed a sigh of relief. Maybe Mr. Hobbes had come to warn him. But then the clerk described the man as dark-haired. Not Hobnail after all. Panic tore through her. What if Kane had left town at this moment so that he could not be connected to Griffin's death?

She rushed to the window in the front of the Calverson Company office and stared out over the crowds, searching. There, heading rapidly toward the river. Three men surrounding a man in the middle—one on each side, one behind. Surrounding another man. Could it be him?

She tore down the stairs, praying she wasn't following a false trail.

CHAPTER 13

Griffin scowled down at the near-illegible scrap of paper—his father's latest plea for more funds. "Why do you suppose my father would require three thousand dollars for excavation equipment? His crews use garden spades."

The secretary awaiting his dictation shot him a frightened look and uttered a near-silent bleat. "I'm sure I do not know, sir."

Hell, and why had Williams stuck him with the frightened sheep of a man? Maybe it was an attempt to drive Griffin out of the New York office.

Griffin flung his father's letter onto the massive mahogany desk. "I'll deal with this later. We should draft a response to the latest offer to buy the Minnesota property. Oh, and have we had any news yet about Senator Burritt and his lovely daughter, Elizabeth?"

The other names on the list he'd had an assistant draw up had all been disqualified. The girls didn't match the description. Or they'd last been seen in other cities.

The secretary shifted nervously through the stacks of papers.

Griffin attempted to stifle his impatience. "Just check to see if Galvin's man has verified my idea. It will be in Galvin's weekly report."

More scrabbling at papers. "Yes, sir. I mean, no, sir. This says that Miss Smith is still unidentified."

"Fine. We'll deal with the Minnesota issue then." Griffin shifted his chair so he could stare out the window as he droned on about properties and retaining mineral rights. Gazing far off in the direction of the harbor, he could see the masts of ships. He considered standing up, walking out the door and heading straight to one of those ships.

He'd grown sick of travel, but now he'd grown tired of New York. And London, for that matter. A dusty train heading west. A ship heading south or east. Somewhere else, preferably primitive. He didn't need to seek adventure; the simple survival that travel in those areas required would be enough.

Something to scrub his brain clean.

Araminta had said no in her usual forceful fashion. And that was that. He did not need her, and her infernal presence in his thoughts was a useless burden. Perhaps another woman would provide some distraction. . . . The idea irritated him almost more than Araminta's haunting him.

A light knock and one of Williams's assistants opened the door. "I'm sorry to disturb you, sir, but I have a, ah, gentleman here who requires a moment of your time. He insists it's a private matter."

Griffin dismissed the secretary, who gathered papers and fled the office.

One of Galvin's young oxen. Buckler. This one worked in one of Kane's more grimy Tenderloin saloons, where the waiter girls were especially popular.

Griffin tilted his head as the bulky young man shuffled in. Something in the way Buckler didn't look him in the face alerted him. Or the grip with which the oaf clutched his hat, while his other hand remained jammed in his jacket pocket. The day was too warm for a jacket that heavy. And Buckler was sweating.

Stealthily, Griffin reached into his own jacket pocket to check for his knife. Good.

"Sir." Buckler cleared his throat.

Griffin could manage hearty when the occasion called for it. "How is your new assignment, Buckler? Is Kane a good employer? Very pleasant for you, I'd say, drawing pay from two masters. What can I do for you today?"

Buckler's mouth opened, but nothing came out. He made another attempt. "Sir," he croaked. "I'm worried. Er. There's something I think you ought to see. At the place. Where I'm working for Mr. Kane."

Griffin managed not to roll his eyes. Buckler was the worst actor he'd ever encountered. "Why haven't you shown whatever it is to Mr. Galvin? He is your supervisor."

"I, er, have. He—Mr. Galvin says you need to see it too, sir. So if you're not busy, I wonder if I could, ah, have some of your time?"

Griffin was busy.

And he was not stupid enough to walk into a possible trap. Except when he was very, very restless and curious. What was Buckler up to? Could Galvin actually know what was going on?

He only wished he could figure out if the young fool had a gun or a knife in the jacket pocket.

Feeling almost cheerful, he got to his feet and reached for his hat and coat. Good, he'd forgotten he'd left his gold-headed cane here. A foolish bit of work, but the hidden blade might come in handy soon.

He grabbed that, too. "Shall we go then?" He gestured to the door. "After you."

The other two men waited at the sidewalk entrance. Obviously more professional than Buckler, they smoothly fell into step, one on either side of him. He waited for someone to growl out words such as "Don't move, or you're dead," but no one spoke. So he came to a sudden stop. Buckler slammed into him.

Griffin turned and put out a steadying hand. "I'm sorry, Mr. Buckler. Are you hurt?"

Buckler stammered, and one of the other men grabbed Griffin's arm. "No funny business, you."

"Excuse me?" Griffin looked him up and down, assuming an air of confusion.

The man, the taller of the two escorts, stared back. Not a familiar face, at any rate. The man took in a breath and let it out with a slight snoring sound. Aha, thought Griffin, Araminta's friend from the basement? This could be a bigger problem than Griffin had anticipated.

"Um," Buckler said. "Sir. Mr. Calverson. Um."

"Christ almighty, you didn't say anything, did you, you idiot," the other man snarled under his breath. "Calverson, you're coming with us."

"Yes?" Griffin turned to examine him. "Pardon me, have we been introduced?"

Buckler whimpered, "Um. Sir. I, that is we, have to take you somewhere."

"But of course, Mr. Buckler. That is why I am here." Griffin managed an aggrieved, befuddled glare to match his still mild tone. "Yet you still haven't explained what is so terribly important. And I want to know what it is that I—"

"Shut it," one of the other hoods spoke with a harsh growl.

Griffin, who was thoroughly enjoying playing the confused but outraged citizen, caught sight of a woman racing along the sidewalk, her dark honey skin flushed, long curling tendrils of her hair coming down in the back under a sky-blue hat.

Araminta. Searching for him. His heart, which should have been filled with fear, lifted, and he wanted nothing more than to run after her. He would, too, once he was finished with this nuisance.

He turned away at once. "I understand," he muttered. "Keep your hands off me and I won't raise a fuss. Let's go."

Behind him, Buckler heaved a deep sigh. Regret or relief, Griffin wondered, as they marched him off the bustling financial block onto a side street.

He gripped his newfangled knife. A present from his sister, it opened almost silently with only a press of a finger.

At the corner of an alley and the street, he gave a sudden twist, ducked and raised a knee hard in the shorter man's groin.

The tall one pulled out a revolver and appeared to have a steady hand, so Griffin regretfully threw the blade at his arm. He would have rather held on to the knife.

The gun clattered to the ground. The confusion lasted long enough for Griffin to slam his cane into Buckler's legs and then use it to hit the gun so it skittered in his direction.

He had the gun in his hand when something slammed into his hip and then his side, and he felt a kind of horrible ripping thrust that could only mean he'd been attacked by something sharp. A blade. He turned and saw Buckler staring, horror-struck, at a bloody paring knife in his own hand. Thank goodness the man was too much of a nitwit to bring a real weapon.

Griffin yanked his arm from his coat sleeve and looked down at his side. The blood was oozing rather than spurting from the two wounds. "Buckler, you fool."

Buckler turned white and collapsed. In a dead faint.

With one hand clutching the heavy revolver and the

other pressed tight to his side, Griffin pivoted to face the taller of the two ruffians. The man took one look at the gun, turned and bolted down the alley. Griffin considered firing off a shot at him, but didn't want to deal with the trouble of the noise and its aftermath. He now knew the man's face and suspected the man's nickname was Bacon; that would suffice.

A woman's scream rent the air. So much for keeping the incident quiet.

At a dead run, her hands outstretched, Araminta plowed into the smaller man, who was still hunched in pain. He toppled onto the pavement and groaned. She fell to her hands and knees but clambered up at once, and ran to Griffin.

She grabbed his arm, the one that held the gun. "Put that away. You are hurt."

Griffin, who knew the pain would start any second, raised his eyebrows. "What does one have to do with the other?"

Someone shouted. Running footsteps.

Araminta's voice was in his ear. "I'm taking you back to the office."

"No. Too disruptive. I need to . . ."

At that moment, the pain slammed through him so he had to clench his teeth to keep from groaning aloud. She snatched the gun from him. She shoved her shoulder under his arm and looped her arm around him. He wondered if he was going to be sick. The pain seemed to throb with every heartbeat. He'd suffered worse injuries in his life, he reminded himself.

"Perhaps I have grown too old for these kinds of larks," he admitted in a croak.

"Don't you dare faint." Her voice came from far away. "You are too heavy for me to carry."

"Araminta?"

"Yes."

"Where are we going?"

"Just walk. A half-block more." She sounded out of breath. After what felt like years, she stopped and waved her arm. It took Griffin, fighting the pain, a few seconds to realize she was hailing a cab.

The coachman shouted down angrily, "He's all covered with blood."

"It was an accident," Araminta called back. "You can't refuse to give a ride to an injured man."

Despite his discomfort, Griffin was amused by her innocence about New York cabbies. "Assure the man he'll get a large tip," he muttered.

During the ride uptown, he leaned against her, counting the jolts. The circle of her arms around him almost made up for the pain.

Her voice in his ear again. "I'm taking you to my house. It's closer."

He nodded.

Then she was urging him up a mountain of stairs. A dark, cool breath of spicy air touched him. Air with her luscious, comforting scent. He felt his legs grow weak, and the ground rushed at him.

"Oh no, no, Griffin. Not yet."

"Araminta. Come to bed." And the world turned black.

CHAPTER 14

The next time Griffin woke, he wondered if someone had thrown him into a dark cellar. No, he lay on a floor on top of a blanket.

A familiar voice spoke—a man. "It might be best to leave him lying here."

"I'd ask the blasted doctor," a woman answered. Araminta. "But he refuses to come to my house."

The familiar man said, "I'll find another one, then."

Griffin opened his eyes and saw he lay just inside a small parlor, not far from a marble fireplace where a cheery fire had been built.

Araminta's house; and the man, he realized, was Hobnail.

His side might have been on fire. For a brief instant Griffin wondered if she had somehow enacted revenge for the insult she imagined he'd paid her. And then he recalled. She'd saved him, or thought she had, which was as good.

He felt like hell, but his spirits, which he hadn't known were downcast, suddenly flew. Good. No, perfect. This was what he'd longed for. Not endless, dull days at sea or traveling through uncomfortable jungles. And not taking up with some other, more acquiescent woman. Another opportunity to wrestle with Araminta, to tease her and watch her smile.

He closed his eyes and wondered if being stabbed could turn a man into a dreadful sentimentalist.

The next time he came to, a gray-haired man was causing excruciating pain by ripping his clothes and fiddling with his side.

"Not so bad." The man sounded disappointed. "I'll just need to stitch this one and then wrap him up. The big fellow can haul him into a proper bed."

Griffin tried to sit.

"You there, stop him. He's writhing."

"No, I'm not. I am attempting to stand up."

"Wait a few days before you try that kind of trick, Mr. Mouton."

Mouton?

Griffin peered over his shoulder at the scowling man with beetling black eyebrows. "Are you a doctor?"

"Yes, and I'd appreciate it if you'd stop moving about."

Something cold dribbled on his bare skin, and then stinging hit. "Ho! Ouch."

"That's the alcohol," the doctor explained, almost cheerful for the first time. He began stitching. "I like to use plenty."

"Ruddy doctors," Griffin mumbled and settled back for the far less painful stitching and bandaging.

After a few minutes, the doctor slapped Griffin's shoulder. "Fine. Now you can take him to the bed."

Huge hands grabbed him and Griffin was face to face with Hobnail, who hauled him up and wrapped a beefy arm around him.

"I can walk by myself."

"Not a problem, sir. Miss Araminta thinks this best. You're bigger than you look, sir," Hobnail wheezed, as they started up the stairs.

The doctor and Araminta were in a corner speaking together. Arguing.

"No, the patient will not be moved yet. He stays here," the doctor pronounced. He pulled out a notebook, scribbled something and handed the sheet of paper to Araminta. "Directions to a good, reliable visiting nurse. If you require more help, call on me again."

He turned and glared up at Griffin. "Good day, ma'am, Mr. Mouton. Try not to apprehend any more pickpockets, sir."

Hobnail deposited him on a wide, comfortable bed.

"Just a moment, Hobnail. Explain. Mr. Mouton? Pickpockets?"

"Miss Araminta told that story to the doctor, sir, because she wasn't sure he'd keep quiet. She's a suspicious woman now. She worries they'll come after you here if she gives your real name."

"My kind of woman," Griffin muttered.

He thought he heard Hobnail say, "No, sir."

When he twisted to look at the big man, a wave of pain washed through Griffin's side. He shut his eyes tight for a moment, and forced away the weakness.

"I'm gonna write up a report on this, sir," Hobnail said, his pale, mild eyes exceptionally stern.

"Fine, yes. But later, if you don't mind."

Hobnail scratched a bristly sideburn and pursed his lips. "I'll agree to later, sir, if you promise to be forthcoming. What should I do now?"

"Right now I need you to get Williams. Tell him to bring a couple of the boys. I'll need a few. Some to do some work, and others to keep an eye open around here. He'll know which. And I'll need an efficient secretary. Not the one I had today."

"Anything else?"

"Go back to Kane's. Keep an eye on Miss Woodhall."

Hobnail's heavy footsteps thudded down the stairs. Griffin closed his eyes again and rubbed his palms against his eyelids. Even lifting his arm caused a spasm of pain, but he had no desire to give in and stay still.

A rustle of cloth, a change in the air, meant someone had come in. And he sensed who it was.

Without opening his eyes, he said, "Araminta, I apologize for inconveniencing you."

"Who were those people? They could have killed you. They wanted to." Her voice was raw with anger.

A sense of warmth stole over him before he could stop himself. Her anger showed that she cared. But really, she'd be indignant if she'd witnessed an attack on a lice-ridden pigeon. The woman championed the downtrodden. Had he ever known anyone so passionate about justice? Warm, strong, real sentiment, not the trite piety so popular these days . . .

Ha. No doubt about it. He was in danger of becoming a weak and pious fool himself.

Griffin shifted in the bed so he could see up into her face, which was etched with a frown of horror. He wouldn't hide the truth from her, though. Maybe it would be enough to get her the hell out of the place. "They were Kane's men. One of them breathed oddly. Perhaps he is your friend Bacon from the basement."

She stood very still, clutching a tray. Her lips parted and her large eyes widened. "Good Lord. It's all true, then. I think I feel sick."

Damn, he hated the fact that he couldn't stand up and comfort her. "Araminta? No. Don't worry."

"I'll be well in a minute. It is just the thought of that basement. I don't think I actually believed it. Oh, and what might have happened to you. Oh! To think, when I went to work for him, Kane seemed so genial."

Griffin attempted to sit up. Pain lanced through him, but it wasn't unbearable. "I won't let him hurt you."

She put the tray on the lace-covered table near his

Get 4 FREE Books!

We created our convenient Home Subscription Service so you'll be sure to have the hottest new romances delivered each month right to your doorstep—usually before they are available in book stores. Just to show you how convenient the Zebra Home Subscription Service is, we would like to send you 4 FREE Kensington Choice Historical Romances. The books are worth up to $24.96, but you only pay $1.99 for shipping and handling. There's no obligation to buy additional books—ever!

 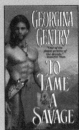  

Save Up To 30% With Home Delivery!

Accept your FREE books and each month we'll deliver 4 brand new titles as soon as they are published. They'll be yours to examine FREE for 10 days. Then if you decide to keep the books, you'll pay the preferred subscriber's price (up to 30% off the cover price!), plus shipping and handling. Remember, you are under no obligation to buy any of these books at any time! If you are not delighted with them, simply return them and owe nothing. But if you enjoy Kensington Choice Historical Romances as much as we think you will, pay the special preferred subscriber rate and save over $8.00 off the cover price!

We have 4 **FREE BOOKS** for you as your
introduction to
KENSINGTON CHOICE!
To get your FREE BOOKS, worth up to $24.96, mail
the card below or call TOLL-FREE 1-800-770-1963.
Visit our website at www.kensingtonbooks.com.

Get 4 FREE Kensington Choice Historical Romances!

YES! Please send me my 4 FREE KENSINGTON CHOICE HISTORICAL ROMANCES (without obligation to purchase other books). I only pay $1.99 for shipping and handling. Unless you hear from me after I receive my 4 FREE BOOKS, you may send me 4 new novels—as soon as they are published—to preview each month FREE for 10 days. If I am not satisfied, I may return them and owe nothing. Otherwise, I will pay the money-saving preferred subscriber's price (over $8.00 off the cover price), plus shipping and handling. I may return any shipment within 10 days and owe nothing, and I may cancel any time I wish. In any case the 4 FREE books will be mine to keep.

Name_____

Address_____ Apt._____

City_____ State_____ Zip_____

Telephone (____)_____

Signature_____

(If under 18, parent or guardian must sign)

Offer limited to one per household and not to current subscribers. Terms, offer and prices subject to change. Orders subject to acceptance by Kensington Choice Book Club.
Offer Valid in the U.S. only.

KN114A

4 FREE

Kensington
Choice
Historical
Romances
(worth up to
$24.96)
are waiting
for you to
claim them!

See details
inside....

KENSINGTON CHOICE
Zebra Home Subscription Service, Inc.
P.O. Box 5214
Clifton NJ 07015-5214

head. "Lie down, would you? As if you're in any shape to offer protection. Here, I brought you brandy. The doctor said I could give you something for the pain."

"No. I will not allow myself to be drugged."

Araminta sat down at the edge of the bed, a glass clutched in her hand. She refused to so much as glance into his face. "For heaven's sake. It is only brandy. You look dreadful—certainly it must help."

She hated seeing the powerful Griffin lying ashen and helpless. God knew she must no longer have a notion of him as someone she might love, but she couldn't help appreciating him as she might any dangerous, sleek and wild animal.

She carefully slid her hand under his head to lift it so he could sip the brandy. The slight contact sent a charge of desire sizzling through her body. Thank goodness she managed to hold back the small sound of longing that rose to her throat.

He still could move her. Why had she imagined that might change? Her body's craving had grown worse, now she knew what the two of them could do and feel—oh, heavens, what he could do to her. But she'd bite off her tongue before she let him know she pined for him as she touched his soft hair, and the warmth of his skin, to raise him for the brandy.

"Come now, Araminta, I'm capable of lifting my own head." The chiding interrupted her thoughts. His sleek voice deepened as he continued, "Although the sensation of your hand on my neck soothes me. Cool, gentle fingers. Run them over my forehead. After all, I might be growing feverish."

With one motion, she put down the glass, yanked away her hand and stood up.

She'd been mistaken—the power of the man was not dimmed. He was like any dangerous animal. Even caught and caged, it would not lose its fierce nature. "Griffin Calverson, let me make one thing clear. You must stay in my house—"

"For how long?"

"The doctor said if nothing goes wrong, and you do not develop an infection, only a few days. The second, higher wound that could have been very serious is shallow. He feels certain no vital organs were injured, for you don't show any sign of bleeding inside."

She couldn't help glancing at the belly in question. Under the white bandage it lay flat and muscular . . . and oh, dear, he saw where she stared. His eyes glittered.

She frowned at him.

"While you're here," she continued, "you will abide by my rules." She paused to consider what those rules could possibly be, and then ticked them off on her fingers. "No attempts at—at seduction."

"The thought would never cross my mind."

She looked over at him, suspicious of that thin tone, but he did not meet her eyes.

She continued, "You will be a patient and behave like one. Nor will you use your lord-of-the-manor behavior to intimidate the girl who cleans and sews for me."

He smiled at her.

She supposed he must have been weak to forget himself enough to flat-out smile at her. In her presence he'd laughed and he'd occasionally twitched up the corner of his mouth, but she couldn't recall seeing this glorious transformation. And she at last understood why he disliked his own smile.

The man did have dimples, charming, deep ones. Along with white teeth, and eyes framed by delightful crinkles. He changed into something enchanting, almost angelic. All of the menace drained from his face. Not the visage of a man who wanted to provoke fear.

She stared, and wondered which man was illusory—the one who wore that smile or the one with the customary scowl.

To her disappointment, the smile faded. "I shall not interfere with the running of your household," he said. "Anything else?"

"I must go to work. And I worry about leaving you here—"

"Someone will fetch help for me." He studied her for a long moment. "I wonder if we should summon a lady to stay here so that your reputation is not ruined beyond repair."

His concern for her took her aback. No one since her mother had expressed any such concern for her. She walked to the window and stared down at the cobblestones. "The house is too small. And it is too late to worry about my reputation."

"My two visits here have caused harm?" He did not sound particularly worried.

"No, it has been almost since I moved in." She did not want to tell him that she had often had trouble with leering men too eager to start conversations and tight-lipped women who refused to return her greetings.

"Ah, I think I understand. A reputation is so very fragile. You, living in this house alone. A single woman with no man and no visible source of income beyond a day job, with a figure like a slice of heaven, would cause talk and—"

"Yes, yes. Enough!" Araminta exhaled a long breath.

She would not allow herself to be teased into a temper by Griffin. In fact, she reminded herself, his stay would give her a chance to recover from his unwelcome ability to bring out the worst in her. Then again, perhaps not, as a fleeting memory of how he'd turned her into a wanton stirred something deep in her belly.

She strode to the door. "Good day, sir. I hope you are comfortable."

She refused to turn back.

Maybe the smile put the thought into her mind, or maybe the remark he'd muttered about being too old for larks. Whatever the reason, for the first time it occurred to her that perhaps Griffin was something of a boy. She hoped that seeing him as a mischievous child, instead of a dangerous man, would reduce his appeal. Instead it only added another rather charming layer to him.

CHAPTER 15

Griffin grinned to himself. He had missed rattling Araminta. He had missed her scent, the swish of her skirts when she moved so energetically, her rounded, delightful body and that mouth. Why the devil was the woman so stiff-necked and unreasonable? She ought to take his offer gladly, especially since she'd already been labeled a loose woman and seemed to have survived with her customary strength.

Perhaps he could seduce her again, and this time keep his mouth shut about hiring her as a mistress. But that would be dishonest and leave too many untidy ends—for he knew that one more night with Araminta would not be enough to cure him of his fever for her.

His need for a formal arrangement had more to do with his own peace of mind than hers. Marriage had always struck him as a fool's idea of happiness—only children believed in Father Christmas and the myth that a married man was happier than a single one.

Since he was not interested in an institution he did not trust, he would not take a woman without recompense, especially a woman outside of his sphere. Or to be honest, a strong woman like her. Without a businesslike agreement in place, she would attempt to take her compensation in other ways—perhaps she would try to control him, or try to delve too far in where no man or woman was welcome.

Griffin had no interest in sharing more than some entertainment—and his body and his wealth. With both of those, he would be delighted to be extremely generous.

Assuming he did not die of some dreadful infection caused by Buckler's wound. He settled back on the pillow and grimaced at the throbbing in his side.

He looked around the room with approval. Graceful, well-made, carved furniture. Fresh flowers on the washstand, a touch of lace over the bureau, more watercolors on the wall, a thick carpet on the floor. Simple but luxurious. A woman lived in this room, but he did not feel stifled by feminine clutter. She did not have satin cloth edged with fringes or pompons covering every surface.

With a grunt he pulled himself into a sitting position. Sweat poured down his face, but he did not feel faint. He had not lost very much blood. Just a matter of good luck that the knife had not hit some artery or another.

He examined his side, which had been thoroughly and painfully washed. The doctor adhered to the theory that extreme cleanliness helped healing.

Araminta's room was not large, so the huge, worn leather and metal trunk that lay open in the middle of the floor and took up a great deal of room must surely have been dragged down from an attic. Was she packing or unpacking?

He pulled himself slowly out of the bed. The doctor had ordered him not to move from the bed for at least a few days, but Griffin had been injured before. His dearest friends, who lived in Central America, believed that after an injury one should move as much as one could. His own experiences had borne out that theory.

He made his slow, painful way to the trunk and saw letters scattered across the top of the clothing and items. For a full minute, Griffin considered leaving the letters alone.

But he wanted Araminta, and she was a formidable adversary. He'd almost rather face a cowardly rat like Kane in some ways. Griffin would use anything he could find to help him in his pursuit. All was fair in this sort of battle, after all.

He did not hold out much hope of the letters being a key to her. She had strewn them in such a careless manner rather than tucking them into a secret corner, all tied up with ribbon or some other private female manner.

Griffin gathered them up. And gave an exclamation of surprise when he saw to whom they were addressed.

Her grandfather?

He'd already found out about the basic facts of Araminta. She was illegitimate. Her mother, Charlotte, was the daughter of the banker Griffin had met. Charlotte had been sent to the country when the baby was born, and had never returned to London. Griffin knew that Araminta's grandfather had pretended the child did not exist.

And the old man had never again mentioned his daughter.

Yet Woodhall hadn't been able to destroy the rumors that circled London and that Griffin easily uncovered years later.

The story went that Araminta's father was a family servant, a butler who died mysteriously. Murdered, they said, by an intruder.

The first letter hinted that the murderer lived much closer to home.

Sitting on the carpet, wearing only his bloodstained trousers, Griffin read the letter and forgot about the pain, forgot about being stabbed.

Only the thump of the front door brought him back. He clutched the pile of letters. After he found a few others in the trunk, he carried his stash and placed them on the table next to the brandy, and then slowly and carefully pulled himself back under the covers on Araminta's bed.

A minute later, several people burst into the room talking at once. A strange collection of businessmen and a rougher class of men crowded in, and stood in astonishment at the foot of the bed.

"Boss!"

"Sir, when I heard what happened—"

"Mr. Calverson—"

"Quiet." He raised a hand, but not his voice. They fell silent at once. "Gentlemen, I am not in the best of moods at the moment. And we have business to attend to."

He sent Williams's secretary off to arrange work to be sent to him. Then he turned to the three men who worked for Galvin, and described the tall man and the short man who'd assaulted him.

He finished with, "I don't think we need to start some sort of war here, so merely send a message to Kane and his employees rather than conduct a battle, hmmm? And we will leave Hobnail out of these plans."

Griffin considered what else they might do. Kane would know who sent the message, but once Griffin got Araminta out of there it would be time to show that Calverson could not be intimidated. He'd already tried to ignore the man and then attempted to jolly the idiot along. Neither had worked.

And if his guess about the Smith girl proved correct, he'd manage to thwart some of Kane's plans and gain a useful ally.

A half-hour after the other men had been sent on their way to track down Griffin's attackers, Galvin burst into the room, dressed in an impeccable black suit. His usual battered homburg had been replaced with a silk top hat.

He must have been working at one of Kane's better establishments.

"Damn it, sir!" Galvin shouted. "Why the hell did you do a fool thing like that? Didn't you give me hell about traps early on? What's happening to you? You just about deserve to get killed."

"Galvin, no need to get sentimental. I imagine I'll survive."

Galvin pulled the chair from the small escritoire and plopped down by the bed. He threw the hat on the floor next to him. "What about Buckler?" he growled.

"He's off my payroll at the very least."

"He's a dead man."

"No need for my sake," Griffin assured him.

Galvin stared at him. "You *are* getting soft."

Griffin would have shrugged, but he suspected it would be painful. "Rumors."

"Humph," Galvin grunted. "Buckler's my problem, sir. I hired him."

Griffin sighed. "He did very little damage and nearly wet himself with fear. I'm going to throw him to Hobnail—that should be enough. If you want worse, maybe turn him loose with some damage, if you absolutely must, but I don't think it's a good idea. He won't be a threat in the future."

Galvin spat his disgust. Griffin considered telling him to clean up Araminta's floor, but the poor man was so disappointed.

"And Kane?" Galvin sounded hopeful.

"Ah. Well, first I'll ruin his latest scheme, I think, and then we'll stick to the plan and close him down. Is that bad enough?"

"Kane's a big moneymaker for Tammany—you'll have to pay a lot. Easier to just give the man a shiv in the gut. It's what he intended for you."

"I have no intention of letting that menace Kane off that easily, and we'll let the man's deeds do the job for him. Murder him? After all the work your boys and Hobnail have done? No, no. I want to go the more complicated route. Get as much dirt as we can."

Now that he knew Araminta would be kept safe, he'd make sure clearing up Kane would take at least a couple of weeks—time that he'd spend with Araminta. Without the injury in his side to bother him. Perhaps that would cure his obsession with the woman.

Then maybe he'd be able to concentrate on the more important matters: finishing up the sale of his father's land in England, researching a possible investment in a new steel plant near Pittsburgh. There were the less important matters as well—avoiding invitations from new and old members of New York society, and ignoring his aunt's long-distance attempts to marry him off to some heiress or titled female.

All part of his routine.

Left alone at last, he pulled out Araminta's letters and glanced down at them. Her bold voice rang out in each word. He found himself smiling down at the small sheets of paper.

The first one was written when Araminta was sixteen. The date at the top showed it less than a month after her mother had died. He read it again.

> *Dear Grandfather,*
> *You were foolish to banish my mother. You did not*
> *know me, of course, so I was no great loss. But*
> *you knew her well. How would anyone who knew*
> *darling Charlotte reject her? Why couldn't you*
> *forgive her for your own sake, you nonsensical,*
> *pig-headed creature?*

Griffin riffled through the piles of papers. Were they all filled with Araminta at her most indignant? This was positively poisonous. "You have my sympathy, old man," he muttered to her grandfather, and then continued to read the letter.

I take up my pen to write because I wish to punish you for her sake. Charlotte never spoke badly of you, though she did not withhold the facts of what you did to her and my father. She spent her life in mourning because of you.

She mourned for your soul. Most of all, she mourned for my father, a good, kind man worth a thousand of you.

But she was not bitter and she did not hate you. I do.

Gentle Charlotte, you old fool, was too good for you. And too good for me, for that matter. For here is the real meat of the matter: my mother often told me that I am quite like you. She meant it as a compliment. Indeed, she said more than once that I have a temperament similar to yours.

This is my vengeance then: a colored woman shares your blood. And your loud laugh, your taste for spicy foods apparently, and your foul temper.

I will write again, to remind you that I exist. Did you know that your daughter wished for a reconciliation with you? She said it was your choice to write or no. You didn't do your duty, so I will write again, and again.

Sincerely,
Your granddaughter

Griffin read through the little pile of papers. Apparently she had more than lived up to her promise to keep writing to him.

She wrote letters about her childhood—an apparently happy time until she understood how her darker skin kept her apart. She wrote of her mother's dreams for her, and her own dreams. She wrote of the two other people who accepted and loved her, both cooks.

One she described as "a round, happy woman who took care of my mother and me."

The other was a chef, her teacher from France who, according to Araminta's letter, "had a way with sugar, flour and eggs that no one could hope to imitate."

Griffin reread the missives that mentioned the chef. He wondered if Woodhall had also seen between the lines and figured out the chef was Araminta's lover. The mentions of the French chef ended abruptly.

Over the years, the letters changed. She grew away from bitterness and melodrama. Eventually she wrote the kind of letters any grandchild would write to her family.

She wrote about the weather and about her successes and failures, usually in the kitchen.

Griffin finished reading the last small sheet of paper and released a long breath. He frowned and flipped back to look at one dated 1880. Hadn't Woodhall died around 1878? And yet she kept writing to him, telling her dead grandfather about her life.

And where were the man's answers to the earlier letters? He shuffled through the pile and even eased himself out of bed to look through the trunk on the floor.

There were none.

Yet Woodhall must have answered in his own way.

"I know I have you to thank for the package of vanilla beans that came after I complained of having none," she'd written. *"Just as I know you*

*must have sent the lemons as well. If you tell me
this is so, I shall give formal thanks. In the meantime I'll use the beans with pleasure. And I shan't
think of you at all as I do so."*

He could tell that some of the letters had been destroyed, for she made references to her own words that he
couldn't find, and he found himself wishing he could
read the missing letters. In his current weakened mood,
he found he enjoyed reading the life of a young girl dis-
covering the world.

The full-grown woman's angry voice dragged him
from his musings. "I don't recall giving you leave to read
my correspondence."

He looked up and cocked an eyebrow at the flushed
and frowning Araminta. "They were spread across the top
of the open trunk. But I apologize if you are annoyed."
He held up the stacks. "Here. Take them."

He'd read them all anyway. Most of them more than
once.

She marched to the bed and snatched away the piles of
letters, and then left the room clutching them to her
breast.

She soon returned, still glowering.

Bemused, he examined her scowling face. "You seem
more upset than is necessary. You wrote nothing terrible."

"It is none of your business what I wrote. I cannot believe that you are such a sneak."

He feigned a yawn, one of her tricks. "I was bored."

"I shall fetch you some books then."

"I'd rather talk to you."

She perched on the edge of a chair, ready for flight.
"Five minutes."

He settled back on the pillows and gazed into her wary
eyes. "Are you happy, Araminta?"

The question had obviously hit her amidships. She
brushed her hand down her sleeve and chewed on her lip.
He wondered what she'd expected from him. Mockery
perhaps.

"I shall be," was her cautious answer. He'd forgotten
that she was almost always honest.

"But you aren't, yet. Is there anything I can do for you?
Or your friend Miss Smith?"

For the first time, her brow cleared and her eyes
smiled. "You are generous."

"Not really." He could be honest too.

She tilted her head. One of her curls slipped from its
mooring and came to rest against her long neck. "Why do
you say that?"

"Can't you guess, Araminta? I still have hopes." And
he knew from her blush that she understood him. Really,
the woman blushed often for such a strong creature.

She did not grow indignant, however. She merely rose
from her chair and went to the door, her shoulders set in
a stiff, proud line. He knew she fought the urge to dress
him down and wondered why she did not give in. He
waited expectantly. Instead she stared at him with shadowed eyes that made his mouth go dry with longing.
When had such a glanced cause the world to reel? At last
she twisted away and, with her back to him, remarked,
"You said you were bored. I will send up some books."

Araminta went down the stairs, skirting the two large,
taciturn men who rested on her sofa, reading a newspaper. She wanted to ignore them, but her mother had
trained her too well.

"May I offer you some refreshment?" she asked at last.

"No, ma'am," one of them spoke up. "We have had
plenty to eat. And we took the liberty of putting some

food in your kitchen. Mr. Calverson's orders. He doesn't want you to be disturbed."

"How long will you remain in my parlor?"

"Would you like us somewhere else? The kitchen, maybe? We gotta stay on the premises until we get orders we can go. Sorry," he added.

Araminta smiled politely. It wasn't their fault she'd dragged the pestilential Griffin Calverson to her house. If only she'd had sense enough to haul him back to his office!

He had hopes, he'd said. What nonsense. Why would such a canny man practically announce his plan to seduce her? It flustered her more than a subtler method such as flirtation. Ah, of course. That must be why he said the words. Araminta realized her lips had crooked into a smile, and forced it from her mouth at once.

She found a few books, including a copy of Lady Asquith's on proper etiquette, and asked one of the men to deliver them upstairs. Then she went to the kitchen and started to assemble a tray of food for the dratted Griffin. One of the bruisers appeared in the doorway. "We're supposed to take care of that. We're going to order in food for Mr. Calverson."

She raised her eyebrows. "I'd rather prepare it myself. I promise you. No arsenic in his food, no matter how tempted I might be."

The man gave her a dubious frown, and sat down at the kitchen table to watch her. Perhaps he wasn't convinced her arsenic remark was a joke. He must know Griffin well.

The man, who said his name was Wurth, insisted on accompanying her up the stairs—and on carrying the tray.

Wurth left, but she lingered in the doorway and watched Griffin eat.

He sipped the tea and watched her over the rim of the cup. "You might as well come in and sit down."

She came far enough to lean against the wall just inside the door. Even from several safe feet away, the lure of his body and eyes tempted her.

"Why not? I shan't bite. Remember, I'm an injured man."

Who had managed to get out of bed and rifle though her trunk. "I am happy enough here," she said and crossed her arms across her chest.

He put down the cup. "Timona met you at some baroness's house, didn't she?"

"For a man who appreciates details, you're almost as slipshod as Timona about titles. Really, I can't believe you don't know the difference between a duke and a viscount. Aha!" She flashed a triumphant smile at him. "No doubt you pretend ignorance because it drives your aunt insane. I saw her while I worked in London. She is a dragon, and you can't bear to leave monsters unchallenged."

He rubbed a hand across his chin. She could hear the rasp of his stubble. His golden brown hair was rumpled, too. The normally immaculate Griffin was disheveled— and as horribly appealing as ever. More perhaps.

The corner of his mouth twitched. "So says the pot to the kettle. Yes, fine, I'll admit that Aunt Winifred is dreadful. And expensive, as well."

"You pay for her upkeep?" She hid her amazement, yet truly she should have guessed that he was a generous overlord to his subjects and family. No, she knew her sneering thought was unfair. She recognized that Griffin had a strong sense of morality, though his principles were unlike others she knew.

His mouth wore a faintly annoyed scowl, as if he hadn't meant to reveal the fact that he paid for Lady Bronclarke. "My aunt is hardly worth the attention one pays to more dangerous dragons."

He picked up his spoon and stared at the tray that lay across his lap.

Araminta folded her arms. "The doctor said that you must eat if you want to regain your strength."

He gave the custard a halfhearted poke with the spoon.

"The doctor ordered mild, easily digestible foods," she explained.

"If I must eat such nonsense, at least you do them well," he grumbled.

Araminta laughed, and at his enquiring look, explained, "You are as much a child as any man is when he is ill."

He laid the spoon on the tray and regarded her with hauteur. "And where have you had experience with ill men?"

"At my work, naturally." Feeling more in control of the situation, Araminta strolled into the room and began tidying it—and rooting around for other embarrassing writings or objects she did not want him to find. "I had a position cooking for invalids."

"Ah, of course. At the Krankauer Institute."

The letters. Indignation filled her again. "You had no right to read those letters."

"No, and I can see that you dislike being reminded that I know about all about you."

The words seemed to echo through sudden, heavy silence. Knew all about her. He knew that she was a bastard, that her grandfather had murdered her father, a servant, and had never been accused of the crime.

The snake Griffin knew more than anyone else alive about Araminta's shameful heritage. She frowned down at her hands and saw they trembled. She would leave before she made a fool of herself and did something disgraceful like crying.

Griffin spoke so softly she barely heard him. "You are

a brave woman, Araminta. That is what I learned from your letters."

"And the rest? You already knew?" Oh bother, her voice trembled, and she knew that the tears were close. To stay calm, she squeezed her hands into tight fists. "I'll leave you to your dinner, Mr. Calverson. I believe that you have a handbell now to summon help. Good evening." And she fled the room rather than look in his face. She wouldn't risk seeing anything like scorn, or even worse, sympathy, in that handsome, cold face.

She had trouble sleeping that night. Since Griffin lay in her bed, she had taken the spare bedroom. She stared at the walls, aware of the males all around in her small house. Several men kept watch downstairs, and Griffin lay in her bed.

She shifted to stare at the ceiling, recalling the feel of his body on hers. No, she did not have to make love, but the warmth of a human so close. She missed that, even though she had never truly experienced it.

The quiet night creaked on with only a few distracting noises. Outside carriages rattled and clopped; inside the house sighed. It was too warm to bother with a fire in the fireplace, so she lay in darkness, thinking.

He would not want to do *that* with a woman, for he had been injured—and he would certainly have drunk the brandy so she'd be safe.

Griffin would go back to his hotel soon. Araminta would have her bed, her house and her life back. No one would be hurt if she simply lay down beside him. Just for one night.

Could it be that lust drove her to pull on her dressing gown and tiptoe across the small hall to her room? Surely women did not suffer from the demon of lust as men did.

Loneliness. The desire to feel the rhythm of another's breathing through the long night.

She stood, heedless of her bare feet on the cold wood floor, and tried to memorize the shadowy picture: Griffin in her bed. At last she pulled back the light counterpane that covered him. He lay on his back asleep, breathing deeply, his head, muscular neck and shoulders such an odd sight against the lace-edged pillows she knew so well. She resisted the urge to reach out and stroke the bare skin. The heat flashed through her as she remembered their evening together. Shame and embarrassment seemed so petty when she saw that powerfully built body again. Even remembering his insulting offer to hire her as his whore could not quench her thirst for his touch and the feel of his body on hers.

Stop. She reminded herself that she came here only to sleep. As she climbed in next to him, she tried hard not to touch his skin and wake him. With tiny movements, she wiggled onto her side to face him. She closed her eyes. Desire swamped her, and pumped through her with every beat of her heart. Though he lay inches away, she swore she could feel the heat radiating from the man. She sat up suddenly. Could he have a fever? She allowed her hand to lightly rest on his forehead, which was cool.

Satisfied, she lowered herself down and matched her breath to his slow, easy breathing. This sort of joy, of simply existing companionably in the middle of the night—this is what she might have had, if she'd ever found someone she could happily marry.

Tonight she could imagine what it would be like to be a wife—impossible outside her imagination, since she'd been born on the wrong side of the blanket, and with the wrong sort of grandmother. Not to mention wanting the sort of man who did not value marriage.

She planned to stay awake and feel the thrum of desire

and soak up the pleasure of another person, of Griffin, in her bed. But perhaps his sleeping presence calmed her enough to release her from anxious wakefulness, for she eventually drifted off.

In the early part of the night, Griffin had lain awake, aware of his injury but not allowing it to fill his body or brain. He'd taught himself to focus on keeping pain at bay and not permitting it to influence his breathing or tighten the rest of his muscles. He found pushing back and controlling painful sensation a useful exercise.

But his late-night concentration was interrupted by the creak of floorboards. He'd frozen, feigning sleep, and waited, ready for an attack—or as ready as he could be with a couple of knife wounds in his side. A second later, he recognized Araminta's scent. She'd drawn back the covers. And though she did not seem to be fond of him just now, she was no assassin.

He almost shouted his delight when the bed tilted as she climbed into it, but her far-too-slow motion told him that she did not want to wake him. If he'd shown her he was wide awake, she would undoubtedly flee the room.

He waited until he heard her breath grow long and steady to turn onto his uninjured side and gaze at her, stroke her delicately with light fingertips. He drew his hand over every inch of the skin he could reach, and unable to resist it, pressed a kiss to her lips, too. She made a soft sound but did not wake, thank goodness.

She finally woke, with a start, as the silver of the setting moon touched her cheek. He'd lain awake and had grown almost mad with needing her by then.

"Araminta," he whispered his demand when he saw the thick veil of lashes lifting and her gaze met his. "Kiss me."

"No." Her heavy-lidded eyes grew wide with horror. "I am sorry. I don't know what I was thinking."

"I do. You were lonely; you ache for someone to touch. Remember how we felt together. You want to taste me just as I am longing to taste you. Mouth, skin, breast. Araminta. God. Let me." He slid closer.

"No," she said more loudly. And slipped out of the bed so quickly she landed with a thump. She gathered her simple cotton nightgown close around her throat. "Good, ah, good night, Mr. Calverson, Griffin. I believe I—oh, dear, I'm sorry."

"Don't you mean good morning, Araminta? The sun will soon rise. We have spent much of the night together, it seems. Finish it out here, with me," he coaxed.

"No," she whispered, horrified, as if he'd suggested she parade naked along Broadway.

She was at the door when he spoke, quietly but using his most authoritative tone. "No, do not leave yet. Araminta, if you could hand me the robe?"

She stopped and turned around. "All right."

In the darkened room, she made her cautious way to the chair where the robe lay. She picked up the heavy robe and tossed it to him as if she were tossing meat to a dangerous animal.

He started to pull it on, then, carefully observing her through mostly closed eyes, he groaned and stopped, his arm halfway into the robe's sleeve.

"Oh, it hurts?" She was at the bedside at once, as he'd expected and hoped.

He nodded. His side didn't actually hurt a great deal, but other parts of his body ached from long, unfulfilled hours of lying in bed with her.

She held the robe, and once he'd pulled it shut, he reached over and gently brushed her cheek with the edge of his thumb. So soft. She only gazed at him; she did not pull away. Or lean forward.

He wet his dry lips and said, "It might kill me, but I promise not to touch you. Come back into the bed."

She'd regained her prickly manner, unfortunately. "Why should I?"

He could not think of an answer. "Please?" was all he could say.

Instead of speaking, she reached for the quilt folded at the bottom of the mattress. Once she'd wrapped herself up in this armor to protect herself from him, she gingerly sat back down, as if afraid something might explode. Not so far off, he mused as he caught a whiff of her fragrance.

He stifled a groan of pain and impatience. "Thank you. It was a great delight to me to find you beside me."

She began to protest, but he cut her short. "I should say a great comfort." He realized that despite the discomfort of his arousal, he didn't lie. Araminta next to him was entirely perfect. "I should also say thank you for letting me stay in your bedchamber."

She sniffed, but spoke with the hint of a smile in her words. "Recall that Hobnail put you in here. I would have asked him to move you if I'd known you'd go through my personal belongings."

"Ah. I ought to apologize, but I learned so much about you that I am not sorry." She made a small stifled sound, but he went on. "I learned that you are courageous and that you follow your dreams."

Her whisper was so quiet, he wasn't sure if he only imagined hearing the words. "Thank you."

They lay in the dark, until her quiet, tense voice broke the silence. "What did you want to be when you were a small child?"

Had he ever been a small child? "An adult."

She chuckled. "No, what profession?"

"I don't recall considering the matter. I didn't have to. In fact, running the Calverson Company is considered gauche by most of my family."

She turned onto her side to face him. Good, she was relaxing again, slipping toward him.

"No dreams of the future when you were a child?"

At her words, he suddenly recalled one of his early dreams: he'd buy a huge house. And then he'd write to his mother about the wonderful things in it—peacocks and elephants were on the list, he recalled—and she'd come back to him. Later on the dream changed: when she wrote back saying she wanted more than anything to come live with him, he'd tell her no, sorry, there was no room.

When did the bitterness leave his dreams? And when did he turn into such a—what was the word Timona liked? Chump. Such a chump to lie in bed with a beautiful woman and think of such useless matters.

"No. No dreams," he said lightly.

She shifted closer. "I do not believe you." Her voice was growing fainter.

He whispered, "Come here. I won't do more than hold you. I promise."

She gave a disbelieving grumble, yet she moved to him. The simple, charming cotton gown slipped from her throat, revealing her slender neck and sweet honey skin. For a moment her breath fanned his face, but when he leaned forward to at last taste her mouth, she twisted her face away. With a strangled sigh, she turned onto her other side, so that her back was to him.

When he kissed the nape of her neck, rubbed his mouth over the curls there, she gave a small squeak and hauled up the quilt to cover her skin. She'd grow too warm soon. He smiled at the idea.

In the meantime, he looped his arm around her, pressed close to her and buried his face in her curls.

"Thank you for staying," he murmured in her ear.

"Thank you for . . . for not trying to indulge your pleasure."

"Or trying to pleasure you," he couldn't resist adding.

"Oh." The word was a sigh that told him she fought off her own desire as well as his, as she tried to squirm away.

He tightened his arms. "No, stay here. Sleep again."

It was wonderful to hold her, feel the tension slowly ebb from her body, each breath coming more slowly. Very pleasant, despite the fact that he had to grit his teeth to restrain his urges to touch her or to move against her, to feel her sweet shape and seek relief for his body.

At last he fell asleep too, curled tight around her. But when he woke up, every muscle in his body complaining, he clutched a pillow and her quilt. She'd disappeared.

"She's gone to work," the guard who brought him breakfast reported.

This was proving more difficult than he'd imagined. Not the campaign for her, which was going better than he'd hoped. Hell, she'd practically thrown herself into his bed. No, the hard part was waiting for her to admit that she belonged there. He could barely wait until she came to her senses.

Keeping her safe from Kane seemed almost easier, though he wished she would gain some sense about that situation, too. He gave a rueful grin at the food on the tray, delicious, and made by her, of course. Did he really want her to be sensible in all matters? Not likely. Not if it would turn her into something less like the Araminta who plagued and delighted him.

CHAPTER 16

After breakfast, Galvin showed up. He trudged through the bedroom door and, with a loud clunk, dropped a burlap sack on the bedside table. It contained the gun Kane's henchman had dropped and Griffin's knife, both of which had been picked up at the scene.

"Cost me a few dollars to grease the sergeant," Galvin said. "'Specially since Hobnail was such a dunderhead about putting in a report. But I knew you wanted the knife back since Miss Timona gave it to you."

"It is a handy item," Griffin admitted. He sat up in bed, reached for the knife, and flicked the blade open.

"Here." Galvin fished through his shapeless jacket's pockets and tossed a hunk of wood onto the bed. "Figured you'd want that, too."

"A man of set habits, am I?" Griffin muttered as he turned the wood in his hands. "Cherry. Thank you."

Galvin grinned. "Going around the bend yet, being trapped here?"

"I am fine." Griffin did not mention that he ached all over, a sad combination of the knife wounds and frustrated lust.

Galvin dropped a case of papers and reports onto the table. "Williams sent along a few pounds of reading material. He'll be scurrying along in a few hours. He's got some meeting with a bunch of Chicago Calverson men who just arrived."

"I was to attend that meeting."

Under his big gray mustache, Galvin grinned. "I suppose he figured you didn't want them all crowding in here." He stretched and rolled his shoulders. "Long night working for Kane. I don't trust my instinct about the boys anymore since that piece of garbage Buckler. So's I'm leaving three at a time. Watch out for you and for each other."

Griffin sniffed with amusement. "I think you overestimate Kane."

"You underestimate him, boss."

Griffin flashed a rare smile. "Not my usual style, is it?"

"Ah, you're worse'n soft," Galvin said with disgust. "I've thought so for a coupla years."

"Sit down," invited Griffin.

"Naw. Got work, but I'll see you—unless you manage to get yourself killed." Galvin slouched through the door and stumped down the stairs.

Through the heating register, Griffin could hear the murmur of conversation as Galvin issued orders and the thud of the front door when he left.

He resigned himself to another day in bed. But unless the situation with Araminta changed dramatically and she crawled into bed with him again—naked this time, he hoped—he would leave the next day. No matter what the doctor ordered.

He flipped through the reports. Nothing of major import. It all could wait. He opened one report and used the folded pages to catch the chips as he began to carve. If he took large strokes it hurt his side, so he used only his hands. It had been far too long since he'd felt wood, worked with something other than paper and ink.

He scraped at the wood and listened to the desultory conversation downstairs.

"The man'll cut the heart out of you soon as look at you."

"Sure. The smooth devil ain't got a heart of his own."

"I hear he had Two-Punch Jack killed just for looking at his sister."

Amused, Griffin understood they were talking about him. They talked nonsense, of course. Two-Punch had kidnapped Timona and attempted to rape her. And actually Griffin hadn't ordered the man's death. He supposed Galvin, who was fond of Timona, had gotten overenthusiastic.

Tired of eavesdropping, he reached for the papers again, when he realized they were speaking of Araminta.

"She puts on airs, talking with that accent."

"Maybe. But there's a filly I'd like to ride."

Griffin rolled his eyes. Why did men always compare women to horses? Hardly an apt comparison in the case of Araminta. She was not skittish or stupid, nor did she attract flies or smell of manure.

One of them gave a rough chuckle. "That one's got some fine curves, but she'll break your balls."

"Yah, maybe, but not if you broke her to saddle first."

"I say it would be worth a fight to get under those skirts and get hands on them tits."

"Mm. Maybe once he's tired of her we can come over for a visit." A low chuckle finished the thought.

Griffin pictured Araminta's eyes wide with fear and anger as men reached for her. He became aware that his hand hurt. When he glanced down, he saw he was gripping the knife handle so tightly his knuckles were white.

Good God, he was on the verge of losing his temper. Always a thorough waste of time. Still, he would not let it go. These men, Galvin's rough boys, might cause mischief.

He eased his hold on the knife and took a few deep breaths.

"Wurth!" He shouted for the one in charge.

The man must have thought he was calling for lunch. A minute or so later, Wurth pushed into the room, holding a tray of food. Griffin eyed the insipid soup and bread and butter. Invalid fare, and he guessed that Araminta hadn't made it.

Wurth deposited the tray next to him. "Here you go, then, sir." He turned to head for the door.

Griffin took a steadying breath and, hoping his aim wasn't off, flipped his handy little knife so it slammed into the jamb several inches from Wurth's head. Not too dreadful, he supposed, although it had hit inches closer to Wurth's face than he'd aimed. His side hurt from the effort of flinging the knife so hard.

Wurth spun around, pale and wide-eyed. "Sir," he gasped.

Griffin held the gun pointed south of Wurth's belly. In a mild voice he said, "You will not touch Miss Woodhall without her permission. Ever. Understand?"

Wurth swallowed. He stared at Griffin, and then glanced around the room, perhaps trying to work out how he'd overheard.

Griffin put down the gun and picked up a piece of bread. "Go on. And tell the others."

Wurth hesitated, gaping, so Griffin waved at the door with the hand holding the bread. "Go."

After Wurth hurried off, Griffin ate the soup and reflected that he'd broken one of his own rules: don't make threats you will never carry out.

It was well and good that Wurth and the others considered him as just this side of insane. It kept them on their toes. The fact was he'd happily break the neck of anyone who hurt Araminta. Yet she was not his worry, for she refused to allow it. The wave of protectiveness he felt for her was as useless as any other strong emotion.

He put down the spoon and glared around the room. Hell, the sooner he could get away from the surroundings that breathed Araminta, the better.

What was it she'd written to her grandfather from France? "I find I cope better with loneliness in strange territories with nothing familiar to remind me of my dear lost past."

Every breath he drew tasted of her already familiar scent and made him ache with lust. Not exactly the same as mourning a dear lost past, but uncomfortable enough to make him wish to be gone.

Work.

Once upon a time, work had absorbed him.

He reached for his pile of papers. The article about new rail lines between New York and Ohio failed to fascinate him, and even the plans he'd jotted to capitalize on the railroad's burgeoning demand for steel seemed less interesting.

He enjoyed business. The tightrope balance between the need for raw materials and new rail cars and equipment could be interesting, and the danger that the process might fall apart appealed to his sense of danger. Making fistfuls of money was fairly pleasant, too. Just now business seemed dull. Even helping to bring down the nuisance Kane failed to fascinate him.

Instead he conducted a silent argument with the absent Araminta. Loneliness would not plague you if you stood firm. Strength could head off any soggy, useless emotions that made a man—or woman—weak.

His hand twitched, and the paper he held crackled, reminding him it would be pleasant to be able to think of subjects other than Araminta.

When exactly had his life begun to center around Araminta? Which moment? It occurred to him that his life had on occasion centered on far worse objects.

When she came to visit him that evening, she was a refreshing sight in a mint-green dress with matching ribbons twisted through her hair. She brought more interesting fare as well, a tray with salad and a crab casserole that she placed on the table. With a swish of skirts, and not a word of conversation, she turned to leave.

"Wait," he called.

She paused, one hand clutching the doorknob, as if she longed to flee. Instead of meeting his eyes, she stared at the foot of the bed. Perhaps she was embarrassed about having spent the night in his bed.

"I have work to do," she told the footboard.

He didn't want her to leave, but had no excuse to keep her in the room. Making mention of the night before would be a mistake, and he thought that a simple request for her company would not ease her awkwardness. A pile of correspondence lay next to him on the bed, and he had an idea.

"Here. You were so dismayed that I read your letters. Read some of my personal correspondence."

With his knife, he slit open the envelopes, and then handed her the stack.

She walked hesitantly back to the bed and took them. Her eyebrows raised, her large eyes gazed at him, filled with curiosity. "Don't you want to read them first?"

He shrugged. "Mostly invitations, I suspect. Oh, my

aunt has written again. You should get some enjoyment from her letter."

The battle between interest and dignity showed on Araminta's face as she glanced down at the letters in her hands. "You are the most absurd man, Griffin. Why would you think I want to meddle in your business?"

"I don't think I'll even answer that question," he said with a chuckle.

The queenly dignity melted away; she gave him a lopsided grin. She picked up the letters and sorted through them.

"Your aunt's letter is particularly heavy," she remarked as she peered into the thick envelope.

He groaned. "Another debutante."

"Excuse me?"

"She will have enclosed a tintype of a candidate. Go on. Let's see which girl she wishes to throw at me this month."

Araminta slid out several sheets of his aunt's crested hot-press stationery and a small photograph.

"Oh dear," she said and read aloud, " 'The Honorable Miss Edyth Gwladys Buttersmyth-Jergen.' Poor girl. What were her parents thinking? Edyth Gwladys."

"Aunt Winifred's last candidate had a reasonable name. She resembled a horse."

Araminta considered the photograph. "This one is more of a hedgehog, I'd say."

He took the picture and stared down at a girl with bleary eyes and a belligerent expression and posture. "You are too polite. I think of hedgehogs as pleasant creatures."

"A rather ill-tempered hedgehog, then."

"I'd say a plucked chicken, or rooster, rather. See the way she stands, chest and chin out as if inviting a fight?"

Araminta laughed. "Poor girl. She is probably a good-natured creature who despised the photographer and that far-too-frilly gown someone forced her to wear." She opened the thick letter from Aunt Winifred and began to read.

Griffin studied the picture, and realized that for the first time in memory, he was enjoying his aunt's correspondence. "That turned-down mouth and those squinting eyes do not belong to a friendly animal."

Araminta turned over the sheet. "Miss Buttersmyth-Jergen has a wonderful pedigree. Related to dukes and ambassadors and bishops. Her sister's husband is apparently not up to the family's standards, being merely a commoner who was knighted, says your aunt, but he already has a GCVO and various other orders. Gracious. And Edyth Gwladys's father is a KT. Your aunt points out that this is the Most Ancient and Most Noble Order of the Thistle. Their motto is *Nemo me impune lacessit*. 'No one provokes me with impunity.'"

Araminta laughed again, and he found he had to smile at the contagious sound. "She does know you, Griffin, for she says that this could be your motto." She read a few more pages. "My heavens, the Buttersmyth-Jergens can trace their lineage back to William the Conqueror. What a family."

Griffin studied the curve of her mouth and the pensive, dreamy expression in her eyes. Could his fiery Araminta sound wistful?

Before he had a chance to probe the question, Araminta gasped. "Your aunt says the most appalling things about Timona's husband."

Griffin adjusted the pillows behind him. "Yes, she feels that by marrying an Irishman, Timona has put herself beyond the pale. My aunt will never receive the McCanns, I imagine. Lucky them," he added thoughtfully.

" 'A blot on the family escutcheon.' You'd think that Timona had done something truly horrible."

"Such as?"

Araminta's smile did not reach her eyes. "Such as committing a murder or bearing a child outside of wedlock?"

"Araminta," he said, exasperated. "My aunt's view of the world allows for no human mistakes, no foibles and no imagination. Unless they are all her own, of course. If you try to live up to her standard you will be trapped in a nightmare of a life."

Araminta's smile was more real. "You are trying to make me feel better, and I appreciate it. Thank you."

"Dammit, I'm doing more than trying to put you in a jolly mood. I mean every word."

"Perhaps, but the words are still considerate. I would never have guessed such a thing of Mr. Cold-as-the-North-Pole Calverson."

To look into her eyes was to see into her heart. What he saw—a combination of mischief, gratitude and a touch of sorrow—made him want to leap out of bed and grab her. How dare she disbelieve him? How dare she be ashamed of her lineage? And how dare she be so entirely appealing?

He again felt weak with something more than simple desire. And weakness was not something he courted. Griffin turned his gaze away from her and gathered the cards and letters to keep his hands busy.

In a light voice, he said, "If you decide to marry, you'll do better than a dyspeptic hedgehog with a perfect pedigree."

"I don't think I will ever marry." She sounded so challenging, he glanced up into her face, and was taken aback by the fierce light in her eyes.

"I don't know why you sound angry about it," he said. "I agree—you should be overjoyed you don't need marriage to survive. You will have a better life than most women. You have ambition for yourself and your future."

She stood and picked up the tray. "And I have work I must do. Will you want any more to eat?"

"No, thank you." He shifted onto his side, so he could see her more clearly. The tension had smoothed from her brow and her mouth curved into an impersonal smile, and he knew that, for once, she successfully hid her thoughts from him. He knew that he was going to have a tough task figuring out how he could turn her back into his eager, sloe-eyed, hot-mouthed bed partner.

"I am much better," he said. "I will return to the hotel as soon as possible."

"The doctor says you cannot leave. You can't even negotiate the stairs."

"I certainly can. But I won't argue with you, Araminta. What sort of work are you supposed to be doing?"

"I must go make some stew," she said. "You must rest."

"What a homely dish for a chef."

She narrowed her eyes. "Nothing wrong with a good stew. Perhaps you'd like it better if I call it pot-au-feu?"

"Is it for me?"

"It's for the Downtown Relief Bureau on Fulton Street. I'll take it to them tomorrow."

"I am not surprised, though I did not know you were a lady of mercy. Who will eat your pot-au-feu?"

"The poor of the lower wards of the city. There is no need to be so glib—I am no lady of mercy. Remember for whom I work. Lie down, Griffin." And with a rustle of skirts and a clink from the tray she held, she was gone.

He waited until her footsteps faded before he picked up the bell. Rather than argue about it, he would show her, and himself, that he could manage the stairs.

Wurth appeared at once.

"Clothes," Griffin ordered.

"Yessir. Right away."

Wurth brought him the standard businessman's suit of morning coat and trousers. "Will you need help, sir?"

"No. I'm not helpless."

He felt like an old man as he dressed and made his painful way down, clutching the banister.

Eyes wide, Araminta stood at the bottom of the stairs, clutching the newel post as if she'd like to yank it up and throw it at him. "What do you imagine you're doing?"

"Proving that I am well enough to leave your house within a day or two."

She aimed a glare of sour disgust at him and put her hands on her hips. "Well now that you're down here, you'd better sit. Do you want to be in the parlor or the breakfast room?"

No point in resisting temptation. "I want to go to the kitchen."

He eased himself into the chair and dismissed the hovering bodyguard. "Go, Wurth. I'll call you if Miss Woodhall turns vicious."

Araminta gave a gentle snort as she set a cup and saucer of tea, a delicate, floral cup, in front of him.

He drank, and watched her fast hands as she peeled and chopped vegetables. Such competent hands, even when they moved less quickly, and he recalled the feel of them on his body.

To distract himself from the nagging desire, he glanced around her kitchen. Clean, well-organized and practical, it was nevertheless cozy. The herbs hanging from the ceiling, the bright plates arranged on shelves—perhaps those touches set it apart from other places he knew? It occurred to him that he did not visit the servants' areas of his residences, and perhaps this was like any kitchen. Yet he'd gamble that Araminta's personality made it feel like home.

"What is your favorite food?" he asked idly.

"Chocolate. Which is yours?"

"I have none. Which food I eat is not terribly important to me." He'd said it carelessly, and usually it was true. He did not often think about food, for unless he was traveling, everything served to him was of first quality. But Araminta couldn't have looked more shocked if he'd screamed an obscenity in a church.

She put down her knife and wiped her hands on her apron. "You cannot believe that. No food that takes you back to the best moments of your life? Nothing that makes your mouth want to cry out with joy?"

"Ah, the flavor of food does not move me the way other tastes might." He was delighted to see her blush at the leer he gave her.

She turned her back, saying, "Oh, you just do not pay attention. Here. Start with the scent of food. Close your eyes."

"Araminta. Don't be foolish."

"Close your eyes. No, I'm not going to play a dirty trick on you. I think that when your eyes are closed your other senses will be more awake."

He listened to her rummage around. "Sniff," she ordered.

A delicate scent of coffee, chocolate and something earthier. Some sort of nut, perhaps.

"Open your mouth."

A delicate sweetness filled his mouth.

"I brought back a piece of hazelnut torte from Kane's."

He hummed his appreciation. "Very good."

"It should bring tears to your eyes, Griffin. It should make you sing."

He laughed and opened his eyes. "Rather conceited about your cooking, aren't you?"

She smiled. "No doubt. But wait."

She went to the pantry and came out with a shriveled lemon. "This should make you sing too, and I had nothing to do with its creation. Pardon its appearance—it's not really the season for the fruit. I know you like it because your soap smells of lemon."

She knew his scent, of course, yet he was stirred by the memories of how she'd been close enough to memorize it. Ridiculous how easily his lust was roused these days. Spring fever.

She scratched its surface and thrust it under his nose. "Take a deep breath of it. Now taste the bitter skin." He obediently chewed the bitter rind she put in his mouth.

She put the lemon on the table and chopped the end off, watching him.

"I can almost see your mouth watering."

It was, but for a taste of her, not the damn lemon. "Hmm," he agreed. "I enjoy your lecture, Dr. Woodhall. Go on, do explain what else I miss when I pay no heed to food."

She grinned at him. "Do you know what the sight of a lemon will do to you if you try to play your flute?"

He watched with amusement as she held the fruit up reverentially in the palm of her hand.

She ruined the solemn effect by waggling the lemon at him. "It is a wondrous, fresh, clean taste. And you don't think there's anything important about flavor?"

"Oh, we'll go back to scent. More scent." She pulled down several branches of dried herbs, took some leaves between her fingers and rolled them. She held her fragrant fingers to his nose. The sharp, musky scent of oregano nearly hid the faint sweet scent of her skin.

She held up herb after herb and commanded him to breathe them in. "I suppose it is like any skill. You must practice discerning scent and flavor. What in life is important," she demanded, "if it's not the joy of smelling marvelous aromas and eating delicious food?"

Was the question rhetorical? Hardly mattered, for he'd answer it. "Feed me more of that hazelnut tart. Just a finger full of the cream."

She wiped her hands clean, dipped her finger into the thick, creamy filling, and pushed it into his mouth. He grabbed her wrist when she tried to pull away. He thoroughly sucked and licked her finger clean. With the tip of his tongue he tasted her palm, a sweet and salty melding of all the flavors she'd passionately shared with him. He pressed a kiss into her palm and for good measure laid his mouth against the warm pulse of her wrist.

"Yes," he agreed. "It is delicious."

With a strangled noise, she wrenched her hand away and turned back to chopping vegetables for her stew.

Griffin leaned back in the chair, closed his eyes and breathed the air of Araminta's kitchen. Practicing.

She did not visit him that night, though he waited, alert to each small squeak.

He gave up waiting when the house had been silent for hours. He lit a candle and began to carve the wood again. He stopped after a moment and lifted the hunk of cherry to give it a sniff.

She was right. The faint scent brought him back to his childhood and the best places he'd lived, the untamed forests where his father had dragged them. He lay for a time and allowed his mind to drift with the scent. He smiled.

CHAPTER 17

Araminta stood in front of the towering, ugly armoire in Olivia's bedroom and pulled out several neatly folded chemises. "Olivia. Listen. I know you're frightened, but we don't have a choice."

They had packed several gowns, but now the girl had cold feet. Olivia sat on her bed and twisted her elegant but too thin hands. "You are so kind to go to such effort on my behalf. But, truthfully, I owe a great deal to—to Mr. Kane."

Araminta clutched the chemises. She counted to ten under her breath. It didn't work.

"Yes," she snapped. "A broken head, a broken arm, countless bruises and perhaps something worse. I cannot imagine you've always been such a spiritless child. I say we leave now, before you change your mind again."

Indeed, at that moment something like spirit flashed in the beautiful Olivia's white face. "You do not know the circumstances. And you have no right to issue orders to me," she said. "You are nothing more—"

She was no match for the disgusted Araminta, who interrupted her at once. "If you are about to remark that I am nothing more than a servant, stop at once. I know exactly what I am, but that doesn't stop me from being your friend. Even when you behave like a ninny and don't heed good advice."

Olivia's face turned pale except for the pink blazing on her cheeks. "Yes. You are right about it all. You are my friend. I'm sorry," she whispered. "I am scared, and no matter how grateful I am to Mr. Kane, he . . . is not a good man. I know that."

Araminta sighed with relief, but then remembered that her house was filled with Griffin and his merry men. She would still have to find a place to put Olivia.

Griffin had mentioned his suites, or he might think of another answer that would serve.

"I have to go back to my house for a brief time," she told Olivia. "You finish packing. No more second thoughts. Promise?"

Olivia smiled. "I promise." She rose from the bed and went to the armoire. "I shall be ready when you come back."

The moment Araminta appeared in the bedroom doorway, out of breath, Griffin knew why she'd left Kane's early.

"I've succeeded," she said. "Olivia will be willing to leave him and come here." She leaned against the doorjamb, obviously unwilling to come any closer.

Griffin laid his pen on the portable desk propped on his lap. He had been about to display too much eagerness. Bad show for a man who knew how to hunt. One should wait for the best opportunity to strike. Move cautiously, he reminded himself.

He picked up the letter he'd been writing and skimmed it. "I shall be departing later today, and so it would make more sense for her to come to me."

She began, "But she is ready now, and the doctor says that you must—"

"I'm nearly well. I require the hotel's services to con-

duct business. This house is too small for my needs."
And, he silently added, *too full of you to keep my brain where it belongs.*

"I don't like the idea of Olivia going to your hotel."

"Fine." He picked up the pen and dipped it in the ink.

She walked to the chair next to the bed and sat down. "I've already made that clear."

"Yes, you have." He scratched out some numbers on an estimate and wrote in new ones.

"But maybe . . ." She hesitated. From the corner of his eye, he saw her pretty forehead furrowed in thought. "You suggested that we find a chaperone for me when you first arrived here. Perhaps for Olivia, we could find some unexceptionable—"

He looked up at last. "No. Not in my suites."

She licked her lips and frowned. *Come on,* he silently urged. *Go ahead and offer.*

Instead she asked, "Why not?"

"I do not like being surrounded by strangers."

"Ah." Her tongue passed over her lower lip again. He glanced down to hide his triumph and interest in that lovely mouth. He waited.

Araminta spoke slowly. "For Olivia. Perhaps. If it were not very long before we made certain she was safe. What I mean is for a few days I could act as chaperone . . ."

She made it almost too easy. Griffin put down his pen at once. "That would be acceptable. A good plan, in fact."

Before she had a chance to change her mind, he called down to his men. When they appeared, he issued orders at once.

"Fetch my carriage from the livery."

"We will move now," he told Araminta. "I know that Kane's business in Albany was fruitless."

"I suppose there's no need to ask why you know that."

He continued as if she hadn't interrupted. "And he might return earlier than you anticipate."

Araminta rose from the chair. "I shall go back Olivia now."

"Good. I shall have your trunk moved to my suites."

At the doorway she stopped and glared at him. "Stay away from my trunk. I'll pack my own things, thank you."

She was down the stairs and out the door almost at once and probably missed his chuckle.

Olivia stared around the largest downstairs gaming parlor, an uncertain frown on her face. With some coaxing, she had almost made it to the front door.

Araminta resisted the urge to pat her yellow hair. "Olivia, love, he has killed women. Come on. Pick up your parasol, and use it to help hide your face if you feel you must. We must leave, for I'm coming back to work after I deposit you at Mr. Calverson's."

"Do we have to go in the front entrance of the hotel?"

Araminta looked at her steadily. "Why not? Will anyone recognize you?"

Olivia took the parasol and did not answer. Araminta followed her out the door and down the block to the corner. She refused to worry that she had volunteered to stay in Griffin's hotel. One problem at a time.

The man Griffin had sent with Araminta had insisted on hiring a hack for Olivia and ordering the coachman to park around the corner. "And no luggage, mind you," he'd said to Araminta.

"For goodness' sake," Araminta grumbled as she tucked her skirt under her and took her place in the carriage next to Olivia. "You'd think that we were sneaking away with the sterling silver. All of this intrigue and carrying on as if we were thieves."

The man sat across from her and gave an apologetic shrug. "Mr. Calverson's orders. Here's the rest of it. At the hotel entrance, you're to ask for a Mr. Bendlow, who'll escort you to a meeting room where you'll meet another gentleman."

"Who are these people?"

"I dunno. I suppose it's just because there's no need to advertise you're there for Mr. Calverson," the man said.

Araminta gave an impatient click of the tongue.

Mr. Bendlow proved to be a small man with thick glasses and impressive ginger muttonchops. A desk clerk at the hotel, Araminta supposed.

"This way, ladies."

He led them across shining marble floors covered with thick carpets to the same private room where she'd met Griffin.

"This is Mr. Williams." Mr. Bendlow introduced them to another well-dressed businessman.

The lean and smiling Mr. Williams bowed, and Mr. Bendlow left the spacious room.

"It's a whole parade of gentlemen, isn't it?" Araminta muttered to Olivia, who wore a pallid, wide-eyed expression of fear. Araminta took her hand and gave it a reassuring squeeze. She needed reassurance too, something to combat the rising unease as she ventured deeper into Griffin's domain.

Mr. Williams escorted them up to Griffin's suite. Araminta watched her friend's face as one of the wide double doors swung open to admit them. Olivia kept her eyes focused on her gloved hands, which clutched the handle of the parasol. She only briefly examined the palatial rooms.

The girl was either too afraid to show interest, or she'd

seen rooms as marvelous and rich as Griffin's suite before. Araminta guessed both were true. Her own heart beat far too quickly. She repressed the nervous laughter that formed in the pit of her stomach when she recalled the title of an unpleasant print hanging on a wall at Kane's mansion: *The Scene of Her Seduction.*

"Mr. Calverson will see you in the drawing room," said the maid, who had a wide smile and a wink for Araminta.

Griffin lounged on an emerald-green velvet divan that matched his eyes. If he'd been a woman or a vainer man, Araminta would have wondered if he'd picked the color for that reason. Though he wore a dressing gown over a loose white shirt and had a rug across his knees, he looked nothing like an invalid, for he exuded his usual quiet strength. He'd been shaved since Araminta had seen him two hours earlier. And except for the lines at the corners of his mouth and circles under his eyes, no one could have guessed that he'd been stabbed three days earlier.

He did seem too washed out, now that she examined him more carefully. She resisted the urge to press her lips to his forehead to see if he had developed a fever. The image of him succumbing to a fever or lockjaw twisted through her—not for the first time. She held her breath with the sharp ache of an imagined loss.

He did not look at her. Instead he directed one of his rare and devastating angelic smiles at Olivia. "Miss Smith. Thank you for agreeing to come here when you felt you had to leave Mr. Kane's household."

Olivia returned his smile, and Araminta saw how gorgeous the two of them would be together. The tableau of angelic Olivia and glorious Griffin almost made her heart catch. The hair of near gold and the hair of moonlight would be a perfect match.

She resisted the urge to kick them both. How long was

she going to have to endure this? And from where did this oh-so-gentle and thoroughly charming Griffin come?

At least he was no longer smiling, though he seemed gravely polite instead of blank faced. "I would conduct you to your chamber, Miss Smith, but I'm afraid I am under the weather. I hear that I have you to thank for my rescue?"

Araminta had told him the story of how Olivia had overheard the men planning the attack. But really, now he acted as if Olivia had blazed in with a sword and fought off the villains. But of course not—ladies would never be so bold as to tackle evil assailants. Araminta's knees still ached from hitting the cobblestones. She'd ripped one of her favorite gowns that day.

Araminta gritted her teeth. She might have been a spoiled child, and her jealousy shamed her. For heaven's sake, she was the one to drag the girl here. And if Griffin fell under Olivia's spell and Olivia succumbed to this new Griffin, she had only herself to blame.

The grinning maid appeared to show them to their rooms.

They crossed the wide front parlor and walked down a hall to Olivia's bedroom, a sunny yellow room with pure white trim.

"It is perfect," Olivia assured the maid. She turned to Araminta. "Will you come say good-bye before you return to work?"

"I'll just go to my room, wash up and meet you here again," Araminta said.

The maid led her back across the huge parlor and through the smaller drawing room.

"This one is yours, ma'am."

The bedroom was also pleasant but more modest and much smaller and—oh, good God . . . as Araminta knew from her previous memorable visit, it lay next to Griffin's.

She drew in a thick breath and grew dizzy. His plans were so obvious he might have shouted them. He would turn on this unexpected charm and polite breeding to entertain Olivia during the day. And at night, he expected Araminta to entertain him. After all, she did not deserve the same consideration as a lady.

She threw her shawl on the bed and directed a new surge of anger at herself. For though she hated the idea and felt she hated him as well, her stupid body hummed with something she knew was excitement. Too bad for the treacherous ache inside her, and too bad for Mr. Calverson. He was doomed to be disappointed in his odious plans.

CHAPTER 18

The maid knocked on her bedroom door. "Mr. Calverson wishes to speak to you."

Five minutes later, Araminta was ready to throw herself on him, but out of pure anger, without a trace of lust.

"No, Araminta, you should not return to Kane's," he repeated in his most annoyingly tranquil manner, watching her from his velvet-covered chair.

Araminta paced the library's thick carpet. "But he will suspect that I have something to do with Olivia's disappearance. And I am sure then he will trace her to you."

"That is of no importance."

"Then why on earth did we bother with the silly sneaking about this afternoon?"

"I did that in part for Miss Smith's peace of mind. I knew that she is terrified of Kane, and she has other worries as well."

Araminta glared at him. "And has she told you about these other worries? Oh, certainly, it makes perfect sense to me that she would tell a man she barely knows all about her troubles when I have been her friend for months and have learned nothing about her."

Griffin raised his eyebrows. "Alas, and here I thought you were breathing fire for other reasons."

"What are you talking about? I was doing no such thing. When did I breathe fire?"

"When I greeted your charming little friend, I thought I saw you about to explode with rage. And since I knew I had made the effort to behave, ah, less like 'a cold toad,' I thought perhaps you were jealous because you suspected I was flirting with her."

All of the air seemed to flow out of Araminta's chest. She could not meet his amused face. "Nonsense," she managed to murmur. Why did he have to remember every horrible word she'd said to him that day so long ago?

"Yes, I understand that now. You were indeed jealous, but only because I managed to get Miss Smith's attention away from you."

She felt the edges of her mouth twitch.

"Good, I'm glad you think it is funny."

"I think *you* are funny."

He heaved a sigh and straightened. She noticed he sat, rather than sprawled, on the chair. Clearly the man was recovering quickly.

He seemed less drawn, as well. "I am an object to be either despised or laughed at, am I, Araminta?"

She eyed him but could not discern if he spoke with any real emotion. Before she could formulate either a reassuring or a biting answer, he said, "Do you promise not to return to Kane's?"

"I can't make that promise," she said at last. "At the very least I must speak to the people who worked for me."

"Hobnail could do that for you."

She brightened for a moment, then shook her head. "No, if he carries messages from me, someone would tell Kane, and that would put Hobnail under suspicion. I don't want to do anything that might harm him."

"He can take care of himself."

"He has been a good friend," Araminta said, firmly. "I saw what Kane tried to do to you, remember. I would hate to be the reason Kane turned on Hobnail. And at any rate, it would hurt no one if I go say my good-byes."

Griffin raised one eyebrow in an expression she recognized as disgust. "I shall not stop you."

"Very good of you, I'm sure."

"While you're gone, I will have a talk with Miss Olivia Smith."

"What will you tell her?"

He smoothed the edge of his mustache with his forefinger. "Go now. I don't want that bastard coming back early and finding you."

She thought she'd managed to hide her automatic flinch, but he watched her now, a speculative glint in his eyes. "It's because I used that word, bastard, isn't it?"

She pressed her lips tight, ready for his mockery of her overwrought response.

"I'm sorry, Araminta. I should have known better."

She was not ready for a simple apology. And she was not at all sure she liked the way it made her heart beat harder.

She aimed a smile in his general direction, unable to meet his eyes. "I'm used to it by now, you know. I've been a bastard for any number of years."

"It is an ugly word, and you are not an ugly woman."

Oh, no. She would not permit her yearning body to soften at his gentle words. She pushed back her shoulders and groped in her dress's pocket for her gloves. "Well. Now. I'll be back as soon as possible. It's best if I use the back entrance again."

He gave an irritated, dismissive gesture, a single sweep of a hand. "Don't be ridiculous."

She had retrieved enough equilibrium to meet his gaze. "I'm used to being something worse than simply a bastard, Griffin."

His eyes grew cold. Did he think her simple statement

of the truth was self-pity? But then he said, "I ruddy well hope you don't have to put up with any nonsense while you're staying here." And she knew that his anger was for her sake.

She went to say good-bye to Olivia and was delighted to realize the jealousy had evaporated.

Williams came into the apartment soon after Araminta had gone.

"Sir, you were correct."

"Senator Burritt, eh? What's kept his mouth shut?"

"The girl had been writing letters. She sounded perfectly happy. But when she refused to come home for her mother's birthday last month, he grew suspicious. Kane has acted like a concerned constituent and come forth to offer to help find her. But our man will find Burritt and reveal the facts."

"Araminta was right. She did put her father off the trail." Griffin shook his head. "What a greedy man Linder Kane is. He not only wanted to possess the senator, but he wanted the senator's daughter, too."

After Williams returned to the office, Griffin called Annie, the maid.

"I need you to act as chaperone for Miss Smith."

She guffawed. "Me? I like that."

He blew out an impatient breath. "Less of it, Annie. Just come in and keep yourself busy, or pretend to. Do some sewing or what have you. Despite what she's been through, I think she's a proper young lady and will be appalled at being left alone with a man."

Annie gave another hoot of laughter and walked off, her bum swaying as if it were a hammock. She always put on a show for him, but Griffin was not tempted.

He went to the parlor, where the thin and colorless

Miss Smith listlessly flipped through a book, a cup of tea on the table by her side. How did the female live with a chef as superb as Araminta and not grow fat as a pig? She must be ill.

She looked up when he walked toward her, and he was reminded of a startled rabbit cringing in the grass. He longed to tell her that he didn't eat girls—at least not for tea—but knew that would have her hopping away. So he put on a gentle smile and bowed.

Annie came in and began straightening the already perfect room. She tipped him a wink.

All of this smiling felt strange on his face, which he'd trained never to relax. He lightly kissed Miss Burritt's hand and again reassured her that he was more than pleased by her visit.

They spoke of the weather, of the opening of the bridge that would soon take place, of the new opera house in the city that everyone disdained as hideously ugly.

"But I am sure the music will be wonderful. I love good music, don't you?" Olivia said, and Griffin saw the shadow of the coquette she must have been.

"Indeed. You must attend a performance with me."

She started. "I am sorry, but I can't."

Griffin decided she needed a bit of prodding. "Come now. Eventually you must emerge from hiding, now that you've escaped from your prison. It is time to face the world, Miss Burritt. We know your identity."

The girl turned even paler. She gave a cry of dismay and rose from the chair, knocking the book to the ground. "Oh, no, no," she gasped and fled the room.

By the mantel, Annie flipped her dust cloth over her shoulder and rolled her eyes. "You were sort of crusty, but really, what a dope she is."

Griffin didn't bother to reply.

* * *

In the confusion of the kitchen, a red-faced Jack shook a fist at Araminta.

"Where the hell you been?"

Araminta drew herself up, even as she tied her apron in place. "Do not speak to me that way."

"But we're hours behind and you just disappeared and—"

"We'll be fine." She turned to Maggie. "I see you finished the hors d'oeuvres. Good work."

There was so much to do before the evening's entertainment. She could not possibly leave them to work on their own. As she chopped and basted, she spoke to Maggie in a quiet voice. "I shall have to leave my position here."

Maggie nodded so vigorously a couple of red curls slipped from her mobcap. "We're all surprised you stayed as long as you have. Even Jack says you're good enough you ought to be able to work anywhere you like."

Araminta had to smile. "If my plans succeed, Maggie, I hope that you will agree to work with me again?"

Maggie gathered some finely sliced carrots, tossed them in a bowl and grinned. "Just send word and I'll be round at once."

Within two hours, dinner was ready to be served. She decided to leave before cleanup began.

Really, there was no need for all the fuss these men put on. Jack and Griffin both overworried. The dinner for the night's thin crop of gamblers was fine, and Kane had not reappeared.

She managed to privately bid good-bye to all of the people who worked for her. Jack just stared, open mouthed, as she slipped him a few dollars. She gave each of them some money. Kane might grow enraged and seek out someone to take the brunt of his abuse, now that

Olivia was gone. She did not want her assistants to be trapped in his household.

Hobnail, glum and stolid, met her at the kitchen door, and they set off for the hotel. He hailed a hansom cab and handed her in, then climbed in to sit across from her.

"So you're moving in with him." Hobnail's voice was heavy.

"Only until the situation with Miss Smith is straightened out."

"Oh, no. He's set his sights on you. And his boys say he always gets what he wants."

"I don't think so, Hobnail." She tried not to show her annoyance at being discussed as if she were one of the Calverson Company's business deals. "I think he's just been bored."

Hobnail rubbed his stubbled, square jaw and scowled at the hat he'd wedged on his knee. "He always gets what he wants. And I heard him say it myself. He wants you."

She sniffed in disgust, though the quiver that ran through her did not feel entirely like revulsion. "I am not interested in that man. I can't believe he goes about telling the world he wants me. As if I were some sort of decorative item."

As she walked up the back staircase, she found herself balling the fabric of her skirt and wishing it were Griffin's throat.

And when she was met by the flirtatious maid, who said, "He's raging mad because you took so long," she merely frowned. The feudal lord was angry because one of his minions had not jumped through a hoop quickly enough? She clenched her teeth, determined not to lose her temper.

Griffin stood in the middle of the sitting room, feet wide apart, arms folded across his chest, face rigidly inexpressive.

"I am glad to see you are feeling well enough to stand and walk," she remarked distantly.

He apparently did not notice her chilly politeness. He answered in a tone even flatter than usual. "Where the hell have you been? I nearly sent the police after you."

She peeled off her gloves and arranged herself on a sofa. "You sound just like Jack, the rather vulgar man who works for me. I had work to do."

"You are not to go back to that place, do you hear? Hobnail is too busy to watch out for you."

She smoothed her skirt, still puckered from her rough handling as she'd climbed the stairs. "Mr. Calverson. I am here to help my friend. Not to be your menial and follow your orders. I should think you have plenty of servants; you don't need to acquire more."

"Servant?" His voice dropped menacingly low. "If you were my servant, I would have fired you long ago."

"And I would never work for a man like you. Even Kane knows to stay out of my personal business, and not to poke around in my possessions."

Griffin's face had gone as empty of expression as she'd ever seen it, but his eyes were dangerous. She stood and strode toward the door, shaken by her anger—and his. "If you will excuse me, it has been a long day. I am tired and—"

He was in front of her, pulling her into his arms. She did not dare push at him for fear of hurting his injury. Or that's what she told herself as she slipped closer.

"I was so bloody worried," he growled into her hair.

Before she could explore the interesting effect of those words, his mouth came down hard on hers and demanded deep kisses. Oh, Lord, his touch was instantly intoxicating. Passion flared in her, hot, sudden and intense as an electrical charge. She arched up to meet him. This was what she'd longed for, what her body demanded.

He pulled her closer and groaned. "Now, Araminta. Please."

"I won't. And your—your wound. You can't do anything."

"Don't underestimate a desperate man. I most certainly can do anything."

He pulled her against him, and she felt his iron-hard arousal pressed to her belly. She couldn't help writhing a bit in appreciation.

"God. I can right here. Or against the wall. Anywhere," he breathed.

"You make me feel like a trollop," she said, trying to force her conscience back into place.

"Just a woman." Surprisingly gentle, he spread kisses over her face. "A passionate woman. Oh, you're superb. And I know you're interested too, Araminta. I can taste it on your lips. And I see it in your eyes. Ah." He kissed her eyelids. "You can't hide from me."

She groaned as his hands slid beneath her bustle along her bottom and he pulled her close.

"Griffin, stop torturing me. You can have other women. That maid. She looks as if she'd—"

"Other women?" He loosened his grip and stared into her face. "No. I want you, Araminta. I'm starved for you."

She held her breath, for there was no mockery in his hot gaze. Only pure hunger that seemed to reach in and increase her own ache for him.

Too much, she thought, and closed her eyes. She'd always thought of herself as a strong woman, but this man could melt her resolve as if it were butter.

"Look at me," he ordered.

"Griffin. I won't give in. Please. Stop."

With two fingers, he traced her cheek, followed the

line of her jaw. "Why not? You want me, and I'm on the verge of going mad for wanting you."

"I can't think right now. Let me go."

"I'm not holding you."

She opened her eyes. "Oh." She took a few steps back from his solid chest.

He swayed on his feet, but still glared at her. "Why not, Araminta? Tell me that, at least."

"I was wrong and weak to give in before. I will not risk creating another bastard."

"Damn. I told you, it's an ugly word. It doesn't describe you."

"It is how the world sees me."

"It's of no concern, at any rate. I protect us from unwanted, ah, consequences."

"Sometimes such protection fails."

He walked to the divan and sat down heavily. "Araminta, you won't allow yourself to live, will you?"

With trembling knees, she made her way to the other sofa. "I won't allow myself to make a mistake as horrible as bringing an unwanted child into the world."

Silence filled the room. He stared over at the well-brushed and empty grate, an extraordinarily grim set to his face.

She cleared her throat, trying to hold back the tears. He looked over at her, and she realized passion and anger had fully retreated, and he truly was his usual aloof self.

"I'm sorry," he said quietly.

The stab of disappointment was much sharper than the relief she knew she ought to feel.

Araminta could not snap back so easily. Her voice held a quaver. She twisted her hands together to still their slight tremble. "I should see Olivia. I promised to check with her when I got back."

"Ah. About your friend . . ."

Some shift in Griffin's tone froze Araminta's breath. Good heavens, had he ravished the girl? Sent her away somewhere?

"Go on."

"Her real name is Elizabeth Burritt. She is the daughter of a senator. I am arranging to have her reunited with her family."

A horrible thought occurred to Araminta. "How long have you known? Why didn't you tell me?"

Griffin didn't answer, and his gaze returned to the empty fireplace.

Araminta gasped. "Oh, no. You wouldn't tell me because you wanted to use me to get her. She's part of your plot to get Kane, isn't she? A pawn. Both of us are your pawns."

The sketch of a frown creased his brow. At least the cold-blooded face held some semblance of feeling again. "Hush, Araminta. Might I explain?"

"You needn't. You must have learned about her days ago. And you've hidden the truth from me, hoping I'd fetch her here for you. And I'd act as if you were doing me a favor. Maybe I'd be grateful enough to give you a chance to relieve some of that hunger of yours."

Araminta got up so quickly she stumbled and almost fell. Griffin rose from the divan, perhaps to catch her, but she recoiled from his outstretched hand.

She shoved back a curl from her cheek and glared at him. "Well, I'm glad to have been of help to you, Mr. Calverson. Even if I won't service you, you've gotten what you really needed—the heiress."

She paced the room once, feeling the anger rise in her breast. "Oh, and the future is very bright, isn't it? Absolutely perfect. A senator's daughter. The wealthy eligible bachelor who rescues her from the criminal. Oh, my, I can see why you turned on your charm this morning with her. A girl like her fits any ambitious businessman's plans."

He leaned against the mantel, his arms folded across his chest, watching her. "You're absurd," he growled. "How often must I repeat that I don't plan to marry? And if I did, I wouldn't want that girl. She's a damned mouse."

"Even if you don't want to take her to bed, you wanted to bring down Kane, didn't you? And she's going to help you?"

"Yes, I'm delighted that Kane gave me a weapon to use against him. But what is it to you? I didn't keep her identity a secret. She did. I didn't want to drag her out of Kane's house. You did."

"And you helped. Once you knew who she was."

He gave another quiet growl, but didn't deny it.

"I forget that you have to have your company's best interest in heart when you act," she said stiffly. "I should be grateful that you agreed to help."

He shoved a hand through his hair, disheveling his usually perfect locks. "You damn well ought to be."

"Well, then. I shall go see my friend Miss Burritt."

"She hasn't admitted to the name, yet. And I have no idea what she was doing under Kane's thumb or how she got there. Hobnail has been trying to figure that one out."

She eyed him with revulsion. "And you want me to find out the details?"

"I don't actually care." He shrugged extravagantly, then winced. She'd forgotten his wounds.

"Oh, lie down," she snapped. "All of your fine plans will be worthless if you develop an infection."

As she stormed from the room and paced down the short corridor to Elizabeth's bedroom, a weariness filled her heart, dousing the fire that had raged just minutes before.

CHAPTER 19

Olivia—no, Elizabeth—took a few seconds to reply, "Come in," to Araminta's knock at the door.

The girl lay sprawled on the yellow bed, her face red and swollen from crying.

Araminta remembered that, whatever her name, Elizabeth was not trying to manipulate her. Not like some people.

She sat down on the edge of the bed. "How are you? Does your arm still ache?"

Olivia/Elizabeth shook her head. "Not any more. It hasn't for a while. Did he come back? From Albany?"

For Araminta there was only one "he," Griffin, so she was confused for a moment.

"Oh. No. Mr. Kane is still gone."

She reached out and stroked Elizabeth's hair, so thin and fine compared to her own rebellious curls. "Why didn't you tell me who you were?"

Elizabeth's chin quivered, but she managed to hold back the tears. "I knew you'd tell me to leave him more . . . persistently if you knew that I was not just one of the regular girls."

Araminta couldn't help her guffaw. "I've known that since I met you, Oliv—Elizabeth. Even the most innocent girl at Kane's had more worldly experience than you."

The girl shook her head. "But you don't know that."

"Tell me then," Araminta coaxed.

Elizabeth closed her eyes. "It began when I—I fell in with some girls from a rather fast set. We snuck off to an opium den. Three of us. With a college boy who'd been there before.

"We took a Broadway car." She laughed without humor. "I remember thinking it was so very risqué to ride on a streetcar. The house was on Forty-second Street. A plain house on the outside, for it's all very secret, of course. But inside! Pillows, a huge chandelier, paintings of dragons, and elaborate smoking devices. Some of the people there . . . I was shocked by one woman whose dress had come entirely unfastened. But soon I cared only about getting more and more of the drug."

Araminta felt naive once again, and wished she could get as far away as possible from the illnesses of the city.

Elizabeth went on, talking about her almost instant craving for hashish, and her pains to acquire the drug without raising anyone's suspicions. "I bought some preparations from the drugstore, but the house was much better. I hid it from my parents—they thought I was sickening because I had developed a *tendre* for a boy. They offered to send me abroad to help me get over it." She rolled her eyes. "Parents can be so blind sometimes."

"I suppose so," Araminta said, hoping she didn't sound angry. "But your parents love you, don't they?"

Elizabeth gave a tiny nod. "And I love them. And that is why I had to stay with—with him."

Araminta's jaw dropped. "Hey?"

"I was disgusting, a user of drugs. And then, I—I gave myself to men." Elizabeth's voice was almost inaudible now. "I was a disgrace to my upbringing. To the people who loved me."

Araminta had to lean close to hear the rest of her words.

"I was going to kill myself. He found me there. . . He helped me."

"Oh, certainly. He helped you with his fists."

"That was because he loved me. It was slow, but he weaned me from the drug. He wants to marry me, but I said no. And that is what made him lose his temper."

"Ah." Araminta straightened up as a horrible fear seized her. "Do you love him?"

She hesitated. "I am afraid of him. But he has been good to me."

A deep male voice answered. "I don't think that he has, actually. He found you there, eh? Who do you suppose owns that house you first went to? The opium den?"

Elizabeth sat up and stared at Griffin, who leaned against the doorjamb, his hands shoved into his pockets.

Araminta mouthed, "Go away," at him, but he didn't appear to notice her.

"No," whispered Elizabeth. "It wasn't him. He has gambling, not . . . the other."

"You know he conducts all sorts of businesses. Ask yourself this: why else would he venture into the house where he discovered you? Why else would a man who doesn't indulge in drugs be in that place?"

A glistening tear rolled down Elizabeth's cheek. Araminta pulled out a handkerchief and handed it to her.

"Go away. Please." Elizabeth sounded muffled by the white linen. "Oh, God. I want to be by myself for a few minutes."

Araminta patted her shoulder, then went to the door, where she at last caught Griffin's eye. "I was doing quite well until you came along," she murmured as they walked down the hall.

"She has to face the truth. She'll be fine once she cries a few more buckets of tears," Griffin said amiably.

Araminta considered his words. Perhaps she had been

coddling Elizabeth too long. "You could be right. I have avoided pushing her, since she seems so delicate, but she must grow stronger."

"I did not mean to deceive you about the identity of your friend."

She was dismayed that she believed him. Life was far easier when she could stay angry with him. "Then why didn't you tell me?"

"I wasn't certain myself until very recently."

They made their slow way down the corridor in silence. His manner was cool, and he did not look at her. The peculiar, powerful scene between them might never have occurred. Better that way, of course. If she were to live here in order to provide Elizabeth with a chaperone, it would be best if she didn't need one for herself.

He stopped. He winced and pressed a hand to his side. Beneath his dressing gown lay the slightly raised outline of his bandage. "I find I am exhausted."

"Oh, no." Araminta gripped his elbow to steady him, and ignored the clamor of inner warnings that came with their contact. "Shall I ring for help?"

"Not necessary for a woman of your strength. Remember how you dragged me blocks last week?"

His skin was very warm through his clothing. Perhaps he was growing feverish. The light was not good, but she thought she discerned gray smudges of exhaustion under his eyes. "I should have ignored you and taken you back to your office. I wasn't thinking clearly that day."

"I'm still alive, aren't I? But I don't need anyone else's help if you'd be willing to put your arm around me. Ah, yes, perfect. And now . . ."

Instead of walking straight ahead, though, he swiveled, bringing their bodies into instant contact. His mouth came down on hers.

Instant heat thrummed through her, but she tore away, gasping. "Griffin, no. Not again."

The shadowed jade eyes she'd mistakenly thought were tired now glittered with hunger and dangerous amusement. "Just a quick kiss," he murmured. "Gratitude for helping me to my bedroom."

She pulled at his rock-solid arm. "Come on."

They stopped by his door. He wove his fingers firmly through hers and drew her hand to his mouth to brush his lips over her fingertips.

"All the way into my room, Araminta."

She shivered, but managed to speak. "I don't think so."

His finger traced the edge of her jaw. "Tell me, why not a few kisses?"

His momentary weakness caused by his injury seemed to have passed, for he turned and once again held her, his strong hands at the small of her back, pressing her forward against him. "Kiss me and then tell me what is wrong with something so delicious. Just a short embrace. We shan't create any babies." When his warm, rough whisper brushed her ear, she had to agree. A kiss or two wouldn't hurt.

She allowed herself the treat of his hot, strong mouth on hers, the delicate caress of his tongue, which soon became a much fiercer stroke. And she was falling again into the heat of his touch and body.

He kicked the door closed behind them and drew her toward the bed.

Griffin smiled at her. She had almost grown used to his smiling, but whenever he did, she found her own mouth stretched into a broad, silly grin.

He pulled her down, and she was soon lying on her side facing him, trying to gather her muzzy thoughts but succumbing to liquid sensation. He slipped his hand into her bodice as he unbuttoned her blouse.

"Get rid of the bustle," he muttered.

"No. You said. Just a few kisses." She nuzzled her face into his throat, at the opening of the white shirt he wore under the dressing gown. He smelled of lemon, starched cloth and the faint clean scent of him that she'd grown used to haunting her small house. How she would miss it when she returned, but she wouldn't allow herself to dwell on the day she would be alone again.

Her body must have recognized his scent, for just a deep inhalation brought her to the edge of dizzying excitement. Oh, she would give almost anything to be able to spread her legs and lose herself to desire and feel him inside her again. She groaned as his fingers explored her skin. He ducked his head to kiss her exposed breast and left it cool and tingling from his touch.

She'd give almost anything, but not herself. Desire might rule her body, yet Araminta had to become wiser than she'd been when they'd lain together. She would not make the same mistake as her mother.

With a belly-deep sigh of resignation, she pulled her protesting, passion-swollen body away from his. She sat up and began to fasten her blouse.

Griffin moaned. "No. Come back here."

Her skirt was rucked up, and he touched the inside of her leg. She tensed, waiting for him to grab at her, ready to fight off any force. But he did not haul her back; he merely ran his hand up her calf to her thigh, back and forth over the smooth, sensitive skin, and then his light touch ventured farther up. They both gasped as his fingers found her curls, and he gently stroked her between her legs. "I shan't hurt you," he whispered. "I promise."

"But I won't make . . ." He hadn't agreed that they'd made love before, she reminded herself, even as the spiraling tension sucked her body tight. "I won't . . ."

"Hush," he commanded. "Just let me."

She was beyond speech as he caressed her. And when he pushed fingers inside her, the explosion soon struck. She cried out in surprise, though this time she had known what would happen.

His fingers trembled as he unbuttoned his trousers.

"Griffin, I shall not—"

He guided her hand to his erection. "There are other ways," he growled and lay on his back. "Let me describe them."

She squeezed him and enjoyed watching his face crumple into helpless pleasure.

"Go on," she said, and bent to give him an experimental lick. He responded with a very gratifying groan.

Her heart sped up again. "Tell me what to do."

Araminta was an eager student. Interesting how his pleasure seemed to pound through her. She treasured the glassy spark in his heavy eyes as he lost himself to the passion that she gave him. Oh, that defenselessness on his face was almost as exciting as his touch had been on her. He gave a thick cry and was a slave to her touch. He murmured her name, and stared into her eyes as he was seized by ecstasy.

They spent more than an hour doing careful, slow studies of each other. He was far too sore for anything strenuous.

Filled with the luxurious sensation of spent lust, she tried to ignore the sense of shame. Something more nagged at her. She shouldn't have indulged in this pleasure. As she fell asleep, she worried that a part of her had been injured, even more important than her pride or her long-vanished feminine modesty.

Love. The word whispered through her and woke her from the light doze. Next to her on the large bed, bathed in the late-afternoon light, Griffin breathed and twitched restlessly. In sleep, his mouth and the tension around his eyes relaxed, and showed a kinder, more vulnerable man, the hint of the boy he'd been. An achingly beautiful person. One large hand curled over his chest, and she remembered how talented those hands were on her body. She wanted to kiss the scars on the knuckles.

"Oh God damn bloody hell." She whispered the worst curses she could conjure.

She should have avoided his bed, and not only to protect herself from bearing a baby out of wedlock. She had forgotten to protect her heart. Why did she have to learn these lessons only when the pain hit her?

She loved him, irretrievably.

His body, his sarcasm, his gentle fingers, his scowl, his annoying nosiness, his complexity, his cold manner.

She, Araminta Woodhall, unemployed Colored spinster cook, temporary inhabitant of New York City, thoroughly loved Griffin Calverson, millionaire businessman and entrepreneur, relation to British royalty. At least they shared the temporary New York address, she mused.

He wanted her, but didn't love her. And never would. After all, Griffin Calverson did not believe in love. She'd known that even before she'd met him.

She propped herself on one elbow and watched him sleep, but not for long. Despite everything, she retained a trace of pride and didn't want him to wake and see her despair. No doubt she would be incapable of hiding from his sharp vision.

She tiptoed into the hall. From far off, at the other side of the suites, came the low sound of men's voices.

She groaned under her breath. They'd all know. The stiff-backed Williams, Hobnail, all of the Calverson company men would know what she and Griffin had done that afternoon.

When she made the safety of her room, she looked in the mirror. With no brush, she could only finger-comb her wild curls and twist them into a knot at the back of her head.

Perhaps they'd think Griffin was too injured to frolic in bed. She turned sideways to peer at her image. There was no disguising her swollen lips and cheeks reddened with kisses and rubbed by the stubble of shaved male skin.

The memory of his mustache brushing her breast made her shiver. Even after the hours together, she would not have minded a few more kisses. Ha. A few kisses were what got her into trouble.

She smoothed her rose calico dress over her hips and adjusted her bustle, and after making herself as neat as possible, she decided to go talk to Elizabeth. Perhaps she could coax her to return to her father. The sooner Elizabeth went back to her real life, the sooner Araminta could leave this place and the endlessly harmful temptation of Griffin.

Elizabeth sat in the parlor alone, drinking tea. She smiled brightly when Araminta entered the room. The smile did not leave her face, but perhaps she lost a touch of the eagerness, as if she'd been expecting someone else.

Had she already succumbed to Griffin's attraction?

"The maid said you were sleeping. I trust you had a good nap?" Elizabeth asked.

"I needed the rest." That was no lie. Her body vibrated with exhaustion.

"Mr. Williams kept me company for a short while. He is a very agreeable gentleman."

Uh-oh. Poor Griffin had competition. Elizabeth must have seen Araminta's smile, for she blushed. "I mean, he put me at ease."

"Unlike Mr. Calverson."

"Yes, very different from him. Mr. Williams is a gentleman. Mr. Calverson is like—like Mr. Kane."

Araminta crossed to the chair near Elizabeth and

arranged herself on it hoping her dress didn't show signs of having been rumpled in Griffin's bed. She resisted a sudden urge to check the buttons on her gown to be certain she had closed them properly. "I don't think you can compare Mr. Calverson to Kane."

"But how can you say that? They are so similar! Such ruthless men! They care nothing for anything but their power."

Araminta was opening her mouth to argue, but realized she'd said much the same thing to Griffin, and probably also to Elizabeth.

How could anyone prefer Williams to the potent Griffin, or think Griffin resembled the smarmy serpent Kane? At last she settled on, "You must admit that Mr. Calverson has acted as your friend."

Elizabeth pressed her lips tight. "I do not know. Perhaps it would have been better to leave me at Mr. Kane's. At least there I had a home."

"What could you mean?"

"I can't go back to my parents. I can't be the reason for their disgrace. . . . Is something the matter?"

Araminta realized her face had twisted into a thundering frown that reflected the growing dismay inside her.

"Your parents love you." She was surprised at how calm she sounded. "Don't you think they deserve to make that decision?"

Elizabeth shook her head so hard that two carefully pinned ringlets escaped from her hair. "I will not be the cause of their shame. I could never survive that."

Araminta studied her friend for a long minute. Her stomach churned, but she managed to find some dispassionate words.

"Never. You could never be the cause of their shame. People can never . . ." She tried to think of what she meant. "A mother's shame should never reflect on her daughter. And a daughter's actions should never be blamed on her mother."

"I don't understand."

Araminta shook her head. "I'm not sure I understand what I mean either. But please never hide because of mistakes other people have made or even that you've made. Don't waste your life because you brought shame on something as ephemeral as a family's reputation."

"Araminta, it is not something an outsider can understand. You don't know what I mean."

For the first time, Araminta lost her patience with her friend. She rose to her feet, and in a voice shaking with anger exclaimed, "Oh, you are so very wrong. I do know it. No one will ever know better. My very birth was a source of shame. And everything that happened—all of that *stupidity*—happened because I decided to exist."

Elizabeth's mouth fell open.

Araminta's breath slowed. The red-hot glaze of temper had already receded. "Shall I tell you, I wonder?"

Elizabeth nodded, mute. Araminta wondered if she'd scared the timid girl, but she supposed she'd needed the burst of anger to get the story past her lips.

She paced a small area in front of Elizabeth as she talked. "My grandfather was named Hiram Woodhall. He was a very wealthy banker in London. But he began to fall apart when his unmarried daughter discovered she was pregnant."

"Oh." Elizabeth turned red and tried to interrupt. "I didn't—"

But Araminta wouldn't let anything stop her, now that she'd managed to start. "He grew insane the night I was born. He dashed a vase against the wall above the bed where my mother lay with me."

Elizabeth's rosebud mouth opened as if she would say something more, but she didn't speak.

Araminta plowed on. "And then my grandfather ran downstairs to the servants' quarters and found the butler. He stabbed him to death with an ice pick. In the heart."

"Why?" Elizabeth's whisper was almost silent.

Araminta found the rest came far more easily than she would have ever guessed. "The butler was my father. He could not marry my mother because he was still married to a woman he had not seen in ten years."

"Gracious Lord."

"Yes, it is quite the story, isn't it?" Araminta wondered why she'd been so unwilling to ever tell it before. She felt no worse for having confessed the worst of her history aloud.

"You were only a baby."

Araminta sat down again, and ran her damp palms over her skirts. "I was the cause of my father's death and my mother's banishment from society and her estrangement from her family—and subsequent poverty. And I was the reason that her father became a murderer. In other words, I was a source of enormous shame, young lady. So do not tell me that I don't know about ruining a family's name."

"But none of it was your fault. Your mother was to blame."

Araminta shook her head. She had tried that argument with herself before. But she found she had to respect her mother's unswerving love for the two men who'd destroyed her life. "If she had not fallen in love, I would not exist. So I can't find it in my heart to condemn her."

Olivia crumpled the handkerchief she held. "You know what I mean. It is different for me. I—I went to that house."

"Is it your fault that the drug seized you?" Araminta shrugged. "I don't think you chose your fate. You did not look for Kane. He found you."

"Did you ever see your grandfather? Talk to him?"

"Twice. The first time was when I was seventeen."

Funny how long it had been since she'd replayed the scene in her mind. Once she had thought of little else than that private meeting, at a distant inn, soon after the death of her mother.

She'd been hungry and alone, yet Araminta's strongest sensation at the time had been relief that she did not resemble the wraith of a nasty white ghost with boiled, pasty blue eyes.

Her grandfather had looked at the candle burning on the writing desk of the lounge or at the barmaid scrubbing a table. He had never so much as glanced at her.

In a timid voice, Elizabeth asked, "What did he say to you?"

"Very little. And I was angry then. So I threatened him."

"How?"

Araminta gave a rueful smile at the memory. "He asked me what I planned to do with my life. And I said, 'Grandfather, perhaps you would give me an introduction to society.' Oh, when I saw the horror on his face, I knew I would never go hungry again."

"But that was blackmail," Elizabeth said, and she sounded almost as horrified as Araminta's grandfather had all those years ago.

"Yes, I suppose it was. But I had to live and could not find work, not at first. I discovered he'd pay for anything I wanted, as long as I kept myself away from London and pretended I was no relation of his."

Elizabeth frowned. "How horrible it all is."

"Beastly."

"How can you speak of it so lightly?"

Araminta saw her friend's glowering eyes contained fierce condemnation.

Araminta did not feel offended. She only felt far older

than the girl. She also was aware of a curious sensation of freedom, as if she'd been released from a kind of prison.

She reached over and patted Elizabeth's hand. "What would you have me do? Starve? Grandfather had paid for our upkeep. As long as we stayed in that country village, he made sure we would not starve. After my mother's death, I wanted the same arrangement, but with my freedom. No, actually, I didn't want his horrible money, but I took it until I could make my own way. Thanks to my mother, I had a proper education, yet no one would hire me as a governess or teacher."

"To be reduced to blackmail."

"I never asked him for money once I got a job. In fact, I despised his money. He used it to keep my mother prisoner."

Elizabeth drew in a shuddering breath. "I am tired, Araminta. I think perhaps . . ."

Still reveling in a giddy sensation of liberation that she supposed she'd gained by telling her own story at last, Araminta relaxed in the armchair and waited for Elizabeth's excuse. The girl would run and hide.

But then Elizabeth showed another of her flashes of strength. "Blackmail is horrible. I think you're right. I should contact my father. Perhaps the real reason I stayed with—with Mr. Kane had more to do with protecting myself. I will bear my degradation and not try to hide from the consequences."

Araminta wondered what in her story had caused the girl to change her mind. Perhaps Kane had threatened her or her family with blackmail.

She squeezed Elizabeth's fingers. "You'll have love to support you. Real love from people who care about you."

Elizabeth pursed her lips, hesitant.

"If you don't, and your parents make your life

unbearable, I can come fetch you. We could travel to Europe together. You would like France."

The girl's dainty mouth grew thinner, but she smiled. And Araminta knew that her dear Olivia—or rather Elizabeth—would no longer lean on her for comfort or advice. Just as well. Perhaps the girl had discovered her backbone at last. A rather grim backbone, she reflected. How soon would they lose all the closeness they'd shared at Kane's? Araminta was glad Elizabeth would soon return to a better life, but still, she was vaguely bereft.

Elizabeth sipped her tea. They sat in silence until the maid came in and announced that Mr. Williams wished to see Mr. Calverson.

Mr. Williams came into the room after the maid.

Araminta folded her arms and hoped Williams didn't notice her blush. "I believe he is still resting."

"No, I'm not." Griffin strolled into the room, his gait stiff. He settled on the divan. "Good afternoon, Williams."

"Good to see you're feeling better, sir." Thank goodness there was no trace of a smirk in the man's demeanor.

Mr. Williams, his brown hair slick with pomade, and wearing a remarkably high collar, bowed to Araminta, but took Elizabeth's hand in his. "You are well?" he asked her in a low voice. He fingered a pince-nez before placing it on the bridge of his nose.

Araminta glanced at Griffin, who watched Wiliams with a quizzical frown. Then he met Araminta's eyes and for several heartbeats she stared back, held by the warmth she saw in his gaze. A warmth meant only for her.

Williams and Elizabeth sat on chairs near each other and carried the conversation. They blathered about the beauty of Long Island and walks on beaches until Araminta wondered if anyone would notice or mind if she slipped from the room. They were superbly suited, she reflected.

Griffin must have grown impatient. "Miss Burritt, are you ready for us to summon your father?" As usual, Araminta thought him too blunt for Elizabeth, but reflected it was certainly one way to liven up the conversation.

Elizabeth raised her small, determined chin. "Yes, I am ready. Thank you, sir."

Before Araminta's eyes, the girl evolved from fragile victim to elegant young lady. More than ever, she was grateful Elizabeth had been pulled from that place. Even if, during the process, Araminta had lost her heart to a man who didn't want it.

Griffin turned to his assistant. "Williams?"

"At once, sir." With a low apologetic bow to Elizabeth, Mr. Williams hurried from the room.

A quiet bell chimed through the apartment. Griffin slowly rose to his feet. Araminta refused to feel guilty for his winces of pain.

"Dinner." He held out an arm to each woman. "Shall we?"

As always, Elizabeth toyed with her food. Araminta, who loved eating food other people had cooked, enjoyed the meal, although she thought the meat a trifle overcooked and the sauce for the fish contained too much salt.

Griffin drank some wine and stared at Elizabeth. "Not nearly as delicious as Miss Woodhall's cooking, is it?"

Elizabeth murmured something about the wonderful food.

The clink of silver against china was the only sound for several minutes. Araminta reflected that she was in a pitiful state, for, when she didn't take care, her attention wandered to Griffin. She found herself fascinated by every small gesture, or the way his skillful fingers loosely grasped his silverware or lifted his wineglass.

Griffin met her gaze, and the hunger in his eyes caused

her stomach to do the strange flip she so often experienced these days. He turned away from her and focused his attention on Elizabeth. "Have you considered what you will tell your father, Miss Burritt?"

Elizabeth's fork clattered to the plate.

"I should imagine the truth will suffice," Araminta said warningly. "Miss Burritt felt that she protected her parents, you see."

The corner of Griffin's mouth quirked and he had the devil in his eyes as he gazed at her. "Yes, I understood that."

Elizabeth looked politely interested, but Araminta gasped with dismay. She knew what his words meant.

He'd listened to her conversation with Elizabeth. Probably stood with his ear pressed to the door.

He carved a piece from his slice of duck. "I think that might work. What would you like to say about your rescue—I mean for public consumption?"

Araminta's consternation was replaced by another, perhaps even more unpleasant apprehension. She'd overheard conversations like this before, when she traveled with Timona. "Why would anyone need to say anything about the rescue?"

His eyebrows rose. "A story of some sort will come out. I'm afraid that the best thing we can do is make sure that it is the version we want."

"Oh, no," Araminta groaned.

Elizabeth leaned toward her, worried. "Oh, dear, what's wrong? Are you feeling ill?"

"No, it's something worse than illness. The press. He's going to feed a story to the newspapers."

Elizabeth pressed a hand to her mouth. "No," she squeaked faintly. "How could you?"

"Relax, ladies." No doubt about it. Griffin was enjoying himself. "We'll come up with something wholesome. Nothing about sordid drug use."

Elizabeth moaned softly. "How horrible it all is."

"Beastly." Griffin directed a long, blank-faced stare at Araminta as he spoke the same word she had used. She had to dive for her napkin and press it against her mouth to choke back the sudden laughter. Not only had he eavesdropped, he had no shame about it.

Griffin showed no outward emotion, but Araminta knew him well enough now to discern the glint of enjoyment in his eyes. "Are you sure you're not ill?" he asked her, all touching concern.

She put down the napkin, but refused to meet his gaze. "Quite sure."

Odd. She had expected to feel mortification and sorrow following their illicit tryst and her sudden understanding of her heart. She had been certain it would be torture to be near him. Instead he provoked her into laughter.

"I think we should consider our story—" he began, but Annie appeared in the doorway.

"Mr. Tothman has arrived."

Araminta shut her eyes tight. It needed only this. Would the day never end? Solly Tothman, the over-energetic reporter, bounded into the room. Araminta knew the gangling, wiry-haired man appeared harmless, but he would peck at them all until he got a story that would sell the most papers.

"Hello, Solly," she said, as the reporter, all elbows and knees, plunked onto a chair next to her. "Has Mr. Calverson decided to employ you to dupe the public?"

"Sure has. At least I hope so!" He waggled his fingers at Annie. "Hey, you! A plate, please?" He might have been summoning a waiter in a busy tavern.

He beamed at Araminta. "How have you been, love of my life?"

Apparently Annie did not bring his plate quickly enough.

He reached across Araminta and grabbed a bread roll from the bowl and a chicken leg from the platter at the center of the table.

"Gad! How I have missed your cooking!" he said through a mouthful.

"You're still missing it," she muttered, slightly nettled that he didn't recognize the food wasn't as good as a dinner she'd prepare. Solly's saving grace was that he appreciated good food. Though perhaps he would wolf down any food at all.

Griffin turned to Elizabeth. "Miss Burritt, this is Solly Tothman. He will help us by writing an article about you."

Solly bounced up from his chair and held out a hand to Elizabeth. He was a ferret, Araminta decided. Long, lean and excitable to the point where he could not hold still. Even at rest, he sniffed at people. Perhaps considering them for his next meal.

His bright, beady eyes peered at Elizabeth as he spoke. "Came the moment I was needed. Always ready to be of service to the Calversons. And to you, of course. Pleased! Very pleased! Miss Elizabeth Burritt, am I right?"

"Yes," she said.

"Been some speculation about you lately." Solly goggled at her with a wide smile that grew sharper and hungrier as he scrutinized Elizabeth. He didn't let go of her hand. "A breathtaking young lady like you—stands to reason you'll bring attention to yourself simply by being the rose of perfection—"

Griffin reached over and tapped Solly's wrist with a butter knife. "Stick to business, Tothman."

"Yes! Right you are, boss!"

Solly pulled a notepad and the stub of a pencil from his jacket pocket and threw himself onto his chair.

Griffin put down his silverware and leaned back in the chair. "What do you think, Miss Burritt? I think perhaps we'd do best with a severe attack of diphtheria that left you weakened. And several months at a sanitorium in New England."

"No," protested Solly. "Dull! Far too pedestrian!"

"Spice it up with a description of her brush with death. Just make it convincing. Very convincing." Griffin continued to aim a long, thoughtful stare at Elizabeth. "We don't want any of your friends recalling visits to any unfortunate houses to detract from the story. Those rumors must be made to seem impossible, or at least outrageous."

She made a small choking noise. Had the damnable Griffin reduced her to tears? No, Elizabeth recovered herself.

She nodded.

Solly, flipping to a fresh page, apparently didn't notice Miss Burritt's embarrassment. "What about you, Calverson? What part do you play in all this?"

"None," Griffin said firmly.

"And Araminta? So you've taken to eating with your employers?"

She glared at Solly. "I am acting as chaperone for Miss Burritt."

"Not cooking here, then? Where are you working these days?"

"Nowhere." She and Griffin answered simultaneously.

Solly's thin lips curled into a disgusted smirk. "You better give me a nice sum for this story, Calverson. Mysterious houses and all. I've heard the rumors, and I know I'm getting fobbed off with some second-rate ho-hum trash." He stared at his notebook glumly. "At the very least you might come up with something more creative."

"Tothman, you will get your nice sum. And you will write the story as we have presented it."

Solly raised both hands in the air. "I surrender."

They ironed out a few details. Solly even suggested he leave at once to find a sanitorium to fit the story. "I think I know the perfect one. It's small, so you won't have to pay many bribes. I'll do the interviews tomorrow." He slapped his forehead with his small notebook. "Oh, I've come down so far in the world," he moaned. "To think that I managed to present some of the biggest stories ever to grace the pages of—"

"Enough, Tothman."

Solly left with a parcel of food and quite a lot of cash for the trip north.

Griffin inspected Elizabeth. "That was not so dreadful, was it, Miss Burritt?"

She still stared down at her almost untouched dinner. "No. I suppose not. When will I see my father?"

"I think we might have to wait until tomorrow."

After a few minutes, Elizabeth excused herself and went to her room.

Araminta pushed back her chair. "I think Elizabeth expected to see her father, not Solly Tothman."

Griffin gave a small shrug. "I don't know what's keeping the man. If he shows up tonight then it will be a pleasant surprise for the girl. If he doesn't then I'll wait for regular working hours to send someone to drag him over here."

CHAPTER 20

Griffin thought dinner would never end. Miss Burritt was a poor conversationalist, and Araminta too subdued in her friend's presence. When at last the china was removed from the table and Elizabeth had abandoned them for the sanctuary of her rooms, he did not hesitate to stand and hold out his hand to Araminta.

"Thank you," Griffin said in a low voice. "For this afternoon."

He'd been about to say something else to Araminta. She raised her exotic dark eyes to his, her succulent complexion flattered by the peach and gold gown that bared her slender neck. Griffin curled his fingers around hers. *Come with me,* he wanted to say. *To hell with it all, let's go to bed and stay there until they pry us out.*

He wanted to sweep the table clear of dishes and make love on the polished mahogany. Later they could crawl onto the couch in the sitting room. And after that, they would experiment in each of the bedrooms. Long, slow sessions. Furtive, quick ones in the parlor. Araminta in a froth of silk petticoats, wearing nothing but her own fine café-au-lait skin, or also in nothing but her thin chemise with the delicate embroidery.

He kept his fantasies to himself. They needed a plan. An arrangement. He could not fall into unbridled sex without something to guarantee her well-being once their time together was over. He would not look back on any time with Araminta with regret or fear that he'd hurt her.

And if she were the one to end it? The thought made him swallow hard. What if she were to refuse, again?

Ah, well, he'd always appreciated a challenge.

And perhaps he could remind her of her own words to Miss Burritt—that hiding from the world because of a sense of shame was a crime against life.

Candlelight glowed on the rise and fall of the lace bodice covering her full breasts as she drew a deep breath and rose from her chair. "I am quite tired, so perhaps I'll follow Elizabeth's example."

He clasped his hands behind his back. Better that than grab her. He reminded himself he would act the part of a gentleman and woo her, despite the test on his patience. "No. Don't go yet. Come have coffee with me."

She didn't move, and an almost imperceptible pursing of her lush lips betrayed her uncertainty. What inner battle did she wage? he wondered. They wanted each other. Why wasn't that enough? At last, to his relief, she nodded.

He led her to the sitting room, dark and cozy at night, gracious and wide open during the day. The gaslights were off, though several branches of candles glowed on the mantel and a side table.

"Timona told me that the suite's furnishings belong to the company. Who chose them?"

"I selected much of it several years ago."

"Why do you stay in this hotel?" she asked as she arranged her silk skirts and lowered herself into a chair by the window. "Why not rent or buy a house?"

"I don't like being surrounded by servants."

"Ah, your father doesn't like that, either."

"Yes, and both of us like to feel as if we can walk out the door at any time."

She plainly interpreted his meaning as some sinister warning. Her shoulders went back and her chin lifted. Perfect posture. "You restless Calversons. Do you suppose you will ever put down roots in one place? Don't you long for the comfort of a real home?"

He shrugged and sat down on the sofa. This was not the sort of conversation he relished—about himself, at any rate. "Perhaps someday. Since we are speaking of comfort, a sofa is a more pleasant place to settle than a chair, don't you think?" He patted the cushioned seat next to him.

"I am fine, thank you." Then tension melted from her features and proud shoulders. She grinned at him and shook her head. "You are a rogue, you know."

"And why do you say that?"

"You listened to my conversation with Elizabeth."

"You were in the parlor, a public area. And your voice carries, Araminta."

Her eyes went wide with alarm. She even peered around the room as if listeners lurked in the corners.

"Don't worry. I am the only one who heard you. And I think I'm the only one who paid attention."

"What do you mean?"

"Your little friend is too wrapped up in her own misery to hear yours."

"I am not miserable," she said, and her back went straight. No doubt her mother had taught her that ladies sat with perfect posture. "But you will admit that the circumstances of my birth were not ideal."

"I'm mistaken. And you are correct—you do not wallow in misfortune. You turn it to your advantage."

Her shoulders remained stiff, but her lashes dropped over her expressive eyes. "I resorted to blackmail."

He should have known her strict moral code would create twinges of conscience. What a deuced nuisance that code of hers was. He had dearly wished she'd given the self-righteous Elizabeth Burritt a dressing down, but apparently Araminta agreed with Elizabeth's view of the situation. Or perhaps she reserved her best work for Griffin alone.

She sat, head bowed, her hands clasped in her lap, and he wanted to gather her into his arms. Instead he gruffly told her, "Nothing more than the old man deserved. But tell me, what about the other time you met him?"

"Pardon?"

"You said you met him twice. And described only the one meeting. Oh, and was that before or after you wrote the letter in which you called him a ridiculous old fool?"

Her chin went higher and her back straighter, if such a thing was possible. "I do not know why this interests you."

"Your past interests me," he admitted. "It positively fascinates me. No, don't glare. I am not being ironic. Please. Tell me."

She continued to frown at him, but answered, "I think I wrote the letter first. I really cannot recall any longer. I have glanced at them, but I've never reread the letters."

"You should. They will show you a remarkable woman." He stopped and wondered at his own warmth. He did not know if she heard it in his words, but he'd sensed it—a heaviness, a thick ache in his lungs.

"The last meeting?" he reminded her.

"He was dying, but I did not know it at the time. I was in a foul mood, but I'd come despite the fact I did not want to. All I learned from the letter his lawyer sent was that he'd grown ill and for the first time had summoned me."

"But surely after all of your letters, didn't you want to meet him again?"

"I had written hundreds of thousands of words to him.

At that moment I thought that was more attention than he deserved."

"Hundreds of thousands of words?"

"I destroyed most of the letters."

Griffin wished she hadn't. "But you went, anyway."

"Yes. For my mother's sake, I went."

"Tell me more."

She played with a length of her skirt, rubbing it between her fingers. "What else is there to tell?"

He pulled his attention away from the hypnotic play of her hands. "All of it. Was the house crowded? Woodhall was a well-known man in his day."

"They must have shooed off the well-wishers. I was the only visitor." She was silent a moment, as if summoning up the picture from her past. "He was even paler than I'd remembered him, almost invisible against the white sheets of his bed.

"That's when it occurred to me at last that he was dying. I almost fell over in surprise. For some reason I thought him immortal."

"Could he still speak? Did he know you?"

"Oh, yes, he knew me, and he didn't waste any time with maudlin greetings. I think the first words he spoke were, 'I do not acknowledge you still because it is bad for business.'"

She fell silent again and brushed the wrinkles she'd created on her skirt.

Griffin couldn't imagine she'd remained silent that day with her grandfather. "What did you say to that?"

"I had no interest in arguing with an old idiot who was on his deathbed. So I just nodded. But that's when he thoroughly infuriated me.

"He said, 'Araminta, I want you to know you are my granddaughter. I know it. You are truly my granddaughter.'"

Griffin believed he understood. "Ah. And you were annoyed because he acted as if he conferred some wonderful present."

She nodded. "Precisely. I knew he thought I'd crow with delight at his private acknowledgment. Oh, I boiled with rage, and was on the verge of telling him to enjoy his trip to hell, when I recalled my mother, and I knew that she would say it was more than enough."

Griffin wanted to stroke away her sorrow, make her forget the inadequate fool of a grandfather from her past. He'd replace that despondent look with one of delightful eagerness. But he sensed she wouldn't welcome his touch at that moment, so he made a stab at humor. "Poor Araminta. You never got to tell Woodhall off in person."

Apparently still lost in the memory, she stared into a candle flame on the table near her, and didn't smile at his dig. "I held my breath against the stench of the room and his breath. I leaned over and kissed his forehead."

She shook her head. "Ha, I even told him that I loved him, though I wasn't sure if that bit of news pleased either of us.

"His mouth twisted into a terrible grimace. I thought he was having a seizure of some sort, until I realized it was a smile.

"About then, a manservant came in, and I excused myself. That was that. He died that evening."

Griffin wondered if he could have forgiven the old villain. Not likely. He cleared his throat of a strange lump that had formed. "And he left you money."

She looked up at him again, the candle flame reflected in her huge, liquid eyes. "Yes. He left the money in a trust, a very quiet one, administered by lawyers he had never before used. Fifty thousand pounds, all mine."

Griffin had known about the trust, of course, but

hadn't understood she had so much money. "Why on earth did you go back to work?"

"Several reasons. I discovered I dislike using his money."

Of course she'd be moralistic about it. Griffin waved a hand impatiently. "Ridiculous. Money is money."

"You heard what I told Elizabeth. It was tainted money, used to keep my poor mother in place. She was confined to one little cottage by those pounds of his. No, I don't want his horrible money. In fact," she said, and the mischief he cherished returned to her voice, "I plan to leave most of his trust to establish a home for unwed mothers."

He laughed. "Using his name, I hope?"

"Of course." She grinned at him. "But that was not my only reason. I tried to be a lady of leisure, but it did not suit me. I grew too restless and cooked huge meals that only I ate and found that I was still writing letters to my grandfather though he was dead. One day I woke at noon, and knew I had to find something to do with myself."

Any woman of his social circle would have considered it a fine ambition to lead a life of leisure. "During the Season, my aunt rarely rises before noon."

"I was not part of the social whirl."

"No. And I'm not surprised to hear that you don't thrive in indolence."

"I like to cook for multitudes. Chopping up two potatoes seems useless. A twenty-five-pound sack, now that's worth rolling up your sleeves to tackle."

He remembered the sight of her at work in her kitchen and nodded his understanding.

The candlelight picked out a red glow in the dark curls that escaped the bun at the back of her head. No matter how carefully she pinned up her hair, the curls always slipped their bonds. Just like the woman. No matter how polite and calm the surface, a wild, impulsive creature lay beneath.

She was watching him. "I know that you enjoy working with your hands. Do you miss the active life you led on your father's expeditions?"

"We were talking of you."

"I'm tired of the subject."

"Ah, but I am not, and as host I declare the right to steer the conversation."

"My life has been extremely dull, Griffin. Especially compared to yours."

"I don't find anything about you dull." The words came out unbidden, too passionate.

She frowned at him. "Now you sound like the young bucks who'd corner pretty girls at the countess's dances."

"I do, don't I," he said, relieved that she did not take him seriously. "How do you know what the young bucks say? Did you attend those dances?"

"Good heavens, no. The footmen would recount the best of the parties afterward. They overheard the most absurd conversations. William, my favorite, could mimic any accent and voice. Of course he'd only do that when Blackwell the butler wasn't around. Or when he thought I wasn't listening."

For the first time since their meeting at the concert, Griffin saw clearly how Araminta had never quite fit in any of the worlds she'd occupied. Too well-off and well educated to be a servant, yet not accepted as a member of society.

He had moved between worlds all of his life, but they had all welcomed him with open arms. If he felt displaced and out of tune with his world, it was due to something inside him, nothing that came from the outside.

And with an understanding so fierce it made him

dizzy, he realized that she'd had to rely on strength that had never been tested in him. Not entirely true, of course. His own mother had walked away . . . left her family for the last time when he was twelve.

Griffin's hand lay on his knee. He tapped his leg impatiently. Any weakness brought on by stumbling about in his memories served no purpose.

Araminta rose and shook out the skirt of her peach gown, which looked like pure gold in the soft glow.

"I think I will go to bed now, Griffin. I want to awaken before Oli—Elizabeth and tell her she must wait a while longer for her family. Unless we can find someone else? An aunt, perhaps."

He pushed himself to his feet. "She should stay here with us. I do not trust Kane to allow her to go easily." He walked to her and stroked the long line of her jaw and throat. "Araminta. Thank you."

She took a step back, frowned and clasped her hands tightly together. "I'm not sure if we should have . . ."

Blast, she felt shame about the afternoon. "No one was harmed by what we did together. No one."

Her face still wore a look of despondency. She obviously didn't believe him. He tried another tack. "But I meant thank you for keeping me company this evening and allowing me to play Solly Tothman and pry into your past."

She relaxed enough to raise her chin and smile. "At least you did not take notes."

He didn't tell her that he had no need for paper and pencil to memorize facts.

He touched her hand, such soft skin. She'd started the evening with gloves, of course, but had shed them, to his delight. He traced the fine bones of her wrist with his thumb, followed the graceful line to her elbow. When he raised her hand to his mouth, she tried to tug it away.

"I must . . . ah, will you go to bed now?" she whispered, and sounded almost fearful.

He wanted to say yes. If she lay in the next room, he'd find her. He continuously craved the passion they shared. When he touched Araminta, he lost the practiced skills he'd been taught years ago by the most accomplished courtesan in Paris. When her skin touched his, he lost himself.

Though he enjoyed the play in which they indulged, he still had an appetite for all of her. But he'd wait until he knew she was thoroughly receptive. He wanted to demand why she seemed to be worried again. Too caught up in some problems she'd invented, probably.

She was like a partner from one of those interminable country dances. Coming near, offering tantalizing bits of herself, then circling away and moving off to a distant corner.

Very well. He could learn to do a little dancing. He hadn't bothered to before, but she was worth learning for. He'd play a new role. He'd discover the best way to woo her to his bed.

He'd planned to place one of her fingers into his mouth, and suck and nibble on it until she gave in with one of her wonderful throaty moans. But instead he turned over her hand and gave it a lingering kiss. "No. I shall work."

The smile she gave him held relief and told him he'd given the right answer.

As they left the room, Griffin spotted a note on the silver salver. Annie, showing rare discretion, hadn't barged into the closed parlor.

He ripped open the note and groaned as he read it. "It's a telegram. The blasted senator and his blasted wife aren't in Albany. They're down in South Carolina, of all places. Galvin's sent a wire down and will also arrange for someone to meet the senator before Kane does."

Griffin crumpled the note and tossed it back onto the tray.

"Oh." Araminta could not say more. She knew she should be disappointed for Elizabeth and worried for her own sake, but she was perversely glad to hear the news. She would not be leaving here tomorrow.

In the morning, Griffin prowled the rooms like a restless creature. Araminta was relieved when he announced that they would go to the park.

She pinned on her hat, pulled its flimsy veil over her face and gathered up her parasol and gloves. "The Madison Square Park?"

"I think we'll venture all the way to Central Park," he said dryly. Araminta wondered how long he'd stayed in New York. Surely the man who'd traveled his entire life would be on the verge of going mad, trapped here.

"But what about . . ." Elizabeth began.

"There is no need to worry about Mr. Kane." He apparently did not notice her shudder as he pulled on his gray kid-suede gloves. "We will be accompanied by some gentlemen. Nothing short of an army will be able to seize you."

When the men in question met them in the hotel lobby, Elizabeth turned pale. Araminta could hardly blame her. Except for the genteel Mr. Williams, they seemed very much like the rougher types who'd guarded Kane.

"These are our friends," Araminta reassured her in a low voice.

"They are not gentlemen. It will not do to be seen in the company of such coarse men," Elizabeth whispered.

Araminta reflected that Elizabeth's disagreeable

comment must be considered a good sign. After all, it was another sign the girl was turning back into the society miss she'd once been.

Araminta had a plan. "You, Mr. Calverson, Mr. Williams and I will walk together. And the other gentlemen will merely stroll along nearby."

The carriage ride with the four of them seemed too silent, but Araminta did not care about awkwardness once they climbed down from the carriage and entered the park.

They strolled past a stand of recently planted trees, out into the delicious sunshine. The pale green leaves, the tender grass made the world seem new again.

She'd spent so much time indoors or on city streets that the fresh green world intoxicated her. She forged ahead quickly, and Griffin kept up. He had a loose, easy stride, a man used to using his body for work, and she saw why Elizabeth thought of him as less of a gentleman than Williams, who had the city dweller's hunched shuffle.

Elizabeth and Williams soon fell behind. She and Griffin paused to wait and admire a vista of a sloping hillside.

"I wish I could lie down and roll straight down the hill," Araminta said under her breath.

"Hmmm." Griffin's hum was pure sensuality.

She rolled her eyes. Everything was a reference to bed sports to the man. "As I did when I was a child."

"I imagine you were a hoyden as a girl."

"I was a most ladylike and quiet child," she informed him. "For several minutes together. On at least two occasions."

He laughed, reached over and clasped her wrist lightly. As always, sensual warmth from his touch radiated through her, but she felt even more moved because it was a gesture of a friend.

They made their way to the terrace and the fountain.

As they walked across the wide esplanade, Elizabeth at last looked up from the conversation she conducted with Williams. "Oh dear, there're so many people about. Ought we be out in the open? Perhaps it would be best to stay under more cover?"

Griffin watched Miss Burritt scurry to a path among the trees, Williams in tow, Galvin's men not far behind. As he and Araminta followed, he growled, "I am growing tired of the timid little creature."

Araminta, attempting to open a ruffled blue parasol, stopped fidgeting with the thing in order to give him a severe frown. "She has been through an ordeal."

He took the parasol from her, shoved it open and handed it back. "The ordeal is over. Where is her spirit?"

"You are judgmental. You can't criticize someone until you know what she is experiencing."

He raised his eyebrows. "You do."

She stopped twirling the parasol that rested on her shoulder. "What do you mean?"

"Your impressive list of my faults."

"Oh. That. I was worse than judgmental. I do wish you'd forget that temper tantrum of mine." She blushed and her mouth quirked into a brief smile. "But about Elizabeth, perhaps it is impossible for you to imagine her pain."

Griffin snorted. "Why?"

"There is such a difference between you. She has been through a terrible experience and didn't have your strength to begin with."

"And you think I am incapable of understanding suffering?"

"You are a robust male who has every advantage possible: wealth, power, intelligence and, ah, an attractive appearance."

The woman apparently did not believe him human. He

might have been affronted, but she was so captivating in her pastel blue dress he had trouble taking offense. "Thank you for the comment concerning my intelligence and appearance. But I know that you long to add 'arrogance.'"

She shook a finger at him. "Do not attempt to change the subject. Yes, you know physical pain. But your spirit is so strong. A man with every advantage—what could he know of suffering?"

Loneliness, he almost retorted. But he hadn't consciously endured that pain. He hadn't been aware that he was lonely. Not until he met Miss Woodhall.

He saw that she watched him closely. Her question was not rhetorical. The blasted woman was digging again, pushing at him.

"You're correct. Men with every advantage never experience any pain whatsoever," he assured her. "Except upstart women who attempt to put them in their place." Putting her off was still easy.

She laughed and began twirling the parasol again.

They watched the children going round in the goat carts. Williams strolled next to the Burritt girl, their heads bent close together as they talked.

Miss Burritt flinched when one of Galvin's men came too close to her. Griffin, watching, muttered, "She needs to spend time with males so that she'll see that we don't all want to cause her pain." He shook his head. "The silly goose. No, I believe she is more of a rabbit."

"Yes, but such a lovely, soft rabbit." Araminta gasped and put a hand over her mouth. "Oh, no, stop laughing. She is my friend."

"And you never mock your friends?"

"Of course, but not behind their backs. Or not often," she added.

Griffin laughed again and was struck by how, lately, mirth bubbled through him almost continuously.

Araminta, of course. He repressed the urge to wrap her in his arms and, under the gaze of all these witnesses, thoroughly kiss her. To show his gratitude, of course.

That night Araminta couldn't sleep. She wished she could hunt down Griffin and tell him how he'd robbed her of her peace by forcing her to fall in love with him—but even she could never be that bold.

A book might help her mind drift away from thoughts of the pestilential Griffin. She pulled on her wrapper and made her way through the dark, silent apartment. She paused at the door of the library, for a light flickered inside.

Griffin sat at the desk. He'd shed his jacket, waistcoat and neckcloth and had rolled up his shirtsleeves. In the halo of the candle burning at his desk, with his strong forearms revealed, he resembled a magnificent thief.

Papers of all sorts were spread on the thick rug by his feet. She felt like an intruder. The well-kept suite rarely had any sign of disorder, and this little nest of work seemed as if he had created the only private area she'd seen.

Perhaps she could find a book and leave without bothering him. She crept into the room, and he showed no sign of noticing her until he leaned back and looked over at her. "Feeling restless?"

She shook her head. "You?"

"I need very little sleep. I am refreshed after six hours." He flipped through another pile of papers. "I saved this for you. My aunt has sent another candidate. Here."

Araminta felt her hunched shoulders relax. This friendly conversation surely could not hurt her.

He handed her the picture of a delicate girl, with a tiny mouth curled into a smile.

"Oh." She settled on an armchair on the opposite side of the wide desk, tucking her bare feet under her. "I wish I could find a flaw in this one." And she also wished she hadn't allowed the wistful note to creep into her voice.

He leaned his elbows on the ink blotter and steepled his fingers. "Yes, I happen to know Julie very well. We grew up together, and she has always been the most charming and lively creature. But . . ."

Araminta glanced up. "Well? What is wrong with her?"

"She prefers the company of other women."

Araminta shrugged. "Many women are so. Elizabeth, for instance, is uneasy when around men."

In the candlelight, his green eyes held a wicked gleam. "I mean in her bed."

Araminta blushed and, as so often happened in New York, felt like an innocent. "But surely if she were to marry she would learn to like . . ." Her voice trailed off. She tightened her wrap across her front.

"If I were searching for a wife, I would not be willing to risk marrying Julie. I imagine she will continue to regard men as amusing but essentially repulsive creatures." Griffin wore a grin, dimples and all. "So you think women should enjoy their time in bed? You express an unusual attitude."

She sat forward and quickly tossed the picture of the pretty young woman onto the desk. "Yes, I know it is not considered normal to enjoy, er, that." She pressed her lips tight and decided she'd said more than enough on the topic as it was.

"But you do, Araminta." Such an insinuating, soft voice.

She narrowed her eyes at him. "If I were a proper lady

I would deny even knowing what you're talking about.
But you know I do. Enjoy it, I mean."

"If you were a proper young lady I would have no interest in listening to you talk about the subject."

A dull sorrow settled on her heart, but she managed
to keep her voice playful. "Pray, don't mock me, Griffin. I've done my best to lead a worthy life."

"And you do so well. You have something better than
moral rectitude. Passion. So much more satisfying." As
he spoke, he rose and strolled around the desk. So much
for her plan to keep that broad surface between them.
"Life is too short to abandon passion."

"Carpe diem. An argument as old as time itself, Griffin." She wiggled farther back into the shelter of the
chair's shadow, wishing she wore real clothing instead of
a thin nightgown and wrapper.

"Ah, but that doesn't mean it's a faulty argument."

He stood in front of her now and startled her by dropping a velvet package on her lap, saying, "Do not grow
indignant, Araminta. I bought them with no expectation
of any kind of repayment."

She untied the sack and pulled a string of pearls from
it. The rich ivory beads glowed in the faint light, almost
luminescent. "I can't take these from you," she breathed.
"No. I can't wear them."

"I knew you'd be tiresome," he said in his most bored
manner. "They are to go with the earrings I saw you
wearing at Kane's. If you must insist that I have motives
for my gift, consider it payment for delivering Elizabeth
Burritt to safety, eh? You said it yourself, it's advanta-
geous for me."

"No," she murmured. She wanted to be indignant, to
throw them in his face and tell him she was not for sale.
But she was caught on the image of Griffin thinking
of her mother's earrings as he'd walked into a shop.

Thinking of her. She did not protest when he took the pearls from her and leaned down so close she could feel his breath and his heat, so he could hook them around her neck. She shivered as his fingers brushed the nape of her neck.

He straightened. "Now let me see if they're as lovely on you as I'd imagined." Gently grasping her hands, he pulled her up and out of her comfortable chair.

Disconcertingly aware that her nightgown and dressing gown were too thin, she crossed her arms over her breasts. "How long ago did you buy them?"

He ignored the question and gently grabbed her wrists to pull her arms down and move closer to her. "They are lovelier." The words tickled her ear as he breathed them. And then a soft nibble on her earlobe made her gasp.

A shiver passed through her like a breath; his skin and mouth on her made her weak with need. She whispered, "If I had a jot of sense, I'd flee this room and you and your gifts."

But her senses and heart were suffused with the man. She pulled away from his grip, only to be confronted by the sight of a tender smile that lit his eyes.

She pressed her forehead hard to his shoulder in order to escape the magnificent smile, but that was no better. Now she rested close to the splendid column of his throat, and she could easily kiss that warm skin. The reasons to say no didn't seem to matter when his heartbeat pulsed against her mouth. Griffin and her body conspired against her good sense.

She could only pray that Senator Burritt would hurry so she could pick up her life again. Surely away from Griffin she'd grow strong again—strong enough to resist him.

CHAPTER 21

Senator Burritt had rushed north to be with his daughter, just as a father ought, but Araminta did not like the man. His falsely jolly manner seemed to have little to do with the anticipation of a reunion with his daughter. He directed all of it at Griffin, beaming at him as if Griffin, and not Elizabeth, was the reason he sat in the gold and cream sitting room.

Araminta wondered if Griffin's injury hurt him or if he disliked the senator as much as she did. He sounded more brisk than usual. "I assure you, Senator, I have only provided a safe haven for your daughter. I had nothing to do with removing her from Mr. Kane's house."

"Pish, Mr. Calverson. You do not do yourself justice." The senator had white hair and a pink face and the combination reminded Araminta of a raspberry cloud pudding she occasionally made. The rich voice and the wide, white smile were eerily reminiscent of Kane.

The senator shifted in his chair. "So where is Elizabeth?"

"In her bedroom," Araminta said.

"Oh? Go on and fetch her then."

Griffin's face could have been made of stone. "Senator, Miss Woodhall is my guest and I will—"

She bounded to her feet. "I'd be glad to, Senator." Her back to the senator, she directed a scowl at Griffin.

Elizabeth sat on her bed, her hands folded on her lap.

Araminta smiled at her and touched her cheek. "You know your father is here, love. Are you ready?"

"Of course. I'm so glad you came to get me because then I can tell you thank you, Araminta. For everything."

She stood, and Araminta pulled her into a hard squeeze of a hug.

The men were standing as Elizabeth and Araminta walked into the sitting room.

"Papa," Elizabeth whispered.

The senator did not open his arms to his daughter, and Araminta resisted the urge to shout at him.

Sedate and ladylike, Elizabeth crossed the room. She held out her hand, and he raised one of his to clasp hers. Araminta was somewhat mollified when she noted that his hand trembled. He must have felt some strong emotion after all.

"I am glad you are safe," he said as she kissed his cheek. "And your mother and I will endeavor to keep you safe from now on."

Araminta, standing near Griffin, whispered, "The old fool."

"What's wrong?" Griffin murmured.

Wasn't it obvious? Probably not to a man like him. "Her father should tell her he loves her, of course."

"You are an entirely mawkish female."

"You have only just now discovered that?"

She doubted he heard her response, for the senator was addressing Griffin again, and he might have been giving a speech from the floor. "I want you to know again that I appreciate all that you've done for us, Mr. Calverson."

"Not at all," was Griffin's repressive answer.

The senator beamed. "I am grateful for the story that you and my daughter created to explain her absence from society. I fear that the plans her mother and I have made for her future must be changed. Yet I am certain that even though she has forfeited her chances of the marriage we'd hoped for, I feel that she is still a gem. And will make the right man happy." He paused significantly. "Very happy."

Araminta wished she could see Griffin's face.

As they drank tea, the senator pontificated on his favorite political causes and his thrilled ecstasy that Mr. Calverson had deigned to do business in the best city in the best country in the world. "As Mr. Wilde said, 'The God of this century is wealth. To succeed one must have wealth. At all costs one must have wealth.'"

Araminta wondered how Griffin would point out that Wilde's words were not meant to be taken at face value, but Griffin merely listened, his eyebrows raised a quarter of an inch.

Araminta, who'd grown expert at reading his face, decided this was an expression of astonished revulsion.

She and Elizabeth took their teacups and went across the wide room to sit on a sofa, side by side.

"I will see you soon," Elizabeth promised.

Araminta knew that soon Elizabeth would not want to think of her nightmare time with Kane. And since Araminta was part of that world, her friend would forget her. She patted Elizabeth's hand. "Don't fret yourself. I know you'll be busy."

"I wish you could come with me. Just for now." Elizabeth hesitantly returned Araminta's pat with a feeble squeeze of her fingers. "I—I admit I am feeling a little dazed."

Across the room the senator's voice boomed, "Will you come to my house for what we common folk think of as our midday dinner, sir? My dear wife would be delighted to meet our daughter's savior."

Griffin did his level best to freeze the man. Araminta

had a chance to again admire how well Griffin could turn as frigid as the haughtiest aristocrat. Even his aunt could not have done better. But Burritt must have had a hide as thick as an elephant's, for he was able to ignore insults and even a direct refusal.

Elizabeth watched her father's efforts to cajole Griffin, her eyes growing round with dismay. "I hoped Araminta might accompany us, but I heard Mr. Calverson say he will be busy."

"A man has to eat, Elizabeth. We won't take much of your time, sir. And you'll be glad you stopped by to share our fine repast."

Griffin met Araminta's eyes and raised his brows slightly. She gave a tiny nod and an apologetic shrug. She wanted to make sure at least Elizabeth's mother would take care of the girl. And she doubted she'd receive an invitation from the senator without Griffin's influence.

"Very well, Miss Woodhall and I would be glad to escort you and your daughter home. I will not have time to dine with you but—"

The senator was on his feet, shaking Griffin's hand. "Very good, very good, sir."

As they passed the library, Griffin stopped to talk to two Calverson company men who were bent over examining some sort of map spread across the floor.

"Gentlemen, I shall be back as soon as possible."

Williams smiled weakly. "Take your time, sir."

In a moment of inspiration, Araminta said, "Oh, Mr. Williams, perhaps you should accompany us? I know that Mr. Calverson mentioned that he had some questions about . . ." Her voice petered out as she realized she had no notion what sort of questions Griffin might have.

"About the Minnesota sale," Griffin finished for her. "What a very, very good idea, Miss Woodhall."

The senator's shaggy white eyebrows knit.

"Mr. Williams heads our New York office," Griffin remarked casually.

The senator's brow cleared. "Certainly, sir. Plenty of room in the landau."

Williams scurried back into the library and emerged with a much more convincing smile and carrying a leather portfolio under his arm.

As they walked across the lobby, Araminta instinctively dropped back from the group. Griffin twisted on his heel and gave her an impatient scowl.

"Come on." He strode to her, took her hand and tucked it firmly into his arm. "This was your idea," he whispered as the three others surged through the hotel doors. "You will at least offer me some moral support."

She stifled a chuckle.

The senator's hard-topped carriage waited out front of the hotel, with a beautifully matched pair of bay horses and a liveried driver and footman.

The footman jumped down and threw open the carriage door.

"Look," Araminta whispered to Griffin. "Their uniforms are the same color as the coach."

The senator, who apparently had superhuman hearing, beamed at her for the first time. "I have a lovely canary-yellow carriage as well, and, of course, matching uniforms for my men."

"Good heavens," Araminta said in a quaking voice.

"My aunt," Griffin informed her with great solemnity, his mouth set in a severe line, "has four carriages with matching livery."

Araminta nodded. "Yes, I can imagine."

The three gentlemen jammed onto the seat with their backs to the horses. As they jolted up the avenue toward Central Park, the senator began to pontificate about another subject obviously dear to his heart.

"You see how young I appear to be, Mr. Calverson?"

Griffin muttered something even the senator couldn't have heard.

It was apparently enough to encourage the senator. "I don't take my health for granted, sir."

He listed the activities he did to maintain his health, and Araminta soon understood the senator's other favorite subject was quackery.

Mr. Williams listened gravely, and nodded at each of the senator's ridiculous pronouncements.

Araminta gazed out the window at the stylish houses and even more stylish pedestrians, knowing that to meet Griffin's eye would be fatal. As it was, her teeth hurt from holding back her laughter.

The senator went on, "Have you visited the Hygienic Turkish Bath Institute? It is an old institution, the first in Manhattan, but Dr. Holbrook runs a fine, clean establishment. And in addition to the solely oatmeal diet and the baths, I have been delighted to use the services of Madame LaSeur, an expert electrician. Her cures with electricity are remarkable. I had a fit of catarrh, sir, that lasted for months. Two sessions with Madame and I haven't so much as sniffed since. And my other diet, of whole raw fruits, sir. Most efficacious in improving the brain power. I must send you the regime. I trust you will be astounded."

"Indeed," Griffin muttered. "I already am."

Araminta risked gazing at him. A mistake.

He tilted his head back and stared down his nose at her. The austere aristocrat. For less than a second, he cringed and his eyes widened, showing mock panic. She had to hurriedly pull out her handkerchief and pretend the laughter was coughing. Of course Griffin was a superb actor. He'd been acting the part of a heartless brute much of his adult life. That thought sobered her, at least temporarily.

The large carriage and matching bays trundled through the heavy traffic, driving in fits and starts. Near the fashionable shops, they passed a crowd of ladies in the first stare of fashion. Araminta admired a particularly elegant woman in lilac wearing a hat containing a jungle of matching plumes.

The senator must have seen the woman too. "Don't see beauties like that everywhere. Even in England, do you?" He shoved an elbow at Griffin. "What's the name of that place where everyone buys their fancy duds? Barn Street?"

Griffin inched away from the senator. "I believe you mean Bond Street," he said more politely than Araminta would have guessed possible. Out of respect for Elizabeth, perhaps? His mouth twitched, and she realized he was also having trouble with self-control. Griffin? Holding back anger or laughter? Now that was absurd.

Good thing she did not lace her stays tightly, or she would explode with the mirth she repressed. Funny how often she found herself on the edge of laughter. She recalled thinking that she could never be comfortable with Griffin, for he did not laugh. Perhaps he didn't, often. She, however, could not recall a time she had felt such merriment. When she wasn't on the verge of tears.

The footman handed her down with great ceremony. The red and black brick building, lumpy with turrets and strange little balconies, wasn't the largest on the street, but it was the newest.

In the front hall, she had to stand still and wait for her eyes to adjust to the darkness. The sensation of entering a busy cave was not helped by the silver and gold stenciling done over maroon walls and the immense, dark, carved wood furniture. Even after she'd thought her eyes were ready for the gloom, she almost toppled over a large maroon velvet sofa in the middle of the room.

"If you'll follow me." A butler had appeared from nowhere. "Mrs. Burritt is awaiting you in the red room."

"I find it hard to imagine how anything could be any more red than this room," Griffin muttered into her ear.

The red salon managed. Floor-to-ceiling red velvet drapes covered unseen windows. The wallpaper depicted red and pink roses. The sofa and matching stuffed chairs were covered in brilliant crimson satin.

Dressed in gray half-mourning, with jet beads, Mrs. Burritt stood waiting to greet them.

"A cheerful pigeon." Griffin's soft whisper in her ear made Araminta wish she could stomp down hard on his shining boot. If only he had not been so entirely accurate, Araminta might have recovered from her dangerous sensation of teetering at the edge of laughter. Now she was afraid to open her mouth.

Mrs. Burritt's bosom was shoved up and out by tight corseting. And her bustle in the back with its long train could have been a tail. One almost expected her to coo.

Instead she shrieked. "Elizabeth, my love!"

Rushing past Araminta in a flurry of pale blue skirts, Elizabeth flew into her mother's arms.

Griffin muttered, "Meets with your approval, I see. You're beaming like a lighthouse."

Araminta edged away from him but still prickled with the awareness of his watching presence next to her.

Mrs. Burritt hugged Elizabeth, then held her at arm's length. Her smile faltered. "But your clothes! What is that dreadful thing on your head? Could it be a straw bonnet?"

Araminta sighed. A fool, but at least the woman was a loving fool.

* * *

"Lovely, very touching, the reunion of mother and daughter," said the senator, and Griffin thought that despite the clichéd words, for once the man's sentiments were sincere. "But I'm sure they'll want to be alone, and the gentlemen would prefer to discuss more interesting subjects?"

He hustled Griffin and Williams from the salon into a library across the large, gloomy hall.

They settled in huge armchairs arranged around the empty fireplace.

"Try these cigars. Straight from one of my constituents' Cuban farms." The senator thrust the foul objects at Griffin and at Williams. "So, gentlemen, thank you for agreeing to visit us. And giving me the time to talk about some of my ideas."

Within a few minutes, Griffin understood that Burritt was seeking sources of funding for his next election.

Williams nodded, smiled and made agreeable noises. He appeared to be entranced by the senator's conversation.

A future politician.

That had to be the reason Williams had always struck Griffin as not quite trustworthy. At least he wasn't a regular thief or a thug, like previous Calverson Company crooks.

Law books and philosophical tomes crammed the floor-to-ceiling mahogany shelves of Burritt's impressive but dusty library.

Under a bell jar next to the mantel, a stuffed snowy owl stared back at Griffin, a baleful, superior expression on its face. Did the senator notice the fact that with his jutting white eyebrows and beak of a nose he resembled the dead bird? Griffin supposed so. The man seemed very aware of his own image and likely wanted to associate himself with the bird of wisdom. A thick-headed bull, the white-headed breed, was more appropriate.

Griffin settled into the armchair with a glass of brandy and a cigar. People as animals again. It was a disease he'd caught from Araminta, one that left its victim with a propensity for the absurd.

He'd give the eager Williams a gift of fifteen minutes of this tedium, and then he'd flee the dismal Burritt ménage and spend some time with Araminta. He daydreamed about what they'd do together, as the two other men droned on.

Williams actually protested when Griffin issued his farewell.

"Stay and discuss the bill," Griffin said, indifferent. "I shall expect you back by five."

Williams agreed at once. "Yes, sir."

The senator pouted at Griffin as if, by departing, he was taking away a favorite toy. "I am sorry that you did not get more time with my daughter, Mr. Calverson."

"I've had several days with your daughter." Griffin was so tired of the man, he hardly cared about the sinister insinuation of this remark. "Good-bye, Senator."

Burritt insisted on walking him to the sitting room and left Williams reading informative literature about future farming bills.

Griffin took the opportunity to play up Williams, using words he knew would impress the senator. "A good, steady fellow. He's come up through the ranks of the company. I trust him implicitly. And he seemed very taken with your daughter."

He was pleased to see a thoughtful gleam in the old blighter's eye as they entered the parlor.

When Griffin announced they were leaving, Araminta eagerly jumped up from the sofa. "Thank you, Mrs. Burritt, for the delicious pastry."

She embraced Elizabeth and allowed Griffin to escort her from the house.

As they rode back to the hotel, he examined her

furrowed brow and compressed lips. "That bad?" he asked as he propped his booted feet on the bench next to her.

"The discussion consisted of nothing but planning a new wardrobe for Elizabeth. But Elizabeth seemed happy enough. And she assured me that she will never go near any kind of opium again. I believe her." She sighed and absently nibbled the end of one of her gloves, a strange but endearing habit he'd noticed recently.

"What else is bothering you?"

Her brow grew darker and she burst out, "If only I could be as certain about the happiness of the others still at Kane's. I worry most about Maggie and Alice."

"Kane will need to hang on to his help now. He won't hurt anyone in the kitchen now that you've flown the coop."

"What on earth does that mean?"

"Idiom for escaping prison," Griffin explained. "Speaking of birds, I met one today." He told her about the snowy owl in Burritt's library.

Araminta laughed so hard she had to grab the handle dangling from the corner and pull herself upright. "Oh, dear. Perhaps we should move away from animals and consider the plant kingdom? I am afraid we are growing too impertinent and cruel."

Griffin raised his eyebrows. "Only when we are too accurate."

Araminta still grinned, but her amusement faded as she recalled the senator. "I wish I could like Elizabeth's father."

"That man will be a pest, I imagine," Griffin said as he climbed from the carriage. When she descended, Griffin instead of the footman waited to help. His strong fingers gripped her arm.

Araminta gently disengaged her arm as she made a

show of smoothing her skirts. Any public display made her uneasy. "But aren't you glad to have him as an ally? I thought he is terribly important."

"As far as I'm concerned, he is merely terrible. I have no need to own any more politicians."

She smiled. "How many do you have as pets, then?"

"Pols are not pets. Merely domesticated animals."

"I was right. You are the worst sort of cynic," she teased.

"Nonsense." He gave her a brief smile—an almost common occurrence lately when they were alone together, though she was not yet accustomed to the kindliness it lent his features, and those smiles still could send a jolt of longing through her.

They walked across the wide lobby of the hotel. Araminta no longer hesitated before stepping into the lift. As the doors rattled open, Griffin moved close to her. Araminta ordered herself not to jump when his warm hand covered the small of her back. Hungry for more, she fought off the urge to lean against him.

He must have noticed her discomfort. He shot a glance at the elevator operator, and she could have sworn she heard Griffin give a tiny growl. "Come," he said as they stepped off the elevator. "Listening to Burritt talk has made me thirsty. I shall order some tea." They walked companionably toward the suite, chatting about the ideal times to drink tea.

As she watched him, she realized, *This is what it would be like to be his wife.* Living with the passionate undercurrent of attraction, but more than that, a friendship that grew with each conversation, each shared folly. The thought was as sharp as one of her best-honed blades. It forced her to recall the truth: He did not want a wife, or even a companion. He wanted an employee.

Restlessness seized her. She stopped in the doorway. Polite as always, he waited for her to enter first.

She paused to covertly study his face, and wondered how she could have thought him an iceberg of a man. Ah, no, she'd always instinctively understood his core consisted of pure passion. From the first moment she'd seen him, she'd likely felt his hidden passion in her body's response to him. She had selfishly wanted his heat for herself.

She'd had her taste of him, and her time with him had perhaps ruined her for anything less delicious.

"I have changed my mind about the tea, thank you. I— I think I shall go for a walk," she said.

They'd drawn close, of course, as inevitably as a magnet and metal, and his fingers made gentle circles on her arm. Becky came into the room, but he did not stop his caress.

Araminta sidestepped away. "Please," she whispered.

"Eh?"

With her chin, she indicated the maid.

He gave a small sniff of amusement, no doubt at her desire for propriety, then pulled out his watch and flipped it open. "Blast. I forgot Marcus is still here. I'll send him back to the office. And I need to pen a note to send along with him. You might want to take Annie with you if you go for a walk—I imagine she could use the exercise."

He flashed her a smile, and stroked her cheek before he strolled away. She listened to the echo of his footsteps as he walked across the parquet floor to the library.

She forced herself to face the truth: the moment to say good-bye had arrived.

It was over.

Elizabeth was gone. There was no need to remain as chaperone. And anything else was out of the question.

Now she would leave this apartment, leave the hotel, make her way back to her small, snug and empty house.

What then?

She absently rubbed at her arm, the small patch Griffin had stroked.

Instead of anguish, dead calm filled her. Perhaps the storm would come later, once she was home and alone and drearily safe.

She forced herself to make plans. A few weeks to explore New York. She would not open her restaurant here, after all. And then, before she grew too restless with the life of leisure, a boat back to Europe. A small café. Not London. Which smaller city in England would accept the food she enjoyed preparing?

The thoughts, familiar lists of her goals, flitted through her brain, but she barely paid attention to them. Reassuring words reminding her that life would carry on, even if she didn't believe it at the moment.

She walked across the spacious rooms, her mind so filled with a disarray of thought and emotion, she was rather surprised to find herself in her bedroom.

The room had been straightened, the three gowns she'd brought hung in the armoire.

She pulled the portmanteau from under the bed and packed quickly. She lifted the little velvet sack containing the pearls he'd given her. It lay heavy on her palm. She imagined his disgust if she left them, and she shoved the sack into her bag.

Would she dare to say good-bye to him? She wanted to, more than anything. But she'd finally learned that what she wanted wasn't necessarily what was best for her.

If he touched her . . . No. She couldn't risk it. Contact with Griffin would ruin her resolve. No matter how he looked at her—with a smile or amusement or scorn or even as coldly as he could manage—she'd be trapped.

She would turn into the creature Richardson had mistaken her for that night in the restaurant.

By continuously biting hard on the inside of her cheek, she managed to keep the tears at bay. She went to the yellow bedroom, where Annie was cleaning up after Elizabeth.

"I've come to say good-bye, Annie," she said. "Please say good-bye to Becky. And to the others."

The maid tilted her head and frowned at the bag in Araminta's hand. "You're going then, miss?"

"Yes, I must."

"Aren't you going to say anythng to him?"

Araminta shook her head.

Annie absently tucked a glossy black sausage curl back under her cap. "What'll I say when he asks?"

"Anything you'd like. No. Wait. Tell him I'm gone. Say good-bye."

"You know, miss, he's not so rotten as he likes to pretend."

Araminta nodded. "Yes, I know." Her words quavered a little, so she bit her cheek again.

Annie tossed a dusting cloth onto the bureau and flopped down on the bed. "I've heard about you, miss."

Despite the weight in her heart, Araminta's curiosity was pricked. "Have you? What do you know about me?"

Annie held up a hand and ticked a list off her fingers as she recited, "You're a kind person, you're a good friend, and you cook the best food in the universe."

"My goodness. Who told you all of that? Mr. Calverson?"

"No, his sister did. She's a good 'un."

Araminta stared at the maid, remembering bits of a story Timona had once told her, of a girl who'd worked in a brothel. A girl named . . . "Oh, my. You're that Annie. The, ah, one . . ."

"Yep. The strumpet," Annie replied cheerily. "I worked in a rotten bagnio. The ab-so-lute worst. But then Mr. Calverson broke it up and gathered us up before we were pulled in by the cops. He offered work to me and some of the other girls who wanted out of the life."

She got up and began thumping a pillow.

"Annie, why are you telling me this?"

"So's you'd know he's got a heart. Until you came along I wasn't sure if he had a prick."

Araminta winced.

Annie shot her a hopeful grin. "Did I offend you?"

She sounded so childishly eager, Araminta almost smiled. "Did you intend to?"

"Sure."

"Then yes, I'm deeply offended."

Annie giggled and for a moment seemed absurdly young. Araminta wondered if she was even seventeen yet. Annie's story reminded her that there were worse things in life than falling in love with the wrong man. The reminder didn't diminish her pain.

The girl squinted at Araminta. "Still saying good-bye?"

"Yes. I—I must."

"Huh. If I was you, I'd take the job. I tried for months to get him interested. I stay on because the money's good, but I'm hoping one of his flush pals will give me a go."

"Is that so?" Araminta said faintly, feeling extremely naive once again. "Thank you for your advice, but I already have gainful employment and don't need to take another job."

"Oh well." Annie shrugged. She went to a chintz chair in the corner of the room and gathered an armful of folded bedsheets. "Nothing to me. Just thought I'd do you a favor. And him one, too."

"It's very kind of you." Araminta managed a smile, but Annie had already turned back to spreading the clean sheets on the bed. All evidence of Elizabeth was gone, and soon Araminta would be erased from the other bedroom.

Araminta left.

CHAPTER 22

Araminta's house was too small to contain both her and the hints of Griffin. She knew that he had paid to have her house thoroughly cleaned after his stay, yet she found too many small reminders. One of his guards' racing forms lay folded on a table. The wizened lemon sat in the kitchen. She paced the house, hunting for the evidence of him.

Upstairs, she pressed her face to the sheets, but her bed had been remade and his scent was gone. The books she'd sent up for him to read lay neatly stacked near the bed.

By the books sat a small, nearly finished carving of a horse. She knew he'd been whittling wood, but had no idea that he possessed such skill. The little horse lay in her palm as she marveled at the delicate features. Another new facet of Griffin. And this was the man she'd once assumed cared only for money and had no appreciation for life or beauty.

Work had always drawn her out of her doldrums, and so she trotted downstairs and into the kitchen. Perhaps she'd experiment with some new recipes and send the results over to the soup kitchen.

As she rummaged through the pantry, however, she realized with dismay that her favorite knives and pans were still at Kane's. Oh bother. Could she march in there and take it all back?

She brewed some tea and sat at the kitchen table to sip it, pondering how to retrieve her belongings.

Perhaps she could ask Hobnail to help—but the only way she knew how to contact him was through Griffin, and she knew she could not see Griffin yet. The sight of him would create mayhem, and if he smiled at her, she'd be undone. Pride, self-preservation would fall away, and she'd go straight into his arms.

Perhaps in a few days or weeks or months she'd gain some strength. . . .

She slumped in the chair and knew that it would more likely be years before she could resist the man, if ever.

No. She'd have to go to Kane's herself and soon, before the evening's activities were in full swing. If she went in the servants' entrance, chances were good that Kane wouldn't see her. She could gather her things together, and even better, make sure Maggie and the scullery maids were all right. She could be gone before he found out she'd been on the premises.

A flour sack would hold her cooking tools. She'd sneak in and out like a thief.

Relieved to have a plan of action and something to do that took her out of the silent house, she set off for Kane's. She even hummed a little as she swung down the street, the flour sack tucked under her arm.

She went through the garden and peered into the kitchen, where Jack and Maggie moved about quickly. It seemed to her they worked faster than she'd seen them go before. Sweat poured down Jack's bald scalp. It was all she could do to keep herself from bellowing at him to wear something wrapped around his head to keep the food clean.

She opened the kitchen door. "Good afternoon," she called out cheerily, as if paying a social call. "I'm here to pick up my knives and so on."

Jack and Maggie looked up from what they were

doing. Maggie's hands stilled above the pastry she'd been rolling. Jack put down the oyster he'd been shucking.

"He won't be too glad to see you," Jack said, a smile—or perhaps a smirk—on his face. "He thinks you stole his doxy."

Araminta walked to the cutting board and wrapped the paring knife she found there in one of the soft cloths she had brought along. She wouldn't take the time to clean it. Being in this house made her skin crawl, and Jack seemed even more insolent than before. "He is wrong. Miss Smith left on her own accord. She is not an object that can be stolen away."

"Still," said Jack, "you best watch yourself."

He peeled off the thick glove he wore to protect his hand from the shucking knife.

"Be right back," he told Maggie. "Gotta make sure that girl isn't eating the walnuts I told her to bring out. You get straight to work on the oysters, hear?"

Right after he left, Maggie turned to Araminta and groaned. "Please hire me. Won't you, please? Everyone complains about the food now. Jack has been awful since you left. He's a tyrant worse'n Kane."

Araminta sighed. "I'm sorry, but I can't. Because I've left this place, I won't be able to open my own restaurant as quickly. But the moment I can, I'll be back for you and the girls." She thrust another covered knife into the bag.

Maggie's pale, freckled face puckered in thought. "But maybe you could borrow the money?"

"Is it that bad here, Maggie?"

"Just about."

Araminta paused for a moment, her nutmeg grinder in her hand, and watched Maggie deftly scrape out the oysters, dip them in flour and spices, and place them on a wide platter.

Borrow the funds?

Why not? She had always been determined to use her own money to have her restaurant. Make it a creation of her own hands. But . . . would it be cheating to temporarily use the money from the Woodhall Home, as she called the money her grandfather had left her? No, for she would pay it back.

She'd dearly love to give Maggie, and the others, too, a chance to escape, and this might be it.

"You might have something there, Maggie," she said slowly. "It could be a good plan. In fact, we could probably—"

At that moment, the swinging door slammed open.

Kane stood on the threshold, his face wreathed in smiles. Behind him stood Jack.

Kane's amiable face was bad enough. His words chilled her. "Hello, Miss Woodhall. Will you come into my office, please? I have something I need to discuss with you."

Araminta picked up a heavy black skillet with both hands.

"No, Mr. Kane. We don't have anything to talk about, sir."

"Oh, I think we do. Where is she?"

"Who?"

He stared at her. His hands formed blocky fists and a harsh red tide swept from his neck to his clean-shaven face, but the disconcerting smile never faltered.

Araminta forced herself to keep her chin high and stare back. "I don't know whom you mean."

She couldn't tell from his pleasant expression if he believed her. The brute was a smiling version of Griffin, she thought, with a face that gave nothing away.

"Jack," he said, still amiable, "would you go fetch a couple of lads from the Seventh Avenue address? I think I need some time alone with Araminta."

Jack turned and trotted away.

Kane limped into the kitchen. The door swooshed shut behind him, and Araminta saw he held a black, two-foot-long wooden stick, a club of some sort.

"A few taps with this and maybe we can finally get your memory moving." The tip of his tongue briefly touched his upper lip, and, with a sinking feeling, Araminta suspected the idea excited him. Talking would do no good.

She remembered the story of the woman he'd mistreated and then had murdered—perhaps had murdered himself—and she adjusted her grasp on the pan.

"Mr. Kane?" Maggie's voice quavered. Her thin lips trembled.

The smile momentarily vanished, but when it reappeared, his face beamed with joviality.

"Oh, dear," he said to no one. "Perhaps I ought to start with someone smaller and less full of herself than our Araminta."

Keeping his gaze steady on Araminta, he strode toward Maggie. He moved far faster than Araminta would have guessed possible for a man with a limp, and before Maggie realized his intention, he'd grabbed her wrist.

With a shout that sounded like joy, he sliced the cane down so hard it whistled as it flew through the air to crack across Maggie's shoulders. Araminta's heart congealed with anger at the brute and fear for Maggie.

Still clutching Maggie's slender wrist, he spoke over the sound of her loud sobs. "Shall I do it again, Araminta? Or will you come with me to my office so we might discuss Miss Smith's whereabouts?"

Araminta reluctantly lowered her skillet but decided he'd have to attack her to get her to drop it. "Leave Maggie alone."

He didn't take his gaze from Araminta as she walked across the kitchen. The skillet dangled loosely at her side.

"Put down the pan, Araminta." He raised the cane in the air, ready to strike Maggie again.

"Of course, Mr. Kane," said Araminta as she drew near. And she did.

First she put the fifteen-pound skillet down, hard, on his upraised hand, and then, as he swung around to get at her, she put it down on the side of his head.

CHAPTER 23

Annie wandered around Griffin's library, humming a show-tune, adjusting a tall, opalescent Chinese vase, running her finger over the binding of some embossed leather books and then checking for dust.

"Here, look," she said, holding up her finger. "Me and Becky do a good job. Better than the hotel staff, I'll tell you."

Griffin, seated at the desk, bit back the urge to bellow. Instead he patiently repeated the question he'd just asked. "What do you mean Miss Woodhall left no other message? Simply 'good-bye'?"

"She didn't seem real happy." The maid squinted at the edge of her thumb and rubbed it. "I think she was fit to be tied."

Griffin pushed back his chair. He went to the window and stared down at the teeming street. Araminta had been relaxing lately, been less prickly. Why would she run away? "I only had to write a quick message to Galvin. Why didn't she wait to say good-bye if she decided to go home?" he muttered.

Annie apparently thought he was addressing her. "She said she already had gainful employment."

He quickly pivoted and frowned at her. "What? What are you talking about? What in God's name did you discuss with her?"

"I said she ought to take a job working for you. I even put in a good word for you."

Griffin did not want to imagine what that meant. He went to the desk, and shoved some money and his watch into his waistcoat pocket. "Thank you, Annie. That will be all."

"She's got Negro blood, don't she?"

"I said that will be all."

"Still a nice lady, though."

"Annie. Go!"

She sauntered from the room.

He shoved fingers through his hair and reconsidered what he should do about Araminta.

He'd been on the verge of storming after her, demanding to know what was wrong. But he realized that it did not do to be too aggressive with her. In their dance together, when he grabbed, she ran off, but if he gently touched her, she blossomed. She was worth it—all of this nonsense he would never have tolerated in an earlier life.

He would give her time. No point in rushing her. He sat back down at his desk, picked up a letter opener and began a halfhearted look through his personal posts. Nothing but unwanted invitations. If he spent any more time in this city, he'd have to hire his own secretary instead of taking whichever was available from the company. The one characteristic he shared with his father was a dislike of companions. He'd rather travel alone.

Although he wouldn't mind hiring one particular chef.

Why on earth had Araminta stormed off as if she were angry? Had he somehow offended her?

He reviewed their conversations but could not see where the rift had come from. Araminta was not the type of woman who'd stay silent and nurse a grudge. Even if she attempted to hide her feelings, Griffin could read her too well. Or he could, once upon a time. Lately he had not been as sure.

Perhaps she mourned the loss of her friend. She'd kept a job with a man she'd grown to despise, mostly to protect Miss Burritt. Araminta was worth a hundred Elizabeth Burritts.

He leaned back in his chair and tucked his laced fingers behind his head.

She'd go to her house. Perhaps make a huge batch of soup for the indigents. Delicious soup, with the scents of oregano and basil. Perhaps even a touch of cinnamon. Sensual delights. She'd brought scent and flavor into his life, and without her his life would be bland gruel.

She couldn't have meant good-bye, except for the moment. And hellfire, even if she did, he would not allow it. A rush of fear filled him at the thought that she'd walk out of his life with no intention of coming back. To the devil with being careful to follow the rules of the dance. He wanted more. Not an acquisitive man, he'd decided to add this one particular woman to his permanent collection of valuables. He'd have to persuade her to add him to hers.

Griffin stalked to the front door and grabbed his hat.

He stood on her doorstep and hammered at the door. Either she was determined to ignore him or she wasn't home.

The coachman called, "Wanna try somewhere else?"

He vaulted back into the cab and gave the address for the Calverson Company offices. Griffin remembered Araminta's worry for Maggie. He had a sudden, unpleasant premonition of where Araminta might have gone. And he wasn't up to confronting Kane on his own yet.

Potter was the only man available at the company

headquarters who could perhaps be of help. Really, this sort of thing was out of the company's purview. Griffin needed Galvin, who was God knew where.

"Afternoon, sir." Potter had run from the back room when he'd been fetched. He panted as he climbed into the carriage next to Griffin.

Griffin briefly outlined their errand.

Potter ran a finger between his starched collar and his neck. "You're still not recovered, sir. Are you sure this is wise?"

Griffin leaned against the greasy leather upholstery of the cab. "On the contrary, I am sure it is lunacy. It might be necessary, however. You go and check—Kane and his men don't know you. No point in causing trouble unless we must."

"I hope that Wurth and the others get the message you left," Potter muttered. "Sir."

"And that they get it soon," Griffin agreed.

At Kane's Park Avenue mansion, no one answered Potter's knock. The double cream-colored front doors were not locked. One even stood a few inches ajar. No one stopped Potter and Griffin as they pounded through the marble foyer into the first parlor and through the dining room, which had been set and lay ready for the evening.

They were too late.

Or so Griffin thought, when he heard the terrible cries from behind the green baize door. And then he realized it wasn't Araminta who screamed.

In the kitchen, Griffin glimpsed a small, plump woman in blue cowering next to the ice box. The screamer, no doubt.

Araminta stood above Kane like an avenging angel, her wild dark hair about her face, her glorious eyes blazing. She clutched a heavy iron skillet in both hands, and at her feet sprawled a groaning Kane. He half sat, half lay against a table leg. Blood covered his wilted collar and starched white front.

"Are you all right?" Griffin demanded.

Araminta turned, and as quickly as their eyes met, her gaze snapped over his shoulder. Her eyes grew wide. "Behind you."

Four men barreled through the kitchen door. Araminta raised her skillet. Griffin, who had only his cane, slipped the sword from the sheath. The brute who'd been trotting toward him skidded to a stop and eyed the unsheathed blade.

From the corner of his eye Griffin caught a glint as another thug charged toward Potter.

Griffin shouted, "Look out! A knife."

Potter, who now wore a happy smile, seized a large strainer and, after a struggle, ripped the knife from a fat, bald man with a huge mustache.

A redheaded gorilla circled Griffin, who held his thin blade en garde and wished that he'd paid better attention to fencing classes—or that he'd brought along a knife.

The redhead lunged and Griffin leaped out of the way—and brought the heavy head of the cane down on the man, who stumbled back, rubbing his head.

Araminta raced over to the bald one still fighting with Potter. She raised her skirt a few inches and gave the bald man a hard kick in the rear quarters. As he fell face forward onto the slate floor, she shouted, "Jack, how could you? I have changed my mind about hiring you."

A skinny young one wearing checked trousers hurtled toward Araminta. Griffin stopped him with a slash of the blade. The man howled in pain and dropped the stuffed eelskin he carried, and clutched his injured arm. For two seconds he stared at Griffin, who slowly moved toward him. Then checked trousers turned and fled the kitchen.

"Where the hell do you think you're going?" bellowed

Kane. Griffin twisted toward Kane, whose face was green, though he had managed to pull himself up and was reaching for an empty bowl.

Griffin pointed his blade at Kane. "Sit."

Kane sat.

The fight did not last long, especially when Hobnail came crashing into the scene, his fists causing considerable damage on the big, bald Jack, who was lurching toward Araminta, arms outstretched. Griffin, feeling aggrieved that he hadn't had the chance to go after Jack, eventually hauled Hobnail off his bellowing victim.

At last the thugs who'd defended Kane sat or lay in a corner near the stove, panting.

Hobnail, standing guard over them, pulled out a blue handkerchief and pressed it to his nose, which streamed blood. "Well now. I figure this means I'm done here," he said in a muffled voice. "Be real glad to get back to regular work. Less nasty."

"Always figured you were soft for the cook," the red-headed bruiser who half lay on the floor in the corner sneered at Hobnail. "Didn't think you'd be a turncoat for the bit—" Griffin didn't have a chance to do anything because Hobnail's foot in the man's side made the bugger change his mind about finishing the sentence.

Araminta stood by the door, holding the small, sobbing woman's hand. Griffin caught her eye. "You all right?" he asked.

After a pause, she nodded and turned her attention back to the woman. Maggie, no doubt. In the midst of the mayhem and blood, Griffin suddenly realized that he'd likely be once again meeting all manner of strange people with Araminta in his life. He subdued the grin that rose at the thought, but he had to clamp down hard on the anger that filled him when he realized his priceless woman had almost gotten herself killed.

Later. He would deal with her later.

He dropped to his haunches and squatted by Kane, who half lay against a table leg. "You're finished, you know," Griffin remarked conversationally. "You're going to be arrested for murder."

Kane peered at him. Despite the blood still dripping down his face, Kane managed to don his usual broad, white smile. "That's old news. I've been arrested and gotten free more than once."

"I know you murdered Pushy Pete Carter because you thought I'd hired him," Griffin continued, as if he hadn't interrupted. "I hadn't, by the way. But several men who did work for me heard you brag about the incident. And they've heard you discuss other murders you've committed or hired out. I'm sure that a more careful search by policemen you haven't paid off will turn up some evidence."

Kane muttered something. He put his hand to the side of his head, and then squinted down at his hand. "Damn female chef." He shuddered as he feebly wiped his blood-covered palm on his once-pristine blue worsted trousers. Araminta must have injured his arm as well. Griffin wished he could have seen her in action.

He pulled out his clean linen handkerchief and handed it to Kane. "Extortion, murder—you have been a nuisance to me and my associates. Why have you been so determined to be a pest?"

"You." Kane spat out the word. "Because of you, ya son of a bitch. I spent years building up my businesses. And you stroll in and doing no work you think you can just park yourself in my territory."

"You purposefully mistook my intentions. I made it very clear I'm not interested in taking up any of your trades."

Kane used the handkerchief to scrub at the blood on

the side of his face and then dropped the soaked cloth to the floor. "Then why the hell were you always poking around?"

"You'd proved you were a nuisance. To me and my friends. I could not very well allow you to do that."

"Oh, no. You're just like that Lord Courtney, just another bogus Brit confidence man. You were gonna use your fancy accent and fancy manners and your flash connections to scoop up my business. You wanted to ruin me. You won't do it. I been in New York longer than you been alive."

Griffin straightened. He propped his hip against the table and folded his arms. "Interesting. If you'd only left Pushy Pete alone we could have avoided all of this nonsense. Actually"—he gave a quick glance at Araminta, who listened with a frown—"if you treated your women with more respect, we could have avoided much of this trouble."

"Says you."

"Yes, I do indeed. But back to the point. I have a great deal more than murder on you, Kane. The springs I found on your rigged equipment when I visited. Very easy to spot. Your gambling was worse than illegal. It was fixed—and shoddily. Never allow your evidence to lie around where it can be pocketed by the help."

He nodded at Hobnail, who pulled some playing cards from his ratty waistcoat. Hobnail held them up and intoned, "This deck of cards, taken from this establishment on the night of May third, are marked in a fashion similar to decks I confiscated earlier. I have . . . Oops—" His nose began to bleed again, and he hastily tucked the cards away.

Kane's smile drifted back onto his face. "You can't prove that those cards were used in my house."

Griffin absently touched the corner of his mouth, where he'd been cut.

Araminta noticed that his eyes gleamed as if he were about to divulge the last line of a wonderful joke.

"No, but Officer Hobbes will be happy to testify that they were," said Griffin. "And so will Gregory Galvin, a man of many trades, including private detection."

One of Kane's men in the corner groaned and buried his face in his hands.

Araminta couldn't believe her ears. "Officer Hobbes?" she gasped.

"Hobnail," Hobbes reminded her, his blue eyes surprisingly gentle in his battered, bloody face.

Griffin still stood propped against the chopping table, calm as always, hardly a seam askew or a golden brown hair out of place. If she hadn't just witnessed his involvement in the imbroglio, she would have thought he'd come in from a stroll in the park. Araminta demanded, "Why didn't you tell me?"

He gazed at her, and then at Hobnail, his face devoid of expression. "It was up to Hobnail to decide whether or not he'd tell you."

She turned to Hobnail. No, Officer Hobbes, her burly protector. "What kind of officer are you?"

"New York City Police Department," he said. "I'm a fly cop, or plainclothes officer."

"No uniform," she said. Of course. No wonder he'd been so sharp-eyed on their walks.

Hobnail swiped at his nose and nodded. "Sorry I didn't say anything. Didn't know if you'd be mad."

"Mad? I don't think that—"

Griffin interrupted. "Might we have this discussion later? I am still busy threatening Mr. Kane."

Araminta's eyes narrowed, but she fell silent.

Kane growled. "Yah, well, it won't work. I got friends in high places—"

"Yes, but you also have enemies in high places. You made those enemies on your own, you know. Murder is frowned upon. And gambling is a crime, of course. However, cheating is an offense that your most important customers, those important friends of yours, will never forgive. And you were insane to mess with Elizabeth Burritt."

Kane started to climb to his feet, but Griffin straightened, and Kane sat back down on the floor again, hard. He glowered up at Griffin. "Ho! You stole her from me."

"Of course I did. And Senator Burritt was extremely grateful to me for my rescue of his darling daughter."

"He wouldn't dare move against me. I'll tell the world the truth about the girl."

Araminta wondered if Hobnail would arrest her if she brought the skillet down on Kane's head again.

Griffin didn't seem particularly disturbed, however. She could swear she still saw the light of amusement in his eyes.

He drawled, "You'd tell the world that you lured an innocent young girl into drug addiction and then used her as your mistress? No. I don't think you want to do that. Oh, and at any rate it would be your word against those of the Dr. Haynes Sanitorium about where the girl spent the last few months. I doubt the maids who observed her here would qualify as reliable witnesses."

Kane stared up at Griffin, but when he spoke, the aggressive cockiness had vanished. "I cared about Olivia. I wanted to marry the girl. I took good care of her."

His blood-streaked face twisted as he fought tears, and Araminta was appalled to realize he thought it was true.

Within minutes, it felt as if every square inch of the room had filled with men. Calverson types, Araminta

saw by the way they deferred to Griffin, and a couple of
policemen who seemed to treat Hobnail with marked respect. She was soothing a confused Alice, who'd just
returned from her half-day off, when someone tapped her
arm.

The man called Galvin jerked his head in Griffin's direction. "He says you gotta leave as soon as possible.
More police are on their way."

"Alice, you go home to your mother's," she said.

Galvin shoved his hands into his baggy trousers' pockets. "Ready?"

Araminta frowned at him. "I will speak to the police
first, and—"

"Later. Maybe." Galvin ignored her protests and led
her to the kitchen door.

But before they were through it, Griffin strode over
and blocked her path. His face was twisted into a scowl
of undisguised rage. He seized her shoulders. "What in
bloody hell were you thinking? Why did you come
here?" he bellowed.

All around the kitchen activity stopped. Griffin Calverson actually shouted?

Araminta ignored the stares in their direction and refused to raise her gaze from his precisely tied white
cravat. "I wanted to get my equipment."

Griffin's voice dropped closer to his usual volume,
though not his usual controlled, unemotional quality.
"Didn't you listen when I told you about Kane? Why
didn't you ask me or Hobnail for help? You knew when
you left the same day as Miss Burritt he'd suspect you in
her disappearance. And I made it clear he was not at all
happy to lose her. Why did you come back? Are you a
fool, Araminta?"

She reflected how peculiar it was that when others raged,
she could more easily control her temper. "Perhaps. But if

I am, it is none of your concern, Griffin. I am grateful for your help, but I'm a grown woman. If I make mistakes they are my problem alone."

She was not so unaffected after all, for her head spun and her hands trembled as she turned and walked out the door.

Hobnail had said he'd take a statement from her at home, so she would go straight there. Halfway down the path, she stopped and turned to Mr. Galvin. "But my things." A rush of dizziness overcame her and she gave a dry sob. "I had them in a bag. And Maggie. I worry about her. I should never have left just because Mr. Calverson told me to."

Galvin fingered his untidy gray mustache and gave an impatient grunt and trotted back to the kitchen. He came out bearing the sack and accompanied by the still-sniffling Maggie.

Galvin said, "Miss Maggie here says she's fine but she was worried about you. Maybe she ought to stay with you, if you don't mind."

"Of course." Araminta started to put an arm around Maggie, but the girl flinched. Kane's hit probably still stung.

She took Maggie's hand and squeezed it instead. "You come home with me and we'll have a cup of tea."

The tension at the corners of Maggie's cinnamon-brown eyes eased, and a ghost of a smile brushed her lips. She wasn't British, but Araminta had managed to teach her about the healing properties of having a hot cup of something when crises struck.

Galvin hustled them to a carriage next to the building. Already several policemen had appeared out front, and a crowd of interested gawkers gathered at the iron fence at the front of the mansion.

Galvin helped Araminta and Maggie climb onto the

gig's bench. He unhitched the horse, clambered up next to Araminta and picked up the reins.

The streets were not horribly congested, and he managed to steer them into the stream of traffic after only a minute of waiting.

Araminta watched the scarred, gray-haired old man for a moment. "Mr. Galvin, you know Kane. Is he as dangerous as Mr. Calverson said?"

Galvin grunted, and she realized he chuckled. "Worse. Calverson underestimated the scum and his connections. He's not in jail yet neither. Kane's got one of the best lawyers in New York. He'll likely get off, unless Calverson pays out some more. Which I'll bet he's willing to do."

He hauled back at the reins to avoid hitting a pushcart vendor who'd steered a rattling cart into the street. "Never seen him get so riled up," he said thoughtfully. "Calverson, I mean."

His sharp, bright eyes gave Araminta a speculative examination that made her feel as if he were boring through her brain.

"I've known Calverson for a dozen or so years," Galvin continued. "He's a cold son of a . . . gun on occasion. But usually when he is, someone's messed with a person or thing he cares about. Like Timona."

Araminta nodded. "Yes, I know."

"You would. You were out in Minnesota, weren't you, when she got married?" He twisted the end of his grizzled mustache and eyed her for another moment before turning his attention back to traffic. "Calverson didn't mind that marriage as much as we all thought he would. In fact, he didn't mind it at all. He said he reckoned the McCanns were a good match. Said that someone he trusted told him they were a perfect pair and would be more'n comfortable together."

She had used those exact phrases, the day she thought he had ignored her every word.

She smiled, warmed by his words and the memory of the McCanns. "They are happy. Very happy."

She turned away from the gray-haired man's careful scrutiny of her, and pretended to watch an organ grinder on a street corner. Griffin had trusted her even then? She did not like how happy Mr. Galvin's words made her.

At her house, she bid good-bye to Mr. Galvin and settled Maggie into the back bedroom. The girl was apparently so excited about the prospect of being Araminta's guest she was down the stairs at once and helping put away her cooking tools.

Araminta had planned to feel sorry for herself, and nurse her broken heart, but she could only be grateful for Maggie's presence.

"I'm sorry you lost your job," Araminta said as she cleaned and dried the knives she'd retrieved from Kane's house. "Kane paid better than I'll be able to at first. And I'm not sure where I shall open my restaurant."

Maggie, sitting at the kitchen table, looked up at her and grinned. "Learning to cook from you, miss, is worth a cut in my pay or even leaving New York. Besides, I'm on my own now. My sister's married and don't need me any longer. But tell me what you'll serve, miss. And do you think we—I mean you—will be able to get Alice, too? She's a biddable girl. Oh, are these your recipes? Might I take a look?"

Her eagerness didn't entirely spark Araminta's enthusiasm for her old dreams. But it kept her from wailing in misery, which, as Griffin would say, would have been a useless exercise. Griffin. Oh bother. For perhaps the hundredth time that day, Araminta chewed on her bottom lip to stop the tears.

Maggie stayed only one night. She declared that she

wanted to gather her few belongings from her bedroom at Kane's and go stay with her sister in Brooklyn.

Araminta hugged her. "I shall come find you the moment I can."

An hour after Maggie left, someone rapped on the door. Araminta assumed Hobnail had come to take her report of Kane.

Griffin stood at her doorstep splendid in a snowy cravat, silk top hat and bored expression.

CHAPTER 24

Her heart pounding, Araminta considered not opening the door at all. She did, of course, but instead of inviting Griffin to enter, she stepped into the doorway. "I'm still not up for company."

If he managed to get into her house, only a miracle would keep her out of his arms. A miracle or, more unlikely, a Griffin Calverson who was too upstanding and noble to try to seduce her again.

He was dressed in tan trousers and a blue morning coat. Griffin never wore the skintight trousers or ridiculous jackets with long tails of the fashionable young men called dudes. But his air seemed more dashing than usual.

He swept off his silk top hat and ran a gloved hand over his glinting hair. A small line of concern appeared between his eyes as he examined her. Everywhere his gaze touched, a wave of heat rose. Heavens, he wouldn't need to seduce her. She'd jump on him.

He replaced his hat at a slightly jaunty angle, and leaned against the doorjamb so she wouldn't be able to close the door without giving him a firm shove. "I am sorry to hear that. Were you injured?"

She shook her head.

"I sent along that girl to keep you company; where is she?"

"Maggie? She left."

His body shifted ever so slightly closer. "So you're alone?"

She closed the door a few inches, blocking him. "Yes."

Instead of appearing pleased, his face darkened. "I worry that you might not feel well enough to stay alone."

She was about to protest that there was nothing wrong with her when she recalled that she was using her weakness as an excuse to not invite him in.

He searched her face. "Araminta, I am sorry if I offended you by berating you yesterday."

She gave him a brief, wan smile. "No, you were right. I was entirely stupid to go there. And I thank you for your concern."

He stepped up, onto the last marble stair, too close to her again. Oh God, she caught the scent of him, warm Griffin. More mouthwatering than fresh bread. She clenched her hands together.

"Then tell me, what is the matter? You won't look at me. You are acting so very . . ."

She waited.

"Very polite," he finished.

She couldn't help tilting her head back. "And that is so unusual?"

"There we go!" he said happily. "I knew you were in there somewhere, Araminta."

When she began to open her mouth to explain, she saw the warmth in his eyes, the painfully magnificent green eyes glowing for her.

He would leave when she explained that she could not be his mistress, and perhaps she could get on with planning her life. But with him next to her, she could not say good-bye, stupid woman. She lied instead. "I think I am still feeling the effects of that dreadful scene in the kitchen."

"Well, then," he said briskly and pulled out an

impressive sheet of parchment from his waistcoat. "Let me help you take your mind off of it, shall I? I have a specific reason for my visit."

For physical relief? she almost asked. *Because you find you want someone under you in your bed again?* He did not deserve the sharp edge of her tongue. He'd never lied.

So she only nodded.

He waved the paper.

"I have an invitation from the trustees of the New York and Brooklyn Bridge to attend the opening ceremony of the Great East River Bridge." He read from the paper and then pulled out his watch. "It's eleven o'clock now. The official festivities commence at two o'clock. But let's wait until the speeches are over. I am rather tired of hearing the phrase 'Eighth Wonder of the World.'"

Before she managed to stop him, he'd walked past her into the house, taking off his hat and still talking. "Might as well join the whole city, eh? Schools and businesses close soon in celebration. Of course," he said as he drew off his gloves and shoved them into his hat, "I can think of wonderful ways we could privately celebrate."

He slipped his arms around her and pulled her to him.

Throbbing hunger blasted through her. With her eyes closed tight, she wiggled from his embrace. She had planned to tell him no, to send him on his way. But a visit to the bridge could not hurt, could it? An hour or two, outside, surrounded by crowds. He could not flay her heart any more than he'd already done.

She had recently learned to think of him as more than a lover. If she could convince him that they might be friends without intimacy, perhaps she might not lose him altogether.

"Griffin. Thank you. I would like to go to the bridge.

With you. But . . . I would appreciate it if you did not allow any overly familiar behavior."

He looked amused. "I'm about as familiar with you as a man can be with a woman. What the devil do you mean?"

"I suppose touching in a—an unacceptable manner. And making references to subjects that you would not speak of in mixed company."

His mouth tightened and his eyes grew hard as he stared at her for a moment. "Damn it, Araminta, I keep waiting for you to burst into laughter and tell me it's a joke."

"Please, Griffin. I know it sounds unreasonable, considering our past, but I hope you understand that I would be more comfortable this way."

He took a step toward her. She folded her arms across her breasts and backed away.

"It's back to the dance, is it?" he muttered. She wondered what he meant, and was about to ask when he shook his head. "You are so polite, and I want to shake you until you grow angry enough to be the real and passionate Araminta I know."

She wet her lips and prepared herself to say the words. To explain that the passionate Araminta must be gone, and that she could never be anything other than polite with him. But before she could open her mouth, he was turning and walking out the door. "Very well, Miss Woodhall. I agree to your terms. I shall return here at two. That should give us enough time to escape most of the speeches, eh?"

As they drove to the bridge, he kept up a stream of polite remarks that flowed past her. Though she was taken aback that he was capable of showing such elegant manners, almost those of a most polished member of the ton, she barely noticed the words he spoke. Her heart thumped far too hard and loud.

As she'd prepared for the outing—frantically changing into a gown and then ruthlessly rooting through her armoire for a prettier one—she discovered the truth about herself: friendship would never work.

At the end of their day together, she would say goodbye and God bless to the man she loved. She could not bear to be around him. She could only hope she could bear to be away from him.

Throngs of people had paid the penny fee and stood waiting to walk across the bridge.

Griffin touched Araminta's silk-covered arm. "Does it make you nervous to see all of these people and vehicles? Do you suppose the bridge will bear all of this weight?"

She turned and at last looked at him with a smile in her shadowed eyes and on her lush mouth. A bit of dark hair blew across her cheek, and she grabbed at her straw boater and arranged it more firmly on her head. She wore a rosy gown that matched the pink of her cheeks. An audacious color, nothing that a prim woman would wear.

"I am going to cross, Griffin. With or without you."

They set off, and at once the cool breeze from the river washed over his face. They tilted their heads—the cables and towers of the bridge soared into the sky.

"Oh, I feel as if I am flying," she murmured.

"A very apt description."

They walked slowly and people strolled past them, chattering and pointing. Everyone on the bridge was caught up in the giddy atmosphere of a celebration. Everyone but Griffin, who could concentrate only on one woman, instead of the impressive vista spread out all around them.

She stopped under an archway to run her hand over the

coarse rock, and closed her eyes. Sensation was heightened when one closed one's eyes, she'd said, and he wished she would rub her hand over him in the same ecstatic fashion.

Unable to resist, he moved close to her, lifted her hand and put it flat against his chest. "Smoother stone, eh?"

Her startled eyes stared into his before she turned away.

"I apologize," he said as he quickly strode after her. "No overly familiar behavior."

She slowed down. "Thank you."

He didn't want her gratitude. He wanted her. "Mind you, I want to howl with frustration, but I shan't touch you again until you ask."

A shadow of a smile crossed her face and she nodded. Agreement about the dreadful frustration, he supposed, or more blasted gratitude.

He'd force himself to enjoy the day, the sights and her company, dammit. And control the urge to seize her and kiss her senseless. Or rather back into sense, as far as he was concerned.

The walk across lasted forty minutes. Along the way, they stopped and rested on a bench and gazed off at the horizon, elegantly framed in the bridge's cables.

Griffin squinted through the sunlight at the vast skyline of the city of Brooklyn. "Should be an even better view going into Manhattan. Unless you wish to hire a carriage back?"

She shook her head. He was glad. The longer they stayed together, the longer he could take to learn why she had changed into this withdrawn, polite woman, so different from the open Araminta he knew.

But on the walk back her answers, though polite, were even more uninformative.

"Do you feel ill?"

"Oh, no. I'm well."

"Would you care for some refreshment?"

"No, I thank you."

When they reached the Manhattan side again, she turned and held out her hand. "Well. It has been a most pleasant day. Thank you for a fine expedition."

He pulled her close, trapping her arm in the crook of his elbow. "No, I shall escort you home, Araminta."

He hailed a hansom cab and handed her in.

"Lucky you found me," called down the cheery driver. "I've been on the bridge. They say it's the eighth wonder of the world, and I don't doubt it. Quite a party it's been all day."

He chirruped to his horse, and they lurched forward into a trot.

Araminta stared out the window of the cab, so all he could see was the curve of her soft cheek. He recalled that not so long ago he'd been pompously certain he could read her face and see what her heart held, but for days he'd been at a loss.

"Araminta."

She turned toward him, but stared at his neckcloth, not into his eyes.

"Tell me, what is wrong? Have I made you angry?"

"No, not at all. It was a very pleasant afternoon." She shook her head, and in a slanting ray of late-afternoon sun, he saw her eyes grow suddenly brighter. Tears.

Enough absurd tiptoeing. He moved close to her but could feel her body stiffen and shift away from him. "For God's sake, Araminta. Is there anything I can do? What is it?"

"Nothing," she said. "I think perhaps I am tired. It was a long walk today, wasn't it?"

He decided to believe her.

Perhaps he could take her inside and start again on a

long, patient seduction, show her again how well they suited one another—hell, far too sedate a term for what they had. How well they caught fire together.

He glanced down at her sturdy brown button-up boots. *Rest time is over, Araminta,* he thought. *Definitely time for the dance again.* He'd move slowly, stroking, not grabbing. Yes, he'd begin with a thorough massage of her feet. And then he would stroke his fingers over her lovely calves. Just the thought of her shapely legs was enough to bring him to uncomfortable arousal. He was desperate for the woman. More than just wanting her in his bed, he wanted to see her smile at him again, hear her throaty, wonderful laugh.

They reached her house.

"Want me to wait?" the cabman called from his perch.

Araminta wasn't sure if she was glad or dismayed to hear Griffin's response as he handed up the fare. "No, thank you."

Araminta could barely breathe. She was a fool to allow the man back into her life even for a single day. She could not function when under his intoxicating influence.

He unlocked the door and ushered her into her own house.

And then he closed the front door and leaned against it.

"I am tired," she began, but her voice died away as he walked close and put a finger on her lips.

"You will rest, then. And I shan't bother you. But I am not ready to leave yet."

Arrogant Griffin. Worse, weak Araminta, for she seemed unable to order him out. She would have licked her lips, but his hand still touched her. She managed to speak anyway. "Perhaps I am not interested in inviting you in. You—you are like wine. I cannot think properly when you are near."

He grinned. "Good. At last you begin to make sense. I understand precisely how you feel."

"No, Griffin. I can't afford to . . ."

His finger glided lightly across her mouth. And slowly, he leaned in close and tilted his head. "On the contrary. You can."

He waited for two heartbeats as he'd done once before, and then took his hand away from her and leaned in to kiss her. Or so she thought, but the kiss did not come.

He angled toward her and placed his warm mouth just above hers. "Oh, no. You see, I promised"—the whispered words gusted against her lips—"not to touch you first."

She could feel his fast breath on her cheek, the soft tickle of his mustache. If it weren't so arousing, their position, frozen this way, would have struck her as funny.

Back away, she thought; *get away from him.* The mew of longing that came from her throat surprised her. She closed the last tiny space between them, and pressed her mouth to his. The delicate touch of his tongue undid her.

Oh, no, I give up, was her only thought, as she moved and her mouth slid against his, silently demanding more. His arms came around her, and the hunger filled her at once. She pushed her body to his, opened her lips. Her heart pounded, almost as if it fought to get as close as possible to him.

He broke away from the embrace, and she grew red with embarrassment. Had she been too eager?

His hand grasped hers and he pulled her to the stairs.

"A mistake," she whispered. "I didn't mean to."

"Then we shan't," he said. And smiled. His eyes shone with the heat of lust now, but with a fondness, too, that was almost worse. "We will do nothing bad. Nothing that you don't want."

She allowed him to lead her up to her bedroom. Ever so passive.

Reality set in again as she watched him undo his neckcloth, unbutton his waistcoat and then begin on his shirt. She suppressed her eagerness to see more of that warm golden skin.

With a strangled voice, she took a stand. "No. I will not undress. And you must stop."

He nodded, and immediately his hands dropped away from his shirt. But he did not refasten his shirt, and she caught fascinating glimpses of his beautiful torso beneath the starched white front. He folded up his sleeves, exposing tanned forearms. She remembered when they'd made love how she'd run her tongue over that skin, tasting the fine hair. And tried to encircle his substantial wrists with her fingers.

"I imagine your limbs are tired?" he asked in a tone appropriate for a drawing room.

They were. She sat down on the edge of her bed. Better to have picked the chair, but she did not want to push past him. The solid presence of the man against her again would perhaps be too much, and her unruly body would take control away from her good sense. Again.

"Allow me." He knelt, one knee on the floor by her feet. For a moment she wondered why the position seemed familiar. Of course. The traditional position for a marriage proposal.

She closed her eyes and let herself fall backward on the bed, in desolation or in heat—she no longer knew which. His strong hand reached under her skirt and petticoat and she held her breath, dizzy and unsure how she would respond. Her body trembled. But he didn't reach up and between her thighs. Instead he fumbled at the top of her garter, undid it and pulled down her stocking.

His hands, large, warm and strong, touched her feet. She jumped. "I'm ticklish," she whispered.

But his thumbs on her arches rubbed hard. She had not known that the feet's sensitivity could turn them into yet another part of her body that he could command to respond. His hands moved to her calves and thighs, rubbing, stroking her muscles, making circles on her flesh and melting her resolve. She could hear his breath, harsh and uneven, and knew his touch affected him as well as her. Which of course made her swirl even deeper into passion.

Someone banged at the door.

Araminta jumped up as if she'd been stuck by a pin. Ignoring her stockings she hastily shoved her feet into a pair of denim half boots that lay by the bed.

Griffin watched her rush off; fierce longing pushed him close to bellowing with frustrated need. He buttoned his shirt and waistcoat, folded his neckcloth and shoved it into his trousers pocket. He stood in the hall above, listening, and heard the deep voice of Hobnail Hobbes.

CHAPTER 25

Griffin strolled down the stairs.

Hobnail stood in the parlor, his hair slicked back. He held a hat, a far less battered homburg than he wore at Kane's, and thumped it rhythmically against the side of his leg. He'd been saying something about a last-minute desire to see the fireworks, a halting invitation to Araminta, but fell silent when he saw Griffin.

For a long minute he met Griffin's eyes, and his lips pressed together with what might have been disgust. Araminta couldn't have seen them exchange glares. She was apparently unable to look up from the floor.

This was the way the wind blew, then. But naturally a woman like Araminta would have other admirers.

Hobnail spoke at last. "Well. I see that you were busy with company. I won't keep you, then."

He turned to leave, but suddenly he dropped his hat onto the sofa and put a hand on Araminta's shoulder. Even from across the room, Griffin could see her start of surprise.

Hobnail drew in a deep breath. "I must say this. I'll hate myself if I don't."

His face turned red and his Adam's apple bobbed as he swallowed nervously. He gazed at Araminta and did not so much as glance in Griffin's direction again. "I pray you don't end up with him, Araminta. He doesn't treat you like you deserve. I'd offer you more. I said it before and I mean it—I'd be honored to marry you."

Griffin considered himself a fair man. What the hell didn't he do that she deserved? He expected her to say no at once, to put poor Hobnail out of his misery. Instead, she hesitated. Her head tilted back and she smiled at the large man as if he'd offered her some kind of amazing gift.

God, no. Not Hobnail. But then again, why not? He was an honest, clean, trustworthy copper. And a dead man if she said yes.

Griffin wanted to howl with rage. Why hadn't she said anything? Had she been too polite—or too cowardly—to explain that this was the reason she had grown so distant? She longed for a large, inarticulate and modest copper. Instead of a midsize, articulate and arrogant businessman.

He knew that none of his despair showed on his face. And he knew that even if it had, the two people standing across the room would not even notice, for they seemed lost in each other's eyes.

Could life hold any moment more miserable than this? Frantic greediness for Araminta filled him. Why on God's green earth had he ever allowed her to escape from him? If only there was a legal way he could have bound her to him, never allowed her to escape. . . . Oh, bloody hell. Bloody stinking pits of hell.

Then Araminta shook her head. "No. But Hobnail, you do me great honor," and when she said the stock words of refusal, she plainly meant them with every fiber of her being. "I will always, always be grateful. And thank you for coming here today. I rather think you saved me."

She stood on tiptoe and kissed Hobnail's cheek.

"Araminta," Griffin began, but she walked out of the room without so much as a glance at him.

From the front of the house she called back, "Please

just close the door behind you when you leave, gentlemen. There's no need to lock it."

The door slammed.

Hobnail's blue eyes stared daggers at him. "Don't you
hurt her, Calverson. You don't deserve a woman like her."

Griffin suspected the man was right, and so had no answer. Hobnail, walking quietly for so large a man, left
him alone in the silent house.

Marriage. No matter what she said, that's what she
wanted. He could tell by the way her eyes had shone at
the not-so-dim-witted cop.

Griffin had long ago promised himself he'd never
marry. What was the point of marriage for a man unless
he wished to create children? There were more than
enough children in the world, especially neglected,
unloved children. He had never felt the need to make any
more.

But as Griffin strode purposefully toward the front
door, he had a vision. He saw a baby with Araminta's
smile and those dark, bottomless eyes. She was not going
to make that child with any other man if he could help
it.

And even without that baby, marriage was what she
wanted, the liar. And he wanted her. More than that—he
ruddy well needed her.

He swore, and snatched his hat from the tree in the
hall.

Twilight approached, but he spotted her perhaps a half-
block from her house. She had not gotten far, though she
walked quickly. He trotted after her, and easily caught up.
The quick staccato echo of her steps sped up when she
caught sight of him.

He fell into step next to her. "Where are you going?
Running away from your own home? I thought you were
exhausted."

"Leave me alone, please." She pulled gloves from her pocket, and instead of putting them on, began twisting them.

The sight of her familiar mannerism created a strange sensation. He desperately wanted to laugh or kiss her. Or both. "I wonder how many pairs a year you destroy."

She at once shoved them back into her pocket. Her steps quickened, and he matched her stride.

"I saw your face, Araminta, when Hobnail asked. You want to be married, don't you? You lied when you said you didn't. Dammit, I've heard you say you'd never marry. More than once. You spoke of the subject with convincing fervor."

She didn't answer. Her arms swung at her sides in a most unladylike manner as she increased her pace.

He continued, managing to capture a more conversational tone. "I've said it myself many times, you know. I never planned on marrying. Unlike you, however, I meant it."

"I know. Because you don't believe in love." Her voice was as sour as the lemon she'd made him taste in her kitchen. Just a matter of days, really, though it might have been a lifetime ago.

"But you. If you're fond of the institution, why haven't you married? I understand that Hobnail's not your dream mate, but a woman like you—surely you could find a good man who'd marry you?"

She stopped at last, and glared at him as if he were filth, her lip curling. "I will not marry without love. I happen to believe that the emotion exists."

She might have been observing a fly that had landed in her *poulet au champagne avec fromage et champignons*. "But at the moment, I wish there were no such thing as love. In fact, as far as I'm concerned, it is a terrible source of anguish."

"Why is that?"

"Because I love you, Griffin."

Other women had said the phrase to him before. And he knew one or two who'd uttered the words actually believed they did care about him. But never before had the phrase given him a tangible sensation so strong it might have been pain. He thought perhaps he understood what she meant by a source of anguish.

"Ah," he breathed. "I wondered."

"Is that all you have to say? 'I wondered?'" She turned on her heel and walked away so quickly her rosy silk skirt swung like a bell.

"No, no. Stop. Let us go where we can discuss this more sensibly."

She turned to him again, but all the anger and disgust were gone. The sorrow he saw in her lovely eyes hurt him as much as a blow to his chest. More tangible evidence of love, he supposed.

"Your idea of sense will kill me, Griffin. There is no heart in your sense. Nothing but business. Details, arrangements. I can't live as if I were your employee or some project in which you've decided to invest. No." Her mouth tightened and her eyes squeezed tight. He knew she held back tears and couldn't stop himself from walking to her and pulling her into his arms.

She did not struggle, thank God, but pushed her face into his shoulder. Her body shook as she gave over to crying. He clutched her against him and ignored the people walking past, slowing down to have a gander. The sky wasn't dark enough yet to hide their embrace. A wagon loaded with barrels trundled past, and the driver whistled and shouted, "Whoa, lookie at the sideshow." Griffin didn't glance up or loosen his grip on her. If he let go of her she might try to run away. He wasn't going to let her.

She spoke in a breathy whisper, and he bent his head to hear. "Pardon? I didn't catch that."

"I said, take away the business. No money. No contracts."

"And then what?"

She drew a deep breath that shuddered all down his front where she pressed close. "Yes. Then I'll say yes, to you. What you want. Friendship. The bed. All of it. Oh, it would be worth it."

He held her tighter, the pain of love expanding inside him.

"And if there was a baby?" he whispered.

"I'd love it as much as I love you." She pushed him away and fished blindly through her pockets for a handkerchief. A scrap of paper floated down, and Griffin bent to pick up a scribbled recipe. He tucked it into his waistcoat pocket, next to a white glove.

The night he'd picked up that glove from his floor he should have recognized that he was lost, transformed from a sensible man into a thoroughly maudlin, sentimental fool. The first time he discovered the joy of real passion. Making love.

"No," he said.

She finished dabbing at her eyes and then shoved the handkerchief into her pocket.

"What do you mean by that? I know you want me in your bed, Griffin Calverson. You've made that abundantly clear. What exactly is the matter with keeping the contracts and the money out of it? You did not seriously think that if you paid me a certain amount each quarter that I would keep my mouth shut and never criticize you? That I'd—I'd turn into . . ."

"One of my 'toad-eating sycophants,'" he reminded her.

"Yes, one of them."

She rubbed her hands over her face, turning her already pink nose and eyes even redder. She looked adorable.

She took in a deep breath, as if preparing herself for an ordeal. "Do you know what else I think, Griffin Calverson?"

He tried not to show his glee that her formal, polite manner had dissolved and she was going to keep on telling him exactly what she thought of him. About time she reminded him he was a heartless wretch. Nothing he didn't deserve. And he knew it meant he'd nearly won. "No. Tell me, Araminta," he whispered. "Please, please tell me."

"I think it's your horrible parents' fault that you think there's no such thing as love."

He blinked at her, confused. "Eh? What?"

Her large eyes, steady and solemn, gazed into his. "Yes. Especially your mother, if only because she left you without a word. Timona described how your father as much as said your mother took off because she didn't want children anymore. Yes, and Timona said you were always getting into scrapes. I can only imagine what a strong-willed, smart child could do with that. My oh my."

She stumbled for a second. But Griffin didn't interrupt. He might have been frozen and watching her from inside a shell of ice. He had expected anger. Not this.

She hesitated at each word, perhaps thinking them through as she spoke.

"A child must feel he was wicked, and he'd feel invincible. And truly evil. His own mother couldn't stand him. And—and invincible because he had the power to drive off a grown woman.

"It wouldn't be the happy baby girl, Timona, who drove off Mama. No indeed, it would be the stubborn, bad-tempered boy, Griffin. And once his heart was broken, he was set for life. He didn't need to worry about love again. He did need to protect the little girl he left without a mother, though, didn't he?

"That's why you always were so fierce about your sister, or so I've imagined. But, oh, that's a quality I admire in you, Griffin—the way you cared for Timona."

She stopped and drew another deep, shuddering breath. In a quavering voice she continued, "Of course, you might disagree with my theory. Do you have another reason? Why would a sane person believe there is no such thing as good, healthy love? Perhaps the poor child thought he'd grow up and turn into something like that mother and did not want to take the risk. . . ."

He, too, had to suck in a lungful of reviving air. With a few careless words she had unearthed an old, half-comprehended fear. The unshrouded knowledge lay in a corner of his mind now, rather than wrapped up tight. Nothing more than an injured child's fear.

This was the woman he'd wanted to keep from poking and prodding into his life? He had been a fool. And the sting of knowing how ridiculous he'd been hardly bothered him. He'd better get used to being shoved off balance and feeling absurd. He planned to be in for a lifetime of it.

Might as well learn to push back.

"Araminta, when was the last time I said that?"

"Eh?"

"The last time I said that rot about how I didn't believe in love?"

"I'm not sure."

"I've never said those words to you, have I?"

Her brow beetled, and she didn't answer.

"God knows it's the maxim of my family. I think Timona was the first of a long line of miserable fools to marry for love."

"But Timona said that you . . . For so long she believed it. Because of you."

"Yes, I admit it. I told her I didn't believe love existed. More than once I gave her a lecture about the subject. But that was when I was young and therefore an idiot. I have changed. Granted the change is fairly recent, but I most certainly do believe in love."

Her mouth opened, and then closed. "Oh."

"At a loss for words for once, hey?"

He grinned down at her, and she traced a still healing cut on his cheek—or perhaps his humiliating dimple. In a choked voice she said, "We can? You will? You do?"

"Yes. I love you. If that's what you're attempting to ask me."

She buried her face against his shoulder again. He wrapped his arms around her, and the exquisite warmth of her seeped right into his bones. He didn't want to let go, ever.

"Thank you," she whispered. "And thank you for letting me have it my way."

"And that is?"

He could barely make out her words. "No money, no contracts. Secret because it will be less difficult that way, but nothing sordid."

"I never agreed to that."

She grew still in his arms. "I shan't be your paid mistress, Griffin. No matter how much I want you."

"Hmmm. I like hearing that bit about how much you want me."

"Please. I am serious."

"Oh, I am too."

She shook her head, rubbing against his blue jacket. A few curls pulled free and sprang to life around her face. "I can't. And if you did love me you wouldn't keep asking me to become your—your employee."

"Fine. I won't. I'll ask you to marry me instead."

She drew back her head, but instead of smiling up at him as she had when she'd gazed at Hobnail, her mouth was an O, and under knit brows, her eyes were wide. A portrait of pure horror.

"Good Lord, no." She almost whimpered the words.

"Araminta, you just told me that you would be my secret lover. Live a life of shame. Have my illegitimate babies."

She wrinkled her nose. "It sounds ugly, but I don't think that anything we'd have could be so . . . so dreadful."

"Oh, my dearest, silliest Araminta, I heard you talking to Elizabeth. I read your letters—some of them more than once. I don't know how I could possibly have asked you, of all people, to lead such a life. I know that you would have to hide, and you've seen the worst of what happens when people try to conceal evidence of love."

She closed her eyes and shook her head again. "No. It would not be fair to marry you. Not a man like you. A gentleman."

"Why not? Because I can't cook so much as an egg and you've been with an expert chef?"

Her brow puckered in confusion, but that almost at once shifted into a glare. "What do you know about Jean-Pierre?"

"Quite a bit, all from your letters. But I don't know the end of the story. What happened to him?"

"He could not marry me."

"Why not?"

She bit her wonderful lower lip. "You know that, too."

"All I know is that the man was obviously an ass."

Her grim scowl softened. She raised a hand, and for a moment he thought she would stroke his face again. Her hand faltered, and instead she brushed a stray dark curl from her cheek. "Griffin, you are only pretending to be obtuse."

"And you are being a coward."

"No, I'm not."

"As much of a coward as your grandfather."

She turned her head away from him, to stare down the street. She pressed her lips tight. "No. I don't understand what you mean."

"Now who's being obtuse? Here, I shall spell it out for you. You think that because you are colored, our lives will be forever ruined if we choose to make our love public. You know that we will be drummed out of society—a society neither of us cares much about—and shunned by a bunch of snobs. And you think that I will grow to hate you because my Aunt Winifred will refuse to speak to me again. Good heavens, she might even refuse to live off of our money."

Still seemingly fascinated by a ragged man pulling a wagon full of cabbages, she tilted her head as if considering his words.

"Well?" he demanded. "Am I correct?"

"I . . . I am not sure. But it is hard, Griffin." She swallowed. "I am not complaining, but you must understand that it's hard to live with what I am. You would lose the respect of more than your aunt. You would grow to resent—"

"No. Wait. You think I won't be able to bear up under the strain of loving you? You think I'm as weak as your chef?"

Her gaze shifted, going perhaps as far as his collar before she restlessly fiddled with the pearl button on her bodice. "No, I know you're strong. You sweep me away. No one else has ever done that."

He had to pull her in for a kiss. A fast brush of her lips, for almost at once, he put his hands on her shoulders and held her back so that he could look into her eyes, which were unfocused and blurry from even that tiny kiss. She still wouldn't meet his searching gaze, but at last he could read her again.

He loved her bemused, shining eyes—Araminta's dazed expression, which he had christened "rising passion," was one of his favorites. He had many favorites—nearly as many as her expressive features could show.

He'd nearly won and decided to gloat at his victory.

"I know why you won't agree that you are wrong and we should marry. You simply do not wish to say, 'Yes, Griffin, you are correct.' Get used to the words, my love—you will have to say them on occasion." He crowed with pleasure. "Oh, I had not thought of these marvelous advantages to our marriage. Hearing you admit on a regular basis that I am right. And even better, never having to darken Aunt Winifred's doors again."

The corners of her mouth twitched slightly, and she finally met his eyes. For a moment, his throat closed and his chest ached with the unbearable heaviness of love.

When he managed to speak again, he went on. "Of course, you shall have some fun as well. There will be plenty of occasions to remind me that I am a cold stick."

He raised his voice to an outrageous falsetto. "'Until I came along, Griffin, you did not know how to laugh or love or even how to eat properly.'"

Her brow furrowed and she studied him. "Wait. I have never said those things."

"No," he agreed. "I did. And it's true, every word. Just like the rest of . . . what you said. You have always been too sharp for my own good. Hearing you say those words aloud. About my, er, nature."

He seemed to have some difficulty dragging up the right phrases to tell her what he meant. "Those words of yours seemed entirely ludicrous, yet somehow they echoed through me. . . ."

He shook his head to clear it. "If you do not agree to marry me, Araminta Woodhall, I shall be surrounded by nothing but yea-sayers who will allow me to become outrageously arrogant until I am as impossible as the man you thought I was to begin with. And Aunt Winifred might actually get her way and marry me off to one of her creatures."

Her mouth curved into a real smile at last. "What on earth was that about?"

"Never mind. I'm not sure. I need you. Marry me. To hell with your grandfather—if he isn't there already."

Araminta's smile broadened and lit with a sparkle he could see even in the fast-falling darkness. "No, I don't think he ended up there," she said. "My mother's prayers on his behalf had to have saved his wretched soul. My prayers, too."

Of course she'd forgiven the old idiot. Her heart was large enough. "Araminta. My love."

In the middle of the sidewalk on a busy street, he pulled her to him, and they exchanged the sweetest kiss that he'd ever tasted. Nearby, a man who'd been pushing a wheel down the street and shouting his singsong advertisement for knife sharpening broke off in mid-chant to shout, "Will you look at that?"

When the kiss ended, Griffin drew back a few inches and smiled at Araminta. He moved his hands to her waist, and he gave the lightest of shakes.

"Listen, I am not your blasted grandfather. And I will not allow anything about your past or your ancestors or my ruddy ancestors to keep me from my chance at happiness. Araminta. Love. I will make sure you are happy, even if I have to beat every usher in New York into a bloody pulp."

Her small hand stroked the back of his neck. "My kiss brings out vicious behavior?"